MW00860656

Shift

ALLY WAGNER

Shift away from the dark

Au

Copyright © 2021 by Ally Wagner, MK Publishing

All rights reserved. No part of this book may be reproduced or used in any manner without written permission of the copyright owner except for the use of quotations in a book review.

This is a work of fiction. Names, characters, places, and incidents either are the product of the author's imagination or are used fictitiously. Any resemblance to actual persons, living or dead, events, or locales is entirely coincidental.

Cover art by Matthew Weatherston

Edited by Christina Ramos

Layout by Eddy Espina

ISBN 978-1-7367220-0-8 (paperback)

Library of Congress Control Number : 2021921864

First paperback edition November 2021

To my hubby, thank you for putting up with my doubts and insecurities.

To my family, thank you for being more supportive than I could have ever imagined.

To my partner in crime for all things books and writing, thank you for seeing an author in me when I didn't.

One

A frown marred Cain's face as he traced over the pale scars on Kee's stomach for the third time. Her shirt had slid up her ribs as she slept, partially baring the four lines that dragged across her torso. He couldn't help but lightly run his rough, warm fingertips along the raised skin.

Lucas had shown him the attack almost a week ago and still it plagued his dreams. So much so that he spent the majority of the night holding her instead of sleeping. When she got too hot and rolled out of his arms, he held her hand just to reassure himself she was still there.

Still alive.

He stilled his hand and splayed his fingers out across her stomach. Logically, he knew she was safe from the wolves who hurt her. They were dead, killed by her own hand as soon as she recovered. She had eliminated his pack members before he even knew they were at fault. Still, his beast whined at him to keep her safe. He should have been there to protect her. He realized too late that she meant far more to him than Warren's wrath, and it nearly cost them both their lives.

Cain remembered how relieved he had been when she showed up

on his doorstep last night and confessed she couldn't kill him. A part of him had been unsure, especially after seeing glimpses of the cold, ruthless side of her he never knew existed. Not once had he seen it since she arrived last night, only his gentle Kee. Just as she was before she was taken from him.

His eyes softened when she rolled on her side towards him, his hand moving to the dip in her waist. When her sleepy grey eyes met his, he pulled her in closer. "Good morning," he rumbled affectionately, rubbing their noses together.

"Morning," Kee mumbled and tilted her head back when he began to plant hot kisses on her neck. The familiar wakeup routine brought a comforting smile to her lips. "Someone's happy."

He smiled against her skin and pulled back. He propped himself up on one elbow and used his free hand to push the long, dark blonde strands from her face. "I went over a month without seeing you. I'm making up for lost time."

She cupped the back of his neck and brought his head down so she could press their foreheads together. "Oh? And how do you plan to do that?" She whispered, easily falling into their usual playful banter.

He kissed her, tongue flicking over her bottom lip. "Let me show you."

The butterflies that used to flutter in her belly never came. Pushing the thought away, she teasingly nipped at his lip with her teeth. "You have my attention," she responded, but the grin fell away as Lucas flashed in her mind. A sudden pang of guilt punched her in the gut, putting a sudden halt to the mood. She leaned back from him with a soft sigh. "Cain, wait. We need to talk about what I was going to tell you last night."

His smile slipped off his face, concern etching his features. She had tried to tell him something serious last night, but he had been scared to hear it. He had sensed the anxiety that had radiated off of her, but he didn't want it to ruin the bliss of their reunion.

He looked down at the white scars again and frowned. "I think I already know." He glanced up at her and saw the tension around her eyes. "The vampire, right?"

She squeezed her eyes shut as Lucas' image appeared again, her heart clenching painfully. "Yeah," she breathed.

He tightened his jaw and abruptly sat up, swinging his legs over the side of the bed. Instinctually, he had already known, but it still stung to hear. "I didn't even know you liked him." His wolf growled when he remembered how he found her in her apartment after Lucas had fed on her. *Had that all been a lie?*

She sighed and sat up as well, hugging her knees to her chest. "I've always been attracted to him, Cain," she admitted. "But nothing happened until we broke up."

"When did we break up, Kee?" He asked quietly, not looking at her.

She frowned at his bare back but couldn't keep the anger out of her voice. "The night I denied your pack because I refused to fuck Warren. We were both angry and upset. And with how things ended, it was the only conclusion I could come to." When he didn't respond, she pushed. "You had to have felt the same way, Cain."

He clenched his hands into tight fists. She wasn't wrong; he *had* assumed the same thing. He wanted to say it but couldn't get the words out. Yes, she had denied her initiation into his pack. Things had been tense and awkward, but he had been determined to get her back and make it work. But, hearing that she had been with someone else afterwards wounded him.

"So, something happened before your attack," he accused as he looked over his shoulder at her.

She ran her hand into her hair. "Lucas and I kissed the night we fought," she confessed. "There was a lot going on, and I got caught up in the moment." Again, something in her chest fluttered.

Cain stood from the bed, body tense. *So soon after?* "Is that your excuse for after the attack, too?" He asked harshly, his inner wolf growling. His beast wanted to mount her, desired to reclaim her body as theirs. He needed to show her, and everyone else for that matter, who her alpha was by licking every inch of her skin to saturate it in his scent.

Kee sighed and rubbed her face. "No, I'm not going to make excuses, Cain. We had sex." *A lot*, she refrained from adding. *And it was amazing.*

His dark blue eyes narrowed as he whirled around to face her. "Did you think of me at all during those times?"

She knew he was hurt, but she wouldn't lie to him. "Not during, no. You have to remember that I thought you had planned the attack, Cain. I was trying to make myself hate you so that it would be easier for me to kill you." She watched as his muscles flexed, making the tattooed Celtic knots and braids on his left arm ripple.

The wolf couldn't hold back the growl in his throat. "You had to have sex with him to hate me?"

"No, I had sex because I wanted to," she clarified in a firm tone. "He was there for me when I was broken. Helped put me back together when I was lost. I was so upset, so confused and angry with what happened to me. I wanted to hit and break everything in sight. Honestly, I had so much animosity that it scared me," she told him, absentmindedly running her fingers over the edge of her scars that started at her collar bone. "Lucas kept me together. Conrad, too. Without them I'm not sure where I would be right now."

He scratched his chin in frustration, messing up the short hair along his jawline. He wanted to argue with her, to scold her for screwing a walking corpse, but couldn't. How could he when he had failed her? He hadn't been there for her when she needed him most. She had no one to lean on except Conrad and Lucas. *But at what cost?*

"Kee, he made you a different person."

She winced slightly before looking up at him. "He made me into a weapon," she agreed solemnly. "He admitted it when I found out that he's the reason for the attack in the first place." She mumbled and looked away as he moved towards her. "But I don't regret it, Cain. I like my new strength."

He tipped up her chin, drawing her eyes back to his. "You were always strong, babe."

She gave him a weak, knowing smile. "No, I wasn't."

His hand slid up to cup the side of her face, his thumb brushing her cheekbone. "You were to me. You didn't need to change."

"I did. I can protect myself now, and I'm grateful to Lucas for that," she said.

His hand dropped back to his side when she brought up the vampire once again. Did she even realize she kept doing so? "Do you care about him?"

Kee didn't hesitate. "Yes."

Goddamn it. He scowled. "Do you love him?"

A flash of one of Lucas' rare smiles killed the denial on the tip of her tongue. Her brow furrowed as the missing butterflies made an appearance.

"I don't know." She responded honestly. She felt something for Lucas but wasn't sure what exactly those feelings were. She felt comfortable and safe around him. He made her smile but also put her in her place when she was angry. She felt they had grown close the past month, but the truth of everything had destroyed that. Or, so she thought.

"So, you're not sure." He pressed with a sneer.

She looked up at him again. "I know I love you," she said, but something felt off about that statement. "But, I'm confused about Lucas."

He turned and buried his face in his hands in frustration. "If I had just been there, this wouldn't be happening," he grumbled angrily, albeit miserably. "I can't share you!"

No, she's ours. Our mate, came the primal voice inside him. The beast, the inner wolf that made him what he was.

Kee rose from the bed. "I'm not asking you to share me," she responded. "But Lucas and I share a bond that draws us together."

"I know that's how he saved you, but it's hard for me to accept that he's always going to have a tie to you." Cain turned to her and wrapped his arms around her stiff shoulders "It's like there's a small part of you that will always be his and not mine."

She pressed her lips together in a hard line. "I'm not a toy to be possessed by either of you. I belong to myself, Cain."

She belongs to us. His wolf argued.

He slid his hands up her neck and cupped her face. "I know that, Kee. My wolf just gets possessive and doesn't like the idea of someone else having a claim on our mate."

Kee gaped at him, stunned by his declaration. Trying to calm the irritation rising within her, she took a deep breath and slowly let it out as she chose the next words cautiously. "Cain, how can I be your mate after everything that's happened?"

"We will figure it out. You did what you had to, Kee. If I had been there, I would have killed them before they had a chance to touch you," he told her vehemently. "I'll explain what happened to the pack."

Her brow furrowed in disbelief. "You think Warren and Katie will forgive me for killing Wyatt? How about Mason? You think he'll forgive me for murdering his mate? I'm nothing to them, Cain. I'll forever be the outsider who took their loved ones away." Her eyes hardened. "And I don't regret it. I'm sorry I caused them pain, but I'm not sorry for killing the people who tried to do the same to me."

Cain saw that cold side of her slide into place and clenched his jaw. His wolf howled within him to dominate that dark side of her. To tame it and make it theirs. "I know," he replied tersely. "But they'll have to accept my choice once I'm alpha."

The ice thawed from her eyes. "You told me you're Katie's alpha now. You helped keep her together through everything. The truth is going to destroy her."

"Everything will work out." He repeated.

"And what about Conrad? What happens to him if we mate? He's my wolf."

His brows lifted in surprise. "You're still serious about being his alpha?"

Instantly the cold glare reappeared. He wasn't going to accept this side of her, was he? She knocked his hands away and stepped back, just as she did back in her apartment. "As long as he'll have me, yes. He doesn't want to be a part of Warren's pack, and I won't make him do anything he doesn't want to do."

"It'll be different when I take over the pack, Kee. It's already happening. Katie is my wolf now, not Warren's. It's only a matter of time before the other wolves start submitting to me. Once that happens, I'll challenge Warren. When I win, I'll be alpha."

"Conrad still won't listen to you, Cain," she stressed. "I am his alpha, not you."

"You will be an alpha female, just like Nat. My pack will obey you as they do me." He argued.

Her hands balled into fists. Lucas fully embraced her alpha side, why couldn't Cain? "Unless your orders differ from mine."

"Well, yeah. There can't be two alphas, Kee."

"That's exactly the problem!" She threw up her hands in frustration. "Now do you see what I'm saying?"

He sighed and rubbed his face again. "So, Conrad's loyalty will be to you. Fine, I can accept that. Especially since he's been there for you when I haven't," he conceded, despite his wolf growling unhappily.

She blinked at him in surprise. "You'll let me stay Conrad's alpha if we mate?" She asked wearily.

"As long as he doesn't challenge or blatantly disrespect me, yes." He gave her a small smile. "I would do anything for you, Kee. Don't you get that yet?"

An alpha giving up control of a wolf in their pack was no small thing. The fact that Cain was offering her that meant more than anything else he had said or offered her.

She looked up at him when he closed the distance between them once again. "You mean it?"

"Yes," he replied as he pulled her against him, his hands sliding down to palm her ass through her leggings. "I love you, Kee. If it means learning to bend to you sometimes, I will."

We'll see about that. Deciding to test his declaration, she pressed her hands against his chest and walked forward, making him back up towards the bed. She pushed him onto the blankets and began to climb over him, stopping at his hips. She glanced up and saw his wolf's eyes, the shining dark blue pools staring at her with a carnal hunger.

Why did a part of her wish they were green?

Cain muscles tensed with anticipation. She was being dominant, but he and his wolf tolerated it. Kee was an alpha female. *His* alpha female. As he said, he would sometimes bend to her wishes, but he would always take control when needed.

He let out a groan when she palmed his erection through the fabric of his sweats, her smirk widening. His fingers threaded into her hair as she gave him a firm squeeze. Before he could guide her down, a knock rapped against the bedroom door. He jumped but recovered with a low, warning growl. "What?" He snapped with a sharp swell of his aura.

"It's Katie," came the hesitant response from the other side of the door. "Um, Conrad is here. He's...he's in his human form!" She stated in disbelief.

Kee leaned back on to her knees and swatted Cain's hands away when he tried to pull her back. She laughed at his pout as she stood and went to the door. She flashed a smile at Katie as she opened it and headed to the living room to where her wolf was standing.

"Morning, Con," she greeted as she approached him, her shoulders sagging in relief. *Relief of what, though?*

"It's nearly one in the afternoon." He mumbled with a tired smile.

When his honey colored eyes fell on her, she frowned at the exhaustion reflected in them. His blonde hair was tied back in a disheveled bun, his plain white shirt rumpled. She put her hands on his stiff shoulders and frowned with concern. "Are you okay? What's wrong?"

He closed his eyes and relaxed at his alpha's soothing touch. "I didn't sleep well," he admitted. His mind had kept him up all night, plagued with thoughts of Liam, Mia, and Warren. His brain had tried to wrap itself around everything he discovered and refused to let him sleep. Also, he was so used to sleeping next to Kee that his wolf had been restless without his pack member nearby. "I should have known you would have come here."

She shrugged unapologetically, letting her hands drop to her sides. "It was the only place nearby I could think of."

Conrad rubbed the bridge of his nose. "Was that smart? Lucas was pretty pissed last night."

Kee sighed and looked away from him. "So was I. It was a lot to take in, and I was completely blindsided by it." She clenched her jaw. "I trusted him, Con, and he broke that."

He threw his hands up in irritation, the frustration from last night immediately resurfacing. "He didn't plan it, Kee!" He shouted exasperatedly. "He didn't break your trust!"

She pursed her lips and glanced back at him as he yelled at her. "It's still his fault!"

"You're looking for someone to blame and I get that, but he's not the right outlet for your rage!"

"He admitted that I was a perfect weapon, Conrad! He had planned on shaping me into this all along!"

"You're more to him than a weapon, Kee! You *know* that! Just talk to him! Don't let this ruin everything!"

"Don't raise your voice at her," Cain growled as he came into the room, Katie trailing close behind him.

Conrad glared at the beta. "This isn't your business, Cain."

"Watch your tone, Conrad. I won't warn you again," Cain said, lip lifted in a snarl.

"Don't threaten my wolf!" Kee snapped as she whirled on Cain. "I'm his alpha, not you, remember? He's off limits to you."

"He shouldn't be talking to you like that! Put him in his place, Kee!" He said, pointing at the blonde wolf.

She met his fierce stare. "No, he's allowed to have an opinion and tell me when he thinks I'm wrong. I won't just rule over him like a dictator."

"Wait, you're Conrad's alpha? How? You're a woman. What about Warren?" Katie's brow furrowed as the other three wolves in the room immediately tensed and exchanged a knowing look. "Did I miss something?"

Cain cleared his throat and straightened his spine. "Katie, Conrad chose Kee as his alpha because he wasn't treated right in our pack."

She frowned. "But, doesn't an alpha have to overpower a wolf and make them submit?"

"I submit to her." Conrad stated without embarrassment. "She doesn't need to overpower me. She can, but she doesn't need to."

Kee flinched when she remembered how her aura had crashed down and forced him to his knees last night. She grasped his hand in hers, rubbing the top of it with her thumb in apology. "I'm sorry."

His anger left him at her touch, and he gave her a reassuring smile. "It's fine. You were mad, I get it."

"Still, that's no excuse." She looked at Katie. "I respect Conrad, and Warren's pack didn't."

Katie tilted her head at them. "Does Warren know?"

Kee shook her head. "No, and I'd rather keep it that way for at least a little bit longer."

Conrad glanced at his alpha. "We should also refrain from telling them that you're alive. I was talking to Dante, and he told me some things about Lucas. We think someone told Alexander about you," he said before repeating to her what Dante told him last night. "Lucas kept your existence a secret from everyone. Do you think he would tell his enemy? No. Someone *told* Alexander about you."

She frowned at him once he was done with his retelling. "But, who?"

Cain crossed his arms over his chest. "Maybe someone was following you at work."

"No, I would have noticed." Kee replied softly as she tried to rack her brain for someone who may have revealed her to Alexander.

Katie rubbed her arms, feeling completely lost in the conversation. "What's going on?"

Cain looked at Kee, silently asking for permission to tell his wolf the truth. When her lips pursed and brow furrowed, he sighed and gave Katie a modified version. "You know how we thought Kee was dead? Well, she went into hiding after she was attacked. That's why she was gone for so long," he began. "We are still trying to figure out who's behind it."

Katie sucked in a gasp. "What?" Her bottom lip trembled. "Is it the same person who attacked Wyatt and the others?" She asked quietly.

Kee tensed at the obvious pain Katie was in at the mention of Wyatt. "I don't know." She lied. "I've been recovering and hiding while I try to figure it out. It's why I let everyone think I was dead. I wasn't sure who I could trust."

She bit her lip. "I—I may have texted Nat last night after you showed up." She looked at Cain and felt her wolf whine when his eyes fluttered shut in exasperation. "I'm sorry! I didn't know! I was just so excited to see her. I thought—" Tears welled in her eyes. "I thought maybe it meant that Wyatt was alive, too. That maybe there's a chance he's out there."

Cain's irritation dissipated as soon as she started crying. He walked over to her and put his hand on her head, petting her hair in gentle, soothing strokes. "It's alright, you didn't know," he reassured. "The less people who know she's alive, the better. At least until we find out who's behind the attack, okay?"

She nodded then rubbed her eyes as a sob jerked her body. "I just want to be reunited with Wyatt like you were with Kee." She cried.

Guilt hit Kee like a sledgehammer to the stomach. A bitter taste hit her tongue, and her throat closed. She looked down at the floor, her lips pressed hard together. Conrad wrapped his arms around her, pulling her into a comforting embrace. She pressed her face to his shoulder and closed her eyes tightly.

Don't cry. She scolded herself.

Conrad patted her back, and she could almost hear him telling her she had nothing to feel guilty about. How did he know her so well after such a short amount of time?

"Just remember what happened to you," he murmured, running his hand up and down her back. When he felt her nod, he pulled away, but kept a hand on her shoulder.

Cain patted Katie's head one more time before turning to Kee.

"I'll call Nat right now and talk to her, okay?" When she nodded, he headed to the bedroom to make the call.

"Are you mad at me, Kee?" Katie asked with a sniffle after Cain left.

She sighed softly. "No, you didn't know. It's my fault for not telling you. We just need to talk to Nat. Hopefully she didn't tell anyone else yet." Even as she said it, she knew the chances were slim. She was Warren's mate, and she doubted the wolf queen kept anything from her king.

Two

"Where are you going?"

Natalie paused at the door that led to the garage, hand resting on the knob. She glanced over her shoulder at her mate and felt a shudder run through her body at his icy blue glare. Brushing off the feeling, she squared her shoulders and tilted up her chin in a forced air of confidence. "Out." She replied curtly.

Warren's scowl deepened. "Where?"

"To visit Katie." She explained simply, turning back to the door. She pulled it open and jumped when it was slammed back into place. She looked at the hand holding the door shut and took a shaky inhale. He wasn't touching her, but she could feel the heat of his body. She tightened her hold on the doorknob. "Is it a problem that I want to go visit our wolf?"

His lip lifted into a snarl. "She's not our wolf anymore. She's *Cain's*." He pointed out, venom dripping in his tone. "He came into his alpha power and took her from me!"

"We are the same pack, Warren." She turned enough so she could look at him from the corner of her eye. "Don't forget that."

He pressed his chest to her back as his wolf growled. "Don't talk to me like that."

She clenched her jaw as his beast's wild aura began to press on hers, his growl vibrating along her spine. Her wolf bared its teeth in response. "I'm your wife. Your *mate*. I'm allowed to remind you of important things when you clearly forget them."

The alpha of the LA wolf pack spun his woman around and grabbed her jaw. Angling her head up, he stared down into her wide hazel eyes. "You're allowed to do what I tell you to," he sneered. "And I'm telling you to stay put. You're not allowed to leave the house without my permission."

Nat's eyes hardened at his words despite the tendril of cold fear that curled in her belly. She knocked his hand away and shoved him back. "Since when do I need your permission to do anything? I'll do what I want to, Warren!"

"Don't test me!"

Her stomach dropped as his wolf's eyes took over his icy blue ones. Teal irises glared down at her as his energy fell oppressively upon hers. Her bottom lip trembled and her knees wobbled, but she tried to remain brave. "What has gotten into you? You've never spoken to me like this before, and I won't tolerate it now!"

His wolf snarled at her defiance. She was *his* wolf. She needed to obey *him*. He wouldn't lose another member of his pack. *He* was alpha, not Cain! Him!

He grabbed her wrist and shouted, "You'll tolerate what I tell you to!"

Fear kicked her instincts in gear, making her react without thinking. She swung back her hand and slapped him hard across the face. What she hadn't expected was for him to reciprocate the action.

He hadn't expected to, either.

Warren stared down at his hand with a mix of shock and horror as his mate stumbled back against the door, cradling her cheek. His beast instantly receded in shame, taking its wild energy with it. Making his mate submit to him was one thing, but physical harm was something he told himself he would never do. He had never hurt her, never touched her that way before. How could he have crossed that line? He loved Nat with every fiber of his being. She completed him, and he knew that from the moment he saved her all those years ago.

Hearing her whimper, he snapped his head up. His heart seemed to stop as he saw the side of her face rapidly turning red. "Natalie—"

"Don't," she whispered harshly as she regained her footing. She turned her back to him, her hand shaking as it gripped the doorknob tightly once again. Her eyes misted with tears of pain and betrayal. "I don't know what's going on with you, Warren. For a month you've been acting strange. Aggressive. Different. I don't know exactly what to call it, but I can't see my mate in you any longer."

His eyes widened at her words. "Please, Nat—"

She felt him reach for her and her body tensed, muscles coiling tightly as she ducked her head. "No!" She snapped, refusing to look at him. "Don't play the victim. You need to find the man that I love before it's too late."

He dropped his hand, both of them fisting at his sides. "Too late?"

"Before you lose everything, including yourself." She warned before pulling open the garage door and slamming it shut behind her.

Self-pity and anger consumed him as he released a loud, animalistic snarl. Shifting into his hybrid wolf form, he turned his frustration to the house. He tore the couch apart, splintered the coffee table, and shattered the sliding back door. With another echoing howl, he took off into the woods of his backyard.

—

Natalie took a deep breath before knocking on Cain's door. She crossed her arms, trying to hide the shaking in her hands. Tears stung her eyes as the scene with Warren replayed in her head on repeat. What was happening to her mate? It was as if he was losing himself more and more each day.

But why? She asked herself miserably. *Was it guilt? I know he did something. He knows what happened to Wyatt, knows why Brandon and Noah were killed. But, what about Kee? He and Noah were too suspicious when Cain came to us about her disappearance. Yet, Katie and Cain said she's alive.*

"Nat?"

She jerked her head up to meet Cain's concerned blue eyes. She watched as they narrowed into a glare, his hand reaching up to touch her swollen cheek. Her bottom lip trembled at the contact. "I-I don't know what's going on with him."

"Warren did this to you," he stated angrily. He clenched his jaw as he took in the red, puffy skin. "Has he lost his fucking mind?" He asked in a low growl.

A sob escaped her throat without permission, and she leaned into Cain's chest. "I don't know!" She cried. "He's never been like this, Cain! He's angry all the time. He's tense, and his wolf is always on the surface. He thinks you're trying to take all of us from him! He thinks you'll challenge him any day now!"

He hugged her, rubbing her back to soothe her like she had for him. This woman had always been like a sister to him, her mate like a brother. He guided her into the house, kicking the door shut behind them. He glanced at the others as they stood quietly in the living room, watching with concerned, furrowed brows.

"Nat, can I get you anything?" Kee asked softly, frowning when she saw the condition of Nat's face.

Natalie gave a soft gasp and pulled away from Cain. Katie and Cain had said that Kee was alive, but seeing her in person lifted some weight from her shoulders. Was Warren innocent after all? "Kee!" She cried as she pulled the girl into a tight hug. "You're alive."

Kee awkwardly hugged her back, not knowing what to say. She blinked when the other woman pulled back and cupped her cheeks. Hazel clashed with grey as they stared at each other. "Nat?" She asked softly.

"I have so many questions," she muttered. "Where have you been? What happened? Why did you disappear?"

Kee sighed softly and grabbed the other woman's hands, removing them from her face. "I have been recuperating at a friend's place," she answered. "I was attacked."

"Like the others then," she breathed, sinking down onto Cain's couch with a heavy sigh. "Then I'm back to square one."

"Square one?" Katie asked as she sat down on the couch next to her.

Conrad stood next to his alpha, his amber eyes on Nat. "You have suspicions as to who did this?"

Nat's eyes widened as they took in the new wolf. "Conrad, you're human! I know Katie texted me and told me, but I didn't believe it. We thought you were stuck in your wolf form. You're so handsome."

He flushed and looked away from her, his cheeks pink. "I just prefer my wolf form."

Katie steered the conversation back to the attacks. "Who do you think did this to our pack?"

Natalie sighed and lifted her hand to her cheek, fingertips ghosting over the bruising flesh. "I don't know if I should say."

Conrad's body tensed as he watched her. Did she also think Warren was behind it? "Nat, do you know of a vampire named Alexander?"

The skin between her eyebrows knitted together at his question. "Alexander?"

"Alexander was the reigning vampire lord for the Pasadena coven," Kee explained. "He's my boss's enemy and admitted to attacking me, but we don't know how he found out about my existence."

"I certainly didn't tell anyone named Alexander about you," Natalie countered with a frown.

"That's not what we're insinuating," Cain quickly corrected. "Alexander wasn't the one who attacked Kee directly. He sent people to do it."

"How do you know he didn't just find out about you through your boss?"

Kee sighed. "He kept my employment a strict secret even from his most trusted friends. He didn't want people to know about me, and I doubt he messed up. He's smarter than that." She ignored the two very different looks Cain and Conrad shot her.

"So, you're certain someone told him about you. He put a hit out on you?" When Kee nodded, Nat sighed. "Are you sure it's not just a vendetta against the pack? Since four of us have been attacked?"

Cain and Kee glanced at each other. "They might be two different attackers," Cain suggested with a forced shrug. "Right, Kee?"

His tone made Kee's palms sweat with nerves. He wanted to tell them. He wanted them to know what his pack mates did to her. What she did to them in return. What would they do? Would they try to kill her? She was certain of it. Would Cain interfere? What side would he take?

She couldn't answer that. He had already abandoned her once for his pack. She didn't trust him to not do it again.

Her stomach sank. *I can't trust him.*

Kee swallowed dryly and clenched her hands into fists. She took a step back and bumped into Conrad. When he patted her shoulder in support, she shook her head and looked at Nat. "I'm sure they are separate affairs." She ignored Cain's disappointed frown. "Are you sure you've never heard of an Alexander?"

"I've heard of one," Natalie told her honestly. "Warren talks to one on occasion. He said he's a business partner."

"Bullshit!" Conrad suddenly shouted.

Kee jumped at his outburst, startled. "What the fuck, Con?"

"Warren is the one who told Alexander about you, Kee!" He sneered, hands balling into fists.

Kee stiffened when the energy in the room shifted to a thick tension. The LA pack members clearly weren't pleased with the accusation. She put a hand on her wolf's arm. "We don't know that for sure, Conrad."

"The fuck we don't!" He snapped and glared at Cain. "Think of who attacked Kee. Who else could have told them to do that?"

Kee paled at his not-so-subtle reference and tightened her hold on his arm. "Stop."

Cain bared his teeth. "Watch yourself, Conrad. You're about to cross a line you wish you hadn't."

"You know it makes perfect sense!" The other male snarled back. "Pull your head out of your ass and look at the situation! Warren did this to your so-called mate!"

"I said stop!" Kee shouted, turning on Conrad as her aura flared.

He flinched at the lash of her energy and growled low in his throat in stubborn acknowledgment. His inner wolf submitted to her, making his head dip down as he dropped to one knee. "I won't apologize," he grumbled.

"I know," she said before glancing over at the tense trio near the couch. She pursed her lips into a hard line. "I think we should go."

Cain put his hand on Katie's shoulder when she shot up from the couch, keeping her quiet and firmly in place. "That might be a good idea," he replied stiffly. He met Kee's hardened eyes with a torn expression. "Will you come back tonight?"

"No," she replied instantly. At his wounded look, she sighed. "It's not a good idea. I think we'll both have our hands full with this revelation."

He nodded once in agreement then nodded at the two she-wolves. One was furious, the other distraught. "What do I tell them, Kee? I can't leave things like this."

She gestured for Conrad to stand and looped her arm through his to keep him beside her. "I think at this point they're going to figure it out. You may as well tell them the truth." Her eyes narrowed in warning. "But remember what happened last time someone tried to attack me."

Cain watched as she left, a chill running down his spine. When the front door clicked shut, he removed his hand from Katie's shoulder and braced himself for the shouting. Instantly Katie exploded at him, demanding answers to what seemed like a million questions.

"You know who attacked Kee, don't you?" Natalie asked, cutting off Katie's tirade.

He ran his hand through his short hair. "Yeah."

"Wolves, I presume? Our pack nonetheless." When he nodded solemnly, she buried her face in her hands. "And you know who killed our wolves?" She asked, but she had already started to put two and two together.

It was muffled by her hands and as soft as a whisper, but he heard her. He gave a heavy, defeated sigh and sunk down on the couch next to her. "Yeah."

Three

"What the actual fuck, Conrad?" Kee all but screeched at him after settling into the Jeep's passenger seat.

The wolf's nostrils flared as he started the engine and took off down the street. "They had to know, Kee! Their alpha isn't innocent!"

She turned in her seat to face him with a savage glare. "And you didn't think to talk to me about your theory first? They shouldn't have found out that way! I should have talked to Cain!"

"That's why I came over! I figured it out last night! It's been right in front of us, and we haven't even considered it! We were fucking blind, Kee!" He punched the steering wheel, the horn blaring.

She grabbed the handle when he took a sharp right turn. "I should have considered it, yes, but this wasn't the way to go about it! Warren is their alpha! What you spewed is going to have a chain reaction that can end in a blow up! For all of them!"

"So fucking what? Why is that any concern of yours? Look what that pack did to you, Kee!"

"Because I don't want to be the reason a pack breaks apart!" She shouted.

"Warren's the fucking reason! *Fuck*!" He cursed as he hit the horn again, denting the plastic cover.

His anger caused his cheeks to blotch with angry red patches that went down his neck. She had never seen this side of Conrad before. He was usually so easy-going and passive. He was encouraging and supportive, but livid?

She took a deep, calming breath and reached out to place a hand on his tense shoulder. He jerked slightly under her touch, but she rubbed the taught muscle. "Calm down, Con." She cooed softly. "I'm sorry I yelled at you."

His knuckles were white as he gripped the steering wheel. His breath came out in shallow pants as he tried to regain his composure. After a minute, his fingers loosened around the wheel. "No, I'm sorry. You're right; I handled that wrong. I'm just frustrated."

Kee massaged his shoulder until it finally relaxed. "Let's talk about this. How did you come to the conclusion that it was Warren?"

He let out a heavy sigh and chose to eliminate his conversation with Liam. "Like I said earlier, I was talking to Dante about your fight with Lucas. He said that Lucas had kept you a secret from all of them until you were hurt. Do you really think he would let his enemy learn about you? And why would the wolves obey anything a vampire says?"

She kept her hand on his shoulder as she mulled that around in her head. "I get why you came to the assumption, but why would Warren tell Alexander? What did he have to gain from it?"

That was the million-dollar question. Why would Warren care enough to tell Alexander? "I guess we need to start with who wanted you dead."

"What do you mean?" She asked.

"Think about it. Did Warren tell Alexander because he wanted you dead? Maybe he was threatened by Cain. Maybe he knew Cain was close to becoming alpha and wanted to prolong it." Conrad suggested, glancing at her from the corner of his eye. "You're Cain's weakness, and Warren could have wanted to take advantage of that so he remained alpha."

Kee pressed her lips tightly together. It made sense, especially with how Warren had treated Nat today. "But that wouldn't explain the note Alexander sent to Lucas."

"It could. Alexander might have just been reaping the benefits. You know, kicking Lucas while he's down."

"If that's true, then why would Warren have told Alexander about me at all? What was the point?" She sighed and pulled her hand away from him to set it in her lap. "He could have just ordered his pack to kill me and left Alexander out of it. Why purposefully tell him?"

"That's a good question," he hummed as he turned down Olympic Boulevard towards Byte. "Would they both have something to gain by crippling Lucas?"

"Alexander would, but Warren? I don't see how." She frowned and raked her hand through her hair. "I feel like we're still missing something."

Conrad nodded. "We have the pieces of the puzzle, just have to get them to fit together."

She chewed on her lip and stared down at her hands. "What if Warren and Alexander were working together?"

"Working together towards what though? Why would a wolf and vampire be—" he cut himself off, his whole body tensing in realization. He came to a red light and turned to look at Kee. Her body was stiff, eyes wide. Clearly, she had come to the same conclusion he had.

"Do you think they're blood bonded? Like me and Lucas?" She murmured and bit on the side of her thumb. Warren and Alexander had the same bond she and Lucas did.

"They have to be," Conrad agreed. "Nothing else really makes sense."

"They would both know each other's enemies and would want to weaken them." She threw her head back against the headrest. "Fuck that complicates things."

"I wonder how much Warren knows about you." He frowned as he pulled into Byte's parking lot. He parked and turned to meet her questioning look. "How did he know you were connected to Lucas to begin with?"

"Oh." She furrowed her brow. "I didn't think about that. How *does* he know? I doubt Cain told him, but I suppose it's an option. I'll have to ask him."

He nodded. "That might be a good idea. Also, does he know you're a shapeshifter?"

She bit her lip again. "Noah and Brandon knew since I shifted into a bear in front of them. So, I'm going to assume they told him." She sighed and opened the car door. She climbed out, closed the door, and stopped when she realized where they were. She scowled at Conrad. "Why?"

He shrugged innocently as he started walking towards Byte. "Why, what?"

"Why did you bring me here?"

"I'm not sure what you mean."

"Conrad! I don't want to see him! I'm not ready!" She huffed and crossed her arms.

He rolled his eyes. "Kee, the sun is up and he's asleep. You won't even see him until tonight."

"I won't be here that long." She huffed and stormed past him towards the back entrance.

"Señora Quinn, *buenos dias*." Miguel greeted with a bright smile, brown eyes warm. The werebear stepped aside and held the door open for them.

"Hey Miguel," she replied with a smile of her own, her irritation subsiding. "How are you?"

"I'm well, *gracias*. There's nothing to report for today yet. The boss said to up security around the building but didn't say as to why. Do you know?"

Her smiled turned forced. "Just being cautious, I'm sure. He got a threat yesterday and wants to ensure everyone stays safe."

Miguel smiled. "You know, I'll be honest, I wasn't sure how I felt about working with a bunch of vampires, especially the Lord of Los Angeles. But, he's a good man, isn't he?" He was oblivious to the way her smile became strained. "Always looking out for his employees."

"Yes, *always*." Conrad echoed with emphasis, staring pointedly at Kee.

She ignored him and gave the bear shifter another smile. "Report if you find anyone, or anything, suspicious."

"Will do," he replied as the pair disappeared into the club.

She stepped into the back kitchen area of Byte and instantly went to the well-stocked walk-in fridge. "How do you feel about French toast?" She asked as she tied her hair back into a low ponytail.

Conrad lifted a brow at her as he sat on one of the counters. "It's almost two-thirty in the afternoon."

"It's never too late for breakfast!" Lucy chimed in as she sauntered in from the double hinge doors that led to the empty club. Her platinum blond hair was pulled up into a messy bun, her face bare of any makeup. She had on a pair of faded jeans and a long sleeve baby pink shirt accompanied by black ankle boots with a short heel.

Kee grinned at her friend as she pulled out the ingredients from the fridge. "See, this is why we are friends." She pointed out as she began cracking eggs in a bowl.

Conrad rolled his eyes, but a smile was on his lips. "Why are you here so early, Luce?"

She waved the clipboard in her hand before setting it down next to Conrad. "Bar inventory. I have to put the order in today before the club opens." She leaned against the counter and crossed her arms over her chest, pale green eyes on Kee. "So, I take it that it didn't go well with you and the boss man last night."

Kee flinched and hit the egg too hard against the bowl, the shell shattering. She cursed and picked out the white pieces from the yolks. After throwing them in the sink, she grabbed the loaf of bread and began pressing slices into the bowl. When the werefox cleared her throat, Kee glanced up to see both of them staring at her. She pressed her lips together in a hard line. "No, it didn't go well."

"What happened? Was it from a girl after all?" She pressed. When Kee remained quiet she scoffed. "Kiki, you—" She jumped when Kee suddenly slammed the metal bowl down, eyes hard.

"Don't call me that," she snipped. When her friend's brow furrowed in confusion, she swallowed down her anger. "*Please*. It's a nickname someone in my past used to call me, and they're not very fond memories." She turned around and lit the burner on the stove before placing a frying pan on it.

"Oh, I'm sorry, I didn't know," Lucy replied calmly. "But you need to talk about what happened last night. It's not good to bottle it up."

"It wasn't another woman, Luce. I just found out some things that I didn't like," she answered quietly as she set the soaked pieces of bread in the pan.

"Did you talk about it with Lucas? What did he say?" She questioned as she hoisted herself up on the counter next to Conrad.

"He didn't really defend himself or say otherwise."

"Okay," she drawled out. "Let's ask the real question, did you let him explain himself?" When her friend went silent again, she threw up her hands and shoved Conrad. "How do you get through to her? She's so stubborn!"

A knowing smirk curved his lips. "I usually state the obvious."

"Do you tell her when she's being an idiot?"

"That's usually Lucas' job; though he does it in an elegant way."

Lucy turned towards Kee and pointed an accusing finger at her. "You're being a fucking idiot!"

Kee turned towards her friend with an amused smile. "That wasn't elegant at all, Luce."

She huffed and crossed her arms across her chest again. "I don't care. You need to listen to me, woman. I have seen the way he looks at you. Hell, I've seen the way you guys look at each other when the other isn't looking. Kee, I've worked at this bar for three years, and I've never seen someone capture his attention like you do."

Her heart skipped a beat, and she bit down on her lip as she began to cook the next two pieces of French toast. She missed Lucas. Before their falling out yesterday, they hadn't talked for a few days. She had stayed upstairs on the fourth story in one of the guest suites, not wanting to be the reason he didn't sleep in his own bed. Conrad had gone with her, supporting her even though he thought they were being ridiculous.

The hollow, empty feeling in her stomach returned when she remembered their argument again. "He considers me a weapon."

The fox frowned. "What does that even mean?"

She shrugged, momentarily forgetting that Lucy didn't know what she truly was. "Did you know I've actually been here for over a month, Lucy? I've been hiding in the basement or upstairs in the training room." *Or in plain sight as someone else completely.*

She blinked. "Have you really? I heard someone talking about Lucas' wolf, but I didn't know that you had been here for so long."

"Yeah, something bad happened to me. I was recovering and plotting some revenge." She finished the French toast and divided them on three different plates. She grabbed syrup from the fridge and some silverware before handing them their plates. She met Lucy's confused expression and continued. "It turns out Lucas was *indirectly*—" she cut a sharp look at Conrad when he glared at her. "Responsible for what happened. He had wanted me to become, uh, stronger so he can more accurately use me."

"Use you?" She repeated.

She nodded. "I do surveillance work for Lucas sometimes."

Lucy took a bite of her food, trying to figure out the missing pieces of Kee's story. She was being evasive, but as a fox, Lucy was naturally calculating. "So, the question still stands, Kee. Did you ask him to explain himself?"

Conrad snorted after he swallowed a bite. "No, she didn't. She's blaming him for everything when someone else is truly responsible."

"Kee! You need to talk to him. There has to be something else here that you are missing. And let me point this out to you, friend: if you were only a weapon, why would he make you his bonded wereanimal?"

"How did you know I wasn't one before this event?" Kee shot back defensively.

She hummed in satisfaction. "I didn't, but you just confirmed it."

"Tricky fox," Kee pointed an accusing fork at her. "He did it to save me."

Pale green eyes looked at her expectantly. "Why would he save someone who's just a tool?" She tore her gaze away when her phone went off.

Kee watched as the fox's face flushed red as she read the message on her phone. "Okay, enough about my love life. Who's getting you all flustered?"

Lucy cleared her throat and set her phone down on the counter next to her. "It's Derrick."

She lifted a brow. "From the LA skulk? I thought you didn't want anything to do with the fox pack."

She pursed her lips and stabbed a piece of French toast with her fork before dragging it through the syrup on her plate. "I don't," she started. "But, he's charming."

Conrad looked at Lucy, amber eyes unreadable. "Do you like him?"

The werefox blushed again, unable to meet the wolf's gaze. "I don't really know him." She mumbled, avoiding his gaze. "But he asked me out on a date last night, and I got sucked into agreeing. Cunning bastard."

"Oh," he replied curtly and looked down at his plate. "Are you going to go?"

She shrugged and ate the saturated French toast without tasting it. "He wants to go tonight, but I have to work so I don't think I can make it."

Kee looked between the two of them, chewing thoughtfully. Why did she have the sudden need to play matchmaker? "Why don't I work the bar for you tonight?" They both looked at her with equally shocked expressions. *Interesting.*

"You don't have to, Kee. I know you're fighting with Lucas," Lucy quickly rebutted.

"Didn't you tell me to get over it? Besides, he'll be holed up in his office and I'll be busy behind the bar. It'll be fine." She answered. "Or, do you not want to go?" She tilted her head innocently.

"I don't know." Lucy shifted uncomfortably. "I guess I don't really have a reason not to go if you cover my shift." She snuck a peek at Conrad as she said it.

He abruptly slid off the counter and picked up his plate. "You should go," he commented before dropping his plate in the sink with a loud *clang.* "I'm going to try to nap before my shift. I'll see you later," he said quickly before heading out the double doors to the club.

Kee watched him go and looked at Lucy to see her frowning down at her plate. *Very interesting.*

Four

While Lucas was still asleep, Kee stole a bartender's uniform from his office before getting ready for Lucy's shift. The black, form fitting tank top had 'Byte' scrawled across the chest in white cursive. She accompanied it with black jeans, black non-slip shoes, and smoky eye makeup. Finishing the look with a high ponytail, she made her way down to the first level.

"Oh, Kee! What are you doing here?" The other female bartender asked in surprise as Kee walked towards the bar.

Kee didn't know who she was, but she wasn't surprised the vampire knew her. Everyone knew who Kee was since she became Lucas' bonded 'wolf'.

"I'm covering Lucy's shift." She replied as she stepped behind the bar and went to one of the three wells by the bar top.

Each well had an ice bin at thigh level as well as a plastic grid container that held the house brands of hard alcohol. She turned around and quickly scanned the rows of name brand bottles that lined the glass shelves on the mirrored wall. She tried to commit them to memory so she could easily find them throughout the night. She checked one of the bottom fridges for garnishes, making mental notes as she did.

"I am Mirabella, by the way," the vampire introduced, a slight British accent playing on the words. "Is she alright? I know she was speaking to that persistent fox last night." She continued as she stacked empty glasses next to her own ice bin.

Oh, she still wants to talk. "Yeah, she has a date with him."

She grinned, showing the tips of her fangs. "That will make quite a few of the girls happy."

Kee stopped her mental inventory and glanced up at her co-worker for the night. "And why is that?" She could tell Mirabella was an older vampire. She looked young with her layered, sandy blonde hair and natural makeup, but her enunciations gave her away. Especially with her lack of contractions.

Mirabella narrowed her blue eyes at the cold tone she received. "I just mean that a lot of them are infatuated with your beta."

"Beta?" Kee echoed but knew exactly who she was talking about. It was just her and Conrad. Was he her beta by default? Honestly, she couldn't imagine anyone else in that position even if their small pack had more members. A small smile tugged at her lips. He definitely deserved the title.

"Conrad, of course," she replied with a guarded look. Her eyes fell on the four white scars visible on the bare part of Kee's chest. "He is your beta, is he not?"

"Yeah." She straightened her spine and tried to ignore the scrutinizing look directed at her scars. "He is. I guess I just didn't realize how many people wanted him."

Mirabella smirked. "Your wolf is delicious to look at. Everyone thought he was courting Lucy." Her smile almost turned predatory.

"Delicious?" She bit out protectively, her hackles rising. "You can think he's delicious, but no one is to taste him." She warned, staring the vampire down. She kept her face impassive, but the warning was clear.

"Is that a threat?" The vampire asked, all humor wiped from her face.

"Yes." Kee instantly replied. "You and the other vampires will keep your fangs out of him."

"Or what, little wolf? Will you go tell the lord?" Mirabella sneered.

"Lucas doesn't handle my fights, and I don't need him to," she growled. "Remember that he chose me for a reason."

The two glared at each other for a few moments longer before the first group of customers made their way to the bar once it opened. They broke eye contact and instantly went into playful customer service mode, acting as if their tense conversation hadn't happened. Even so, Kee made sure to keep the vampire in her peripheral the rest of the night.

Several hours later, at almost 1am, Kee felt an angry aura flaring behind her. As she turned towards the bar top, a beer bottle struck the side of her face. She felt the bottle shatter against her cheek, a jagged edge slicing into her skin. The impact jarred her senses, momentarily disorienting her. She stumbled as her equilibrium tilted, black spots dancing in front of her eyes.

Feeling something wet drip down her cleavage, as well as hearing several gasps, she snapped out of her haze. She jerked her head up and met the fierce stare of Katie's beast. She was still in her human form, but her aqua eyes were nearly mint with her wolf. Kee's nostrils flared as the scent of alcohol and rage radiated off her in waves.

Well, it's safe to say Cain told her what happened.

"You murdering bitch! You killed Wyatt!" Katie snarled.

The people who hadn't turned at the initial sound of breaking glass joined the current gawkers at the werewolf's exclamation. Kee could feel them watching her with baited breath as she touched the growing wet spot on her chest. She drew her fingertips away to see them caked in blood. She then lifted them to her cheek and fingered the deep laceration right under her cheek bone. Her breath hitched slightly at the pain before she turned a cold, blank look on Katie.

She briefly had flashes of the men who ambushed her a month ago but quickly pushed them away. *No, I'm not a victim anymore, and Katie will pay just as they had.*

One second she was just staring at Katie, the next she was stepping onto the ice bin under the counter and leaping over the bar to tackle the werewolf. Katie tried to brace herself for the impact but was knocked to the ground. The patrons of the bar stepped back, forming a wide girth around the duo, but Kee ignored them as she sat on Katie's chest and landed two punches to her face. Katie yelped in pain before grabbing Kee's ponytail and pulling hard, forcing her head back.

Kee followed the motion, leaning back as Katie tugged her ponytail. She was practically lying back against Katie's legs as she kicked at her. Katie released the ponytail and caught Kee's heel before it connected with her face. She shoved the blonde off her and quickly leapt to her feet unsteadily. She wiped at her bloodied nose and kept her glowing eyes on Kee.

Kee flipped back and jumped to her feet as well. She saw Conrad pushing his way through the crowd towards them from the corner of her eye, but she was too angry to let him interfere. She lifted her lip in a snarl and deepened her voice. "Stay, Conrad!"

He immediately stopped at his alpha's forceful command, his feet suddenly frozen in place. However, that didn't stop him from moving his lips. "Kee, stop!" But he knew it was futile; she wasn't listening to anyone. If he hadn't been on break to call Liam, Katie wouldn't have gotten into the club. He would have smelled her drunk state and denied her access. Unfortunately, the other security team at the door didn't care as much. A drunk wolf was still a high for a vampire.

As the two girls went at it again with flying fists, he eyed the vampires around them. They were too still. Their wide, unblinking eyes were trained on the blood coating the women's flesh. A surge of panic went through him. They needed to stop before more blood was shed, but neither were in a listening mood. Katie's aura was wild and sporadic, her inner wolf fueling her anger. Kee's was just as deadly, but hers suffocated him, made his beast cower and submit.

Relief sagged Conrad's shoulders when he saw Lucas' two right-hand men appear in the crowd. Giovanni and Dante were staring down the thirsty vampires, having to touch a few stubborn ones to break their fixation on the blood. Most of them backed away to find their human partners for the night, but others stayed to watch the fight, wanting to see the strength of Lucas' wolf.

"Say something!" Katie screeched at Kee when the two leapt apart from each other once again. She was panting, one eye swollen shut. She hated to admit it, but Kee was stronger than her. For every hit she landed on the murdering bitch, she received three in return. She swayed on her feet, whether from alcohol or the blows to her head, she wasn't sure.

Kee stood there with her hands up in a defensive stance. "There's nothing to say, Katie. Cain told you what happened. I was protecting myself from Wyatt. He would have killed me." Her cheek hurt like a bitch, like fire spreading across the side of her face. Katie managed to get a punch to her ribs, but those didn't hurt nearly as much.

"He was following orders!" She cried and released a mournful howl. "And you killed him!"

"Go home, Katie. You can't win." Kee warned as she felt the ire in the wolf rise again.

"No! I'll kill you!" Katie snarled and surged forward.

Kee was ready for her. She waited until Katie threw her fist and caught her wrist. Using the momentum from Katie's sprint, she pulled the wolf's hand behind her. Kee's other hand fisted in Katie's black hair as she spun so she was almost behind her assailant. She eyed the edge of the polished metal bar top and tightened her hold on Katie's hair. She had every intention of slamming her face onto the edge, but cool fingers wrapped around her wrist.

She didn't have to look behind her to know who it was. Her mind was buzzing with warmth at his closeness, her lower stomach tingling with need despite their fight. She felt him move closer and her heart skipped a beat.

"No destroying faces tonight." Lucas scolded her softly. When she didn't let go, he flexed his fingers on her wrist before tightening his hold. "Release her, Keira."

Her name rolled off his tongue in a sensual, albeit chiding tone. She wasn't going to listen to him. Her hand twitched with the need to break Katie's face on the bar's counter, to show her just how strong she was.

Katie whimpered in her hold and Kee tightened her grip. *I can do it. Make her pay for attacking me.*

His lips brushed the shell of her ear. "Not here, Keira. Not with so many patrons here to witness."

Her eyes broke away from Katie and scanned the circle that surrounded them. There were at least twenty people staring, not including the people sitting at the bar. She noticed vampires staring at her longingly but continued to gaze over the crowd. She paused at seeing Gio and Dante, both their faces unreadable, and then looked at her beta. His brow was furrowed, but his golden eyes softened when she looked at him. With a reluctant sigh, she released Katie.

Kee tilted her chin up and went to step away, but Lucas' hold remained on her. She glared down at the pale hand, not looking at him. "Let go."

"No." He answered dismissively before looking at Dante and

Conrad. "Please see to it that she has a ride home. Perhaps calling her alpha would be beneficial in case her wolf rises again." When Conrad hesitated, Lucas patted Kee's head with his free hand. "Everything will be fine, Mr Novak."

Kee met Conrad's eyes and nodded at his silent question. "Go ahead."

He stepped forward with Dante, and they each grabbed one of Katie's arms. They hauled her to her feet and steered her towards the front door. Conrad was surprised when she didn't put up a fight, instead keeping her head bowed, eyes on the floor.

"Giovanni, if you would please meet us in my office with your medical kit. I think my wolf may need some help with her cheek." Lucas said in a light tone.

Lucas' face was calm, almost pleasant, but Kee could feel his true emotions from the bond. Anger, along with a mix of hunger and desire, swelled in her. She could taste some other dark, sour emotion but wasn't sure what it was. She wasn't used to feeling his emotions. He usually kept them in check and hidden away from her, something she couldn't do yet. She didn't know what it meant that she could feel them now.

She tried to tug her arm from his hold again, but he didn't budge. She felt him look at her and she couldn't help but look up at the heavy feel of his stare. His emerald green eyes shined with an intensity that made her shrink back. "Let go." She demanded again, but her tone was softer.

"No." He repeated as he bent low enough to shove his shoulder in her stomach. He then straightened with her draped over his shoulder, his arm wrapped around the back of her thighs. He felt her thump against his back with her fists but ignored it as he carried her upstairs to his office.

Kee protested the entire way until she was finally dropped onto the leather couch in his office. She went to sit up, but Lucas climbed over her, his green eyes finally blazing with the anger she felt from the bond. She swallowed once and put her hand on his firm chest, giving it a futile shove. "Get off me."

"No, you are going to listen to me, Keira." He let out a growl that would have impressed a werewolf. "What did you think you were doing down there?"

She glared up at him. "I was defending myself!"

"You call almost breaking her face defense? You could have killed her. I do not need that attention in my club." He sneered.

"Do you see *my* face? She hit me with a fucking beer bottle!"

"Oh, I see *your* face," he gripped her chin and jerked her head to the side to see the smear of blood on her cheek. His mouth salivated as the heady scent filled his nose. His fangs throbbed with longing.

She flinched as he traced the cut with his thumb but felt her chest tighten at his touch. She didn't realize how much she missed it. Angry at her body's response to him, she tried to push against him. "You said you wouldn't feed from me again." She protested.

"I know what I said," Lucas replied coldly. He turned her head back to face him, eyes narrowed into a hard glare. "But clearly you wish others to do what I swore not to."

"What—" She shuddered when he dropped his hand to her collar bone, following the trail of blood. His cool fingertips slipped over her scars, making her jerk under him.

The vampire rumbled hungrily as the blood thinned and spread along her skin as he touched it. *I almost wish I had not vowed to not feed from her. It would be so easy to lick her clean, to lap up the intoxicating blood from her until she begged for more.* With a clenched jaw, he tugged the hem of her shirt up and wiped away the blood before it could tempt him further.

"Lucas, stop." She demanded, thinking he had different intentions as he brought her shirt up. She sucked in a breath when he looked at her with crimson eyes. She remembered what he said about the effect her blood had on him. Her jaw clenched with nerves and she quickly brought up her knee, aiming for his groin. He was quicker, catching her knee before it made contact.

"Do you think I would hurt you?" He asked, voice deep but quiet. Did she *really* think he would hurt her just now? From simply lifting her shirt? Or had she been anticipating a more sensual moment?

"I don't know anymore," she said, meeting his stare. Her stomach dropped when she saw a brief, fleeting glimmer of hurt in those blood red eyes.

His face turned expressionless, devoid of any emotion. He opened his mouth to say something but stilled when a soft knock rapped on his door. His eyes faded back to green as he removed himself from her. He sat down on the arm of his sofa before beckoning Giovanni into the room.

Kee sat up as Gio entered, tugging her shirt back into place. She gave him a stiff, forced smile as he sat down next to her on the couch. "Sorry you always have to patch me up, Gio."

"It is of no consequence, Kee," Gio replied as he got out his hydrogen peroxide and some cotton balls. He tilted her face up and to the side so he could inspect the damage. "It looks like it's already stopped bleeding, which is good," he stated as he soaked a cotton ball and gently dabbed it along the cut. "Looks like your healing is kicking in quicker this time."

She refrained from nodding and looked at the stoic Lucas on the arm of the couch. Did she really hurt his feelings? She wanted to apologize, but her lingering anger chased the words away. "So, you want to explain what that was all about?"

Lucas looked at her sharply. If she thought he was going to be embarrassed, or taken off guard, she was sorely mistaken. "You seem to want someone to feed off of you." He repeated.

"Yes, you mentioned that, but I'm pretty sure I didn't ask for anyone to drink from me. I'm also fairly certain you said you wouldn't feed from me again." She scowled, ignoring Gio's surprised look.

He gave an exasperated sigh. "*As I said*, I know what I promised, Keira. However, I also told you to be cautious of your blood. You did not heed me. You continued to engage in a fight, causing more bloodshed and tempting my vampires further. Did I not warn you against this?"

She narrowed her eyes at him. "You expected me to just let her hit me and walk away?"

"That is exactly what I expected of you," he countered in a cold tone. "If Giovanni and Dante had not been there to calm the vampires and steer them away, I am certain they would have attacked you. And, as a result, there would have been bloodshed by my hand."

She opened her mouth but hissed when Gio pressed a little too hard on her gash. "Fuck, that hurts!"

Giovanni pressed the cotton ball hard against her cut one more time after gaining her attention. "Lucas' vampires will behave for him, but we often get vampires who visit from all over. He would have torn apart any vampire who touched you, and it could have caused a feud with neighboring lords."

Her heart fluttered. Would he really have started a war for her? She frowned at Lucas again. "Why didn't you just tell me?"

"Because words are wasted on you." He replied icily, his anger from last night resurfacing with a vengeance. Her stupidly flaunting her blood moments ago hadn't helped his ire. "Actions, it seems, are the only way to get through to you. How does the saying go? *Actions speak louder than words?*"

She tensed, her spine going rigid at his harsh words. "Maybe you just don't know how to communicate."

"No, I believe you just do not know how to listen, little shifter."

Kee abruptly stood from the couch, nearly toppling Gio over as he applied Neosporin to her cut. Her chest flushed with embarrassment as she remembered how foolish he made her feel for offering her blood to him. "You expect me to listen to you after everything? How about how you left me to wallow in my regret before that? I tried to apologize to you, Lucas! I tried to talk to you about what I said, about what I offered to you! What did you do instead? Ignored me for a week like a fucking child!"

Lucas' normal ironclad control snapped as their fury surged within the bond and collided. He was on his feet and moving towards her with lethal grace. "*I* am fucking child? If we are pointing fingers then perhaps you should look at yourself. Who childishly ran off into their *other* lover's arms when they jumped to a poor conclusion? When they heard something they did not like? Where were your words when we *really* needed to speak about something?" Her lips parted to speak, but he silenced her by continuing. "Tell me, *Kee*, did Cain comfort your naked body like I had? Did you writhe in his arms like you had with me? Did you sleep with him before or after foolishly telling his pack that you are alive and well?"

The one time he ever used her nickname and it sounded like a scorned curse. She breathed hard through her nose, her eyes wide with anger and hurt. There were so many things she wanted to say back to him, to yell and scream at him, but they died on the tip of her tongue. What had he said to her before?

Ah, yes.

She drew her hand back and slapped him hard across the face. His head barely turned, but her hand stung as if she had hit steel. "You're right, actions *do* speak louder than words." She spat before turning and storming out of his office.

Gio looked at his fuming maker and took a step back. Lucas' eyes were red, his hands clenched so tightly into fists, Gio feared he would break his own fingers. "Lucas, you cannot leave things like this," he advised softly. "Alexander has broken this relationship between the two of you. Do not let him win."

"Some things are not meant to be mended," he bit out, both of their anger still raging like a storm within the bond.

"True, but this is not one of those things." Giovanni replied calmly. "You both need to cool off and then you need to have a long conversation with her. She's your bonded wereanimal and you share a connection."

He did not want to hear it, not now. "Giovanni, go downstairs and make sure there is no remaining damage from *my wolf's-*" he nearly spat, "-actions. If so, see to it that they are properly corrected."

He sighed but dipped his head into a nod. "Yes, sir."

Lucas waited until his second was gone before he dropped down onto his couch and let out a stream of curses in Greek. He took a deep breath and tried to calm the anger that made his heart beat once again with purpose. How had this gone so poorly? When he felt Keira in the bar when he woke, he had plans to talk to her about everything. He wanted to talk in length about Alexander and her being a so-called weapon.

However, as soon as he smelled her blood and saw all the ravenous vampires staring longingly at it, he had become enraged. A wave of possessiveness and a sprinkle of fear had gripped him. He had not only feared for her safety, but for his vampires' as well. He could have burned the foreign vampires should they have attacked Keira, but he also realized his own would not have been spared should they have joined the feast. Not only would he have hurt his own coven, but as Giovanni had said, he could have instigated a war with the lords from other cities.

I do not need another Alexander on my hands. Lucas told himself firmly, but his hands balled into fists once again. *But I* will *kill for her. She is dangerous for my control. I nearly broke my promise to not feed from her. And this rage, it is so raw and potent. I do not lose my composure and yet this is not the first time this month I have lost the hold on my emotions.*

He leaned back against the cushions and stared up at the ceiling where he could imagine her two stories up, pacing in the room she had taken residence in. He knew the note from Alexander had messed things up between them, but he had no doubt he made them worse tonight.

Good intentions only get you so far, he mused.

He let out a sigh as he remembered Gio's words. He was right, this was something he knew wasn't meant to be broken. He would make sure he fixed it. He felt a surge of ire vibrate through the bond and pressed his lips in a firm line.

Perhaps not tonight.

He went to rub his face with his hands but stilled when he noticed that her blood was still on his fingers. He tried to stop, but before he knew it, he had his pointer and middle finger between his lips, his tongue thoroughly removing every trace of her blood on his skin. He moaned when the exotic taste pleasantly scorched his tongue. It slid down his throat and warmed his chest, his heart fluttering. His body felt hot; a sensation he hadn't really felt since he was human. Sure, he felt it when he used his golden flame, but that was a part of him. Every time he tasted Keira's blood he was reminded what it felt like to *feel* a temperature from within.

He wanted more.

He covered his mouth with both hands and could feel his fangs throbbing against his lips, begging for more.

Definitely not tonight.

Five

Kee stepped out of the shower, disappointed that she felt only marginally better. The adrenaline rush from fighting Katie and arguing with Lucas had worn off, making her body feel heavy. She dried off and wrapped her hair in the towel before examining the cut on her face in the mirror. It was angry from the hot water but wasn't as big as she originally thought.

Dumb bitch, she thought as she walked back into the large bedroom and towards the black, six drawer dresser. She pulled on a pair of clean underwear, black leggings, and one of Conrad's plain black t-shirts. She sat on the edge of the king-sized bed and toweled her hair until most of the water was gone. Pushing the damp strands from her face, she reached for her phone on the nightstand. She snorted when she saw a missed call and text from Cain.

Call me. We need to talk about Katie.

She scoffed again but clicked on his name to call him back. She pressed the cool glass of the screen to her unwounded cheek and only had to wait a few seconds before he answered. "Hey," she said awkwardly.

"*Hey,*" came his quiet reply.

She sighed when the silence stretched on between them. "Cain, I know you're mad."

"*I don't know how I feel.*"

"I beat the shit out of your wolf; I know exactly how you feel. You're angry because you're responsible for her now." Kee pressed her lips together in a hard line. What else did he expect? They both knew this was going to happen.

He growled softly, but it wasn't necessarily in anger. "*She said you could have killed her, but Lucas stopped you. She said she didn't have an option to submit to you.*"

Katie wouldn't have submitted. Not with that much pain and rage. "I don't know about killing her, but I almost smashed her face on the bar top, yes." When he didn't immediately respond she added, "She attacked me, Cain. I warned you what would happen in return."

"*I know.*" She could picture him rubbing his face like he always did when he was stressed. "*I didn't know she had left until she was already gone. I thought I had convinced her not to go after you, but I should have ordered her as her alpha.*"

"Are you really surprised? She loved Wyatt and I killed him. Just like Mason's mate." She plucked at loose lint on her leggings. Tonight had been proof that Cain's pack would never accept her. How could they? It didn't matter that she had been attacked first. She wasn't one of them and she killed three of their own.

When he still didn't respond, she rubbed her eyes. "Now do you see what I mean about being mates?" She asked quietly after another stretch of silence, "Cain?"

"*I'm here,*" he rumbled. "*I just don't know what to say, babe.*"

"How did Natalie take the news?" She asked, trying to change the subject until she could figure out exactly how to put her thoughts into words.

"*How do you think? She's also sure Warren is the one who ordered the attack, but she's terrified to face him. He's her world, Kee. They've been together for so long and to find out that her mate is the reason for all this death?"* He sighed. *"It's tearing her up. She just left my house hoping to avoid seeing him tonight."*

She frowned again, eyes softening. She liked Nat; she really did. She could only imagine how she was feeling. "I'm sorry," she said but then mentally berated herself for apologizing. "This isn't exactly my fault, but I don't want other people to suffer because of what happened."

"With a death in a pack, everyone suffers," he sighed. *"Three deaths are hard enough for everyone, but Warren being the base cause is going to throw everything into chaos. He's our alpha and he failed to protect us."*

"Base cause," she repeated emotionlessly. "If I had died then your pack would still be a perfect, tight knit family."

"Don't turn that on me, Kee," he groaned. *"That's not how I meant it."*

"I know."

"Do you? Because even if you had died, I would be broken. I was broken until I found out you were alive. A depressed beta could easily be challenged for his spot in the pack."

"Challenged, maybe, but no one could defeat you, Cain. You're too strong." She complimented. He had once told her of the times when he had been challenged by ambitious wolves. Each time he had triumphed without question.

"You make me weak." Cain admitted in a whisper.

Kee tensed and looked up when Conrad suddenly opened the door. She gave him a feeble smile before turning her attention back to her conversation. "I don't want to be your weakness. People in relationships are supposed to strengthen each other, not the opposite." At Conrad's confused head tilt, she patted the spot on the bed next to her.

"What are you saying?" The beta asked defensively.

She took Conrad's hand when he sat down next to her and squeezed it as if she could siphon strength from him. "I think you know what I'm saying." She repeated, her heart skipping a beat, though it didn't twist as painfully as she thought it would have. She had known for a while that they couldn't continue their relationship.

"*Kee, baby, please,*" he practically whined. "*Don't do this.*"

"Cain, think about what I'm saying."

"*I just got you back. I can't lose you again.*"

"I'm not dying." She told him firmly as Conrad gripped her hand in encouragement. "This just won't work. I can never be your mate; your pack will turn on you."

"*I can talk to them. You said it yourself that no one can defeat me. We've already talked about this. I will be their alpha; my word is law.*"

"They'll constantly challenge you. You're going to take a mate who killed three of your wolves? How do you think that's going to make them feel?" She pressed.

"*You're an alpha female. They'll fear you, just as they should!*"

"But they won't trust me. They won't trust you or your judgement. Plus, I can't live my life constantly watching my back to make sure none of your wolves jump me."

"*I will watch your back for you. It's what mates do, Kee!*" He growled into the phone.

She pinched the bridge of her nose and closed her eyes tightly as they stung with unshed tears. She couldn't believe she was hurting him like this again. She was tired. So, so tired. "Cain, your pack is everything to you. I know this. I understand and accept it. That's why I don't want to come between you. I can't be responsible for further discomfort in your pack." She clenched Conrad's hand again. "You will find another mate."

"*I don't want another mate!*" He snarled loudly, making her jerk the phone away from her ear. "*I love you, Keira! You're the only one I want!*"

She sucked in a breath but sternly said, "You can't have me."

This time he did whine. "*Baby, please.*"

"I'm sorry, Cain. But it's better this way." She told him gently.

"*Better for who? You're breaking my heart.*"

Kee tried to blink away the tears at the anguish in his voice. "For both of us. I'm not trying to hurt you. Especially since we've just come to an understanding, but this *is* better for both of us. We just aren't compatible anymore, Cain. Please understand."

"*I can't,*" he mumbled. "*You don't mean this.*"

"I do, Cain. Look, I have to go." She heard him growl before the line went dead. Sighing, she dropped the phone and looked at Conrad. At his concerned expression, she gave him a forced smile. "Done for the night?"

The wolf pulled her into a hug and stroked the top of her wet hair. "I'm sorry you had to do that."

She hugged him back, enjoying his warmth and support. "It had to be done. I should have realized sooner that we were never going to work. I guess Katie was just the wakeup call I needed." She tightened her hold. "I'm sorry for being forceful tonight." She winced when she realized just how much she apologized to him as of late. She pulled back and frowned at him. "I'm not very nice to you, am I?"

He furrowed his brow. "What do you mean?"

"I'm always apologizing for being mean to you. Oh gods, am I abusive?" She asked, truly horrified. She hated alphas. She witnessed how some of them treated their pack and it disgusted her. Had she sunken to that level? Was it in her genes to be abusive?

"Kee, stop," he told her as he cupped her face in his hands, looking down into her panicked eyes. "You're not abusive at all. Trust me, I know abusive." He grimaced as he remembered his situation with Liam.

"But, I've been so cruel to you."

"How in the hell do you even figure that? You took me in, Kee. You've been here for me. Yes, you've been an alpha but never cruel. Today is the first day you've ever actually influenced me to do as you say and both times it was to stop me from meddling in your business." He smiled at her. "You're not abusive. Please don't say that."

Words failed her, so she hugged him once again. Conrad had become such a crucial pillar of support for her. Honestly, it amazed her. Even before her attack, he had been there to lean on. What did he see in her to make him want to follow her? She wasn't sure, but she didn't want to question it. He was by her side, and for that she was thankful. Nothing would come between them.

He pet the top of her head again when they pulled apart. His amber eyes inspected her cheek, looking at the gash. "This looks a lot better already. It was pretty nasty earlier."

Kee nodded. "Gio said it was healing pretty quickly. I wonder if that's because of my bond with Lucas?"

He shrugged. "Maybe. He would know better than I would." He peered at her expectantly. "So, did you guys talk everything out?"

She gave a harsh bark of a laugh. "Not at all. We ended up fighting even worse than before. He insinuated that I'm a whore, by the way."

That's not true, she scolded herself. *He assumed I slept with Cain and called me out on it. I just felt guilty.*

Conrad was stunned before fury crept over him. "What? Are you kidding me?" Was Lucas crazy? The vampire had told Conrad he planned on smoothing everything out with Kee. What the hell had changed?

"He thinks I slept with Cain last night." She shrugged one shoulder. "I didn't, but I might have this morning if you didn't show up. Some pretty nasty words were exchanged between us and I slapped him."

He stared at her with his mouth slightly agape. "What the fuck is wrong with the two of you?"

"I don't trust him, Con. He hurt me. I thought maybe he was going to try to talk to me about it, but we just ended up fighting again. I don't know what to do anymore." She flopped back against the duvet with a heavy sigh.

He rubbed his face in exasperation. "You two are like children."

She let out a real laugh. "We both accused each other of the same thing."

He rolled his eyes and stood from the bed. "You guys just need to talk it out. I'm going to shower."

"Okay," she responded and then glanced at her phone when it started to ring again. She softly groaned, expecting it to be Cain but was surprised to see Nana's name on the screen. She quickly answered it. "Hi, Nana."

"Kee, where have you been?"

Kee smiled at the familiar Irish accent. It wasn't very prominent, but she heard it in the brisk greeting. Her great-grandmother always got straight to the point. She didn't like idle chitchat and was usually blunt when she did speak about things. "Sorry, Nan, I've been dealing with some things."

A hum came through the phone. *"Bad things? Are you in trouble?"* Not a lick of panic was in her tone, just curiosity.

"Yes, to your first question. And no, not anymore. At least, nothing I can't handle." *Or so I hope.*

"Is it because of your abilities?" Kee heard her take a long inhale and knew she was smoking on her front porch. All these years and the woman still refused to give up the bad habit.

"Kind of," she mumbled.

"Is it that beta you're dating? I told you not to tell him." She accused, but not in a scolding manner. *"No one should know our secret, Kee. It's not safe. I even have doubts about your vampire."*

She rubbed her face. "It's a long story, Nana."

"*You can tell me at Thanksgiving.*" As always, Nana had a way of stating rather than asking.

"Thanksgiving?" Kee echoed and pulled up the calendar on her phone. "That's this Thursday."

"*Yes, two days from now. You will come tomorrow, of course. Your great-uncle and his grandson are coming.*"

"I have a great-uncle? Is he grandma's brother?" She asked incredulously. How did Nana fail to mention that she had more relatives? "I didn't know you had another kid, Nana."

"*I don't,*" she corrected. "*He is your great-grandfather's son.*"

"Your mate's son?" She asked. She remembered her mother telling her how she didn't know Nana. The older woman had locked herself away when her mate died years before Trinity was even born.

"*Yes. His name is Christopher. His grandson, Gabriel, is basically your cousin.*" Nana informed her. "*Christopher is a wolf, of course, but Gabriel isn't. It turns out that Gabriel's mother was a witch. Although, I believe 'bruja' is the correct term since she in Hispanic. Anyways, he didn't inherit his father's wolf gene.*"

"Cross-breeding is rare," Kee commented, partially in shock. Two different species of preternatural creatures usually didn't result in a full-term pregnancy. The woman's body naturally attacked the fetus, treating it as if it were a foreign object or virus.

"*Yes, but it does happen sometimes. It seems his mother used some powerful blood magic to make sure Gabriel was not lost during pregnancy. She's still paying the price for it with the head warlock of Texas.*"

She winced. "And his father?"

"*The pack killed him.*" Nana stated in a cynical tone. "*As soon as Gabriel's seventh year came and he didn't turn, they knew he would be a warlock. If his mother had been human, it would have been different, but he was a threat. He tried to flee with Gabriel, but they caught him. They always do. You know how it is, Kee."*

She nodded but realized Nana couldn't see it. "Yeah, I do. How old is Gabriel now?"

"Sixteen, I believe." she answered.

"Ah, he's pretty young." The two fell into silence before Kee broke it with another question. "Nana, not that I'm not happy, but why the visit?"

Nana was quiet for a few heartbeats before replying. *"Perhaps I am just starting to feel lonely."*

Her brow furrowed and she frowned. That didn't sound like Nana at all, but she knew better than to pry into her great-grandmother's feelings. "Okay, Nan. I'll be there tomorrow." She heard the water in the bathroom turn off and quickly added. "Is it okay if I bring someone?"

"Your boyfriend?" She asked wearily.

Kee laughed. "No, my beta."

"Isn't that your boyfriend?"

"No, Nana, we broke up. I'm talking about *my* beta." She clarified with a proud smile. "I told you, it's a long story."

"Apparently so. Bring whomever you wish."

"Would you like me to bring anything for Thanksgiving?" She asked but already knew the answer.

Nana scoffed. *"Do not insult me, child. I know how to provide a more than adequate meal."*

Kee chuckled again when the line went dead and looked up at Conrad as he came out of the bathroom with a towel wrapped around his waist, another one in his hands as he dried his hair. "Hey, what are you doing for Thanksgiving?"

He blinked in surprise at the sudden question. "Nothing. Lucas has Byte closed. He said something about a dinner party for his coven."

She lifted an eyebrow. "How does a vampire dinner party even work?"

"I have no idea," he responded with a wry smile. "Either way, he only wants vampires here on Thursday. I guess I assumed I would be hanging out with you. That okay?" He had hoped he would be with her on the holiday. It would be his first one without Mia.

Kee grinned at him. "How do you feel about meeting an old lady who's more stoic than a statue?" When he tilted his head, she laughed. "My great-grandma wants me to come over. She said I can bring you."

Conrad's lips parted in surprise. "Your great-grandma? Will your whole family be there as well?"

"Nana is my only family," she explained. "She took me in when I was seven."

Cautiously, he asked, "What city does she live in?" He didn't want to run into Liam and have the alpha ruin everything he had been working towards.

"She lives in Riverside. She's considered a lone wolf by the Riverside pack, but they respect her. Her mate had been the reigning alpha for nearly eighty years. He died before my mom was born. Nana went into a recluse state when he died so my mom never really knew her. I didn't either until she adopted me." She gave a small, embarrassed laugh. "Sorry, that was a bit more information than you asked."

He sat down on the bed next to her, his brow furrowed. "I have so many questions, but I don't want to pry."

"I appreciate that. In short, my parents are dead and my grandparents didn't want me so Nana adopted me. She knows what I am and is the one who taught me how to control it. She's not the nicest person, but she's the only family I have. You'll get use to her bluntness."

He smiled at the warm tone she used when talking about her grandmother. "I would love to meet your Nana, Kee."

She beamed at him. "If nothing else, the food will be worth it.

Nana and her mate came from Ireland so she cooks an authentic Irish feast."

"I can't wait." He said truthfully and then looked at the door when a series of scratches came from it. He softly padded to the door and cracked it open. He blinked in surprise and pulled it all the way open when he saw an arctic fox with black paws standing there. Her pale green eyes were glassy, her white fur matted and dirty. "Lucy?" He asked, his beast growling at the sight of her disheveled state.

She looked up at him and let out a high pitched whine. She rose up on her back legs, her front paws reaching out to him. When he lifted her from the ground, she buried her face in his neck and started shaking, her fluffy tail tucked firmly between her legs.

"Luce?" Kee asked in alarm as Conrad brought the fox to the bed. She took Lucy from his arms and held her close, gently petting the fur between her ears as the fox mewled. "Shh, it's okay. We're here. You're safe now." She told her as she laid back against the bed, keeping Lucy tucked close against her.

What the hell happened? Had Derrick done this to her? Why? If that bastard hurt her—! Her thoughts cut off as her anger fizzled out, body still exhausted from earlier.

Conrad quickly threw on a pair of sweats and joined them on the bed. He slipped under the duvet and brought it up over the two girls. He turned towards them, his hand resting on Lucy's side, his fingers lightly petting her as her trembling eased.

"If he hurt you, Lucy, I'll fucking kill him." He told her seriously, a growl rumbling in his chest.

Kee looked at Conrad's angry glare and nodded, glad he still had the energy to be furious for them both. "We both will." She agreed as Lucy tucked her head under Kee's chin and closed her eyes. She stayed awake with Conrad until her friend's quivering stopped, the small fox finally in a deep sleep. She met Conrad's raging eyes and nodded tiredly. "We'll find out everything in the morning, Con. Even if that means kidnapping her to Nana's with us."

Six

Kee felt uncomfortably hot. She parted her eyes and was met with a head of white-blonde hair on her chest. She blinked away the fog of sleep, but it still took a second to register that Lucy was curled up next to her. She looked over at Conrad and saw that he was spooning Lucy from behind, his forehead resting against her shoulder blade. She couldn't help but smile at the sight.

I wonder if they'll ever admit that they like each other.

Lucy released a content sigh and Kee could feel her shimmy her hips back. She stifled a laugh when Conrad's golden eyes snapped open and darted down to where Lucy's ass pressed firmly against his groin. He moved away from the fox, but his legs got caught in the covers, making him trip when he tried to stand. Kee couldn't hold in the laugh a second time.

A blush burned from neck to ears when he realized Kee witnessed it all. No doubt she knew exactly what had happened. "I-I'm going to take a cold shower." He mumbled and grabbed clean clothes from the dresser before disappearing into the bathroom.

Lucy startled awake when he slammed the door. She lifted her head and rubbed her eyes as she processed her surroundings. The large room had white walls and matching lush carpet. There was a wide black dresser off to the side, a matching framed mirror above it. The bed was king-sized with a dark blue comforter and white sheets, the frame a polished black. She quickly sprang up into a sitting position when she saw that she was basically lying on top of her friend.

"Kee?" She asked with flushed cheeks.

"Morning." Kee replied with a smile, sitting up as well.

Lucy's brow furrowed. "What am I doing here?"

Her lips fell into a frown. "You don't remember? You came to our room late last night in your fox form. You were pretty upset." She reached for Lucy's hair, fingering the dirty strands. "You're a mess. What happened?"

The werefox followed her friend's gaze to her hair and looked down at the dirt on her bare skin. She shuddered as the memories came back and clutched the blanket to her chest. "Derrick had ulterior motives," she mumbled and squeezed her eyes shut. "I shouldn't have gone."

"So why did you?" Kee questioned softly, lightly setting her hand on Lucy's shoulder to comfort her. Seconds passed and Kee thought she wouldn't answer. She was about to tell Lucy she didn't have to, but she started talking again.

"I don't know. You said you would cover for me at work and I couldn't come up with a reason to turn him down."

"Not being interested is reason enough to turn someone down, Luce. You didn't owe him an explanation for saying no." She pointed out in a gentle tone.

Lucy sighed and stared down at the navy blue blanket. "I guess I just wanted to see if maybe I could be interested in him. I wanted to see if a date with him could possibly spark something." She leaned into Kee, nestling into her side. "He was charming, but I should have known it was a trap. Tricky bastard."

"Did he hurt you?" Conrad asked as he stepped out of the bath-room, wearing dark blue jeans and a black shirt that showed off his fit form.

Lucy swallowed as she watched him run his fingers through his wet hair, the strands dampening the fabric of the shirt below his collar bones. She blinked when he met her gaze with a sudden fierce inten-sity. She looked away and held the blanket closer to her, suddenly all too aware that she was naked. "Kind of."

A protective growl rumbled in his chest as he approached the bed. He sat down on the edge, putting himself closer to her. He frowned when she shied away, molding herself closer to Kee. He tried to ignore the pang of hurt. "Lucy? What happened?"

She closed her eyes, trying to hide from his angry gaze. "Derrick tried to force a mating bond on me."

Kee looked up at Conrad's sharp inhale as the fox's sudden panic and fear came off her with a pungent, bitter scent. She held Lucy tighter, stroking her hair to try to calm her down. "It's okay, Luce. You're here now."

Conrad scooted closer to them and gingerly pried Lucy's fingers from their tight grip on the blanket. He took her small hand in his, keeping his hold gentle. "What did he do?"

"We met at LA Live and ate at the Yard House there. The date went okay, but I just didn't feel any romantic connection to him. After dinner we walked around for a while until I noticed he was leading me towards the parking garage. I told him I had walked, but he said he could drop me off at my apartment," she shuddered. "He said it in a way that made my hackles rise. I can't explain the tone of it exactly, but my instincts were telling me that something was wrong, that I needed to get away.

"When I stopped walking and turned him down, he grabbed my upper arm and started hauling me towards his car. I instantly struggled, throwing my elbows and kicking my feet. He ignored my blows and picked me up. I bit his shoulder until I drew blood and he dropped me, but we were already at his car. He pressed me against the door and braced me there with his forearm." She clenched Conrad's hand. "Derrick told me he was sorry, but that he was ordered to do it. The alpha wants me as part of his skulk. He told me he wouldn't force his body on me, but that he had to place a mating mark."

Kee hugged her tighter and looked at Conrad, his eyes shining bright gold with his wolf's presence. "Did he do it?" She asked quietly.

Lucy shook her head. "He pulled my shirt down to expose the back of my neck, but I shifted before he could bite me." She shuddered. "He tried to grab me, but I ran under the cars so he couldn't catch me. Once I was out of the parking lot, I booked it until I ended up here. Thank gods Dante knew who I was. He's the one who brought me up here."

"I can't believe the alpha ordered someone to mate you." Kee spat angrily, grey eyes hard with anger. "Was he that desperate to make you a part of his pack?"

"I guess so," she muttered, but her gaze was focusing on the warm, tan fingers wrapped around hers. She raised her eyes to meet Conrad's and frowned at how stiff his body was. She pulled away from Kee and leaned towards the wolf. "I'm okay, Con."

A growl rumbled in his chest until her head landed on his shoulder. He rubbed his cheek on her hair but kept his hand on hers. "It doesn't make the situation better." He bit out roughly.

She closed her eyes at the contact. "I know, but I'm here now."

Kee smiled as she watched them. "Luce, would you like to come with us to my Nana's house today? She's having a big Irish feast for Thanksgiving tomorrow. Her house is big enough so we can all spend the night."

The werefox opened her pale green eyes and looked up at Conrad and then at Kee. "I would love to, but I'm scheduled to work the bar tonight."

She grinned in response. "I'll take care of that."

—

Mr Vranas,

I'm kidnapping Lucy and Conrad tonight. It's the night before a big holiday so the bar should be slow. You can expect us back either tomorrow night or Friday morning.

-K.Q.

Kee read the note three times as she stood by Lucas' nightstand. She nervously chewed on the end of the pen in her hand. She wanted to imitate the note he had once written her but was second guessing her words. She had meant it as a joke but wondered if it came off as bitchy. She didn't know how he would interpret it since their last few encounters had been disastrous. Trying to ease the possible tension the note could cause, she drew a heart and a winking face next to the Q.

Hopefully that would be enough.

She set the note down on the black nightstand and turned to leave. She paused as she faced the bed, her eyes falling on Lucas' motionless form. His crimson duvet was pulled up to his waist, leaving his pale chest bare to her. His black hair was tousled, the silky strands falling towards his brow.

She sat down on the edge of the bed and let out a soft sigh. Her anger from the past couple days shrank as she realized just how much she had missed him. She *missed* Lucas. She missed their flirty banter and intense debates. Missed sleeping in his bed and waking up to his arms around her. Shamelessly longed for his skilled hands on her body, for the confident thoroughness of his lovemaking. For the intense pleasure of his fucking.

I'm still angry, she thought bitterly. *I have every right to be and I'm entitled to answers. I want the truth, but I don't want to keep fighting with him. Lucy and Conrad are right. I need to hear him out.*

Brushing his hair back from his cool forehead, she bent to place a soft kiss. She pulled back when a soft grunt reached her ears. Thin slits of emerald green peeked out through barely parted eyelids. She gave him a tentative smile, her heart hammering unexplainably in her chest.

"I'm leaving for a little." Kee whispered to him. When he exhaled through his nose in a huff, her smile widened knowingly. "No, not like that. I'm going to my Nana's for Thanksgiving. I'll be back." Unable to resist, she lightly pressed her lips against his. She started to move back, but a cold hand slid to the back of her neck, keeping her in place. Her lips titled in a smirk as they met his in a hard kiss.

"Promise." He mumbled when they parted.

Her eyes softened and she moved to brush her lips against his ear. "I promise."

Lucas grunted before his hand fell back to his side. When she pulled back, his eyes were closed once again. She smiled and ran the backs of her fingers along his cheek before standing up and quietly leaving the room. She climbed the stairs to the main level, her shoulders feeling a little lighter.

Conrad immediately noticed Kee's happy demeanor as she all but bounced across the parking lot toward them. He smiled at her. "I take it that it went well?"

She nodded with a grin and held out her hand to take the Jeep keys from him. "Yeah, it did." She said as she slipped into the driver seat.

Lucy, dressed in Kee's jeans and sweater, hip bumped Conrad away from the passenger door. She claimed her spot in the front and stuck her tongue out at him in victory when he slid into the backseat.

He leaned forward, lowering his voice when he neared her ear. "Oh, I'll get you back for that."

She couldn't explain the blush that sprang up in response. She didn't—couldn't—reply so she calmly fixed her shoulder length hair in place and gave Kee a smile. "So, tell me about your Nana, Kee."

Kee blew out a sigh as she headed towards the I-10 East. "Well, like I told Conrad, she's not very amiable. She's actually pretty bitchy," she explained with a laugh. "She's blunt and stoic, but she's the only family I have."

Lucy grinned. "You're kind of a bitch too, but I love you."

"Gee, thanks," she replied with a roll of her eyes. "Nana is my great-grandma. When I was seven my parents died. My grandparents didn't want me so Nana adopted me."

The fox balked at her. "Oh gods, Kee, I'm so sorry."

"For what?" She asked curiously.

"For your family situation." She clarified. "Can I ask why your grandparents didn't want you?"

Her hands tightened on the steering wheel as she considered how much to tell the two of them. "My grandma blames me for my mother's death." She finally admitted in a small voice.

Conrad, sensing his alpha's discomfort, leaned forward and put his hand on her shoulder. "You don't have to talk about it."

"The fuck you don't!" Lucy seethed, turning in her seat to stare at her friend. "What kind of demented asshole blames a seven year old for a death?"

"*Lucy.*" The wolf warned gently.

She took a deep breath and released it. "I'm sorry, that was rude of me. Con's right, you don't have to talk about it. I'm just angry for you."

Kee shrugged. "It was a long time ago, Luce. I've gotten over it."

Lucy wrung her hands together, a habit that manifested when she was upset or irritated. "So, your Nana is a wolf as well?"

Kee's spine stiffened as Conrad's hand tightened on her shoulder. *How did I totally forget once again that Lucy doesn't know what I am? Fuck. Is this even the right time to tell her? When she's trapped in a car with me?*

Pale green eyes slid over the suddenly tense duo in the car. Her hands paused their rubbing as she looked between the two of them. "She's not, is she?"

"No." Kee replied.

Lucy's stomach dropped when the air in the car thickened with anxiety. She fumbled with the door until she found the window button and rolled it down halfway. She winced slightly at the harsh sound of rushing wind and loud traffic but greedily inhaled the fresh air. She felt a hand touch her shoulder and saw that it was Conrad. He had kept his left hand on his alpha's shoulder, but his right rested on hers.

Her brow creased slightly as she turned her attention back to her friend. "You're not either. . .are you?"

Kee sucked in a breath, her knuckles white as she gripped the steering wheel. "Do you want me to take you back to Byte?"

"That depends on your answer," she shot back. When Kee's eyes narrowed, she realized her mistake. "Kee, I haven't known you for very long, but you're already closer to me than most people. I'm comfortable around you. As stupid as it sounds, I feel safe. Like, I can be myself instead of putting on the front of being a tough stray." She put her hand on Conrad's so that they were both touching Kee's shoulder. "Even if you're not a werewolf, you're still my friend."

Conrad smiled proudly at the fox before looking at his alpha, meeting her eyes in the rearview mirror. "I think you can trust her, Kee."

Kee finally relented after another bout of quiet hesitation. "Buckle up, buttercup, it's a long story. You can decide afterwards if you still want to be friends."

And so, she told her everything, starting with what she was. She jumped into the night she met Cain's pack and explained why she had been nervous about it. She went into detail about her fight with Cain and her chosen initiation into his pack. When she started to talk about her ambush, she did so in a detached tone. She explained how she had barely survived and only because of Lucas' bond. She briefly went over how she killed her attackers and finished with how and why she had officially ended things with Cain last night.

"I'm sorry." Lucy started as she wiped at her eyes. "I hate that this happened to you."

Kee took Lucy's hand in hers, keeping her left hand on the wheel as she watched the road. She took the Main Street exit and glanced at the other girl as they came to a stop at the light. "I'm alive, Lucy. I may have a little bit of an anger problem now, but I'm alive."

"I can't imagine thinking that the person you love tried to kill you." She cried, tears welling in her eyes again. "The betrayal you must have felt."

"Yeah, it was hard," she murmured. "But if I hadn't believed that at the time, I never would have acted on my attraction to Lucas."

The fox gripped the hand that held hers. "Oh gods, that's why you and Lucas have been fighting haven't you? Because you found out Cain didn't cause your attack? Is that where you were the day before? Why Lucas was so mad?"

Kee nodded. "I went to Cain's house after I found out that Lucas was indirectly responsible for my attack." She glanced over at Lucy's shocked expression. "Remember when he fought Alexander? Well, Alexander is the one who told Warren to have his pack members attack me."

She floundered as she tried to put her thoughts into words. "Fuck!" She finally shouted. "What a fucking shit show!"

She couldn't help but laugh. "Exactly. So, things have been tense between us. Now do you understand what I was saying in the kitchen?"

Lucy sighed. "Yes, and I get it about the weapon thing too," she tilted her head back against the headrest. "A shapeshifter," she murmured in wonder. "I thought your kind was wiped out centuries ago."

"Two hundred years ago," Kee replied, glad for the change of subject even if it wasn't a lighter topic. "Nana's mom was one of the shapeshifters that was slaughtered during the hunt. Nana had been twenty-seven at the time."

"Do shapeshifters age like normal wereanimals then? Werewolves age a lot slower than humans. Is it the same for shapeshifters?" Conrad asked.

She nodded and then continued her story. "Almost 10 years before the genocide of shapeshifters, Nana had been given to the alpha of the local werewolf pack as a mate."

"Wait, wait, wait. At *seventeen*?" Lucy asked incredulously.

"Actually, she was sixteen at the time of her mating. It was a different time period, Luce. Many girls were wed to older men once they got their first period. But Nana was lucky, I think. She told me her mate was kind and never forced her to do anything she didn't want. Anyways, since her mother was a known shapeshifter, Nana had been faced with the same accusations once the hunters came looking. Of course, she and her mate denied it."

"Her mate knew she was a shapeshifter?" The beta questioned.

Kee gave a soft smile. "Yes. I think Nana's mate loved her from the beginning. If he didn't, that would have been his chance to get rid of her."

"What happened when the hunters came? How did she convince

them she wasn't a shapeshifter?" Lucy pressed, wanting to get back to the story.

"Luckily their six-year-old daughter, my grandma, had changed into her wolf form earlier that month. That was all the proof the hunters needed." Her lips fell into a sad frown. "After that though, Nana refused to bear any more children for her mate. She was scared that my grandma had been a fluke, that the next child would surely be a shapeshifter like her and her mother. She knew they would be slaughtered and didn't want to risk it. However, when my mom also turned into a wolf, Nana assumed her mate's strong wolf genes had wiped out the shapeshifter trait all together." She let out a bitter laugh. "Then I was born."

"Holy shit," Conrad commented from the backseat, rubbing his face. "But wait, didn't you say we were meeting your great-uncle? Does that mean your Nana had more kids with her mate after all?"

"Yeah, we're meeting him, but he's not Nana's son. She told me on the phone that it was her mate's son. I guess that means he went and fathered more pups when she refused to bear him more."

"Your poor Nana." Lucy murmured.

Kee let out another laugh. "Don't let her hear you say that. She'll beat your ass with a wooden spoon."

The three shared a laugh before falling into a comfortable, companionable silence.

Lucy looked at the hand still holding hers and gave it a soft squeeze. "C-can," she hesitated, not sure if she was crossing a line. "Can I ask about your parents?" She watched as her friend's face went stony and she released Kee's hand when she tugged it free.

"That's a story for another day," Kee replied with a forced smile as she pulled into a wide driveway. The pavement cut through a large front yard and led to a two-story house with a wide patio. The house was painted beige with a brown trim. The windows were the old-fashion lift kind with white curtains, the front door a heavy oak. The house was as old as Nana appeared to be in human years.

She cut the engine and grinned at her companions. "Brace yourselves, we're here."

Conrad and Lucy followed Kee's suit and got out of the car. They trailed behind her as she approached the large front porch, both surveying their surroundings. They slowed their stride when they saw a woman who looked to be in her late fifties standing on the porch. She had her medium length red hair pulled back into a low ponytail, tiny streaks of grey blending in with the natural curls. Her grey eyes were cold and calculating as they studied Conrad and Lucy.

Both their beasts paced uneasily within them at the probing stare.

Nana stubbed out her cigarette when the trio approached her and nodded towards the front door without greeting them. "Well come in, lunch is almost done."

Conrad and Lucy watched her disappear into the house and looked cautiously at Kee, who smiled in return. "That's Nana's version of hello. If she hadn't invited you in, we would be on our way back to LA."

"That was a hello?" Lucy murmured in disbelief.

Kee laughed again. "I warned you." She commented before following her great-grandma.

Conrad felt Lucy touch his hand and looked down as she wrapped her fingers around his. "In this together?" She asked him shyly.

His eyes softened at her joke, and his beast rumbled. "That may be the only way we survive this." He replied as he laced their fingers and relished in the way she laughed.

This is dangerous. I can't get caught up in her. There's too much at stake. He thought almost miserably as he allowed her to pull him to the front door. She smiled at him over her shoulder and his beast whined. *Fuck.*

Seven

Lucas awoke at 7:26pm feeling much more relaxed than he had the past few days. His body did not usually hold on to the stiffness that came from his undead sleep, but after his spats with Keira, his muscles had been tight. He sat up and stretched before running his hand through his hair. As he swung his legs over the edge of the bed, he noticed the white paper on his nightstand.

He picked up the note, a small smirk tilting up his lips as he read it. He recalled Keira visiting him but had assumed it was one of the rare times he was blessed with dreams instead of a dark void. He smiled again, remembering her kissing him and promising to return.

Perhaps our next encounter will not be as disastrous as the last few.

He set the note down and walked to his attached bathroom for a quick shower. When he was done, he dried off and styled his hair. He kept it cut in gentleman's fashion, the top longer than the bottom and sides. Normally, the style didn't call for the top being quite as long as he kept his, but after having long hair for the majority of his life, he couldn't bring himself to hack it all off. He combed the top back in a neat sweep and smoothed back the shorter side of the part. Stepping into his closet, he dressed in a dark grey button up with a black vest and slacks.

At 8pm sharp, he was at Byte's bar, telling Mirabella about Lucy's absence. "Dante has informed me that Lucy had a rough time so I permitted her the night off."

She nodded. "I understand, Lord Lucas. It is the night before a major holiday. I am sure I can handle it."

"Keira anticipates the same thing," he responded. He lifted a brow when his employee, and coven member, stiffened. "Something you wish to say, Mira?"

She cleared her throat and tossed her blonde ponytail over her shoulder. "Your wolf is bloody stupid, sir." She flinched when he narrowed his eyes. "I mean, she is bold. She threatened me! And the way she fought that other wolf," she shook her head. "She could have made a mess."

"Bold, perhaps, but she is not stupid, Mirabella. See to it that you refrain from speaking such insults against my bonded lycanthrope." He warned calmly but with an assertive tone. "She has been spoken to about the fight with the other wolf. However, do remember that Keira is an alpha female. She responds differently to challenges."

She frowned at him. "Would that have made the blood bath justified? Is your little pet really worth it?" A second after she finished speaking, she dropped to her knees with a strangled cry.

Lucas stared down at her over the bar top, red eyes emotionless as his aura pressed down hard on hers. "You will watch your tone." He seethed. "Just because I allow you to speak freely does not mean I will tolerate a second strike of disrespect."

"S-Sorry, Lord Lucas." She bit out, her body cringing under the weight of his power.

With a blink, he reeled back his aura. He waited until she was back on her feet before continuing. "As I said, she has been spoken to about her antics and it will not happen again," he repeated. "But tell me, why did she feel the need to threaten you?"

Mirabella smoothed her uniform in place. "I informed her that there are females here who find her beta delicious. She told me that we better keep our fangs out of him."

"It would be best to heed her warning." Lucas commented casually. "Conrad is very important to her."

She scoffed, "She said she does not require you to fight her battles."

"She is correct." He stepped back when a couple approached the bar with wide, anticipating smiles. He looked at their red wristbands, signaling that they were looking for a bite, and offered them a professional smile. "Mirabella, see to it that their first drinks are on the house."

"Thank you so much." The human girl said in awe when the bartender nodded.

"Yeah thanks, man!" The male added with a wide grin.

"It is my pleasure. May your night be eventful." He told them before heading for the stairs to the second story. On the way, he passed Dante and told him about Conrad's night off as well as Lucy's.

"So, Kee took Conrad and Lucy?" Dante shook his head with a smirk. "She missed three training sessions. She'll be hurting when I'm done with her."

Lucas let out a soft chuckle. "Well, when she returns, she is mine first." *Though if it goes well enough, she will be in no state to walk, let alone train.*

Dante laughed as well. "On second thought, perhaps I should just plan on four days of missed training."

"That may be best," he answered and glanced around the club. "Have you seen Giovanni?"

"Not since we rose." The dark skinned vampire replied with a small frown, also scanning Byte for the Italian. "We passed each other in the kitchen, but I haven't seen him since. Do you require anything?"

"No." Lucas hummed in his throat and gave an elegant shrug. "I suppose he is with a lover or feeding." He turned and headed up the stairs. "If you need me, I will be in my office."

"Yes sir," Dante replied and turned his back to the stairs, focusing on the club as more customers filtered in.

Once in his office, Lucas sat down behind his new desk. He had it replaced the day after he broke it, Miguel setting it up for him while he was asleep. He really had to give the werebear a raise for everything he did during the day. Making a mental note of it, he slid the chair in closer, fingers gliding over the keys as he checked the reports in his email. His teeth ground together as his informants all answered with negative responses.

No one knew where Alexander was. Lucas was trying to find Aubrey without answering the other vampire's taunt, but it seemed he was running out of options. He had wanted to ask Keira to help in locating him but refrained. Things were rough between them, and he did not want to add tension by asking her to do something for him despite it being her job.

That is not the only reason, he conceded. *I do not want Alexander to get his hands on her should things go awry.*

But Keira wasn't weak anymore.

He sighed and steepled his fingertips. If things went well when she came back, should he ask her? Or would she think he only made up with her in order to ask a favor? Why was this so complicated? If they didn't make amends, would she still deny him his request?

Shaking his head, he turned his attention back to his computer and began to reach out to other contacts. These people were not under the rule of his coven, did not directly serve under him. Hell, some were not even vampires, but he needed to find his bleeder and would do what it took to locate her. If these contacts failed to provide him with information, he would have no choice but to ask Keira.

After staring at his computer for over two hours, the monitor started to go fuzzy, a haze swimming across the screen. It was not until he looked down at the keyboard that he realized it was his vision. He heard someone nearby shout Keira's name and jerked his head up, but there was no one in his office. He tried to blink the black spot from his eyes until he realized he had been pulled into one of Keira's dreams.

"Damn it, Keira! It's not that hard!" Daddy shouted at his daughter's cowering form.

"I can't do it!" She cried, looking away from him as she panted, her lungs wheezing.

"Yet you shifted into a fucking cat! You're a wolf and you'll shift into one! Look at me!" He waited until her wide, frightened grey eyes turned towards him before shifting into his wolf form. He walked closer to her with a snarl.

She closed her eyes tightly, trying to find her wolf. Daddy said I just have to find my wolf, find the inner voice, and I'd be able to turn like him. *But she didn't hear another voice. There was only her thoughts, her fear. She was scared. Terrified. Her dad had pulled her into his study every night that week, trying to get her to shift into her wolf form, but she failed each time.*

This all started because of that cat! *If it hadn't shown up, she wouldn't have to do this. Daddy wouldn't be yelling at her and Uncle Christian wouldn't be mad either. That stupid cat ruined everything! Why did she have to turn into it?*

She panicked when she felt that familiar fire sensation blaze across her body. Her limbs shrunk and sprouted black fur, her back and shoulders popping as she shifted. No, no! *She cried with a wailing meow. She heard a deep, rumbling growl and pressed herself flat against the ground in submission, too petrified to face her father's rage.*

Despite her being in a trembling, submissive form, he snapped his jaws at her, his sharp teeth biting into her small, furry arm. When she let out a pained screech, he released her. He shifted back into his human form, his inner wolf howling with fury. "Get out of that form. Now!" *He snarled down at her.*

Her chest heaved in fear and pain. She didn't know how to shift back. She didn't even know why she turned into what she was now. She couldn't control it, didn't understand any of it. Daddy, help! I don't know how! *She meowed and meowed, trying to get him to help her.*

She glanced up at him, pleading him to help her, but he just glared down at her. He was seething, blue eyes hard with anger.

"Why can't you do this? Why can you shift into this quivering cat before me and not a wolf? What's wrong with you?!" *All of his questions were shouted at her, his volume rising with each one.*

I don't know! I'm sorry, Daddy! *She wailed in her head.*

"Uncle Christian is demanding to see your wolf form!" *He sneered.* "You have to be a wolf, Kee! You won't disgrace me this way!"

She could feel a new wave of anger expand from him and saw his hands shake from the force of it. Sobbing still, she tried to press herself harder against the floor again, ears pinned back and eyes looking away from him. It was just as he had taught her, but it wasn't enough. Something hard hit her across the face and she immediately went silent, shock and pain numbing her senses.

Daddy. . .hit me?

Kee let out a yowl when he grabbed her by the scruff of her neck and hoisted her small feline body off the floor. She dangled from his hold, tail tucked between her legs. He snarled at her, his handsome face red with anger. "If you can turn into this pathetic form, you can turn into a wolf! If you don't, Keira, it will cost us everything!" *He gave her a shake that hurt her restrained neck.* "Do you understand me? Uncle Christian will not tolerate it! I will not tolerate it!"

"Liam!" *Mommy screamed at him as she barged into the room. She ran over to him and put her hands on the cat, trying to support her weight.* "Let *her go!" She growled.*

"She will ruin everything, Trinity." He snarled back.

"I don't care, she's my daughter! Let her go!" When he still didn't, Mom bit down hard on the top of his hand, teeth sinking into his skin. His hand abruptly opened and she cradled Kee's furry form to her chest. She glowered at him over her shoulder. "This training isn't working, Liam. She's just a little girl. Pups don't understand shifting until they reach puberty. Until then, it's only brought on by the full moon."

"And yet she managed to turn into a fucking cat, didn't she?" He snapped.

"Yeah, and how did you get her to do it?" She asked sharply, nostrils flaring as the scent of blood hit them. She looked down at Kee and found black fur matted on her arm. She brushed the fur and came away with bloodied fingertips. She whined in her throat before thrusting her hand out at her mate. "Is this how?" She screeched, her wolf shining in her eyes. "By drawing blood? I don't even know who you are anymore!"

"Don't you raise your voice at me, Trinity. I'm your mate," he warned in a low voice. "I'm doing what I need to in order to protect us."

"Hurting your daughter isn't protecting her!"

"I meant you and me," he replied solemnly.

Her grey eyes widened. "What are you saying?" She whispered.

He looked away from her pained expression, hands clenched in fists. "You are my priority."

Tears welled in her eyes. "Keira is my priority," she retorted stiffly. "I'm ashamed that you don't agree."

"She's a shapeshifter, Trin," he bit out. "She has no future."

"That's not for you to decide!" She snapped, holding Kee tighter to her. "She didn't ask to be this! She has no control over who she is! This isn't her fault!"

Daddy turned back to her, anguish on his face. "No, but it's yours."

Her mother gaped at him. "Excuse me? How is this my fault?"

"Are your grandparents wolves, Trinity?" He asked quietly.

"*They are on my father's side. They were both bit.*" She swallowed thickly. "*I never really knew my grandparents on my mother's side. My mom told me that my grandma went away after her mate died, lost in her grief. But Mom told me they were wolves as well. Her grandfather was the alpha of Riverside until he died!*" She defended.

"*But you don't know for sure?*" He pressed.

"*I've only seen my grandmother a handful of times, Liam. I don't even remember what she looks like. I can only go off of what my mom told me.*" She backed away when he started to approach her. "*You can't blame me.*"

"*My bloodlines are perfect. It has to be yours.*" He looked wounded at her retreat. "*I'm not going to hurt you, Trin.*"

"*But you'll hurt our daughter?*" She breathed as she backed up until she reached the door to the study.

"*I will do what I have to in order to keep you alive,*" he responded. "*I won't lose my mate over a mistake.*"

The tears that filled her eyes spilled down cheeks. "*She's your daughter. How can you say that? How can you just turn off your love for her as if it's a switch?*" This time his face pinched in pain, but he didn't respond. "*I can't do that. I will love her forever no matter what she is.*" He opened his mouth, but she shook her head and hurried out of the room.

"*I'm sorry your dad is acting like this, Kee. I'm going to protect you. I promise,*" she told her vehemently.

Lucas sucked in a breath as he was thrust back into his own reality. He was on the floor by his desk, the chair several feet away. When had he gotten up? Or had he fallen? He sat up and leaned against the drawers of his desk, trying to process everything he had witnessed.

The two in the memory had obviously been Keira's parents. Her father tormented her for being what she was while her mother tried to protect her. Had this been Keira's entire childhood?

What else had she endured?

He swallowed his shapeshifter's lingering emotions and reached for his cellphone. He tapped her name and leaned his head back against the desk as he waited for her to answer.

"*H-hello?*" Keira breathed into the phone.

He took another inhale of air he didn't need at her shaky tone. "Are you alright?" He asked softly.

A slight pause. "*Why do you ask?*"

"It has been a while since I witnessed one of your nightmares," he commented, trying to keep his tone light so he did not upset her further.

He heard her sigh. "*How much of it did you see?*" She murmured with tired chagrin.

"Enough of it," he replied with a frown. "I ask again, are you alright?" He wished that she was next to him. The past few times she had her nightmares, he had been able to wake her and comfort her. He wanted to hold her now. Those memories had not been pleasant, even for him who had merely bared witness to them.

"*Hold on, let me go outside,*" she whispered. He heard her rustling around then a door click open and shut. A few heartbeats later there was another, heavier sound of a door opening and closing. He could hear her walking a few paces before she let out a soft sigh. "*Okay, I can talk now. Sorry, I didn't want to wake up Lucy and Conrad.*"

Yes, that was right, Conrad was usually in bed with her. Why had he not woken her up? "Was Conrad not with you?"

She let out a soft laugh. "*No, I'm playing matchmaker.*"

"Conrad and Lucy?" Lucas mused. "What was your excuse for sleeping alone?" He could almost feel her grin through their bond.

"*After Nana went to bed, we went back to the guest house. We were in the living room watching a movie when I said I was feeling sick and wanted to go to bed early. I locked the door to my bedroom when I went to bed. Pretty easy, really.*"

He couldn't help but smirk. "What makes you think they are

sleeping together? Perhaps Conrad is more gentlemanly than that."

"*Oh, he is, no doubt. I passed him snoring on the couch when I snuck out. Either way, they still got to spend some alone time with each other.*"

"At the expense of your dreams, it seems." He observed.

Another sigh. "*There's that,*" she agreed. "*But I can handle a few bad memories if it means Conrad and Lucy are happy. Besides, I can't keep relying on him to keep the bad stuff away. I might not always have him beside me like this.*"

"Perhaps, but you have me, Keira." Lucas reminded her softly. He frowned when she went silent for a few moments.

"*Do I?*" She whispered back. "*After everything that's happened?*"

"A lot has occurred, yes," he agreed. "And there is much we need to discuss, but that does not change the fact that you have me. Even miles away, I am here for you."

She took in a shaky breath. "*You're making me feel guilty over here,*" she murmured, but her tone was a gentle teasing. "*I can't stay mad at you when you say things like that.*"

"That is not my intention, but if it forces me into your good graces then I can deal with it." He jested back.

She laughed and it echoed pleasantly in his ear. "*I'm sorry about the fight with Katie, Lucas. You're right, it was stupid. I didn't even think of where I was. I just wanted to pay her back for attacking me.*"

"I understand, Miss Alpha," he teased again. "And you are forgiven. I also reacted a bit too harshly. I was," he paused, searching for the right word, "*nervous* to see the other vampires looking at you like that."

"*Nervous?*"

He hummed in his throat. "Perhaps frightened is the better word, though it is not one I use to describe myself often. It is as Giovanni told you, I would have killed them if they touched you. Brethren, or not."

"I'm sorry I put you in that position. If there's a next time, I will handle it better."

He gave a small smile. "I have a feeling that your definition of better and mine are very different." His smile widened as she laughed again. It was easily one of his favorite sounds.

"How about I promise not to flaunt my blood to any vampires while in your bar?"

"I will take what I can get." Another laugh and the two fell into a comfortable silence. "I take it you are feeling better now."

"Yeah, thanks to you."

He looked up at the ceiling as he told her, "I am sorry that you had to deal with that as a child."

She shushed him. *"Don't apologize. It's in the past, okay? I'm just sorry I couldn't keep you from seeing it. It must have been triggered by telling Lucy about myself. I also told her and Conrad about Nana and her past."*

"Oh?" He asked, surprised she had told Lucy her secret. She took his question differently and instead told him of Nana's past. When she was finished, he scoffed. "Fear is a powerful motivator. Unfortunately, the motives are not always pleasant. It saddens me that your kind was wiped out, Keira, but I am fortunate to have met you."

"Just fortunate, hm?" She joked.

"I feel that saying 'blessed' would be in bad taste, given my nature." He should have said more. Should have told her that she was precious to him but didn't want to do it over the phone. Still, he could feel a small wave of happiness through their bond. "We will talk more when you come home."

"After your dinner party?"

"Yes. It ends at midnight. Will you be returning by then?"

"I think I can make that work." Again, he could almost feel her smile.

"Then it is a date." He confirmed and stood from the floor, walking towards his chair. "Sleep well, Keira. If you have another nightmare and I do not feel it, call me."

"*I will,*" she told him, but he could sense her lie. He didn't comment on it, knowing she was just trying to be strong on her own. "*Oh, and there's something I want to tell you before I hang up.*"

"Yes, my sweet?"

"*I officially ended things with Cain. I just thought you should know. Have a good night, Lucas.*" She told him before hanging up.

He stared down at his phone in surprise, but a smile curved up his lips. Yes, they would have a very long talk when she came back. And after, well, Dante wouldn't be getting her back for a while.

Eight

Kee smiled down at her phone, her cheeks slightly flushed despite the chill of the night. She felt the tingle of his pleasure through the bond and couldn't stifle the giggle that bubbled out of her lips.

"Shouldn't you be sleeping?" Came a voice with a light Irish accent.

She looked up from her spot on the main house's porch steps and smiled at her Nana. "Shouldn't *you*?"

"I heard someone having a conversation." Nana mused as she sat down next to her great-granddaughter. She pulled out a pack of fresh cigarettes and tapped the lid against her palm before opening them. She selected one of the thin white sticks and raised it to her lips as she lit it. Taking a deep drag, she looked at the younger woman. "Who were you speaking to?"

"Lucas," Kee replied, turning down a cigarette when it was offered to her. "Smoking is bad for you, you know."

"Your vampire," Nana scoffed. "And if I can endure the hunt and the death of my mate, I'm sure I can handle these just fine."

She frowned as she looked at the woman who had been her guardian. Her hair was pulled back in a messy braid, strands sticking out at every knot. Her heart clenched when she remembered how her mother had always worn her hair in the same manner. The dream had left her raw with emotion.

"Speaking of your mate, how did you feel when he had a baby with someone else?" She asked, trying to distract herself.

Nana blinked once at the random question and took another drag from her cigarette. "I was happy for him."

This time Kee blinked in surprise. "Happy?"

She sighed. "I denied him pups. We were together for almost two centuries and I gave him one child, Kee. *One.*" She flicked away the ash. "I encouraged him to go rut with one of the other pack females."

She gaped at her. "You told your mate to cheat on you?"

Nana clucked her tongue. "No, child, I told him to go sire another heir."

"But he still had to sleep with another woman," she murmured. "How can you do that to your mate?"

"How much do you know about mating?" She countered in a bland tone.

Kee pursed her lips together. "Only what Cain told me. He said it forms a bond between the lovers, makes them inseparable. He told me that they are loyal to each other, that there will be no other for them."

"That is the fairytale version of it," she mused bitterly. "The less dominant one in the relationship, usually the female, is bitten on the back of the neck by the male. It can be done in any form, but it's most potent with their hybrid or wolf form."

Her eyes widened. "What if they miss the scruff and bite the bone? Couldn't they snap their necks?"

"That's why it makes a stronger link. It takes more reserved strength and trust." She put out the cigarette and flicked it into her yard. "The dominant male will mix their own blood in with their chosen mate's and that's what makes the bond."

That's almost identical to my bond with Lucas. She thought with a furrowed brow. *I thought it was vampire magic, but maybe it's just blood magic.*

"The bond is solidified once they have sex after the bite. Wolves mate for life so they are only supposed to have eyes for their partner. The good wolves honor that, the bad ones do not," she said simply. "But even the bad ones usually only go for occasional flings. It's just a primal urge that needs satisfying, so they don't tend to develop feelings for a different wolf."

"Is that why you let your mate do what he did?"

"John was a good man, a great alpha, and an even better mate. He treated me like his queen despite our mating being arranged. We fell in love with each other over time. But I knew I was holding him back from having more children. He was alpha and he deserved more heirs." Her lips turned into a sad smile. "I wish I could have given him more, but the risk was too great. I still pleasured his body, let him satisfy both our needs, but he knew my fear so he respected it by not coming in me."

Kee flushed at her Nana's words, despite them being spoken in a factual manner. "That must have been hard."

She continued as if the younger girl hadn't spoken. "He refused to sleep with someone else for so long," she gave a quiet laugh. "Said he didn't want to dishonor me and our bond. You see, he was a strong alpha. He helped many females resist the shift on full moons. I knew he could have another pup if he tried, so I told him to.

"I nagged and nagged at him because I *knew* he wanted more pups. So, he eventually caved and did." She steeled her expression. "I knew when it happened. That's the cost of the bond. You know when your mate is doing something wrong, is hurting, in trouble, or hell, even if they're happy. You may not know exactly what is happening, but your instincts will tell you something is wrong. It's a mental and physical connection."

Kee turned on the step so she faced Nana. "Did it hurt when he did it?"

"Not in the way you think. I just felt...worthless."

She balked. "Why?"

"My mate had given me everything, but I couldn't give him the one thing he wanted," she explained. "As soon as he started screwing that girl, I felt it. I was bitter and jealous. Which is completely irrational since I made him do it, but I couldn't help it. He must have known how it affected me from our bond because he rushed and returned to me as fast as he could." Another bitter laugh. "He put his head in my lap and *apologized* to me, told me he was ashamed. I was so angry that he had the gall to say sorry for something I told him to do. For doing something that would give him what I know he wanted."

Kee hesitantly reached out and put her hand on Nana's knee. The older shapeshifter had never spoken so much about herself before. Had never expressed such emotions. It worried her yet intrigued her at the same time. She wanted to know more about the mysterious person who had raised her, but the display of emotions was so unlike Nana.

"His death nearly broke me, Kee." She admitted softly. "He was my everything and to have literally half of my soul ripped from me was almost too much. I think if I had been a real werewolf I would have died shortly after him, as some mates do if bonded for as long as we were." She met Kee's eyes, grey staring into grey. "I don't know why I didn't die with him. I questioned it every single day until I got the distraught phone call from your mother. Then I knew why the goddess spared me. I was meant to have one more daughter; one just like me."

Kee's eyes stung with unshed tears. "Me?"

Nana snorted and looked away. "Are you daft, child? Of course *you*.

Who else?"

Leave it to Nana to ruin a moment. Still, she leaned into her great-grandma and rested her head on her shoulder. "Thank you for everything, Nan. I don't know if I ever told you that. I'm not sure I would be here if you hadn't taken me in."

"Don't be dramatic." She huffed but rubbed her cheek on Kee's head. "You are strong, Kee. How else would a shapeshifter become an alpha to a wolf and a fox?"

"Conrad chose me and—wait, what?" She asked, pulling back to look at her.

Nana lifted a brow at her. "Do you not understand your own connections and pack bonds? The werefox is your pack; it's in her aura."

Kee immediately bristled. "I can't force her into my pack." She snipped defensively. Though she wouldn't deny that she liked the idea of Lucy being a part of her pack.

"You didn't, it doesn't have that feel to it. I doubt she is aware of it either. It's not as strong as your bond with the wolf, but it's there. Have you asked her?"

"No, I guess I never really thought of it," she answered honestly and looked down at her pajama pants. "But I would like her to be part of my pack. I already feel responsible for her and want to protect her."

"Then ask. Do they know what you are?"

"What we are, yeah." She clarified and looked up at the other woman. "Does that upset you? That I told them our secret?"

"You are smart, Kee. You always have been. I will take credit and say you got it from our side of the family, just like you got your strength from your father. If you trust them, then I will as well." She cleared her throat and turned serious as she gazed at her adopted daughter. "Speaking of your strength," she began. "You've changed. You're more confident and surer of yourself. You said you had a long story to tell me, so get on with it."

She was tired of telling the story, hated having to repeat it over and over, but Nana had asked and so she complied. She told Nana everything that had happened to her, the other shapeshifter just listened with an expressionless mask.

"You can shift into people now," she commented when Kee finished. "You learned that much faster than I had. I'm impressed."

Her eyes widened. "Why didn't you tell me we could shift into people?"

"Because it's a very dangerous skill, Kee. There's a risk that comes with shifting into people." She warned.

She tilted her head. "What risk?"

Nana pursed her lips in a hard line. "How many people have you shifted into?"

"Two, both of them werewolves."

"Did one of these happen to be your boyfriend?"

"Ex-boyfriend," Kee corrected. "And yes, he was. Why?"

She sighed. "Was there anything different about shifting into him rather than the other?"

Kee was about to tell her no but froze. That wasn't right. Shifting into Cain *had* been different. She normally felt a wave of warmth when she shifted, but Cain's had been painfully cold followed by a stab of heat through her body, her mind and chest throbbing. And then there was the fact that she had heard his inner wolf. "Yes," She murmured. "I could hear his beast. That didn't happen with the other two."

Nana nodded gravely. "That's because you *became* him."

"What? I became the other two as well and didn't hear their wolf."

She closed her eyes and tried to put her explanation into words. "There are two different types of shifting, Kee. Copying a person is one, becoming a person is the other," she stopped Kee from speaking when she tried to ask a question. "Hold on, let me explain. I should have told this to you when you were younger, but I didn't want you to abuse your power.

"When we shapeshifters touch something, we make a copy of the image in our mind. We don't have to touch an animal to become one because we know what that generic animal looks like. Just like how we can change the color of our hair or eyes because we know how it's *supposed* to look. However, if we touch a specific animal then we can make *that* exact one. That's what happened to you when you shifted for the first time, Kee. You pet the cat and then copied its image."

Kee's mouth hung open unintelligently before she shot to her feet in anger. "You couldn't have fucking told me this years ago?!"

Nana snarled at her. "Don't you use crass language with me, child! Do you want to hear the rest? Yes? Then sit down!"

She grumbled unhappily but did as she was told. She took a deep, calming breath. "You should have told me. I didn't know that merely touching someone would allow me to shift into them."

"You copy their image," she reiterated. "Didn't you find it odd that you could so easily copy the wolves you had shifted into? You must have touched them, no?"

"Cain is obvious, but Mason?" She tried to think of when she had ever touched him. Her eyes widened. "I shook his hand when I met him."

She gave a single nod. "That's all it takes."

She rubbed her face hard with her hands and tried to sort through her thoughts for a moment. She pulled her hands away and looked at Nana. "So why was it different with Cain? Is it because I spent over a year touching him?"

"No, you didn't just copy an image of him, you became him. This doesn't happen just from touching; it comes from taking in someone else's essence." At Kee's confused look, she scoffed. "Their DNA, child. Whether it be saliva, blood, or semen."

Kee's cheeks reddened. She literally had all three of those from Cain. Saliva had come from kisses. The blood from when he had gotten into a fight with a pack member. The other wolf managed to split his lip and scrape him up, but Cain had won. Whenever he won a fight, he would always be on a dominance high. She had kissed all his wounds, acknowledging and praising his win, before he took her to bed. Obviously, unprotected sex explained the last part.

Nana rolled her eyes at Kee's embarrassment. "As long as you were safe during your ovulation, I don't care. You're twenty-five, I'm not blind to the habits of the current day and age. Saving sex for marriage is something that is rarely valued anymore."

Still, she didn't like Nana to know about her sex life. "I became Cain?" She asked quietly and received a nod in response. "His beast, it was so real. I finally understood what Liam had talked about when I was little. The voice within that talked to me. He's the reason I didn't lose the fight to Noah."

"That doesn't surprise me. From what you've told me, and what I've seen when I met him, Cain is supposed to be an alpha. His wolf is strong." She explained in a tired voice. "That is why you have to be careful when shifting into people. You never know what you're truly becoming. You need to be self-aware. You may be a shapeshifter, but you were born between two wolves. You are drawn to them and your body might adapt to their beast."

"What does that mean?" She questioned with a furrowed brow. "Adapt to their beast?"

"You make a copy of their beast. Don't give it a reason to stay." She simply said before she stood up and brushed the dirt from the back of her nightgown. "Go to bed. Breakfast will be ready early in the morning."

Seeing that Nana was clearly done talking for the night, Kee rose to her feet and awkwardly hugged her great-grandma. "Thank you again, Nan."

She stroked the top of her head, not hugging her back but returning the affection. "Sleep well."

———

Kee snuck back into the guest house and tiptoed past the living room. She paused slightly by the couch when she realized that Conrad was no longer alone. A grin curved up her lips when she saw Lucy lying on top of him, her head on his chest while one of his arms was draped across her back.

She quietly walked past them and slipped into her room, silently shutting the door behind her. She flopped onto her bed with a soft moan of delight. She was so, so tired. She had a long day and had been jolted awake from her nightmare. She then had a pleasant conversation with Lucas and world shattering talk with Nana.

Okay, maybe not world shattering, but it had definitely confused me. Yet, at the same time, it answered so many questions.

She shook her head and grabbed her phone, seeing that it was now past midnight. She brought up her text messages and sent a quick one to Lucas, needing the distraction.

Mission matchmaker is a success!

She smiled tiredly at her phone and set it down. As she burrowed under the covers and nestled in her pillow, her phone buzzed with an incoming text.

Well done. Now, Miss Matchmaker, your next mission will be waiting for you in my room tomorrow evening. Wear something nice. Or, nothing at all. The choice is yours.

Warmth shot through her body and she pressed her thighs tight together. "Cocky bastard," she mumbled and didn't bother writing him back. At the amusement she felt in the bond, he must have felt her body's reaction. Thoroughly distracted from her conversation with Nana, she put her phone on the nightstand and went to sleep.

Nine

Kee sat on Nana's couch with a hot coffee mixed with an Irish liqueur. She sipped the beverage, her stomach full from the feast Nana had prepared. She had made a traditional corned beef and cabbage, champ potatoes, Irish stew, roasted lamb leg, biscuits, and Shepard's pie. She didn't realize how much she missed Nana's cooking. The woman easily put her to shame in the kitchen.

Conrad and Lucy sat on the living room floor with Gabriel, each eating a slice of apple cake drizzled with custard sauce for dessert. Gabriel was five foot five with a mess of brown hair and matching eyes. He was a good kid, smart and polite when needed, but also had that snarky side that every teenager tended to possess.

His grandpa, Christopher, was pleasant and relaxed but had that lingering alertness that all werewolves seemed to have. He had greying, dark brown hair cut short to his head and blue eyes. He was five foot seven and a little pudgy around the middle, which was odd for a werewolf. Even without shifting, wereanimals tended to burn through calories faster than most preternatural creatures.

"So, Keira, what do you do?" Christopher asked as he sat on the couch next to her, a plate of apple cake in his hand.

Kee looked up at the question. When the pair arrived, there had barely been time for greetings before Nana ushered them all into the dining room. While at dinner, everyone had been too busy stuffing their faces and moaning in delight at Nana's cooking.

"I'm a bartender." She replied and took a sip from her drink. "At least, I used to be. I fill in whenever I'm needed. Otherwise I, um, gather information for people."

"Like a detective?" Gabriel chimed in, turning to look at her.

"Ah, you could say that," she answered. "But I just follow people around."

"That's really cool." He added. "Do you help catch bad guys?"

"No," she laughed. "I just investigate what someone is doing and then tell someone else. It's actually pretty boring."

He hummed softly. "Have you been to downtown Riverside?"

"Not since I moved to LA. Why?"

Gabriel seemed to think for a moment before replying. "There's a new preternatural store that opened up, but they only let certain people in. I sense magic, but there's a weird feeling to it."

Christopher huffed. "I told you to leave it alone, Gabriel. I didn't sense anything."

"You're not a warlock, grandpa!" He shot back angrily. "You don't feel what I do!"

"And you think she will?" He snapped back. "Don't get others involved in your wild theories!"

Kee glanced at her great-uncle before looking back at Gabriel. "What's your theory?"

He studied her for a second, making sure she wasn't just trying to appease him like one would a child. "They don't allow just anyone in. I tried to go in, but they said I was too young. I asked grandpa to go without me, but they told him that wereanimals weren't allowed. What does that leave? Humans, vampires, and warlocks, right? Maybe the forest creatures, but they don't ever come to the city."

"Maybe what they sell is only for particular clients?" She suggested.

He snorted. "Obviously," he drawled out. "But the place radiates magic, and not the good kind. What kind of place would sell that stuff? I've watched the shop for hours. High class people go in, witches, wizards, and vampires, and they always come out seemingly empty handed. At night, I've seen them bring in big wooden crates with holes drilled into them. They're doing something wrong; I just know it."

"I've sensed none of this." Christopher scoffed as he took another bite of his cake. "The alpha of Riverside would know if something was amiss."

"Would he though? If it didn't concern werewolves?" Kee defended before Gabriel could.

"Of course, it's his territory! Every alpha knows what's going on with the other monsters in his area. That's just what they do."

"Unless he doesn't know, which is possible. I'm an alpha and I don't know everything going on in my city." She pointed out.

Conrad was at Kee's side the instant Christopher's aura snapped out like an explosion. He bared his teeth at the older wolf, eyes taking on the bright gold color of his beast. "Watch yourself." He growled in warning.

"Don't sneer at me, pup!" Christopher snarled as he leapt to his feet, plate crashing to the floor. He ignored Lucy when she stood beside Conrad, echoing his growl. "A woman claiming to be alpha is blasphemy! Women cannot be alphas! I should tell the alpha of LA County on you for claiming such a disgraceful thing!"

Kee calmly grabbed Conrad's belt loop and yanked him back when he moved to lunge at her uncle. She set her coffee down on the end table and stood. She rubbed the back of her beta's neck, easing down his hackles. "It's okay, Con. Calm down," she cooed softly. She glanced at Lucy and put her other hand on her shoulder. "You, too. Take a breather."

"He threatened you." He huffed out, nostrils flared. He didn't want the alpha of LA County anywhere near her. Liam was bad news, and a part of him feared he would tear Kee apart.

"He threatened to tattle on me like a little bitch," she replied, cutting a cold gaze sharply to Christopher. "Besides Con, if you got blood or cake on Nana's cream carpet, she'd kick your ass."

Christopher glanced down at the smooshed cake on the carpet and hesitantly looked at his dead father's mate. His beast shrunk back at the ruthless look in her eye. "I'm sorry, Nanette. I didn't mean to soil your house."

"I welcome you into my home and this is how you repay me? By attacking my great-granddaughter and dropping my hard work onto the floor like it is nothing? Such disrespect. Go home, Christopher, and think about your actions." Nana scorned.

His wolf rose to the surface at her demand. "You can't make me leave, Nanette. I'm here to honor you and my father."

"Are you challenging me?" She asked calmly, but her aura expanded in the room. Conrad and Lucy winced, but Kee stood unaffected. She kept her hands on her pack mates, watching as Christopher tried not to cower. "I am stronger than you, Christopher. I would rank higher than you in a pack regardless of being female. Do you want to find out for certain?"

He tilted his head back in submission. "No," he bit out. "I'm sorry."

She wheeled her aura back in and put her hands on her hips. "Out you go then. Gabriel can stay. There's no reason his night should be ruined because of you. I will take him home tomorrow." Her tone left no room for argument.

"Fine," he huffed and looked at his grandson. "You behave yourself for Nana."

"I will." The teen replied and watched him storm out the door before letting out a low whistle. "I'm impressed, Nana. I've only seen my grandma do that to him."

"He's always been a handful." Nana scoffed as she kneeled on the ground to pick up the cake. She thanked Lucy when she came back from the kitchen with a wet rag to help her.

"So, Gabriel, what kind of stuff do you think this shop is selling?" Kee asked as she took up her spot on the couch again. She patted Conrad's knee when he sat down next to her. She could tell his beast was still pacing within him with irritation.

"Honestly? Black market stuff." He answered as he turned to look at her.

"A monster black market, hm? I can't see the Council being okay with that." She mused and checked her phone when it vibrated in her pocket. She frowned when she saw Cain's name but read the message regardless.

Happy Turkey Day. I miss you.

Her eyes softened a little. As much as she tried to deny it, a part of her would always have some sort of feelings for Cain. She had admitted that to herself when she had been hell-bent on revenge. Despite that, she felt lighter once she broke up with him. They had too much between them, too much in their way, for it to ever work out.

Happy Thanksgiving, Cain. Tell your family I say hello. She wrote back and then turned her attention on Gabriel when he huffed at her.

"Of course, the Council wouldn't know. That's *why* it's the black market. It has to be totally underground. Like, the actual store is probably a front. There's probably a clue or gesture a buyer has to do to be shown the real stuff." He said. A second later his face brightened. "We should go check it out!"

Kee glanced at the time on her phone. "It's almost seven on a holiday, you think they're open?"

"Yep! They're always open. Black market, remember?" He looked at Nana as she and Lucy stood, the carpet thoroughly cleaned from the mess. "Can we, Nana?"

Nana hummed softly. "If you're right and there is something odd going on there, it may be dangerous to be sniffing about."

"But what they're doing could be *more* dangerous." He pointed out. "We should do what Kee does! Gather information and then go tell someone else."

Kee didn't see the harm in humoring him. "As long as I'm back in LA by midnight, I don't see why not. That means we have to be back here by ten-thirty, okay?"

He jumped to his feet in excitement. "Fuck yeah!"

"Language, Gabriel." Nana chided then looked at Kee. "Are you sure you want to go? You don't have to do this."

"Why not? If he's right, then it's something that should be exposed. If he's not, then at least we checked, right?" She smiled at the young warlock when he nodded enthusiastically. She stood up and put her hand on Conrad's shoulder to prevent him from following. "You and Lucy stay here."

He blinked up at her in confusion. "What? Why?"

"Because you're still riled up." She patted his head when he looked off to the side with a frown. "It's okay. Thank you for being upset for me, but you don't need to. You and Lucy should just stay here and relax. Think of it as a little vacation from home."

Lucy smiled and plopped down on the couch next to Conrad. She bumped her shoulder into his when he glanced at her. "We can get another slice of apple cake and watch a movie with Nana." When she saw him hesitate, she put her hand on his knee and sweetened her smile. "Stay with me?"

His cheeks flushed, and he nodded once in agreement. "Alright," he conceded and looked back up at his alpha. "Be careful."

"I will. I have a little warlock as my right-hand man." His frown deepened and she laughed. "Don't worry, Con, you'll always be my right-hand man. That's why you're my beta."

He started at that, eyes widening. His heart picked up speed while his wolf rumbled happily. "Beta?" He echoed softly, but he couldn't deny the elation that coursed through him.

No, Conrad couldn't get excited. She didn't know what was going on. Didn't know the real reason why he was there. *I need to tell her before she makes this decision.* His whole body was torn between misery and happiness. *But if she trusts me enough to make me her beta, maybe she can help me with Liam. Maybe she can help me get my Emilia back.*

His amber eyes cut towards Lucy, her face beaming with happiness for him. *Fuck, I need to tell her about Mia before this goes any further.*

"Con, if you don't want to be my beta, you don't have to be." Kee told him in a gentle tone, though she would be lying if she didn't say she was disappointed by his reaction. He seemed happy at first, but then his mood shifted to something. . .muddled. She couldn't quite place it.

He jerked as if he had been slapped. "N-no! That's not it, Kee. I'm honored, really."

She smiled at him, deciding not to comment on his odd behavior. Not tonight, at least. She turned to Gabriel. "Ready?"

"Yep! Let's go!" He replied as he bounded out the door.

—

"This is it," Gabriel told her as they stopped in front of small shop in the heart of downtown Riverside. It was across the street from the Mission Inn but down towards where the ice skating rink was set up. "See, look," he whispered as a woman walked out of the shop, dressed in a silk dress, fur coat, and red bottom heels. "Fancy people."

As the lady walked by them, the scent of clover and spice hit her nose. "Definitely a witch," she agreed as she looked at the shop again. The wide storefront window had an old antique table in it with a faded, vintage lace table cloth. Various worn books, random bottles with aged glass, and tarnished jewelry were spread artistically across the surface. But, just as Gabriel had said, the shop pulsed with magic. "Well, you're right about the magic. I can sense it."

He stared up at her in disbelief. "You can sense it? My grandpa couldn't."

She shrugged. "I'm not a normal wereanimal," she said simply. "Witches and wizards smell like clove and spice. Any wereanimal can scent one. Magic doesn't necessarily give off a scent, just its wielder. Good magic feels like someone is tickling your aura, almost like they're running a feather over it." She narrowed her eyes at the shop. "But this. . .this makes my hackles rise. It feels like someone is clawing at my aura, but in a 'nails on a chalkboard' kind of way. Does that even make sense?"

His mouth had fallen open at her as she explained everything he felt to a T. "It makes perfect sense," he mumbled and then looked at the store. "Should we try to go in?"

"Might as well since we're here." She answered, but her stomach fluttered nervously. She didn't want to get closer to the bad magic, but if something forbidden was happening, she would tell Lucas. He would know what to do.

"But, what should we say? They know who I am. I tried to come in before and they said I was too young. You're a werewolf, you won't be allowed in either."

He had a point.

I could shift into something else, but I don't want Gabriel to see, or anyone else for that matter. Didn't he said vampires could go in? Hmm. "I have an idea that may get us in. Let me go first, but stay close behind me."

"What are you going to do?" He asked cautiously as he followed her towards the door.

"Just follow my lead." Kee told him before pulling open the old door to the shop.

The store was dimly lit, rows of bookcases and tables much like the one in the window were lined up perfectly against the walls. Towards the back of the building was a small glass countertop with an old-fashion register. A pleasant-looking, elderly gentleman stood behind it, hands clasped in front of him. He was dressed in a pressed white shirt with black suspenders that dropped down his chest and hooked onto his black slacks. A small grey mustache framed his thin upper lip, making his face look even thinner than it already was. The look was completed with a black bowler hat that covered up his dark grey hair. His eyes were squinted shut, but Kee knew he could see them clearly. She could feel him watching them.

He's not a vampire, but he doesn't smell like a wizard either.

"Welcome to The Street," he said in an affable tone. "However, I do regret to inform you that neither one of you are allowed in here. We do not cater to young wizards or wereanimals. Do please see to the exit."

Kee didn't break stride as she walked confidently up to the counter, Gabriel only hesitating for a moment before following close behind her. "My apologies," she began as she reached the man. He was smiling, but it looked fake, as if it were painted on. "But I thought you served vampires?"

He tilted his head marginally as he looked at her with eyes still closed. "Ah, we do, yes, but neither of you seem to be, so your observation is irrelevant." He turned his head towards the younger man behind her. "I do believe I have already told you to come back when you are older."

"You are to speak to me, not my assistant," Kee snipped, making the strange man turn his attention to her once again. She was still trying to figure out what he was, but she couldn't put quite her finger on it.

"My apologies, baby wolf, but I have nothing more to say to you." He said and gestured towards the door, his smile still frozen on his face.

She looked at Gabriel, trying not to look miffed at being called a baby. "No wonder you weren't able to get the items I need. Oh well, I will just have to tell Lucas," she said with forced dismay and tucked her long, dark blonde hair behind her ear. "He won't be pleased that we both came back to Byte empty handed."

Come on, take the bait. She thought when the man just stared at them through his eyelids. She turned to leave, putting her hand on her cousin's shoulder to steer him out, when the man made a small noise of protest.

"Lucas, you said? As in, Lucas Vranas? The Lord of LA County?" He hummed pleasantly.

Gotcha. "Is there another?" She shot back in a bored tone, trying to keep her breathing even. "Don't worry, I'll tell him we need to acquire what he needs at some other store."

"Why, may I ask, would he send you?" He questioned lightly, but Kee could sense his unease.

She lifted a brow at him in mockery. "Because I am his bonded wolf, of course. I, however, was tied up in other matters so I sent my assistant instead. I figured that since he was a warlock, he would have passed your test, but I didn't think age would be a factor."

His lips twitched before the smile widened. "Ah, I see. A simple miscommunication then. Although, I will admit, we were unaware that the LA lord would know of our humble shop all the way out here."

"Humble shops often spread in name if they are worth it," she bluffed. "But if we're mistaken, we will take our leave."

"No, no, I was hasty, Miss Wolf of Vranas." He stepped out from behind the counter. He walked towards the bookcase closest to him and pulled out a book with a tattered, dark blue spine. The bookcase spit in half down the middle with a loud crack. Each side pulled itself open and a set of narrow wooden stairs materialized between them.

"Follow me, if you will." The smiling man said in the same relaxed manner as he began to descend the stairs.

Kee looked over her shoulder at Gabriel and saw his terrified, albeit excited expression. "You can go back to the car, if you want." She offered.

He shook his head, forcing an air of confidence. "No, I have a job to do remember, *boss?*" He said and ushered her to go on.

A part of her had hoped he would have gone back. As soon as the bookcase had opened, the feeling of magic and the sense of foreboding nearly choked her. But she couldn't back out now. She had no idea what would happen if she simply turned and fled after flaunting Lucas' title.

There was no harm looking, right? After all I don't actually have *to buy anything.*

She reached the bottom of the winding staircase and stopped short at the sight. Gabriel ran into her, but she was too busy looking at the street to care. On the right side of the paved, stark white street were little stands and stalls with various items for purchase. On the left side was a tent similar to that of a circus big top. The colors were black and grey, the woman standing outside almost blending in with the colors.

The fake smiling man bowed to Kee with a sweeping gesture, book still in hand. "Miss Wolf of Vranas, Mr Young Assistant, allow me to welcome you once again to the The Street."

Ten

"Holy shit," Gabriel muttered under his breath behind her. "This place is crazy."

"Yeah," she agreed as she started to follow Mr Smiley—that was the name she had given him in return for hers—down the street. There were other shoppers walking along the pavement and some who stopped to browse the items for sale at certain booths.

"So, Miss Wolf of Vranas, Mr Young Assistant, what is it that the lord is looking to buy?" Their guide asked as he clasped his hands behind his back.

Fuck, I don't even know what they're selling down here. "I'll know it when I see it." She replied evasively, eyes scanning the contents of the tables they passed.

Many of them sold various dried plants, but none of them were familiar to her. A couple held small vials of various liquids, others having a collection of rough cut different colored gems. She noticed dried animal parts on one stall; specifically, a reptilian tail and a large claw of some sort of bird.

"Perhaps a blade for his scuffle with the Pasadena lord?" He offered in his unwavering light, humorous tone.

Kee glanced at the stall he referred to, seeing swords and knives laid out in neat rows. The metal of the blades ranged from matte black to gleaming silver. Some were different hues of blue, and there was a green one that was the same shade as Lucas' eyes.

Seeing her gaze, the merchant swept his hands out over his stock in a welcoming gesture. "Come closer and browse! I will answer any of your questions." His words were drowned in a thick accent. It almost sounded French, but she couldn't be sure. His dark brown hair was draped over his shoulder in an intricate braid with little flowers tucked. His skin was a sickly white, his eyes an odd shade of hazel.

She blinked and his features changed. His eyes were purple, hair green, and skin almost translucent. She blinked again and everything was back the way it had been. She stared at him a few more seconds, but his appearance didn't waver a second time.

What the hell?

Kee saw that Mr Smiley had tilted his head so he could look at her over his shoulder. His face was blank, his eyes still squinted shut, but she had a feeling she was being judged. She straightened her spine. "Lord Lucas doesn't need a weapon to fight Alexander. He *is* the weapon." She said and nodded once at the stall. "I was looking at something for myself, but it would be best to focus on my job first."

Seemingly pleased by her answer, he turned back forward and continued to lead them through The Street. The scent of clove and spice flooded her nose, but there was a distinct smell of old blood mixed within it. She looked at the dark skinned witch sitting behind a stall that had a black table cloth with matching jewelry. Her hair was a tangle of black locks tied up high on her head with a bright yellow cloth. Her eyes were a pale, milky brown.

Feeling Gabriel tug the back of her plum colored sweater, she looked over her shoulder and down at him. "Hm?"

"Voodoo witch," he mumbled uncomfortably, eyeing all the dried skulls and bones laid out next to the pendants on her table.

"Stay close." She repeated firmly in a hushed tone. She resisted the urge to hold his hand and mentally berated herself for not taking this more seriously. Gabriel's safety was in her hands. If anything went wrong, she was responsible. She didn't fear Christopher, but Nana scared the shit out of her.

After a few more minutes of walking the strip of pavement, Mr Smiley turned around to face her. "Nothing suitable to your quest, Miss Wolf of Vranas? I am afraid we are at the end of The Street."

Kee glanced at the big top that hadn't been explored. She wanted to say they didn't have what he needed, wanted to turn around and leave, but felt a pull towards the tent. Something was tugging ever so slightly on her senses, beckoning her closer.

I swear, if this gets Gabriel hurt, it better kill me in the process. Otherwise, Nana will do it instead.

"You say we've reached the end." She jerked her head towards the tent. "But we haven't been inside there yet."

"Ah," he commented pleasantly. "This is The Top. You may find what you are looking for in there." His fake smile twitched before widening a small fraction. "But admittance is only granted by the Ringmaster."

Kee looked at the tall, rail thin woman standing outside the tent. She wore a black form fitting coat that fell to her knees. Her undershirt was dark grey, a lace bow tied neatly around the collar. Her slacks were a striped black and grey material that hugged her thighs before disappearing into knee high, black leather boots. Her hair was ashy white and tied into a knot at the back of her neck. On top of her head was a black top hat, a grey lace ribbon wrapped around the base.

"You must ask the Ringmaster." Mr Smiley told her.

She slowly approached the Ringmaster's reclined form against the tent entrance. The Ringmaster's image shifted so that her hair was white feathers, her skin a glittering grey. Kee blinked and everything was back to how it was. She cursed when she realized just what kind of people were behind The Street.

"Ringmaster? May we enter your tent?" She asked, now cautiously choosing her words and paying more attention to the ones spoken to her.

The Ringmaster opened her eyes, revealing irises the color of curdled milk. "You wish to enter my tent? To witness my treasures? You think you are worthy of such a feat?"

She was growing tired of these fucking tests, but it made it all the more obvious as to what these people were. She almost said never mind, fuck dealing with it, and was about turn around when she heard it.

Please. It was a soft, muffled plea that echoed in her head. She thought at first Gabriel had said it, but the voice was too deep. It sounded exhausted. And very much in pain.

Where are you? She thought back to him. It should have creeped her out, or scared her, that someone had whispered in her mind, but the man's tone had instead made her concerned. He seemed so defeated and drained. *What happened to you?*

When she didn't receive an answer, she stared at the The Top as if she could magically peer through the thick fabric and see what hid inside. A muscle in her cheek twitched. Damn it all. She had to find the man asking for help.

She looked at the woman once again. "Ringmaster," she began, trying to phrase her next words carefully. She wanted to match how these people had spoken to her. "I claim no such thing. Your treasures are surely worth more than my interest or coin, but I would be flattered if you allowed me and my assistant to gander at them in awe."

The Ringmaster studied her for a moment before giving a wide, pleased grin. "I like your eyes as much as I like your words," she purred. "They match my tent. I will allow you in." She sauntered over to the tent flap and held it open.

Gabriel tightened his hold on her shirt and she could hear his heartbeat hammering hard. "K—"

She shushed him before he could say her name. Ever since she had seen the flickering image of the arms dealer, she had a suspicion of who ran The Street. It made sense why Mr Smiley called her and Gabriel what he did and why the Ringmaster's image had faltered as well.

"Names should not be spoken on The Street." She warned him.

"Very clever." The Ringmaster commented with a grin, her teeth all sharp points for a brief moment before switching to rounded human teeth.

"What?" Gabriel questioned, tightening his hold on his cousin's sweater.

"The fae don't use names. They believe there's power in learning someone's name." Kee told him lightly, trying not to convey her unease or make his fear worse.

"T-the fae?" He squeaked. "As in faeries?"

"Exactly, Mr Young Assistant." Mr Smiley replied with his cemented smile. "Is that troublesome for you?"

"N-no!" He squeaked. He cleared his throat and tried again. "No, of course not!"

Kee turned and put a protective hand on his shoulder while facing the Ringmaster and Mr Smiley. "He's barely sixteen," she said with a smirk. "He's not used to anything outside of wolves and vampires."

"Ah, of course, of course. A young wizard indeed." Mr Smiley replied with a twitch in his smile.

"Exactly. That is also why I thought this would be a good experience for him," she admitted. "I apologize for underestimating your business."

His smile widened knowingly. "It is forgiven. We aim to please the Lord of Los Angeles."

She nodded once. "I will inform him of your accommodations."

He inclined his head. "Appreciated. Enjoy The Top."

"I'm sure we will," she replied with a forced smile as she led Gabriel into the big top, the Ringmaster close behind. The inside of the tent was dark, only lanterns and little candles provided small, soft patches of light. Once her eyes adjusted, she could see five metal cages. They were large, at least fifteen feet tall, and practically brushed the top of the tent. Two of the cages were empty, but she could make out dark shadows within the other three.

Help. Came the distraught voice again.

I'm here. Which one are you?

"Ringmaster, what prize should we look at first?" Kee asked and swallowed as a sudden wave of anxiety swelled inside her. Whoever, or whatever, was in these cages was terrified. She could feel it surrounding her like a thick, heavy blanket.

She grinned. "Any you would like. I am afraid my selection has dwindled some due to a recent purchase and an unforeseen death."

Kee tried not to look aghast at her response. *Death?* Her body tensed when she remembered the voice in her head. *Is he dying?*

"It's unfortunate when the unplanned happens." Kee commented flippantly even though her heart constricted at the possible fate for the person who had cried out to her.

"Indeed! Not to worry though, I am sure I will restock my inventory soon! They are not easy to come by, but I do get them." Ringmaster grinned again and walked past them so she could lead the way to the first cage. The shadow within it shifted and tried to shrink back as its owner approached the bars. "None of that! Come closer and show them your face!"

A whimper sounded in the large cage before the shadow inched closer. Gabriel sucked in a breath when it came into view within the dim light. "A griffin?" He asked incredulously.

"Yes!" The Ringmaster agreed in a proud exclamation. "Isn't he beautiful? Feathers of a griffin are essential in flying potions."

Kee stared at the animal in silent shock. The talons twitched open but curled back together so they could hide under the feathery chest. The large, balding wings curled around its furry, lion-like body. She could see that his wings bent at odd angles in certain spots. Her stomach tightening when she noticed that some of the feathers had been torn out, blood seeping into the white and golden feathers that remained. His beak was cracked, one beady black eye swollen shut.

"Is a feather what you require? He has plenty more. Wing feathers are more costly than the body ones, unfortunately." Ringmaster informed her, oblivious to her thoughts.

She cleared her throat. "No, Lord Lucas doesn't need to fly." She responded, and it was sheer will that her voice hadn't faltered.

"Ah, of course. To the next one, then!" She said merrily as she led them to the next cage.

The sound of splashing water made Kee's brow furrow. She stopped in front of the cage and looked up at the single lantern hanging from above it. She followed the light down and saw a small plastic pool meant for toddlers. It was filled less than halfway with water, causing the poor creature inside it to lay sideways. Her pale green skin was dry and cracked where it rested outside the water. Her hair was damp but brittle as if she had been out in the sun for too long. Kee couldn't tell if her tail was black, or a dark blue under the murky water, but she could smell the salt and blood that oozed from it.

"A mermaid," Gabriel squeaked.

Kee couldn't stop from voicing her dismay. "That isn't enough water for her." She accused, watching as the malnourished, frail creature tried to lie flat on her stomach in the water. It exposed the skin on her back and the scales on the top of her tail to the air. The mermaid glared weakly at them with black eyes over the plastic rim of the poor excuse for a pool.

"It is enough," Ringmaster defended. "It keeps her weak so that we can get the scales from her tail. It also helps for when we need to draw tears from her."

The young warlock squinted at the mermaid, looking at the gaping holes where her scales should have been on her backside. "Do they regrow their scales?" He asked quietly, his lip trembling at the cruelty.

The Ringmaster shrugged. "If they do, hers have not yet."

"Perhaps they would if you fed her or gave her more water," Kee snipped and then immediately tried to remedy her slip up. "I mean, that way you have more merchandise for the future, no?"

"I suppose, but I find it to be easier to get a new one." She turned to the pair. "The LA Lord should not need to breathe under water or charm someone to his bed. Or am I mistaken?" She asked coyly.

"No, he has no use for either of those." Kee replied with a forced chuckle despite her anger fueling her pounding heartbeat. "What else do you have?"

"My last treasure is my most popular one." the Ringmaster stated happily as she skipped over to the final cage. "My beauty." She cooed as she picked up a lantern from the closest post that held up the tent. She swung it closer to the cage and clicked her tongue in disapproval. "Who said you could change back?"

"Fuck you." A voice snarled in return. It would have been a vicious sound had he not sounded so tired.

He's the one who called me, Kee thought as she approached the cage.

A naked man stumbled closer to the bars of the cage when she did. He seemed to be tall, but she couldn't tell with his hunched shoulders. His eyes were black, almost like the mermaids, but he had whites to his eyes when she did not. His hair was black and shaved on one side, the other side falling in a mess that curled below his chin. His bruised cheekbones were high with cheeks sunken in and smeared with dried blood.

You can hear me. He echoed in her mind as he stared at her. She saw one of his eyes had a cut similar to her scar except it ran down his brow, through the top of his eyelid and then continued down to stop right above his cheek bone. It was maybe a day old, but the wound looked angry with infection.

I heard you calling for me, Kee responded and moved closer to the bars. *We didn't know you were here, that this market even existed.* She hesitated before asking a foolish question. *Are you alright? How can I help you?*

He suddenly snarled at her, baring his teeth. *What do you think?*

She looked at the Ringmaster and noticed the fae staring at her in question. "What's so special about him?" She questioned with a forced air of boredom.

She beamed at her, as if hoping she would ask. "Allow me to show you!" She grabbed a pole next to her, and Kee could see that it was silver. Of course, the metal didn't hurt the fae's long fingers as they wrapped around the rod. Iron was their weakness, not silver.

"No—" She tried to stop the Ringmaster from prodding him like cattle, but the fae had moved too fast. As soon as the silver touched the man, he let out a roar of pain as his skin sizzled. It was then that Kee noticed he had puncture wounds all over his body. They weren't caused by the pole. No, these were deliberate cuts and gouges. Pieces of his flesh were missing, old and new blood splattering and marring his naked flesh like war paint.

"You know what I want," the Ringmaster chided. "How else can I make a sale?"

"Fuck off." He hissed through his pain.

She poked him again and he snarled. Kee put her hands on the bars but gave a cry of pain when they were scalded. She pried them away and stared down at her blistered hands. She glared at the silver bars that had been painted dark grey to match steel. "Silver cages?"

"Oh, I should have warned you, Miss Wolf of Vranas," the Ringmaster laughed humorlessly. "These cages are meant to keep my treasures in and nosey wereanimals out."

You're a wolf? He whispered in a tortured tone. *Get out. Go!*

I can't leave you guys like this. She protested.

The mermaid will be dead by the end of the night and the griffin has been purchased. It's just me and my time is coming. So just go before they grab you, too.

Her heart hurt for the mermaid, but she wasn't sure there was anything she could do for her currently. She could only hope the griffin would be able to escape his new owners. However, something told her his fate had been sealed with his mangled wings.

Then I will get you out. She felt Gabriel tug on her shirt. She couldn't endanger him more than she already had. *I can't tonight, but I know they won't let me back in alone. I'm going to have to bring someone with me tomorrow.*

He scoffed in her head. *Do yourself a favor and stay the fuck away. I'll be dead soon anyways.*

Don't say that! What's your name? The voice in her mind went silent as he was prodded again with the silver rod. He screamed in agony and she flinched, her chest tight with the pain of not being able to help him.

Samson, he wheezed before his body started to contort and twist. With a painful, roaring cry he shifted.

Kee watched with her lips parted in awe as a dragon took the place of the naked man. His scales were a dark crimson red that faded to black towards his underbelly. His black eyes were slits and they stared at her for a moment before they squeezed shut in agony. His spiked tail fell uselessly to the floor as he collapsed. His large, black webbed wings tried to shield him from further pain by curling over him, but they brushed against the silver bars of the cage and he cried out again. His long neck dipped down so his head could tuck under one of his wings, trying desperately to not hurt anymore. His talons on each claw and point of his wings were black like the horns on his head and down his spine.

"T-that's a dragon." Gabriel stammered in disbelief. "They're extinct."

"No, just very hard to find." The Ringmaster smirked.

Kee ignored them as she stared at Samson. She noticed one of his front claws had broken off. A couple horns along his neck and one of the two large ones on his forehead seemed to have been cut away. Even lying down, the top of his back was several inches above her head. The length of him was probably 20 feet long, but she couldn't be sure with his tail.

I'm sorry, she told him softly as her eyes threatened to sting with tears. *Please hold on until tomorrow.*

I won't hold my breath. He whispered bitterly.

Kee mentally counted to three before she pulled away to look at the expectant Ringmaster. "He is truly a treasure," she complimented even as her stomach tensed with the need to vomit. "But it is still not what Lord Lucas was looking for. I think, if it is acceptable to you and Mr Smiley, I will return tomorrow night with my master." She nearly choked on that last word. "Something tells me he will be very interested in your dragon, but I'm not authorized to make a sale under his name without his consent."

The Ringmaster brightened at the idea of a lord coming to see her treasures. "I think that would be lovely." She set the silver pole down and ushered them towards the tent entrance.

Mr Smiley stood waiting for them outside. He tilted his head at her, eyes squinted shut. "Still not what you were looking for?" This time his light tone had a taunting tease to it.

Kee looked at him, focusing on the spot between his brow so she wasn't staring directly at his eyes, regardless of the eyelids being in the way. She didn't know enough about fae to look one straight in the eye. "No, but I think he will be interested in what inventory is here," she said evasively. When the skin around his eyes tightened, she cursed. She needed to smooth it over. "I told the Ringmaster that I will bring Lord Lucas back tomorrow evening, if that is acceptable?"

His head tilted at her before his smile quirked. "We would be honored to receive him," he stated as he clasped his hands behind his back once again.

She nodded and tried to appease the faerie in front of her. She wanted to make sure she didn't leave them any doubt of her intentions. "Although I did not find anything on my list, is it acceptable if I purchase something for myself?"

His smile widened. "But of course."

She inclined her head, avoiding thanking him with words. She put her hand on Gabriel's shoulder and guided him towards the arms stall they had passed earlier. "Just wait until we leave," she murmured to him as his lips trembled with unspoken words.

"Welcome back!" The merchant grinned. "Which of these caught your eyes earlier?"

Kee gave him a forced smile and pointed at a small knife. "This green one here. What can you tell me about it?"

"It's a switchblade made with emerald. Emeralds hold healing powers, both physical and mental," he explained, his smile never faltering. "It helps clear the mind and promotes harmony."

"That sounds perfect. How much?" She asked, reaching into her back pocket. She was glad she had grabbed her ID and some bills from her wallet.

"$1,500." He replied with wide grin. "I take PayPal as well."

Well, at least he's a modern faerie.

It wasn't a problem, considering she had a decent amount in her account from working for Lucas, but it was still a hefty price for a blade smaller than her forearm. Grabbing her phone from her other pocket, she ignored the four text messages waiting for her and brought up the money app. She found his merchant email and sent the amount. Once he received the notification, he folded the knife so the blade tucked into its handle and handed it to her. She took it from him with a nod and tucked it into her back pocket where her money was.

She turned around and Mr Smiley was there with his usual pleased smile. "You have been most gracious, but I believe we are done for the evening. If you would show us the exit, we will be on our way."

"We look forward to your return." He replied as he took them back up the stairs and through the bookcase.

Gabriel gave a small bow to Mr Smiley. "Tha—" his words were promptly cut off when Kee covered his mouth with her hand.

She looked at Mr Smiley and gave an exaggerated eye roll. "He still has a lot to learn," she laughed without humor. When the fae simply nodded, she released Gabriel's mouth and turned him by the shoulders so she could push him out the door.

"No, wait until we get to the car." She told him when he opened his mouth. She kept her hand on one of his shoulders, making him keep a normal pace with her until they were blocks away from the shop.

Once they got to the Jeep, Gabriel threw his hands into his hair. "Holy shit, holy shit, *holy shit!*" He cursed, his bottom lip quivering. "What the hell did we just see, Kee?"

The forced confidence she had put on melted away, and she stumbled to her knees next to the driver's door. She covered her mouth as the hollowness in her stomach filled with disgust and dread. She flared her nostrils as she tried to take in deep breaths of air.

They're being tortured. She cried to herself, the image of all three of them flashing before her. She squeezed her eyes tightly as she gagged.

"What are we going to do?!" He exclaimed, oblivious to her current state. "Oh gods, those poor creatures."

She removed her hand and took deep breaths to try to calm her racing heart and queasy stomach. She forced herself to her feet and dug the key out of her pocket. She unlocked the doors and slid into the driver's seat. She waited until Gabriel was in before turning to look at him. "*We* are not going to do anything."

He turned wide eyes on her. "What do you mean? We can't leave them there!"

"I don't plan on leaving them there, but you aren't coming. You were already in enough danger tonight. I should have taken it more seriously before we went in. You could have been seriously hurt if things went wrong." She started the car and put her hands on the steering wheel. She grabbed it tightly, hoping it would stop the trembling in her hands.

"Everything was fine, Kee! I want to help them!" He protested as she drove them towards Nana's house.

"No, it wasn't. You didn't know they were fae. You almost gave away my name and thanked them. If you thank them then they feel you owe them. A favor for a favor. That's how they work. Names help them glamor you." She explained in a tight tone. Her mind was reeling, Samson's gouged flesh and broken horns searing her mind.

It's not right.

Gabriel crossed his arms across his chest with a loud huff. "I can be useful."

She glanced at him. "I'm not saying you can't be, but I can't put you at risk. Lucas and I will come back tomorrow. He'll know what to do."

He stared at her. "Wait, you weren't lying? You really *are* bonded to the LA lord?"

She blew out a sigh. "Yes. The fae can't lie, but that doesn't mean they like being lied to."

Gabriel frowned and hugged his arms tighter across his chest. "I-is he strong?"

"Lucas? Yeah, probably the strongest person I've ever met." She answered honestly.

"Can he save them?"

She clenched her jaw and tightened her hold on the steering wheel again. "I hope so."

Eleven

Kee pulled into the driveway of Nana's house to see Conrad and Lucy waiting outside. Conrad had been pacing but stopped mid stride and jerked his head towards the car when it pulled in. She turned off the engine and got out, walking straight towards her beta.

"Kee? What's wrong? What happened?" He asked when he saw how tense she was. His brow furrowed when her eyes watered as she approached him.

She resisted the urge to hug him, to absorb his strength. "It was horrible," she murmured, balling her hands into fists at her sides. "Gabriel wasn't wrong, the place is run by the fae." She said as Nana and Lucy approached.

Nana stiffened. "The fae? In Riverside? How do you know?"

She told them everything that happened, Gabriel chiming in to add to the story. When she was done, the three of them had gone as white as a sheet.

"It's a black market for monster parts." Gabriel stammered as tears finally filled his eyes. "That poor mermaid. Gods, her cracked skin, her missing scales."

Nana pulled him into her, putting an arm around his shoulders as he broke into a fit of sobs. She stared at Kee with her lips set in a hard line. "This is bad."

She flinched. "I'm sorry, Nan. I didn't mean to put Gabriel in danger. I really didn't know what was going to happen. I sensed the black magic, but I never imagined it would be like that."

Nana waved a hand at her. "I don't fault you. Should you have turned away when you felt the black magic? Probably, but how else would we have discovered this?"

"Now we just need to figure out how to shut it down." Lucy commented, fidgeting uncomfortably.

Conrad drew the fox to him so he could comfort her. She tucked under his arm and nuzzled into his side, making his beast rumble happily. He looked at Kee, "Do you think Lucas will help?"

"I hope so." She answered tiredly. She pulled her phone from her pocket and checked the time. It was a little past 11pm, and it took about an hour to get back to LA. She clicked on her forgotten text messages and quickly read through them. One had been from Cain telling her it wasn't the same without her on a holiday. Conrad had written her twice asking her for updates, and the last was from Lucas asking when they were leaving.

About to pack up and leave. I have something to tell you when I get back to Byte.

She didn't get an immediate response, but she knew he was still entertaining his guests. She shoved the phone back into her pocket and ran her hand through her hair. "We should get going, it's late."

"I'll grab our bags," Lucy offered as she slipped out from under Conrad's arm and went to the guest house.

Kee gave Nana a brief hug and thanked her for dinner. "It was nice to see you again, Nana. I missed you."

"You missed my cooking." The older woman shot back but patted Kee's head in goodbye. "I'll expect you and your pack for Christmas as well. Perhaps even your vampire, should he help solve this issue in my territory."

Conrad grinned when Nana reached up to pet his head as well. "Thank you for having us. I look forward to Christmas." Maybe with Mia.

Her face turned cold, and she shoved a finger in his chest. "You take care of your alpha. She's stubborn and is used to being independent. It'll get her in trouble one day. Make sure you're there to help her out of it."

His face softened. "I will." He gave Gabriel a fist bump and then took the bags from Lucy when she rushed back to them.

Lucy hugged Gabriel then Nana. "Thank you so much for having me! Did I hear correctly about Christmas? I'll be there!"

Kee shook her head with a smile and turned to her cousin. She wrapped her arms around him when he hugged her tightly. "I'll try my best to save them, Gabriel. You just focus on growing your magic, okay?"

He nodded against her shoulder. "I'll try."

She gave him a squeeze before releasing him. She waved at Nana again before getting back into the Jeep. She waited until everyone was settled in before backing out of the driveway. "I wish you guys could have seen it." She muttered.

Lucy frowned. "I'm glad I didn't," she replied softly. "It's sounds horrible."

"It was." She grunted grimly. "They literally skinned and cut out pieces from them. All for a fucking sale."

Conrad let out a soft growl. "That's disgusting."

"Yeah." She pulled onto the freeway and didn't speak again until they got to Byte. She drove on autopilot the whole way back, Samson's plea and the sight of his battered body playing on repeat in her mind.

They pulled into Byte a quarter past midnight. They walked

through the back, nodding at the last few vampires who were leaving the party. The trio made their way through the kitchen and across the empty club. A large banquet table had been set up on the dance floor, but there weren't any chairs in sight. Kee noticed the red table cloth had suspicious, almost black splatters on it and shuddered.

The three climbed the stairs to the fourth story and ventured into the room Kee and Conrad had claimed. Conrad dropped the bags on the floor and moved towards the dresser to pull out pajamas. He looked at Lucy as she stood awkwardly by the door. "Did you want something comfortable to wear?"

She flushed and shook her head. "I should probably get back to my apartment. I've been away for a couple days."

"Oh," he straightened. "Can I walk you out?"

She smiled shyly at him. "Sure."

"Wait, Luce, before you go, I have a question for you." Kee set the simple dress she had pulled out down on the bed and took the werefox's hand in hers. "Now, don't feel obligated or pressured, okay? Especially after what just happened to you."

Lucy's pale green eyes widened slightly in concern. "You're worrying me. Is everything alright?"

She smiled. "Yes. I would just like to invite you to join my pack. I think I speak for us both when I say we love having you around. We want to protect you, and we trust you." She squeezed her friend's hand. "But it's *your* choice and I won't force you."

"Join your pack?" She echoed. "I'm not a wolf."

Kee laughed. "Neither am I," she grinned when Lucy blushed in embarrassment. "I just ask you think about it before saying no."

Still stunned, she nodded. "I will," she promised and hugged her friend. "I'll see you later, Kee." She allowed Conrad to open the door for her and walked out with him.

Alone in her room, she turned to the dark blue dress she had laid out. She gave a soft groan. After the whole fiasco with The Street, she didn't feel like dressing up. Granted, her makeup was already done so all she had to do was change into the dress, but she didn't want to. Then again, he *had* given her the option to not wear anything.

She blushed and felt heat shoot through her. *No, I'm not going to be that easy.*

She huffed and removed her jeans and sweater. Something heavy dropped to the floor and she bent to pick up the switchblade. She set it on the bed before pulling the dress over her head. It was a simple chiffon dress that stopped at her knee. It was sleeveless and had a modest neckline that barely showed her collar bones. The back was open, making her remove her bra. Her shoulders and spine were exposed until the fabric joined back together a few inches above her waist.

She grabbed her hair and tied it in a long, loose braid that hung over her shoulder. She slipped on a pair of black ballet flats and turned towards the door but paused. Biting her lip, she hooked her thumbs in her panties and pulled them off.

Compromise, not easiness, she mused.

She grabbed the thong, along with her jeans and sweater, and tossed them in the hamper. She then grabbed the switchblade and left the room. As she reached the main floor and headed towards the basement, her stomach bunched in nerves. Everything had been fine between them during their phone call and messages, but in person things had been disastrous. How would things be now?

Reaching the bottom of the stairs, she made her way to Lucas' room and hesitated at his door. She swallowed a dry lump in her throat and knocked lightly on it.

"Come in, Keira." She heard him say through the heavy door.

She twisted the knob and pushed the door open to step inside. She closed the door behind her and leaned back against it. Lucas stood by the bookcase, his eyes on her. She drank in his appearance, appreciating the black slacks that hugged his legs. He had a dark green collared shirt on, a black tie knotted perfectly at his throat. She could see a black suit jacket and matching vest were draped onto the back of his couch and she almost mourned the loss of not seeing the full image all together. But still, he was there, and he was as beautiful as always.

Just seeing him made all of her troubles momentarily disappear.

Before she realized it, she was all but running towards him. She threw herself at him and he easily caught her, his arms circling around her waist as hers looped around his neck. They pressed their bodies tight against one another and just held each other. Gods, how she had missed this.

Lucas pulled away first so he could cradle her face in his cool, pale hands. "Keira," he rumbled in his deep baritone voice.

"Lucas," she whispered back, looking up at him. "I missed you."

He gave her a real smile, the tips of his fangs peeking out from under his lip. "And I you." He told her before dipping down to press a soft kiss to her lips. When she made a sound between a whimper and moan, he kissed her again with more force.

Her hands slid down to his chest. One still held the switchblade, the other fisted his tie to pull him closer for a deeper kiss. Her lips parted against his and his tongue met hers. She knew his rule of being careful with his fangs and she refused to have anything ruin the moment, so she stilled her tongue and let his caress hers.

Lucas ran his hands down the exposed flesh of her back. He broke the kiss and trailed his fingertips lightly down her spine again. "I see you chose to wear clothes," he teased in a soft tone. "I cannot say I am not disappointed."

She grinned up at him. "You tempted me so let's just say I compromised."

"Oh?" He asked with a raised brow.

She shook her head at him. "Oh, no. I'm not explaining until you tell me what you have planned for our date."

His face sobered. "Keira, I am sorry, but I had to cancel what I had planned. Something has come up, and I need to remain here." His eyes fluttered shut. "I did have a night planned for us, but I cannot ignore this."

She released his tie and cupped his face with her free hand. "I'm not mad. I honestly have had a really rough night as well and I almost came down here in sweats and a t-shirt."

He let out a soft laugh. "I would have been pleased all the same," he admitted then traced his hand down her naked back again. "Although, I will not complain about your attire. You look lovely as always."

Her cheeks flushed at the compliment, but she shook her head. "You're the good looking one," she corrected. She held up her hand to show him the switchblade. "I was actually reminded of your beauty tonight so I bought this for you."

He blinked and took the offered item. The black polished handle was beautiful, but the emerald blade that flipped out was more so. "Where did you get this?"

"From a market that we'll talk about later. It's emerald. It's supposed to have healing powers for both the body and the mind. It'll help give you mental clarity and harmony."

He smirked at her. "Did you also know that in the past people believed emeralds could help fertility and lust?"

Her face turned bright red. "He didn't say that." She muttered with a curse. "I thought maybe it could help you with everything going on." Her face relaxed into a soft, concerned expression. "Is everything okay? Did something new happen? Can I help with anything?"

Lucas shook his head and brushed his thumb over her bottom lip. "I may not be able to take you out, but I will still share a perfect evening with you. No poor topics for now, agreed? Everything can wait until tomorrow." He saw her face fall when he said tomorrow, her brow furrowing. When she parted her lips to respond, he cut her off. "Shh, tonight then, but I want at least a few blissful hours with you until that time."

Kee looked up at his face, at the pleading gleam in his eyes and could deny him nothing. "Later," she agreed before giving him a wicked grin. "Blissful, hm? It's a good thing I'm not wearing panties then, I suppose."

His eyes dilated, and he ran his hands down to cup her backside and lift her so that her legs wrapped around his waist. "Compromise, you said?" He questioned in a deeper, seductive tone, his accent becoming heavier.

She tightened her legs around him as he carried her to the bed. "I'm wearing *nothing*," she teased. "*Under* my something nice."

"Make it nothing at all." He commanded as he gently tossed her on the bed and pulled off his tie.

"And if I don't want to?" She countered. She lifted her chin defiantly when he stilled, his fingers frozen on the buttons of his shirt. She watched as his eyes sharpened in intensity before he simply tore open the shirt, buttons scattering across the room.

Lucas shrugged off the shirt and grasped her slender calves that had firm muscle beneath the skin. He yanked her down towards the edge of the bed and dropped to his knees. His hands skimmed up her calves, the side of her legs, and then rested on the tops of her bare thighs to part them. He glanced up the length of her body, making sure those dove grey eyes were focused intently on him before slipping his head under her dress and burying his face between her thighs.

She gasped when his tongue slid between her folds and grabbed at the blankets, desperate for an anchor at the sudden tide of pleasure. The tip of his tongue swirled around her clit, just as she liked it, before he sucked on the bundle of nerves.

Her hips bucked and he quickly pulled away so he didn't puncture her most tender flesh with his fangs. He grabbed the hem of her dress and jerked it up. With a last long, slow lick, he lifted his head and looked at her. The tip of his pointer finger circled her opening before sliding in.

"Your mouth is going to get you in trouble one day, my sweet." He warned as he pressed a kiss to her soft thigh.

Kee went up on her elbows and lifted a brow at him. "Maybe you should punish it."

He blinked at her before the green of his eyes darkened. "Be careful of what you ask for."

Her stomach fluttered when she felt the sudden spike of pure desire from his side of the bond. Oh, he liked that idea, did he? She sat up and pushed him back so she could slide off the bed to her knees. "I know what I'm asking for."

Lucas got to his feet and looked down at her. He cupped her cheek and ran his thumb over her bottom lip, staring down at her with a challenge in his eyes. "Do you want me to fuck this mouth of yours, Keira? Is that it?"

Her hands went to the fly of his slacks in response. She carefully lowered the zipper and tugged his pants down past his knees. He stepped out and kicked them aside, leaving him completely nude and erect before her. Slowly, she raked her eyes over his pale, naked form. He told her that he had once been tan, the days he spent outside tending to his family's crops leaving him a golden bronze. Even without the tan skin, he looked like a Greek god.

He traced her bottom lip again and rumbled when she took the thumb into her mouth, giving it a soft suck. Her hand wrapped around his cock, thumb rubbing in the bead of liquid that oozed from the tip. He closed his eyes as she stroked him, her small hand sliding up and down his erection. She continued to suck on his thumb as she did and he soon grew impatient, needing to feel that sensation on his cock instead.

He pressed down on her tongue and grabbed the bottom of her jaw with his fingers. "Open your mouth."

She did as told, opening her mouth for him. He removed his thumb from her mouth and grabbed her jaw, guiding her mouth to his erection. She flicked her tongue over the broad head, tasting the precum she had spread there earlier, before taking the tip into her mouth. When he didn't move her forward, she swirled her tongue around the head and slit.

Lucas released her jaw and grabbed her hands, placing them flat against the tops of his thighs. "Tap my thigh if it becomes too much and I will stop. Do you understand?" He asked. When she looked up at him and nodded, he wrapped her braid around his fist and urged her forward.

Kee's mouth slid further down his cock. He pulled her back before she went too far then guided her back down. When he tightened his hold on her hair and held her in place, she knew she was going to be at his mercy more than she ever had been before.

He kept her head still and pumped his hips in shallow movements, warming her up in a way. He watched her face carefully as he moved a little harder, pushing himself further into her mouth. When he hit the back of her throat, she gagged and he waited for her to relax before going again.

This time when he hit it, Kee was ready. She kept her hands flat on his powerful thighs, but her fingers curled as he moved a little harder. She tried to relax her throat and tongue, breathing deep through her nose as he began to pick up a steady pace with his thrusts.

"Good girl," Lucas rumbled his praise and released her braid so he could cup either side of her head. He held her firmly as he worked his hips, thrusting into her mouth. When she closed her eyes at a particularly deep thrust, he growled, "Eyes on me, Keira."

She looked up at him and heat pooled between her legs when he groaned in response. Strands of his black hair fell over his brow as he stared down at her. He had a look of concentration mixed with adoration that made her press her thighs tighter together.

Lucas felt pure male satisfaction when saliva dribbled out of the corner of her mouth and down her chin. He deepened his thrust, the head of his cock hitting the back of her throat and trying to go deeper. Her fingers twitched on his thighs, but she didn't tap out. Encouraged, he slid one hand to the top of her head while the other cradled the bottom of her jaw once again. With the same aggression as earlier, he continued to thrust deep, seeing how much of him she could take.

Her eyes squeezed shut again as they watered from his rough treatment. When he thrust in and held himself at the very back of her throat, she tried to hold out and breathe through her nose, but it was too much. She tapped his thigh and, true to his word, he immediately pulled back. She gasped in through her mouth and wiped at the slobbery mess her chin had become.

He helped her to her feet and kissed her swollen lips tenderly. "Are you alright?" He asked as he pulled back.

She all but ripped off the dress and tossed it aside before pressing her naked body against his. "Seeing you like that—" she swallowed thickly and looked up at him with pure need. "I need you to fuck me. *Now*."

He didn't need to be told twice. He laid her down on the edge of the bed and salivated when she automatically parted her legs for him in invitation. Still standing, he moved between her sweet thighs and grabbed her hips, pulling her closer to edge of the bed before driving into her wet heat. When she cried out in bliss, he growled and began a hard, fast pace, knowing he wouldn't last long after fucking her mouth the way he had.

Kee cupped her breasts and squeezed them as he rammed into her. She moaned when he lifted her legs and rested her ankles against one of his shoulders. One arm went around her thighs and held her firmly as he quickened his thrusts. "Lucas!"

He leaned forward, making her legs bend towards her body. "Again." He rumbled, nostrils flaring as her walls began to flutter around his cock. The base of his spine began to tingle, but he wouldn't come until she did.

"Lucas," she moaned. When his hand encircled her throat, her body tensed as that building wave inside her started to crest. There was something about being completely dominated by him that turned her on more than anything and he knew it. Suddenly his other hand was between their bodies, his thumb rubbing hard, firm circles into her clit. Her back bowed, hips jerking up as her orgasm slammed into her. "*Fuck!*"

Lucas groaned when her pussy clamped down on him. Two more jerky thrusts and he followed her into orgasm. When he finished emptying his blank seed within her, he released her legs. They dropped to either side of him and he collapsed over her, forehead resting on her shoulder.

A lazy, tired smile tilted her lips as he placed languid kisses along her neck. She stroked his silky hair and down his smooth back. She lingered over his shoulder blade, lightly tracing the scar tissue of his sun.

"Can we just stay like this for a while?" She mumbled.

He smiled against her neck. "I believe we can manage that."

Twelve

Lucas let out a relaxed sigh as Kee nuzzled into his side. Her head rested on the spot between his left shoulder and breast, her leg lying over his. He lightly ran his fingertips down the soft skin of her arm as it draped across his chest. They had been like that for a couple hours, but he could lay there forever and be fully content.

"Do we have to get serious?" She mumbled, splaying her fingers out on his naked chest. A tired smile curved her lips when a laugh rumbled under her hand.

"Yes." He answered. His other hand came up so he could run his fingers through her undone braid, detangling the mess he had made. "There is much left unsaid between us that needs to be discussed."

She groaned softly but nodded in agreement. "Where do we even start?"

"At the beginning," he decided and stared up at ceiling with a frown. "I am sorry about Alexander. I truly did not know he was behind your attack. I would never wish that upon you."

Kee curled her naked body closer to his. "Conrad and I figured out that Warren is Alexander's bonded wolf," she told him. "It would explain how everything is connected." She inhaled a deep breath and slowly let it out. "I'm also sorry I blamed you like that. I know why you didn't kill Alexander. I was hurting, angry, and just looking for someone to blame for my attack."

"You were not wrong, though. Had I killed him, you would never have been ambushed." He shifted out from under her so he could prop himself up on one elbow and look down at her. He traced his fingers down the white scars that ran diagonally across her torso. "These will be my reminder to show no mercy from here on out." He sneered.

She looked up into his suddenly angry eyes and grabbed his hand, lacing their fingers together. "They remind me that I'm alive," she retorted. "And that I only survived because of you, Lucas."

His eyes softened. He brushed his lips against her forehead. "You give me too much credit."

"You give yourself too little," she teased before her face sobered. "We need to talk about me being your weapon."

His body tensed. "When I found you shifting in the back lot of Byte, I wanted you for my own personal gains," he admitted. "You are a rare creature that has such a unique, powerful skill. I will admit that I was disappointed that you could only turn into animals. I never pushed you on the subject, but I had hoped that one day you could surpass your limitations."

Kee remained quiet as hurt ached in her chest. So, she *had* been a tool to him since day one. His cool fingertip lifted her chin, and she reluctantly met his eyes. "Hm?"

"Somewhere along the way you became more than a weapon to me, Keira. I enjoyed spending time with you. I found amusement in pushing your buttons until you were irritated and flustered. I knew there was a confident side of you that was hidden away, and it brought me great pleasure to rip her out of her hiding place." He smirked when she laughed, the hurt from her side of the bond easing. "You have harnessed the strength I knew was inside you, and it suits you wonderfully."

She went up on her elbows as well and kissed him. "Thank you." She breathed against his lips when they parted.

"You need not thank me." He replied and repaid her kiss with one of his own.

After a few heartbeats of comfortable silence, Kee brought up his bleeder. "So, what are we going to do about Aubrey?"

"I have to find her. It is in my contract to care for her wellbeing." Lucas sat up fully with a huff of irritation. "But I am more concerned about Giovanni."

"Gio?" She asked in confusion as she sat up as well, hugging the blanket to her chest. "What's going on with him?"

He ran a hand through his hair in frustration. "He is missing."

She gaped at him. "Missing?" She sucked in a sharp breath. "Do you think Alexander has him?"

He nodded once, the movement no more than a stiff jerk. "I do. I have not received a note like before, but I am almost certain of it. This is how Alexander plays his games."

"Capturing one pawn at a time?" She murmured.

"Exactly." He turned his gaze to her. "I have exhausted all of my options to locate him. My contacts, both vampire and not, cannot find him. I am certain that if we find Alexander, we find Giovanni."

She saw the unspoken words in his torn expression. "You want me to try to find Alexander?"

"That is the question," he sighed. "At first, I was hesitant to ask you because we were fighting. Now I am just nervous that he will get his hands on you."

She dropped the blanket and climbed into his lap. His hands automatically went to her hips, and she framed his face in her hands. "Didn't you just get done telling me how strong I am? I won't let him touch me."

He nipped her palm without drawing blood. "You are strong, but so is Alexander. He was the Lord of Pasadena for a reason." He told her solemnly.

"I'll be okay," she reassured him.

"Promise me if you find him you will not engage him. Swear you will wait for me." He demanded seriously. "I just need you to find out his location, and I will take care of the rest."

Kee stared into his emerald eyes and saw the concern behind the intensity. She pressed her forehead against his. "I promise I will try." When his body tensed, she elaborated. "I mean, I won't attack him, but I'll defend myself if I need to. Hopefully it won't come to that. I promise I'll try my best to be careful."

He wrapped his arms around her waist and brushed their noses together. "That is the best I will get from you considering the circumstances."

She nodded and pulled her head back. She slid her hands up and ran her fingers through his hair. "My turn to ask a favor."

He looked curiously at her as nerves prickled at the bond. "This has something to do with tomorrow night."

"Yeah," she mumbled and stilled her fingers when the images of the caged creatures flashed again. Her eyes watered as her chest tightened. "I saw something horrible tonight."

When a small sob wracked her, he pulled her body flush against his. One of his hands went to the back of her neck, holding her to him. He didn't enjoy seeing her cry. "It must have truly been horrible to bring tears to your eyes." He commented gently. "Tell me."

Kee told him everything about The Street. She told him about Gabriel's suspicions and how she got them in using her status as his wolf. She explained the stalls and their items for sale before telling him about the Ringmaster and The Top. The horrifying conditions of the griffin, mermaid, and dragon shifter. She finished with her purchase of the switchblade and leaving with her cousin.

Lucas had been silent as she retold her encounter with the fae's black market. Once she finished, he smoothed her hair back from her face. "This is not the first time The Street has appeared."

She blinked at him and wiped at her eyes. "It's been around before?"

He nodded. "Yes. By the time any reining preternatural catches on to it, they usually disperse," he gave her a frown. "Unless the lord finds it acceptable."

Her brow furrowed. "How can anyone be okay with the treatment of those creatures?" When he didn't respond, her eyes widened. "You're saying the Riverside lord is fine with it?"

"I am saying the Riverside *County* lord is fine with it. She dabbles in magic users." He explained. "She has been known to turn warlocks into the undead. The Council supposedly put a stop to it, but that just means there is no proof of her current antics."

She clenched her jaw. "Samson is dying, Lucas. He said the mermaid would be dead by the end of tonight and the griffin was bought. It may be too late for the others, but we have to help him."

He stroked the side of her neck with his thumb as he gave her an apologetic look. "Keira, I cannot just barge into another lord's territory and meddle with their affairs."

Her brow creased. "But what they're doing is wrong."

"I know," he agreed. "However, I am the Lord of Los Angeles County, not Riverside County. It is up to the Lord of California to handle this matter."

She grabbed his shoulders tightly as her anxiety swelled. "Lucas, I have to help him! I told him I would come back!" *I can't let him die.*

He gently shushed her. "I understand that," he said patiently. "But I cannot shut down The Street or The Top. It is outside my jurisdiction."

What was she supposed to do? She couldn't return there without him. "What about Samson?"

Lucas pressed a reassuring kiss to her lips when they quivered. "I will accompany you tomorrow evening, my sweet. They are expecting me now, and it should be sufficient reason to enter the territory. If we need to purchase your dragon, then we will do so."

"You would do that?" She muttered. "I can't fathom how much he's going to cost."

He gave her a tender smile. "You ask so little of me and have never requested a favor. I can do this for you."

She gave him a shy smile in return, but it faded away a few seconds later. "That doesn't stop them from gathering new creatures."

He let out a soft sigh. "No, it does not."

She closed her eyes and dropped her forehead to his shoulder. "I can't believe the fae are so horrible."

He stroked her hair, smoothing the dark blonde strands in place. "Every species is capable of evil, Keira. There is always good and bad."

"Are you mad I dragged you in to this?"

"Mad? No. Apprehensive is the better word. The Riverside lord and I have had our issues, but that is history. I am more concerned about people finding out what you are to me. I trust my coven members, but that is it. Every person who learns who you are to me brings you closer to danger. I have enemies, Keira, and they will not hesitate to use you against me." He slid his hand to her cheek and raised her face from his shoulder so they were looking at each other again. "That is why I am so concerned about Alexander."

"I'm sorry. I just didn't know how else to get us in." She pursed her lips together. "Maybe the Riverside lord won't find out? Do you think the faeries will tell her?"

"It is always a possibility." He released her face and looped his arms around her before reclining back against the mattress, bringing her with him.

She snuggled into his chest again. "Thank you."

"For?"

"Going with me tomorrow—today. I know it's a big favor to ask."

He ran his fingers up and down the smooth skin of her back. "Consider it payment for helping me find Alexander."

"You don't need to pay me for that. I would have helped you regardless. I love Gio and I want to get him back, too." She drew circles on his chest. "Are you okay? With everything going on I mean?"

He closed his eyes. "I am considerably better now that you are here. I will be even more so when Giovanni returns."

"And Aubrey?" She teased.

He grimaced. "I suppose I will be less stressed when I find out if she is dead or not. If she *is* dead, I have broken my contract. As a regional lord, I will be up for scrutiny from the Council. If she is dying, I will have to turn her. If she is alive, then everything will be fine."

"You have to turn her if she's dying?" When he nodded, she hummed in thought. "How do you turn someone into a vampire?"

"They have to be near death then receive blood from a lord vampire. The dying condition can be caused by anything except chronic sickness. It can be someone who was in an accident, or it can be a human who was simply drained."

"Drained?"

"A vampire who wants to bring a healthy human over to our side has to drain a great percentage of their blood first. It makes it easier for the vampire's blood to invade their system. There has to be an exchange of blood for five days after the initial bite before the human is officially undead. The fledgling has to be kept in the dark with their maker until the transformation is complete. They are too skittish and blood thirsty to be alone." He let out a tired sigh. "I would rather not spend five days awake and asleep with Aubrey. She already thinks she is entitled to my body."

Kee had to stop the growl that started to vibrate in her chest. *I don't own Lucas. He can do whatever he wants to.*

She cleared her throat. "You *are* pretty addictive."

He smirked. "Is that jealousy I feel, Miss Quinn?"

"I'm not sure what you mean, Mr Vranas." She hummed innocently.

He gave a soft chuckle. "You have nothing to be jealous about. I assure you that the only one I want in my bed is already here."

She blushed. "You're such a charmer, aren't you?"

"Only to you," Lucas replied, his smirk widening when she gave him half-hearted smack on the chest. "But, if I have to turn Aubrey, she will have to be here with me for five days."

She made a face. "Hopefully it won't come to that then."

"Agreed." He glanced at the clock on the wall and frowned at the time. "I will be forced to sleep soon, Keira."

She frowned. "Do you want me to go?"

"Of course not. I was simply giving you the option."

She rolled her eyes at him. She grabbed the covers and pulled them up to her shoulders. She cuddled back up to his side, her head going back to its spot right under his shoulder. "Good night, Lucas."

"Sleep well, my sweet." He reached over and switched off the bedside lamp. He settled his arms around her warm body and closed his eyes, allowing the rising sun to pull him from the world of the living once again.

Thirteen

"Cain?"

The werewolf looked up when his only wolf gently called his name. His dark blue eyes watched as she shuffled into the living room. Tension stiffened her posture and set her jaw in a hard clench. He could smell the fear and nervousness coming off of her in waves.

He tried to hold back the growl in his chest as he rose to his feet from the couch. "You're early."

Katie nodded, not meeting her alpha's eyes. "I didn't want to be late."

"Good," Cain snipped out and grabbed his truck keys as he stormed towards the front door. As he passed her, her small hands grabbed his shirt, and he growled low in his throat in warning.

She quickly released him and kept her eyes cast down. "Cain, please. I'm sorry."

"For what, Katie? What exactly are you sorry for? For attacking my intended mate?" He asked and whirled on her. "For making a fool out of us?"

She shrunk back, her wolf whimpering. "Yes, but also for breaking you guys up," she whispered. "I did it for Wyatt. She killed him, Cain.

She killed the wolf who was going to be *my* mate."

"If she hadn't killed him, he would have killed her. Then your mate would have been the reason I didn't have mine." He told her, voice low with anger. When tears spilled down her cheeks, he softened the edge in his voice. "I'm sorry you're hurting, Katie. I never would have wished Wyatt dead, but he tried to kill Kee and I'm happy he didn't succeed."

She sniffled miserably. "I know."

He groaned and rubbed his face. "Look, if you need someone to be angry at, blame Warren. He's the reason you and I are both without our loved ones."

"But Kee's still alive, Cain," she pointed out softly. "You can still be together."

He swallowed his growl and steadied his voice. "Katie, tell me, what do you think would happen if I mated Kee now? What really happened will come out to the rest of the pack and, regardless of Warren being the one who caused it, they will blame her for killing our pack mates. She's an outsider and she killed our brothers. Even if it was justified, they will never accept her."

It had taken him a while to truly digest what Kee had explained to him. He knew she was right about his pack. She wouldn't be safe while Warren was alpha, and she would constantly be plotted against when he took over the role. His pack would never feel he had their best interest in mind and would question his choices. There was also the issue of her being her own alpha.

She pressed her lips together in a hard line. "Maybe Nat and I could talk to them on her behalf."

He scoffed. "You would defend her? You hate her for killing Wyatt and the others."

"But she makes you happy and you trust her." She countered. "You're an alpha and so is she. You guys would make the best team."

"We *did* make the best team," he corrected. "I'm not alpha of LA yet, but I plan on fixing that today. Come on." He opened the front door and let her walk out in front of him before locking the door behind them.

There was a tense, awkward silence as they drove to Warren and Natalie's house. Katie fidgeted with her seatbelt as she stared out the window. "Do you think he'll admit it?" She asked softly.

He sighed. "I'm not sure. Nat said she tried talking to him about last night, but he turned on her. She locked herself in their room after that. He's losing it, Katie. I don't know if it's from the guilt of what he did, or if it's from me taking the power of alpha from him. Either way, he's a liability to the pack."

"Did he hurt her?" She whimpered.

Cain let a growl rumble in his chest. "When I asked, she said she was fine, but that doesn't mean he didn't hurt her."

She nervously curled a piece of her black hair around her finger. "I'm scared."

The alpha in him made him comfort her, despite the irritation he still felt. He reached out and put his hand on her head, giving it a light pat. "I won't let anything happen to you."

They didn't speak again until he pulled into Warren's driveway. Cain stared at the black Mercedes he parked next to. He looked at Katie when she came to stand next to him and saw that she looked equally confused.

"Who's is this?" She asked with a furrowed brow.

"I have no idea," he replied and nodded towards the house. "Let's go find out."

They approached the front door, and Cain knocked once before opening the door. The open-door policy was the number one rule for alphas. It allowed pack members to come to their alpha's house at any time when a problem roused. He cautiously stepped into the house, making Katie stay behind him in case Warren came at them. He slowly walked towards the living room and stopped when he saw four wolves seated on the couches. Warren and Natalie sat on the same couch but at opposite ends. The other couch had two male wolves he didn't know.

"Cain," Nat called in a relieved tone as she stood. As soon as she was on her feet, she stiffened as if remembering something and slowly turned to face one of the unfamiliar men sitting across from her. She kept her head down and looked away from him once he caught her eye. When the wolf jerked his head towards Cain and Katie, she nodded once and walked over to them.

Cain furrowed his brow when she came up to them. "What's going on? Why are you asking for permission in your own house?" He asked as he scowled at the trio. A growl rumbled in his throat when Warren looked at him, but it stopped when his alpha tensed and turned his attention back to the pair in front of him.

"Shh, Cain," she quickly shushed him in a low voice. "You need to leave. Come back later, okay?"

"Now, now, Natalie, don't send the beta away yet." One of the wolves said as he elegantly rose to his feet from the couch.

Cain noticed Warren kept his head down as the man stood, and the crease in his brow deepened. "Who are you?" His eyes widened when the wolf turned towards him, his aura flaring. Katie dropped to her knees at the new wolf's power, but Cain and Nat remained standing.

The new wolf was about six foot, maybe a little shorter, but his body was hard with muscle. Not the bulging, bodybuilder type but still apparent. His hair was a dark blonde and cut short. His eyes were a light blue but had a cold, calculating look in them.

He was strong, of that Cain had no doubt, but to make Warren, Nat, and Katie submit to him? He didn't seem *that* dominant.

"You must be Cain Donovan." The newcomer grinned and increased the intensity of his aura. He saw Nat tilt her head to the side in submission but was pleased when the beta just met his stare. "I can see why you are Warren's beta. You are prime alpha material."

"Who are you?" He repeated, his wolf snarling within him as Nat finally relented and went to her knees. His eyes took on the shining, dark blue hue of his beast, the need to fight the wolf in front of him overwhelming.

"I am the one who asks questions, not you." He answered dismissively as he watched Cain's eyes change with interest. "Do you want to fight me? To change into your wolf and tear out my throat for hurting your two female pack mates?"

His lip curled up in a snarl when the other man looked pointedly at Nat and Katie. "Leave them alone."

The alpha laughed before his face grew serious. "I am the Alpha of Los Angeles County." His eyes went yellow with his inner wolf, and the force of his aura doubled. He watched as Cain's eyes widened, his body stiffening from the power that crashed down over him. "Submit to me, Cain." He ordered.

Cain bared his teeth. "No. I don't care who you are."

"I am the alpha of your alpha and therefore you are part of my pack. You will answer to my orders because you are beneath me," he growled low in warning. "*Submit.*"

His beast thrashed in him, torn on doing what he was told and fighting for his dominance. When he felt the man's power take another notch up in weight, he decided to go the safe route. He tore his eyes away and tilted his head to the side. His heart beat hard in his chest, his breathing ragged from the effort. "I submit."

The alpha smirked triumphantly and drew his energy back in. "Good boy," he praised then made his way back to the couch. "I have heard a lot about you, Cain. I'm sorry for the loss of your intended mate. Ah, but that's not entirely accurate anymore, is it? She actually survived, right? Have you marked her yet?"

Cain swallowed as he tried to calm his beast and shake off the way the LA County alpha had riled him. He helped Nat and Katie to their feet but stood protectively in front of them. "No, *sir*," he glowered. "We have gone our separate ways." He cut a glare at Warren as he said it. This time, when he looked at his alpha, he noticed how haggard he looked. There were circles under his wild, glowing blue eyes, his shoulder length black hair a mess of tangles.

"Uh oh, an alpha and beta at odds with each other," he mused as he sat down next to the younger wolf he had arrived with. "I sense a lot of disturbance in your pack, Warren. Your beta wants to fight you, and your mate won't touch you. Why is that?"

"Yes, Warren, why is that? Why don't you tell your alpha what you did?" Cain growled as Natalie put a hand on his arm to keep him in place.

"Shut up, Cain. This is not the time for our petty arguments." Warren finally spoke, his voice rough with the presence of his wolf.

"Petty?!" The beta snarled and Nat had to anchor herself to keep him from lunging forward. "You cost me everything! You're the reason three of our brothers are dead! Wyatt, Noah, and Brandon! You call their lives petty?!"

Warren leapt to his feet but flinched when his alpha snarled at him to sit down. He obediently did as told but glared at his beta. "This isn't the time," he grit out between clenched teeth. "We can discuss this later."

"Do you want to discuss how you put your paws on your mate later, too? Or is that also petty?" Cain seethed. Katie and Nat were each holding one of his arms, keeping him from launching at Warren.

"Cain, please." Natalie pleaded, not looking at her mate or the alpha who had turned to look at her. "Not now. Not when we have guests."

"Wait," the blonde alpha said with a low tone as he turned to Warren. "You hurt your mate?"

Warren cringed at the ice in his voice and hunched his shoulders. "I didn't mean to," he answered in a pathetically small voice.

"I do not tolerate mate maiming, Warren." He growled low as he rose to his feet and cracked his knuckles.

"Dad." The other new wolf finally spoke for the first time. "Another car just arrived."

Nat quickly jumped at the opportunity to escape the growing tension. "I-I'll go see who it is. I'll send them away, Alpha." She stilled as she went to turn towards the front door, remembering protocol. "If that's okay?"

He nodded once, not looking at her. "It may be best if you don't see what I do to your mate, Natalie. I don't want to cause you further harm."

She paled but gave a brisk nod. She squeezed Cain's arm once then hurried out the door to steer away the newcomers.

—

Conrad shifted uncomfortably in the driver seat as his alpha stared at him with a sly smile. He cleared his throat and lifted his Starbucks coffee from the cup holder. He took a sip through the green straw and stared straight ahead. After a few more seconds that lasted a lifetime, he groaned and slammed the cup back into the holder.

"Okay, fine!" He caved, throwing his hands up. "I *like* Lucy."

Kee grinned in triumph. "I knew it!" She slid her sunglasses back in place to cover the dark circles under her eyes and took a large swig of her iced espresso.

She was exhausted. She had gone to bed basically at sunrise and had woken up four hours later to start her search for Alexander. She knew exactly where she wanted to go to start her search, but she needed caffeine and a distraction from her nerves on the way. Conrad just happened to be that distraction. "Why don't you ask her out?"

He shrugged with a frown. "I'm not really looking to date, Kee."

"Why not? She likes you, and don't think I didn't see her practical-ly on top of you at Nana's." She pointed out with another grin.

His cheeks turned red. "She had a nightmare about Derrick." He grumbled.

"It was cute." She told him earnestly. "You two seriously make a cute couple, so why not go for it?"

Conrad's hands tightened on the steering wheel. "It has some-thing to do with my past," he commented quietly. *Quit being a bitch and just tell her. I know the longer I wait, the worse it's going to be. Ugh, just get it out! Tell her!* "What about you and Lucas? How did you guys finally make up?" *Pussy.*

She smiled at the reminder of last night. "It started with a night-mare I had about my dad," she started with a soft sigh. "Lucas called me and woke me up from it. He calmed me down and we talked a little. We cleared the air between us." She blushed and took a sip from her drink. "It went well."

"*Went well*, huh? Is that what they're calling it these days?" He teased and laughed when her cheeks turned bright red.

"Okay, I deserved that." Kee mumbled.

Conrad laughed, and they went quiet until his curiosity got the better of him. "What happened in your nightmare? You said it was about your dad, but what does that mean?" He couldn't imagine a father being the cause of his daughter's nightmares. His heart tight-ened at the terrifying thought that someone could mentally scar their child that badly.

She sighed softly and stared down at the lid on her cup. "My dad had some pretty fucked up priorities when I was a kid, Con," she began. "He was the beta of our pack and came from a really strong line of werewolves. When I didn't turn into a wolf during the year of my sixth birthday, everyone was concerned."

"But, seven is usually the latest. A pup technically has up until their eighth birthday to turn, so why was it such a big deal?"

"Because I was the beta's heir. I was supposed to be a strong were-wolf. It was expected that I would turn on the full moon of my birth month, but it didn't happen. Then I turned seven and still didn't shift," she smiled bitterly. "Well, didn't shift into a wolf, anyways."

"What was your first shift?" He asked curiously.

"Did I never tell you?" When he shook his head, she laughed. "A fucking cat! My father hated cats so I suspect that just added more salt to his wound." She gave a shrug. "Anyways, I didn't know how to turn into a wolf. I don't have a beast that calls to me like wereanimals so I couldn't figure out how to shift.

"My father just wouldn't accept it. He believed that if I could turn into a cat that I could turn into a wolf. Every night for a week he pulled me into his office and demonstrated his wolf form. When I still couldn't do it, he just snapped. He bit me, hit me, and told me I would ruin everything. He told me I was a disgrace, that I would cost him everything." She waved her hand in a circle. "Etcetera. After the first day he touched me, my mom tried to keep him away from me."

Conrad was grabbing the steering wheel so tightly, the plastic squeaked in protest. "Did it work?" He questioned in a soft but angry tone.

"Hmm, for a while," she admitted as she adjusted the sunglass-es on her face and gazed out the window. "But then the alpha gave a deadline to see my wolf form and nothing could keep him from me. Let's just say he thought pain would entice my nonexistent inner wolf."

"And you were *seven*?" He growled. "How could a father do that to his little girl?" His own wolf howled in pain at the thought.

She shrugged. "Lucas told me fear is a powerful motivator. My dad was afraid he would lose his pack, lose the status he was sure to have one day." She frowned sadly down at her drink again. "And afraid to lose my mom."

He glanced over at her as he brought the Jeep to a stop and put it in park alongside the curb. "Did he?"

"Yeah," she gave him a wiry smile. "He killed her."

He gaped at her. "What?"

She shook her head, put the cup down, and unbuckled her seat-belt. "Let's save that story for later." She stepped out of the car and blinked at the white truck in the driveway. "Cain's here."

He locked the Jeep and came around to her side. He looked at the truck and then went rigid when he saw the familiar black Mercedes parked next to it. No, he couldn't be here. He said he would wait.

Kee looked at the pale wolf next to her. "Con, it'll be okay. It might be better if Cain is here when we confront Warren. He may be mad at me, but he knows what happened is wrong. He might be able to help persuade Warren to tell us where Alexander is." She patted his shoulder. "Come on."

Conrad was still in shock when she started walking. Without thinking, he quickly grabbed her arm and pulled her to a stop. "Kee, don't."

She looked at the fingers wrapped around her bicep and then at Conrad's distraught expression as he looked between her and the Mercedes. Her brow furrowed. "What's wrong? Whose car is this?"

"Kee, please, just get back in the car. I'll explain everything. Just—"

"Kee? Conrad?"

The two looked up at the sound of Natalie's voice. Kee gently pried her arm out of her beta's tight grip and turned towards Warren's mate. She braced herself when the older woman ran towards her. She went into a defensive stance, ready for the physical backlash that had come with Katie, but was stunned when she was hugged instead.

"Your timing is impeccable." Nat quickly told her and pulled away. "Come, you need to calm Cain down."

"What's wrong with Cain?" Kee asked with a frown, walking with her towards the house. When they got closer to the front door, she paused and looked down the driveway at the frozen wolf. "Con? What's wrong?"

"Please," he tried again, amber eyes wide. "Let's go."

She frowned at him. "Conrad, if Cain is out of control and I can help, I'm going to. Besides, I need to find Alexander, and Warren is my best bet."

Nat tensed and turned to her. "Warren isn't exactly in a spot to be talking right now. We have some guests and they're. . .intense."

"That's exactly the problem. Wait, Kee!" Conrad cursed as she followed Nat into the house.

Cain stiffened when Kee's scent suddenly flooded his nose. He shot Katie a warning look then couldn't help but smile when Kee came into view. "Hey." He rumbled happily.

She gave him a small smile and slid her sunglasses up to sit on the top of her head. "You don't look very riled up to me," she commented as she walked straight towards him, Conrad almost too close to her side. She gave Katie a brief glance over. "You okay?" She asked, trying to ease their mutual tension.

Katie blinked in surprise before looking away from the dominant female. "Fine."

She nodded and then glanced over at Warren, who was staring at her with a stunned expression. It quickly morphed to anger, his upper lip twitching with the need to snarl. He glanced at his alpha and pressed his lips together.

"My alpha, this is—" Warren flinched when his alpha growled low, his eyes glowed gold once again as he whirled towards the newcomers.

Kee's eyes locked on to the man who turned towards her, and every single fiber in her body seemed to freeze. She stopped breathing, her lungs burning with the need for air, but she barely registered it over the cold fear swelling within her. Ice filled her veins and her heart seemed to still in her chest. Her bones ached as she went impossibly still. Her muscles tensed and bunched tightly together, her tendons suddenly so taut she thought they would shatter with the barest twitch.

And then she launched into action.

She and Liam met halfway through the middle of the living room with a harsh sound of flesh hitting flesh. She punched him over and over again until his face was a bloody pulp. She was strong! She would win! Another punch to his face and kick to his ribs. He deserved it all! She felt Cain's arm loop around her as she screamed in rage. But she wasn't done. No. Cain tried to haul her back and she took advantage of the height boost and quickly swung a foot at Liam, catching him in the side of the face.

Take that! She shouted. *I'm going to fucking kill you!*

It all played out so nicely in her head. But her body betrayed her. She remained immobilized with fear.

"Kee? What is it?" Cain asked, concern etching his face as she went deadly still. He thought she was looking at Warren, at the person responsible for all their misery. "Don't worry, I won't let him hurt you." He reached out to hold her, as a reflex from when they were dating, but she flinched away from him as if he was going to strike her. "Kee?"

"Don't make promises you can't keep, pup." Liam scoffed, making Kee shudder and sink to her knees.

Cain growled but didn't meet his eyes. He had already submitted to the alpha and he couldn't take it back so soon. "She's not a part of this pack." He stated tensely. Why would Kee fear the LA County alpha?

"Stop!" Conrad shouted as his old alpha started to approach them. He stood in front of Kee and Cain, panting as dread and nerves pooled within him. His beast paced restlessly, ready to spring into action if needed. "Leave her alone, Liam! Cain's right, she has nothing to do with this!"

Liam snarled at Conrad, his wolf's golden eyes dilated with anger. "You know nothing!"

"Liam?" Cain's eyes widened slightly. "As in Liam Driscoll?"

"Yes," the alpha replied and sneered at Cain when he growled louder. "Something you have to say all of a sudden?"

"You're her father." Cain's face twisted in a snarl as all the stories Kee had told him came rushing back to him. "You abused her!" He made a move towards the alpha but felt a tug on his jeans. He looked down and saw that Kee had reached out to grab the leg of his pants, her grey eyes staring at the floor unblinkingly. He cursed and crouched down next to her, pulling her firmly into his chest as her body trembled.

At Cain's words, Conrad felt his heart stop and plummet through his body. He expected to see it on the floor beneath him, along with his stomach, but he didn't tear his wide eyes from Liam's direction. He couldn't meet the dominant male's eyes, but he would get as close as he could.

Liam was Kee's. . .? But their last names were different. He paled as he remembered Kee saying Nana had adopted her. She must have taken her last name. Fuck! All this fucking time and he had no idea!

Liam watched Cain console his offspring with mild amusement. "Don't tell me that *Keira*," he practically spat her name. "Was supposed to be your mate?" He tossed his head back and laughed. "You were better off if she had died, Cain. You don't want to be tied to that creature. She's not a wolf."

"I know what she is." He snipped, holding her tighter to him when she whined in her throat.

He cocked his head in surprise. "Oh? And you still want to mate her?"

"Yes," he sneered. "I love her."

Liam's face went cold. "As your alpha's alpha, I forbid it. You *will not* mate my spawn."

Cain's whole body tensed as the command settled over him like a sheet wrapped around his body. His wolf snarled and thrashed, howling at the loss the order brought. He knew he and Kee were over, but his wolf hadn't accepted it. He had hoped the wolf's possessiveness would fade with time, but the alpha's command had just infuriated him. Still, he had to obey a direct order.

"And *you*," Liam turned on Conrad with a seething glare. "Is this the pack mate that has been needing your attention so much? The one who's been distracting you from your job? She's not a wolf! She is *not* your pack!"

"She is," Conrad stubbornly bit out, his eyes still cast down. "I also know what she is. She trusted me with that information when I entrusted her with my safety."

"Do you think I care about her trust in you? No! You're just as useless as her!" He snarled, face turning red with anger as his aura snapped out and expanded in the room. Conrad twitched but kept his jaw set firm. Liam wasn't his alpha anymore. Kee was. He submitted to her, not her father.

"Stop." In Kee's head she planned on the word coming out like a loud, forceful command, but it had barely made it past her lips with a squeak. *Pathetic.*

Liam sucked in a breath and turned fuming eyes on the shaking form which was his daughter. "Excuse me? Did you say something, little cat?"

She swallowed thickly and pushed away from Cain so she could get her words out more clearly. "Don't talk to him like that."

His lip lifted. "Or what, Kiki?"

She winced at the nickname. "He's mine." Again, her words came out in a soft, unsure manner.

She cursed her weakness. *Scream at him! Punch him! Do something!* She shrieked at herself, but it was no use. Her body refused to do anything. It was stuck in the past, back when she was seven. She was shutting down, the mental scars opening like fissures inside her head.

He grunted out a harsh laugh. "Oh, is he? You claim him as yours? As what, his alpha?"

Her brows drew together. "Yes?" *Come on, bitch! Fight him!*

Liam barked out another laugh. "Oh, that is too good. Will you fight me for him?" When she remained silent, her bottom lip quivering, he snorted. "You may have my blood, but you are nothing. You are still a pathetic mistake, Kiki. I tried twice before to erase your stain from my life, but then you disappeared. Now that I have you here, you're not even worth raising my hand against."

"Shut up! Don't talk to her like that!" Conrad defended angrily, finally meeting Liam's eyes. It was a mistake. Liam's power crashed over him like a tidal wave as he held his gaze. His wolf whimpered at the power, but he didn't want to submit to him.

"Don't forget why you were here to begin with! You were sent here to do one job and you went and made a little friend who just happens to be the bane of my existence!" Seeing his wolf resist, he pulled out his trump card. "Have you forgotten about your precious Emilia?"

Who's Emilia? Kee wanted to ask, but her lips were pinched shut. *And he was only here for a job? What job?*

Conrad blanched but curled his hands into fists. "I did what you asked. I got the information you needed. Give her back to me."

"You think you're in any position to order me around?" Liam rumbled low and walked closer to Conrad. "You think that pitiful thing over there will save you? No." He put his hand on Conrad's shoulder, and the younger male dropped to his knees under the weight of the alpha's power.

"Don't listen to him, Kee." Cain whispered to her as she pressed her face into his chest again.

Was everything between us a lie? Kee thought miserably as a different type of fear attacked her.

"Zachary." Liam said the name like a command and the younger wolf was at his side in an instant. "I think for today we've had enough. I want you to escort Mrs Erickson to our car."

"Alright," he responded dutifully and ushered Nat out the door, barely giving her time to make hasty goodbyes.

"Conrad." Liam waited until his subordinate looked up at him. "Come."

The command worked its way into his bones and he rose to his feet. He started to follow behind Liam as the alpha walked towards the door. His body tensed when he saw Kee staring up at him with eyes devoid of emotion. He swallowed thickly as they walked past her.

"You used me."

Her accusation cut straight to his heart. He turned towards her with pleading eyes. "Kee, it's not like that. I—"

"I trusted you." She hissed out, her voice harsh and strangled with betrayal.

Conrad's eyes stung. "I wanted to tell you. I didn't know how. There's still so much you don't know."

"*Conrad.*" Liam's voice was tight with impatience. "I said *come.*"

His body jerked forward with the need to comply with his order, but his feet hesitated at the broken look on her face. "Kee, please."

"Go, Conrad. I don't want to see your face again." She whispered bitterly as she looked away from him.

"I'm sorry." He told her sincerely as his body finally shuddered and followed through with the command to follow his alpha.

The living room was silent after they left. Cain was aware of Warren and Katie staring at them, but he ignored them. He held Kee to him, rocking her gently as her body trembled. "It's okay, Kee. He's gone."

Kee wanted to scream. She wanted to cry, to hit something, to kill someone. She was scared, angry, and hurt. So very, very hurt. She had trusted Conrad, confided in him. He was her beta, her right-hand man. Her best friend.

It was all a lie. It was just a job to him.

"I want to go back to Byte." She whispered. She didn't give a fuck about Warren, about Alexander, or even Samson in that moment. She just wanted to go home and wallow in her despair. She wanted to curl up under the covers of her bed and erase today from existence.

Cain sighed and tried to ignore the jab of hurt her words had brought him. "Can you stand? Let alone drive?"

With his help, she shakily got to her feet and patted her pockets. She closed her eyes tightly when she realized Conrad still had the keys to the Jeep. "Fuck!" She finally snapped, throwing up her hands in frustration. "Conrad has the fucking keys! Just had to fuck me over one last fucking time, *didn't he?!*"

Cain waited until she was done shouting and gently grabbed her shoulders so he could lead her to the door. He looked over his shoulder at Warren. "I'll be back. This shit between us is far from done." He jerked his head at the stunned Katie. "Come on, I'm going to drop Kee off at Byte and then I'll take you back to your car."

"Are you sure? I can wait here so you guys can have your alone time." She offered nervously, thinking maybe Kee needed the space. The Kee she had witnessed today was nowhere near the girl who had kicked her ass in the bar. But, could she blame her? Her father, the Alpha of the LA County wolf pack, hated his daughter. Cain said he had abused her. She frowned as a wave of pity for the murderer emerged.

"Get in the fucking truck, Katie," Kee grumbled as she stormed towards Cain's truck. Her knees buckled every few steps, causing Cain to keep a hold on her arm to keep her up right.

Katie would have scoffed at the command a couple days ago, but that was then. Now, she quickly complied, climbing into the back-seat while Kee and Cain took the front. She buckled herself in and snagged a glimpse of Kee's distraught expression in the passenger side mirror. She then looked at her alpha, frowning when he looked at Kee with concern in his eyes. She buried her face in her hands and closed her eyes tightly, wishing the last two months had never happened.

Fourteen

Conrad hadn't said a single word on the drive to the hotel Liam and Zach were staying in. He was in the backseat of the Mercedes with an equally quiet Nat. When the car came to a stop, he stepped out and looked over the JW Marriot. It was part of LA Live which meant they were close to Byte.

Good, it'll make finding Kee easier. A pang gripped his heart as he remembered the look on her face. The anguish. *I need to talk to her. She said she didn't want to see me again, but I need to explain everything.*

As he waited for Liam to hand the keys to the valet, he felt something touch his hand and jerked. He looked down at the hand gripping his, and then looked at Natalie's anxious expression. "I'm sorry, Nat." He whispered to her.

She shook her head, her light blonde hair falling in waves down her shoulders. "I know there has to be a reason behind everything." She responded and kept a hold on his hand as they followed the Driscoll wolves into the hotel.

"There is," he told her quietly. When Liam's sharp gaze fell on him from over his shoulder, he looked down. "I just can't tell you."

"I will tell her once we get to the room," Liam said. The four remained silent until they reached their Junior Suite on the fifteenth floor.

Zach held the door open for Conrad and Natalie after his dad walked in. He shut the door behind them and ushered them into the room. Liam sat on the edge of the bed and gestured at the couch. "Sit."

They did as told. Nat cleared her throat and kept close to Conrad, finding comfort that he was at least somewhat familiar when Liam and his son were not. Oh, she knew who Liam was. Every alpha knew who the Alpha of LA County was, but she had never been in his presence without Warren.

Seeing the tense female, Liam's light blue eyes softened. "You're not in trouble, Natalie. I just didn't want to risk your mate hurting you again."

She relaxed marginally. "I appreciate your concern, but he's my mate."

"Which makes it all the more dangerous," he replied. "Female wolves are treasures and should be treated as such. I don't allow harm to come to them."

"Didn't you kill Kee's mom? She was a female wolf." No sooner had the words left Conrad's mouth did he find a fist smashing into his face. The back of his head was then roughly grabbed and forced down on the coffee table. His cheek was pressed hard against the wood, blood pooling from both nostrils.

Liam growled so loud that his whole body shook with it. He lowered his face so that he made direct eye contact with Conrad. "You speak of my deceased mate or of my abomination again and you will regret it. Do you understand me?"

Conrad could only look at Liam for a brief moment before he looked away. He tried to nod, but Liam's hold was too strong. "*Yes.*" He forced out.

Liam gave his head another shove before releasing him and standing up straight. He ran his hands through his hair, trying to calm himself. "I don't understand why you are suddenly so defiant, Conrad. You used to be one of my best wolves."

Conrad calmly sat back up, glancing down at his jeans as blood dripped on to them. "Do you want me to answer you? Or was that rhetorical?"

Nat put her hand on the wolf's knee. "Don't anger him further." She mumbled, mind reeling. She had just learned that Liam had abused his daughter *and* killed his mate. She had seriously underestimated their alpha.

Zach grabbed some ice from the metal bucket on the dresser and wrapped it in a washcloth. He handed it to Conrad with a solemn expression. He hadn't known his father had killed his old mate. He barely comprehended that he had a sibling. Sure, it had been mentioned briefly and quietly by other pack mates, but to see her and know that she actually existed was something else entirely. But the way his dad had spoken to her, the way she reacted to seeing him, he winced.

Conrad thanked Zach and pressed the makeshift ice pack to his nose. At least Zachary wasn't a little shit like his father. "I'm not trying to make you madder. I'm just not sure what you want from me."

Liam sat back down on the bed and stared at Conrad intently. "Go ahead, tell me. I'm truly curious."

It took Conrad every ounce of his will power to not glare at Liam. "I stopped being one of your best wolves when you used Mia against me."

The alpha tilted his head as if considering that. "I suppose that's right."

He scowled at the blood stains on his jeans. "Mia is everything to me."

Liam looked at Conrad and softened his expression again. "I know," he answered in a gentle tone. He gave a soft sigh and nodded his head at his son. "Go ahead."

Conrad watched as Zach brightened before hurrying out the door. He turned his attention back to Liam without meeting his gaze. "What are you doing?"

"You'll see," he responded before looking at Nat. "Since I have your company, Natalie, perhaps you can tell me what's going on with your mate."

She sighed and clasped her hands together in her lap. "I love my mate, Liam. I won't turn against him."

"I'm not asking you to," he countered. "But he hurt you and his beta has accused him of killing his pack mates. I need to know if this is true." He saw her glance over at Conrad uncertainly, and he growled. "You don't need his permission."

She furrowed her brow. "He did hurt me, but his beast is really unsettled right now. He's never hurt me before. It's not like him."

"And the killing part?"

She clenched her hands. "He's the reason they are dead, but he didn't kill them with his own hands." She looked at him with pleading eyes. "Please, Alpha, it wasn't his intention. Don't hurt Warren."

Conrad clenched his jaw to keep himself from snapping. He had called Liam last night after Lucy left and told him the updated information about Warren. He told Liam the suspicion he had that Warren was Alexander's bonded wolf. Conrad didn't tell him about Kee's involvement and now he was terrified to. Liam had beat Kee when she was child because she couldn't turn into a wolf. What would he do when he found out she had killed three of his wolves?

Liam stared at her, searching for deceit. He didn't sense a lie, but there was something she was omitting. Was she doing it to protect Warren? He respected that, but it still irritated him. He was their alpha. He expected cooperation and honesty.

"Natalie," he rumbled her name in a deep voice, his power of alpha coming forth. "Is it true Warren is Alexander's bonded wolf?"

Her eyes widened. "What?" When he narrowed his eyes at her, she quickly shook her head. "I've never heard that! I mean, I know he has a business partner named Alexander, but to be bonded to a vampire? I would know, wouldn't I?"

"Maybe, maybe not," Liam commented and drew back his power when she gave him nothing but truth. So, what was she hiding from him? "If the vampire is strong enough, they can hide their side of the bond." He approached her and sat down on her other side. "Did you know Conrad has been spying on your pack since I gave him to you?"

Conrad didn't look at Nat but could feel her eyes on him. "I didn't have a choice." He mumbled.

"Before I sent Conrad here, I heard a rumor Warren was plotting against me." When she inhaled sharply and went to deny it, he held up a hand to stop her. "Did you know that the lords of LA and Pasadena had a fight a month and a half ago?"

She nodded once, not sure why it mattered. "Yes, Mason is our informant and told Warren later that night."

"Do you know what their fight was about?"

"Warren didn't say. . ." She trailed off, nerves making her inner wolf pace.

"Alexander wants to take over the humans. He wants to make them personal blood banks. He knows that even if all the vampires joined together, they would be outnumbered by the humans." He explained. "Humans, in general, outnumber *all* preternatural creatures. Monsters make up less than ten percent of the population, and it drops every year since we came out to the public."

She met his eyes with confusion. "What are you trying to tell me, Liam?"

"He wanted the werewolves to join his cause. If all the vampires and werewolves united and fought, they would have a good chance at winning. They may be outnumbered, but their strength would be formidable," he told her calmly. "Warren agreed."

She jumped to her feet and nearly tripped over the coffee table. "No! He wouldn't do that! He wouldn't endanger us all like that! He wouldn't hide something that big from me!"

"If he is bonded to Alexander, he may not have had a choice but to keep it from you," he explained in a calm tone.

Conrad set his icepack down on the coffee table and stood. He put his hand on Nat's shoulder. "I'm sorry I deceived you, but what he's saying is true. Alexander was defeated by Lucas and now he's doing whatever he can to get back at him. That includes using Warren in any way that helps him."

She stared at him in shock. She refrained from glancing at Liam as she spoke her next thoughts. "That explains the attack then? As to why it was ordered?"

"She's connected with Lucas, yes." He answered. "Alexander knew that and thus had Warren issue the order. We won't be one hundred percent sure until he admits it, but we're all pretty certain."

Liam narrowed his eyes at the pair, his mind quickly processing what they had both said. From what Conrad had told him, Cain's woman had been the first one attacked because she worked for Lucas. "So, Kee has involved herself with vampires?" She had been the target of an attack because of her employer. His wolves had tried to kill her because of it. Why did that anger him?

Conrad stiffened but glanced at Liam then down at the coffee table. "She works for him."

He tilted his head slightly. The statement was true but not completely. "There's more you're not telling me." He cut his eyes to Natalie. "Both of you."

Conrad had a reply on his tongue, but it disappeared when the door opened once again. He looked over and saw a little girl standing next to Zachary. Her wavy, golden blonde hair was tied into a side ponytail and spilled over her shoulder. Her amber eyes were wide as she stared back at him.

His heart stilled in his chest, his wolf letting out a high-pitched whine that echoed in his throat. "*Emilia*," he choked out.

Her eyes filled with tears, her bottom lip trembling. "Daddy!" She sobbed as she tugged her hand away from Zach's and ran towards him. She only made it two steps before he was already there, sweeping her up into his arms. She wrapped her arms tightly around his neck, weeping into his shoulder without restraint. "Daddy!"

His heart crumpled at the hysterical sobbing that shook her small frame. "Shh, Mia, I'm here." He tried to calm her down, but his own tears had leaked down his cheeks. He dropped to his knees and cupped the back of her head, trying to engulf her in his scent and presence to soothe her. He nuzzled his nose into her hair and inhaled his daughter's sweet scent.

Two months without her had been excruciating. No hugs, no kisses, no bedtime stories, no chasing her around the house, and none of her bubbling laughter. Random phone privileges every two weeks wasn't enough.

He hugged her tighter to him. "I missed you so much, baby girl."

"I missed you more, Daddy." She cried, barely getting her words out between her sobs. She felt his hand sweep along her back in slow, smoothing gestures and started to calm down. She sniffled loudly and pulled back so she could look into the eyes that matched hers. "Where have you been?"

He grabbed the hem of his shirt and used it to wipe the snot from her face with a tender smile. "I've been doing some work for Liam," he answered her. "And it was too dangerous to bring you with me." It wasn't exactly a lie, he supposed.

She rubbed at her eyes and didn't look at him. "I thought maybe I had done something wrong?" She asked in a watery voice that panged his heart. "That I made you mad?"

He could kill Liam for bringing this pain to his daughter. She didn't deserve it. All she did was love, and for her to have these doubts about herself and about him. . .*no*.

"Baby, look at me," when she hesitantly did so, he cupped her cheeks in his hands. "You could *never* do anything wrong. I will always love you. *Always*. No matter what." He told her vehemently. When her eyes filled with tears again, his stung to do the same. He gently wiped hers away with his thumbs as they fell and let out a low, soothing growl. "Don't cry, Mia. I hate seeing you cry."

She reciprocated the action, her small fingers wiping under his eyes. "You can't either then, Daddy." She frowned and lightly ran her fingertips over his swollen nose. "Why are you hurt?

He just gave her a smile. "I got into an argument with someone. It's fine. It doesn't hurt anymore."

She put her hands on his cheeks with a stern look. "No fighting."

He kissed her palm. "Yes, ma'am." He agreed and then rained kisses all over her face. His heart soared as she giggled. When he stopped, she snuggled into his lap and rested her head on his shoulder. He put his cheek on the top of her head and sighed contently as he held her to him. Everything he had done the past two months was for this precise moment. Everything he did had been for her.

Zachary grinned as he watched the two, genuinely happy for them. He was often the one to babysit the seven-year-old. His dad didn't trust the other pack mates around her, and he was young enough to be a sort of big brother to her. When she would start crying about missing Conrad, he would shift into his wolf form and snuggle her. She was a good kid, smart too, and he hated to see her upset. It wasn't her fault Liam had forced Conrad away.

He glanced over at his dad and almost balked at the tender look on his face as he watched the reunion. He knew his dad wasn't exactly the hard ass alpha that he wanted everyone to think he was. He could be kind and gentle, but he didn't enjoy showing it. He knew Liam was fond of Mia, even though he kept his distance from her. But now, as he looked at the two, Zach could see a glimpse of longing.

Zach swallowed thickly. *Is he thinking of Keira? My sister?* He shook his head. There was no way. He had tried to talk to Liam about his older sister before, but Liam had shut him down as soon as any question about her left his lips. At first, he told him that he didn't have a sister. Then he said she should have died a long time ago and that she wasn't to be mentioned.

I want to meet her, he decided.

Nat covered her mouth as stared at Conrad and Emilia. His daughter, she thought sadly. That was why he had no choice; it had to be. Conrad was given to them eight weeks ago; had it been that long since he saw his daughter? How could Liam be so cruel?

Warren cherished children. Their pack wasn't huge, now only having thirty-two wolves, but any pup in the pack was practically a god in his eyes. When a female wolf announced she was pregnant, he and Cain would do whatever they could to help her keep the pup. On the nights of the full moon, they were both there, commanding her not to change and holding her hands as the need to shift turned to pain from not giving in. Sometimes it worked, sometimes it didn't. Because of it though, their pup survival rate was higher than other packs.

Nat stroked her lower stomach as unease washed through her. Their pack was a mess right now, even she had to admit it. She wanted it fixed, but how? Where did they start? She rubbed her stomach again and looked at Liam, who was looking at her with a knowing gleam in his eyes.

"Alpha, we need to fix our pack," she said softly.

"I can't fix it until I know everything that has happened," he told her in a calm voice. "And I mean everything. No more withholding information."

Conrad looked over at Liam as Mia played with his hair. He then looked at Nat, whose eyes pleaded with him. "I'm not going to betray her." He said sternly. Liam growled, and Conrad held Mia tighter to him.

"Then I will betray Cain," she whispered with disdain. "He told me everything. If I want my pack fixed, I need to do this. But-" she straightened her spine and risked meeting Liam's eyes, "-But I want you to let Conrad and Mia go."

Conrad gaped at her. "Nat—"

"Go? He's my wolf; I won't let him leave," Liam countered sharply.

She hesitated. "Then at least let them have the rest of the day together. Alone. Let this happen and I'll tell you what I know."

Seeing his dad hesitate, Zach stepped in. "I can accompany them, Dad. Make sure they don't run."

Liam looked at his son then at Conrad. He gave in with a sigh. "Fine. Enjoy the day with your daughter, Conrad. You've both earned it."

A little surprised at Liam's agreement, Conrad got to his feet with Mia still in his arms. He looked uncertainly at Natalie. "Are you sure about this? I don't want you to be alone with him."

Liam snorted. "Just because I'm unmated doesn't mean I'm going to go after any tail left alone in my company. Plus, I have more honor than to go after another man's mate." He waved his hand at them. "Go, before I change my mind."

Zach put his hand on Conrad's shoulder and pushed him towards the door. When they were outside the room, they walked down the hall to the elevator. As soon as the doors slid shut, Zach turned and looked at Conrad. "I want to meet my sister."

Conrad blinked at him before giving him a sly smile. "No wonder you agreed to be our chaperone."

He nodded once without shame. "I'm sorry." He fidgeted. "What's she like? Keira?"

"First of all, only one person calls her Keira. She goes by Kee," he began.

Mia tilted her head. "Who's Kee?"

Conrad grinned at her. "Someone who I think you'll like very much. She's funny, kind, and just a little crazy, but in a good way." He looked at Zach as he said the next part. "And strong."

Zach frowned. "She didn't seem strong today."

"She was in shock. She just got done telling me about her past with your guys' dad. She still has nightmares about him, and I'm sure for her to see him in person was too much. But don't be mistaken, Zach, she's strong."

He shuffled his feet. "Is that why she claimed to be your alpha?"

Conrad tilted his head up proudly. "She is my alpha." He tried to ignore the way her distraught face flashed before his eyes. "*Was*, at least. Anyways, I plan on seeing her today regardless. She said she didn't want to see me again, but she needs to hear the truth about everything."

"Daddy, I'm hungry." Mia complained as they stepped into the main lobby from the elevators.

He smiled at her, refusing to put her down since he had missed the comforting weight of her. "What do you want to eat?" He asked then looked at Zach's disappointed expression. "Trust me, Zach, when she's mad or emotional, she needs cooldown time. We'll go out to eat, maybe see a movie, and then go see her, alright? I'm not ready to get punched in the nose a second time today."

"No fighting!" Mia complained as she was carried to where the valet was. "And I want spaghetti!"

"Italian it is," he agreed and laughed when she cheered.

"Do you think she will want to meet me?" Zach suddenly asked in a small voice after handing the valet the ticket for the Mercedes.

"I do," he replied as he shifted Mia from one hip to the other. "She doesn't really have family. Only a great-grandma and even they have an odd relationship."

"Dad kept accusing her of not being a wolf, and both you and the beta said you knew what she was." He furrowed his brow. "What is she if she isn't a wolf?"

Conrad shook his head. "I swore I wouldn't tell anyone. You're going to have to ask her yourself."

Fifteen

Cain drove the truck into the back lot of Byte and pulled up near the door. When Kee unbuckled her seatbelt and fumbled with the handle, he reached over and grabbed her shoulder. He felt her flinch under him but tried not to take it personally.

"Kee, are you sure you want to be here? Why don't you come back with me?" He offered in a soft tone.

"I don't want to be near *any* werewolves." She bit out, not looking at him.

He frowned at her. "Don't punish me because of Liam and Conrad. I'm not them."

She finally got the door open and glanced over at him. "I'm not punishing you, Cain. I just don't know who I can trust anymore."

"You can trust me. When have I betrayed you? You thought I had, but I didn't. You know I didn't. So, why doubt me now?"

She gently pushed his hand off her shoulder. "Because Liam is alpha and he can make you do anything," she shuddered. "I don't know if you can resist his command."

He winced. "I submitted to him today, that doesn't mean I'll do it again." He softened his expression. "Don't alienate yourself, Kee. You can talk to me. You shouldn't be alone right now."

She shook her head and slid out of the truck. "Thank you, but I'm fine." When he looked crestfallen, she sighed. "If I change my mind, I'll call you."

He nodded once but didn't believe it for a second. He hated how things had turned out between them. "Alright." He waited until she closed the truck door before driving away.

She watched him go with a soft sigh and turned towards the door. She went to grab the handle, but the door opened, revealing Miguel with his usual bright smile. She forced her own weak smile. "Hey Miguel."

"Welcome back, Señora Quinn! I was just on my way back out." He greeted, but his smile faltered. "Where is your beta?"

A cold fire ignited in her chest, but she tried to force it down to glowing embers. "He left," she replied with a tense smile and walked past him. The door shut behind her, and she let out a shaky breath as she stepped into the prep area of the kitchen. She debated going through to the main floor and up to her room but decided against it. That was her and Conrad's room. The fire in her chest flared back to life, and she pressed her lips hard together.

She turned to the basement and pulled open the door. She quickly shut it behind her to keep out the sun. The kitchen didn't have any windows, but if Miguel opened the back door at the same time she opened the basement door, a stream of sun would hit the top couple stairs. She knew the vampires were currently dead to the world, but she didn't want to be responsible for any vampire dust.

She closed her eyes and slowly reopened them so they could adjust to the dark. She put her hand on the steel railing and cautiously made her way down the rest of the stairs. She reached the last step, and as she turned to walk down the hall, arms enclosed around her. She let out a scream before a cold hand cut it off.

"Shh, my sweet," Lucas cooed softly in her ear from behind. He could hear her heart beating hard in her chest; it practically made her body thrum against his. "It is just me, calm down."

She sagged against him, but her heart didn't relax. She put her hands on the forearm across her chest and squeezed. "L-Lucas," she stammered out and cleared her throat when her earlier emotions tried to break free again. "Why are you awake?"

"Your emotions," he explained in a suddenly tense tone. "You were terrified and then distraught. I tried calling you multiple times, but you did not answer." He lowered his voice and held her harder against him. "I thought Alexander had somehow gotten to you. It was driving me mad that I was stuck down here unable to go to you."

When his hold tightened around her, her control wavered again. She dropped her chin as angry tears filled her eyes. "I was so stupid. So *fucking* stupid, Lucas."

He released his hold on her and guided her to his room. Once inside, he shut the door, ushered her to the bed, and down next to her. "What happened? Was it Alexander?" He pressed.

Kee shook her head and drew her knees to her chest. "No," she sniffled, still trying to keep a tight hold on her emotions despite the frustrated tears still threatening to spill. "It was my dad."

He stilled as he remembered witnessing her horrible memories. "He is in LA?" He asked in a quiet yet deep tone. A fierce need to avenge his shapeshifter rose like a flood within him.

She nodded once. "Apparently he's the Alpha of LA County," she snorted. "Bastard did well for himself. Started as a beta in Claremont, the very edge of LA County, and now he rules the whole area. I guess it's easier to rise through the ranks without an abomination to hinder your appearance."

"The Alpha of LA County," he repeated unbelievably. A wolf of any lower status he would eliminate for Keira, one of this caliber was trickier. "That is a position as high as my own. This makes it harder to kill him."

She thought back to seeing him, to how immobilized she had been. How disgustingly useless she felt. She couldn't do anything, despite screaming at her body to do something.

"I-" She choked on her own self-pity. "-I couldn't do anything," she admitted in a strained whisper. "I kept telling myself to get up! To hit him, to scream at him, to do *something*! But I couldn't. I was frozen. Paralyzed. All the torment from my childhood had rooted me in place." The tears spilled down her cheeks, and she buried her face in her knees. "I was weak and I hate it. I hate how he still affects me."

Lucas put his hand on her back as she gripped her knees tighter. "How long has it been since you have seen him?"

"When I was twelve. So that was, what, thirteen years ago?" She mumbled, eyes screwed shut. "That was the last time he tried to kill me."

"Shock will numb you, Keira," he told her in a gentle voice. "You are not weak. We both know that. You are an alpha. That is proof enough."

"*Alpha*," she suddenly spat and jerked up from her knees. "I'm no one's fucking alpha." She looked at him with venom in her eyes, her hands balling into tight fists. "Conrad belongs to Liam."

He blinked once as he processed her words. He knew Liam was her father and quickly put two and two together. "You know this for certain?"

"Yes." She growled low in her throat as the control on her emotions snapped. The cold flame lit up in her chest again with a vengeance. It spread across her chest and seared her heart before burning its way to her stomach which churned uncomfortably. She opened her mouth to let out a stream of furious curses, but instead a sob escaped. Shocked, she covered her mouth as another one came out and felt that her cheeks were wet with tears.

Why am I blubbering like this? I'm mad! She chided herself as another sob rocked her body. *Stop it! I'm better than this! I don't cry over people! Especially backstabbers who don't deserve it!*

But she *was* crying. Bawling, actually.

Conrad had meant so much to her. He was the first person who counted on her. Not in the way Lucas counted on her to accomplish a job, or the way Cain counted on her to be a girlfriend, but counted on her to just be there. To provide him with security and not abuse her alpha status over him. It was nice to be relied on by simply being her.

They had spent nearly every day together since he left Warren's pack, and she thought their bond was real. They supported each other and he helped her move past the ambush. He never backed down or was scared of her when she got out of control. He encouraged her revenge and talked reason into her when she did something foolish.

I already miss him so much.

"Keira." Lucas reached for her as her tough bravado fell away. He cradled her head to his chest, her tears making wet trails on his skin. "Talk to me." He prompted, gently running his fingers through her soft hair.

"He used me," she cried. "I'm so stupid, I really thought he meant everything he said! I trusted him and he betrayed me. I let him get close to me and look what happened! He always belonged to Liam. To my *fucking* father of all people!" She sobbed. It was like her heart was splitting behind her ribs. It was so similar to when she woke up from her attack and thought Cain had wronged her. "The whole time he had ulterior motives and I had no idea."

"What were these motives?" He asked, stroking her hair as her shoulders shook with sobs.

She swallowed and shook her head. "Liam sent him here for a job, to gather information for him. That's all I know."

"Hmm," he commented quietly. He waited a few minutes so she could calm down before he spoke again. "I think, perhaps, you need to find out the full story."

She sniffed, making a wet, snotty sound, and pressed her cheek against his skin. "I don't want to see him again. I'm hurt, Lucas. The two of you have been my rock and support these past two months. I feel like one side of my world has been ripped apart and I'm falling."

"That is exactly why you need to speak with him. If he was just using you, I do not believe he would have stayed around for as long as he did. I know he cares for you." The vampire pointed out.

Kee curled into him, running her hand along his smooth flesh to wipe away the evidence of her crying fit. "He lied to me."

"Yes," he agreed. "He broke your trust in that regard. However, Mr Novak is an honorable man, I believe. I have witnessed how much he cares for you, Keira. There is more to this story."

She frowned. "Liam did say something about a girl named Emilia, and then Conrad demanded he have her back." Her brows drew together in anger again. "If he has a girl, he'll pay for hurting Lucy."

He wrapped his arm around her shoulders and shifted so that they were lying down. He pulled the covers over them and pet her hair when she let out a shaky sigh. "I know you are hurt, Keira," he told her softly as his body fought him to go back to sleep. "The stings of betrayal you have felt recently have left you raw and guarded." When she nodded, he continued. "But, think it through. You believed Cain had turned against you and it was not true. You thought I had lied and misled you, but it was also untrue. You should hear out what your wolf has to say before shunning him completely."

Kee frowned as she snuggled into his side. "Why do you have to be so smart and rational?"

He smirked. "Centuries of irrationality will make you that way."

She laughed tiredly. "I supposed it will."

"Why did you not answer your phone?" He asked after a brief lapse in silence.

"It's in the Jeep parked at Warren's. Conrad left with Liam and he still had the keys. Cain dropped me off."

He pressed his lips together for a moment. "Why were you with Cain at Warren's house?"

"If Warren is in fact Alexander's wolf, then he would know where to find him. Warren is my best bet at locating him. Cain was already at Warren's house when we arrived. Liam and another one of his wolves were there, too. It looked like they were having a meeting." She explained.

"How was seeing Cain?" He questioned, trying to make his tenor sound lighter than how he felt.

She let out a soft sigh. "Before we went in, Natalie came out and asked me to help calm Cain down. But when we went in, he seemed fine," she pulled the blanket tighter around her. "He held me when I had my freak out about Liam. I pretty much asked him to without *actually* asking." She felt him still and looked up at him cautiously. "Does that make you mad?"

Lucas' jaw clenched for a few moments before he relaxed it. "Not in the way you think," he admitted in a terse tone. "It bothers me that I cannot be there for you at times such as these. The sun will always prevent me from aiding you during the day. So, I suppose I am pleased that he was there to provide you with the comfort I could not."

She pressed a kiss to his jaw. "I won't ever hold that against you, Lucas."

"I will hold it against myself," he replied bitterly.

She shook her head and let out a tired yawn before resting her head back on his chest. "It's only about 1pm, but I'm exhausted," she said before adding with a tease, "Someone kept me up all night."

"They sound unreasonable. Did they at least make it worth it?"

She pretended to think about it. "I guess."

He looked down at her with hungry eyes. "If the sun were not pushing me to go back to sleep, Keira, I would make you regret those words."

She gave him an innocent smile. "Lucky me then."

"You have no idea, Miss Quinn." He closed his eyes and lightly stroked her shoulder as he felt the sun beginning to claim him again. "I will see you in the evening." He murmured a few moments later. When he didn't get a response, he looked down and saw that she had already fallen asleep. With a tired, fleeting smile, he slipped back into unconsciousness.

"Kiki, come to Uncle Christian." The pack alpha called lightly, looking at the little girl peeking out from behind her mother's legs.

Kee hesitated, gripping Wolfie, her favorite stuffed animal, to her chest. Uncle Christian had been the one to come up with the nickname. He always called her Kiki, only ever using her real name when he scolded her. If he was calling her Kiki, maybe that meant he wasn't mad at her, that she wouldn't be in trouble. She glanced at her dad as he stood beside the older man. When he nodded once at her, she stepped out from behind her mom and slowly walked towards their pack alpha. She hoped she didn't have to feel her dad's anger again.

After Uncle Christian gave a deadline for her to show her wolf form, Daddy harshly trained her again. For the past five nights he kept her away from the pack. He had said he wouldn't allow her to embarrass him. Instead, he spent hours trying to get her to shift into a wolf. He showed her multiple pictures of wolves of all sizes, demanding she shift into one of them. Each time she failed, he would strike her and shout cruel words at her.

Weak, shameful, disgusting; she heard it all.

Mommy had tried to help her, tried to prevent it, but he had over-powered her. His wolf was stronger than hers, and she couldn't refuse his authority. Still, she had tried, and he'd had to lock the door to his study and reinforce it with his desk to stop her from getting to them.

Christian held his hand out to her, and she put her hand in his warm one. She watched as he squatted down to her height so his light brown eyes could look straight into hers. She fidgeted under his gaze, dropping her eyes to Wolfie. "Hi, Uncle Christian." She greeted shyly.

He smiled and pet the top of her hair, momentarily ignoring the fading bruise around her eye. "Did you know I have told others that you are the light of this pack?"

She glanced up at him. "Light?"

He nodded, allowing her to meet his gaze. "You are the only child your age in the pack. Before you, the last pup born was almost twenty years ago." He smiled fondly at her. "Your giggles are contagious, your little tantrums adorable. We love you, Kiki."

She smiled back at him. "I love you, too, Uncle Christian."

"Did you know it's the night of the full moon?" When she nodded, he continued. "Do you feel itchy?"

Her brow furrowed as she felt her dad's heated stare fall on her. Her stomach twisted in knots as she felt the unspoken threat in them. "A little." She squeaked nervously.

His smile widened. "That's a good thing, Kiki," he praised, patting her head. He gently cupped her cheek. "Don't be scared of your wolf. Let it take over, let it happen. Your wolf is your friend. She is a part of you."

She nodded once as he stood back up. When he held his hand out for her stuffed wolf, she reluctantly handed Wolfie to him. She trembled without the shield of her plush. She shifted her weight from one foot to another as Christian and her parents stared at her expectantly.

The alpha exhaled heavily when nothing happened for almost a minute. "Kiki, if I have to, I will command you to shift, but I don't want to force out your wolf. I don't want you to be scared of her." She squeezed her eyes shut and he softened his tone. "Just shift, Kiki. Everything will be okay once you do."

Kee tried to find the inner wolf that everyone was sure she had. Once again, she cried for it to speak to her, begged for it to come forward and help her. If she was supposed to have one, why didn't it speak to her? She jumped when Christian's authoritative growl echoed in the room. She looked up at him with grey eyes wide with fear.

"Keira Marie Driscoll," Christian spoke low, his energy swirling around her and causing tears to gather in her eyes. "As your alpha, I command you to shift."

She felt the weight of his power pushing down on her small shoulders. Her legs gave out from under her and she dropped to the beige carpet of her father's office. She cried when the energy of Christian's wolf pressed down harder on her, demanding her to shift. "I can't!" She cried desperately.

"You can, and you will!" He snarled. "Show me your wolf! Shift!"

Her mind raced as adrenaline coursed through her veins like ice with his command. Fear made her chest heave. She felt trapped. She was suffocating under Christian's power and she thought she was going to die. She had sunk to the bottom of a pool and was trying desperately to swim to the surface, but it was out of reach and her lungs burned with the need to breathe. Her body shuddered as she started gasping, her hands flying to her throat.

"Stop it, Christian! She can't do it!" Mommy shouted as she heard her practically choking on air.

"She has to obey me, Trinity," Christian replied calmly as he stepped closer to her little form.

"You're going to kill her!" Her mom cried as she rushed towards her. Mommy screamed when Daddy ran forward and suddenly grabbed her around the waist, pulling her back. "Let me go, Liam!"

"This is her only chance," he mumbled to her as she struggled in his arms. Her limbs trembled and he held her tighter. "Don't shift, Trin! He'll take it as a challenge!"

"I have to help her!" She howled, her wolf whining with the need to help her daughter.

"She can only help herself now." He told her and pinned her tightly to him as their daughter wailed through her gasps.

"Shift!" Christian barked, baring his teeth.

Kee just wanted it to stop. She didn't want to die. She wanted to breathe, wanted to run into her mother's arms. She tried again to find her wolf, pleaded it to come to her, but the only response she got was a familiar meow. As soon as she heard the sound, she shook her head.

No, no, not you! Stay away! I get hurt because of you! I need my wolf! *She implored, but she already felt the fire flaring across her skin.* No! Daddy doesn't want you! Nobody wants you! I hate you! *She screamed at the image in her mind as black fur sprouted from her arms and her body contorted.*

"Keira, no!" Daddy all but roared at her.

She abruptly felt Christian's aura vanish once she shifted. She could feel him stare down at her twitching body with a blank face. He tore his gaze away from her after a few long seconds and looked at her parents. "Liam, come." He ordered as he turned and walked out of the office.

Uncle Christian, please! I'm sorry! I can't control it! My wolf doesn't listen! *She meowed at him, but she knew it was useless.*

Her father swallowed and released his sobbing mate. On his way to the door, he crouched down next to her cat form. "Anything that happens from here on out is your fault, Keira." He spat with venom before standing back up and following after his alpha.

Mommy ran to her and dropped to her knees. She scooped her up and cradled her to her chest, rocking her like she was baby once again. "Kee, Kee," she called softly. She stared up at her mother with yellow, glassy eyes, a pained meow escaping her. "Oh, baby, it's okay. It's going to be okay."

"It *is* going to be okay," she heard a deep voice mumble tiredly in her ear. "You did not have me then, but you do now."

She whimpered slightly and curled into a small ball on her side. She felt Lucas' firm body press against her back, a strong arm wrapping around her waist and pulling her in tight. "I'm sorry." She breathed.

"Shh, go back to sleep, Keira. I am here." Lucas whispered to her, his head resting against hers.

She closed her eyes and didn't respond. She focused on the strength he surrounded her with and tried to convince herself that her weakness was in the past. She was strong and she would prove it to Liam should she face him again.

Sixteen

Kee groaned when she felt something petting her hair and someone telling her to get up. "No," she mumbled into the pillow and pulled the blanket up over her head. The hand disappeared, and she thought she had won until it reappeared with its twin and began to poke at her sides. She tried to move away, but they persisted. The fingers dug into her sides with just enough pressure to make her squirm.

"Fine!" She huffed and pulled the blanket away from her head. She stuck her tongue out when she saw Lucas' smirking face hovering above hers.

"Do not tempt me," he playfully teased before straightening. "It is time for you to get up and get ready if we are to see your dragon."

She quickly sat up at the reminder of Samson. She ran her eyes over Lucas' pristine appearance. His pale cheeks had a slight flush to them, and she couldn't help but wonder who he had fed from. He wore his usual black slacks but had put on a white button up. He had accompanied it with a black tie and suit jacket that fit his frame perfectly. She admired how good he looked but frowned at what it meant. "Are we dressing up?"

"Yes." He pulled the rest of the blankets off of her. "I went through your wardrobe upstairs and found this," he gestured at the black dress that was hanging now wrinkle-free on his closet door. "It will be perfect for tonight."

She looked at the sleeveless dress. It had a lace neckline that went up her throat and down to the top of her cleavage. The back was also made out of lace that went from her neck to her waist. The rest of the dress was a solid black that hugged her chest and torso before it flared out at her waist. The hem stopped a few inches below her knees. She also noticed her pair of black, four-inch heels by the door next to it.

"That's my favorite dress," she informed him as she climbed out of bed. "Why are we dressing up?"

"I have an appearance to uphold, Keira. They are expecting the Lord of Los Angeles County and so they shall get it. I need my bonded wolf to also look the part." He explained.

"I'll have to call you Lord Lucas," she rolled her eyes. "I think I choked on it last time. It's going to be weird, calling you that."

He smirked at her. "I think I would rather enjoy it."

She shook her finger at him. "Don't get used to it." She rubbed her face and let out a sigh. "Damn, I'm still so tired."

"From the emotional episodes you had earlier, I am sure," he said. "How do you feel?"

"Still disgusted with myself for being so weak," she admitted. "And I still want to punch Conrad in the throat."

"You have every right to be angry, Keira; I will not talk you out of that. I am just saying that from my point of view, I do not believe his feelings towards you are a farce." He sat down on the edge of the bed and watched her. "You are also justified to feel hurt. I know what he means to you."

"*Meant* to me," she corrected with a hiss.

He gave an elegant shrug but didn't comment further. "If we are going to do this, we need to do it soon. I need to be back here as soon as possible in case someone hears back about Giovanni."

Her face fell. "Still no word about Giovanni or Aubrey?"

He let out a heavy sigh. "No, no one has seen them or Alexander."

"We'll find them, Lucas," she said as she grabbed the hanger from his door. "I promise tomorrow I will go back to Warren's and find out where Alexander is. I'm sorry I failed to do so today."

He softened his expression. "I understand."

She gave him a small smile and then bent to grab her heels. "I'm going to run upstairs and do my makeup. It won't take too long."

"I will meet you in the parking lot." He told her.

"Okay, I'll hurry." She reiterated as she rushed out the door. Byte wasn't open yet and she was glad she didn't have to push through a mass of people to get to the stairs.

—

True to her word, Lucas had only waited twenty minutes for his shapeshifter. He felt her presence before he heard the soft clacks of her heels on the asphalt. He looked up and couldn't help the small smile that curled his lips. She had accented her eyes with black liner and mascara, a dark tint smeared on the crease of her eyelids. She had put on dark lipstick that had more purple tones than red, and clipped the top section of her hair back.

Beautiful. He thought and held out his hand towards her as she approached. When she slid her hand into his, he bowed and pressed his lips to the top of it.

She blushed. "What a gentleman," she teased as he straightened.

"I do have my moments," he replied with a smirk as he led her down the row of cars to his favorite. This was his most prized item and he had zero shame admitting it. "I am spoiling you tonight."

Kee stopped when he led her to the passenger side of the sexiest car she had ever seen. It was slick black and waxed to perfection. "Is this really an Aston Martin Vanquish?"

"Yes. It is the best money I have ever spent." He answered as he pulled open the door for her.

She slid into the dark red leather seat of the coupe and gaped at the beauty of it. Everything was spotlessly clean. There wasn't a speck of dust on the dash or a smudge of a fingerprint on the digital display. The two front seats were buckets, the back laughable by comparison. There were merely dips in a cushion, a small center console between them.

She buckled herself in and stared at Lucas when he got in. "Aren't these expensive?"

He laughed at her question. "I think I paid around three hundred thousand after taxes."

"What the fuck," she muttered under her breath as she pointedly kept her hands in her lap even though she wanted to press all the buttons just for the sake of doing so. "Do you really make that much money from Byte?" She balked when she realized how rude the question was. "Ah, sorry, you don't have to answer that."

Lucas shook his head and started the car, enjoying the sound and feel of the engine as it roared to life. "You need not be embarrassed; I have no qualms about telling you." He stated as he pulled out of the parking lot and headed towards the freeway. "Byte brings in a steady income, but I have a generous revenue from centuries of saving."

"Oh," she commented and looked at all the red accent lights. "This is really nice. I'm afraid to touch anything. Unless, of course, you're going to let me drive?"

"Never." He instantly replied and chuckled when she pouted. Once he was on the freeway, he reached across and took her hand in his. He gave a small smile when she laced their fingers together. They drove in a companionable silence, simply enjoying each other's company until her nightmare started to nag at him.

"What happened after Christian saw your cat form?" He asked in a soft tone.

Kee tensed, but she should have expected the question. Honestly, she thought he would have pressed her about it when it woke him up. "Christian ordered my father to kill us," she responded quietly.

He slid his green gaze to her before looking back at the road. "Why both of you?"

"Obviously me because I had shifted into a cat. There could only be two options as for what I was: a werecat, or a shapeshifter. Christian had no way of knowing which one I was so he forced his power on my mother. He demanded she tell him the truth about cheating on Liam. She hadn't of course, so that left him with the only conclusion of what I was." She explained emotionlessly.

"And your mother?"

She pinched her lips tightly together. "He wanted my mother dead because she gave birth to me. If she could birth one shapeshifter, she could bear another. That was his thinking, at least."

Lucas squeezed her hand to try and comfort the ache he felt from her. "Liam just simply complied?"

"I don't know. I've seen an alpha's power at work. I know the commands given are like a biological law that sets deep into your bones, but Da—*Liam*—is strong." She cleared her throat. "The night after the failed demonstration, my mom woke me up. She was telling me to get up and put my shoes on while she stuffed random clothes in a backpack.

"She rushed me downstairs and out the front door to a cab that was waiting for us. We got in and I remember it taking us to a gas station. A lot has changed and been built in the last eighteen years so I can't remember exactly where we were, but I know it was in our hometown of Claremont." She had once made the mistake of stepping into Claremont five years later and nearly died from it.

"Why a gas station?" He asked, urging her to continue.

"She had called her mom on the payphone," she explained. "I can only recall her telling grandma that we were close and to come get them, to meet us at the boundary lines. I didn't know what that meant at the time, but I learned later on that we couldn't cross the territory alone. She told grandma a specific place to meet her, and I can clearly see her saying that *he* was coming after us." She let out a sarcastic laugh. "I should have known she meant Liam.

"After the call, she took my hand and led me quickly up the street until it became just shrubbery and dirt with scattered trees. It was dark and there were no street lights, but my mom pulled me behind a tree and kneeled down in front of me. She told me we were going to run. She said she would carry me on her back in her wolf form and that I needed to carry the bags.

"I was so confused. She was scared and that terrified me, but I agreed. I put my backpack on and stood there trembling. She stripped and shoved her clothes in the pack. I watched as she shifted then put her backpack on over mine and climbed onto her back. I had Wolfie under my arm as I gripped my mom's fur tightly in my hands when she started to run as fast as she could. Somewhere along the way to the boundary lines, I dropped Wolfie, but I had been too frightened to notice."

"Which boundary line were you running towards?" Lucas asked. Boundary lines referred to county lines. He knew why her mother was running to a different county. Once she reached the other county, she entered a new alpha wolf's territory. If a wolf from that pack witnessed a foreign wolf entering their territory without invitation, they had every right to attack.

"San Bernardino County," Kee replied. "The city of Upland borders Claremont and my grandparents happen to live in Alta Loma which is the next city over. I guess my mother had called my grandparents before we left the house so that they would be there at the same time we were. The call at the gas station was letting them know how close we were."

He nodded once. "What happen once you reached the boundary line?"

"We didn't exactly make it to line," she whispered and took in a shaky breath. "Something hit us with a snarl. I remember flying off my mom's back and hitting the ground hard. I remember tasting the dirt and blood that filled my mouth. I was dazed, but I managed to push myself up on my arms. I saw-" She gripped his hand tighter. "-my mom and dad fighting in their wolf forms. The snarls were so. . .*loud* in the dead of night. It was deafening.

"I remember crying, bawling at them to stop. I screamed and begged them to stop as their claws and teeth sank into each other's fur over and over again. I got to my feet and fell, but I had to stop my parents from killing each other. When I was finally able to stand, it was suddenly quiet. I looked to where my parents had been and only my dad was standing. He stared at me with gold eyes, blood all over his snout and paws. Fear rooted me in place as he started to walk towards me.

"I heard my name being called and I looked over my shoulder to see my grandpa waving his arms at me. He was probably only a football field's length away from me, but when I was little it felt like miles away. He shouted at me to run to him. I wasn't going to. I wanted to stay with my dad, with my mom," her voice trembled. "Because they were my parents and they wouldn't hurt me. Even though my dad had already hurt me so much for not being able to turn into a *fucking* wolf, I still had hope that he wouldn't harm me. That none of it was *really* happening."

Kee took a deep breath and closed her eyes, not wanting to cry again. "But as soon as he growled at me, I took off towards my grandpa.

I felt the earth tremble under my feet as Liam chased after me. My grandpa just kept calling my name and telling me he was coming and shouting at me to run faster. I remember running through bushes, the sharp sticks cutting into my nightgown and into my legs. Liam had been getting closer and I knew he was almost on me, but then he was gone. I didn't question it, I just kept running until my grandpa reached me.

"He grabbed me and picked me up before running back the way he had come. From over his shoulder, I saw my dad pin my mom down on her back. I saw him bite down on her throat and shake his head so hard that I could hear her neck crack from where I was, saw the moon reflect off the blood that splattered." Her voice had lost all emotion. She opened her eyes and stared blankly at the road. "His white muzzle was black with her blood. He started towards us, but my grandpa had already reached the boundary line with me. He snarled at Liam and told him he had no authority in San Bernardino County. Said that if Liam crossed over, my grandpa would kill him.

"I think my grandpa wanted him to do it. He wanted to kill him for killing his daughter, but Liam was smarter than that. My mom had hurt him pretty badly and I think he knew he would lose if he took on my grandpa, so he left." She felt Lucas squeeze her hand and looked at him. "My grandma had been waiting in the car. She blamed me for mom's death so she had my great-grandma take me in. That's how I became Keira Quinn instead of Keira Driscoll."

Lucas lifted her hand to his lips and pressed a tender kiss to her knuckles. "That was a lot for a young girl to go through."

Kee let out a heavy sigh. "It's in the past. Don't get me wrong, it clearly still haunts me, but I don't dwell on it anymore."

"If I could kill your father for you, I would." He told her seriously as he parked the car in a parking lot a block away from The Street's store entrance.

She shook her head. "That's for me to do," she told him and watched as he turned off the car. "You ready for this?" She asked as she carefully got out of the car and smoothed down her dress.

"Are you?" He countered as he came around to her side of the car. He held out his arm to her and was pleased when her hand went to the crook of his elbow. He guided her towards the store front. "My questions about your family were ill-timed. I apologize."

She gave him a small smile. "You don't have to apologize, Lucas. If I didn't want to talk about it, I wouldn't have." When they reached The Street, she brought them to a stop and looked up at him. "Anything I should know before we enter?"

"Do not question what I do or say," he replied seriously. "And remember to trust me no matter what happens." He gave her a smile before he placed a cool, neutral look on his face. "Are you ready, Miss Quinn?"

She mirrored his expression. "As ready as I can be, Mr Vranas."

With a nod, he pulled open the door to The Street and the pair stepped inside. His eyes instantly went to the man in the bowler hat standing in front of the register. He glanced down at his wolf with a bored expression. "Is this the man you mentioned?"

She dipped her head once. "Yes, my lord." *Ugh, here we go.*

"Lord of Los Angeles County," Mr Smiley greeted with a formal bow. "Welcome to The Street. I am most pleased that you have come so far to visit us. We appreciate the attention."

His emerald green eyes went back to the man who smiled pleasantly at him. "I appreciate you accommodating my wolf while she and her assistant were here looking for items I require." He began and then tilted his chin up ever so slightly. "It is a shame she came back empty handed. She knows better than to disappoint me."

This asshole, Kee thought as she just barely kept from glaring at him. *It's a good thing he warned me, or I would be ripping him a new one.*

Playing the part of the obedient pet, she lowered her eyes. "I'm sorry, Lord Lucas. I didn't find what you were looking for, but I'm hopeful that The Top still has the item I mentioned." She glanced up at Mr Smiley, trying to convey a hopeful look.

Mr Smiley's smile widened with a small twitch. "Ah, I know the Ringmaster had an unfortunate death and a successful sale, so perhaps what you mentioned is still there. But, as like before, you must get her permission to enter The Top."

"Permission?" Lucas squinted cold eyes on his bonded wolf. "You did not say I needed any sort of authorization." She had, but he wanted to paint Keira in a negative light so that she was underestimated. The best offense is the unexpected one.

She shrunk away from his gaze. "The Ringmaster told me she would be happy to have you, so I thought that meant you already had the approval."

"That was that night, this is this night. Every phase of the moon brings a new change," Mr Smiley told her with a head tilt.

"I'm sorry I assumed otherwise," she said as she glanced up at Lucas.

"Never assume what is not guaranteed, wolf. It will always come back with a vicious bite," he scolded then looked at the fae. "May I ask that you show me to this Ringmaster? I have traveled many miles and do not wish to be disappointed a second time."

Kee pretended to look scared when he shot her another pointed look. *I'm going to show him what disappointed means when we're done here, so help me.*

"Ah, of course, of course," Mr Smiley agreed as he walked over to the bookcase. Pulling out the same worn blue book, the case split in half and parted. "If you would follow me," he said in his usual light tone and began to descend the stairs.

Lucas dipped his head to Keira's ear. "Remember to trust me." He repeated in a hushed whisper. He pulled back, gave her a brief smile, then started down the stairs after the faerie.

Kee followed close behind him without responding. She trusted Lucas, but his warning made her apprehensive. Still, she would deal with whatever he had planned if it meant helping Samson.

I don't know if you can hear me, but we're coming. Just try to hold on.

Seventeen

"Where are we going?" Zachary asked as Conrad parked the Mercedes in a parking lot behind a four-story building.

"This is Byte's parking lot. It's reserved for Lucas' coven members and a few others," the older wolf replied as he turned off the engine. He glanced at the clock on the dash and frowned. He hadn't expected the movie to run so late. It was 8:48pm and Byte was already open. There had already been a line of people waiting to get in when he drove by the front entrance.

"Byte?" He echoed. "The vampire bar? Why are we here?"

"This is where your sister and I are staying," When Zach's brow furrowed in question, he elaborated. "The fourth floor is full of guest rooms for people who aren't vampires."

"Why do you stay here though? And why together?" He pressed. "Are you dating my sister?" The word sister still felt foreign to him, but he liked saying it.

Conrad couldn't help the loud laugh that came out. "No! I don't see Kee that way. I told you she's my alpha. We find comfort in each other's presence, that's all. Besides, she's dating someone else."

"Who? Warren's beta said they broke up. Is that true?" Zachary was turned in his seat now, facing Conrad with a curious expression.

"Yeah, it's true," he answered honestly. "And maybe dating is the wrong word to use. She's *involved* with Lucas."

"Oh," he commented quietly. She wasn't a wolf, nor was she dating one. Was she a vampire then? No, there was no way. She was out in the sun and didn't smell like one. Still, he had so many questions. He opened his mouth to ask them, but Conrad cut him off with a shake of his head.

"You need to ask her whatever questions you have left, Zach." Zach's face fell in disappointment, and he tried to give him an encouraging smile. "I'm sure she'll have questions for you, too."

He nodded. "Yeah, you're right."

Conrad turned his attention back to Byte and saw the guard at the back door. He recognized the bouncer and sighed. Brent had tried to stop Kee from going to Lucas once, and she had broken his nose for it. He glanced at Mia in the rearview mirror and gave an affectionate smile when he saw her passed out. He looked at Zach again. "Can you stay here and watch her while I go in the club?"

"What? No! I want to meet my sister!" He protested.

"I know," he said firmly. "But you're underage and I don't want to take Mia into a bar crawling with vampires. We would have to cross the bar floor to get to the rooms upstairs and I don't want to risk it."

"I'm not being left behind, Conrad," Zach growled. "I'll help protect Mia, but I *won't* stay here."

"You're just like your sister," he grumbled before giving a sigh of defeat and unclicking his seatbelt. "Fine, we'll go together, but stay close to me."

The younger wolf perked up and quickly got out of the car. He watched as Conrad carefully lifted Mia from the backseat and held her against him. He smiled when she instantly wrapped her arms around her father's neck and buried her face in his shoulder. He eagerly followed Conrad as the wolf headed towards the guarded door.

"Stop," the guard said once the trio was close enough. "What the hell do you think you're doing bringing two kids in here?"

Conrad gave him a cool glare. "As you know, I live here."

"I don't give a shit. It's operating hours, wolf, and I can't let two minors in here." Brent made a shooing motion with his hand. "Come back after 2."

"You can't deny me my home." He growled.

"I'm not denying you," the vampire replied with a scoff. "I'm denying *them*."

"This is my daughter," he tried to explain in a calm manner. "And this is Kee's brother. We're here to see her."

Brent gave a menacing grin. "The owner and his pet aren't here, wolf."

Conrad blinked before his brow furrowed in confusion. "What? Where did they go?"

He shrugged. "Don't know, don't care."

His amber eyes narrowed. "When did they leave?"

"When will they be back?" Zachary asked at the same time. "I want to wait for her."

"I'm not their keeper so I don't keep tabs on them." Brent forced a yawn. "And you're not waiting here. Are we done?"

Conrad glared at him once again. "No, I'm still going to my room and they're coming with me."

"I don't think so, punk. The lord and his pet aren't here so what I say, goes."

"Get the fuck out of my way. I won't warn you again." Conrad growled, his lip lifting in a snarl. "I don't want to fight you in front of my daughter, but I will if I have to."

"No fighting," Emilia murmured sleepily against his neck.

He clenched his jaw but tried to put out some of his anger as he spoke to his daughter, "Alright, baby girl, I won't. Go back to sleep." She mumbled something incoherent and was quiet again after that.

Zachary cracked his knuckles and stepped forward. "He might not fight you, but I will. I'm the son of the Alpha of Los Angeles County. I may be young, but I can wipe the floor with you any day."

Brent regarded him for a second before letting out a loud, mocking laugh. "Oh, please do."

The door was yanked open and Dante stood there with a calm look on his face. "There will be no fight," the vampire stated in a tone that left no argument. "Move aside or find yourself without a job, Brent."

The vampire hissed at Dante, eyes narrowed in a defiant glare. "He can't bring kids into a bar!"

"Dante, this is my daughter and Kee's brother. We just want to go up to my room," Conrad quickly explained.

The dark skinned vampire glanced at the three wolves in front of him then at his subordinate. "He's not bringing children into the bar, Brent. He is bringing them *through* the bar to head upstairs. There is a difference and you know it. You are being difficult simply because Kee bested you. Stop being so childish." Dante scolded and shoved Brent out of the way. He looked at the trio and nodded his head towards the door. "Come, I'll walk you to the stairs."

Conrad's face relaxed into a grateful expression. "Thank you, Dante."

"It's no trouble, Conrad, but Brent is correct that your two companions can't be in the bar. Once you get upstairs, you can't come back down until we're closed." He explained.

"Do you think your dad will be okay with that?" He asked, turning to look at the younger blonde wolf.

Zach shrugged. "I don't care." At Conrad's dubious look, he sighed.

"I'll text him and make some sort of excuse. I'm not leaving until I see her."

"He's definitely Kee's little brother," Dante mused as they walked through the kitchen and onto the main floor. "So stubborn."

Conrad gave a soft laugh. When they reached the bar area, he covered Mia's ear with his free hand to try and muffle the loud music. He hoped the ear pressed against his shoulder would be safe from the music as well. As he passed the bar, his stomach dropped when he saw a certain beautiful, blonde werefox staring at him with an apprehensive expression.

"Come see me on your break?" He asked, knowing she would hear him over the loud music. When she gave a brisk nod, he returned a forced smile and followed Dante to the stairs. "So where did Kee and Lucas go?"

"Riverside." Dante answered as they walked by the VIP rooms and past Lucas' office to the next set of stairs hidden behind the black door.

"What? They went tonight?" Conrad had a feeling Kee planned on going back, he just didn't think it would be the next night. "She went without me." He knew she said they didn't allow wereanimals, but he had still hoped she would have taken him with her.

That's what happens when you betray someone, he thought bitterly.

"They went without any of us." Dante replied with a sigh. "I don't even know where they went in Riverside, but I know Lucas and the Lord of Riverside aren't on the best terms. I'm concerned what might happen."

Conrad frowned. "Who's the Lord of Riverside?"

"Jada. She's similar to Lucas. She's the Lord of Riverside the city as well as the Lord of Riverside County." He told him as they reached the fourth floor.

"Why don't they get along?" Zachary asked curiously.

"I believe they used to be involved with each other," Dante answered. "Until Lucas killed one of her vampires. If memory serves me correctly, he killed a member of her coven because they sexually assaulted his bleeder."

Stunned, Conrad asked, "Aubrey?"

"No, this was sixty years ago or so. Lucas had a pleasant, but quiet male bleeder named Robert. Jada had a nasty subordinate named Joseph." They stayed in the hallway of the fourth floor as he finished his story. "There was a party of sorts at the Lord of San Bernardino County's manor for all the reigning lords. Joseph decided to take certain liberties with Robert when everyone was busy discussing politics. It's to my knowledge that Robert was as unwilling participant."

Zach gaped at him but kept his tone quiet. "He raped him?"

"Yes." Dante replied with a grimace. "Lucas was furious when Robert finally revealed what happened to him. Even then, Robert only admitted it when Lucas compelled him to do so. The man had been skittish around everyone for nearly a week and Lucas had had enough."

"So, Lucas killed Joseph after he found out?" Conrad asked.

"Not right after, he had to do it in a way where Robert wouldn't be targeted by Jada afterwards. He started by asking Robert if he wanted his memory wiped of that night. He jumped at the opportunity. Lucas then released Robert from his bleeder contract and let him go." His smile turned wicked. "You see, there is a strict law that vampires can't kill humans. It isn't just a human government ruling, it's a law set up by the Council. That's why Lucas released him."

"Then he killed Joseph." Zachary surmised.

"Pulled off each individual finger and toe before tearing off all four limbs. He even removed his manhood and shoved it exactly where you think he did," Dante's face grew serious. "Then he set him on fire until he was nothing more than a pile of ash."

Conrad winced and was glad that Mia was snoring softly on his shoulder. "Where is Robert now?"

"Happily married with two kids." He replied and then checked the time on his watch. "I have to return to my post. If you hear from Kee, will you inform me? Lucas doesn't always keep us in the loop with his antics and it would be nice to know that he's alive. Well, you know what I mean."

"I will. Thanks again." Conrad said as the vampire walked down the hall towards the stairs. He then opened the door to his room and carried Emilia to the bed. He pulled back the covers with one hand before lying her down. When her head touched his pillow, she nestled into it and he covered her with the blanket. He tucked her in and stroked her soft hair with a tender, loving smile. Gods, he had missed her.

Zachary was being nosey, searching every inch of the room for something that belonged to his sister. His nose led him to where her clothes were, then to the empty side of the bed, and to her discarded shoes by the door, but there was nothing personal. "You say you guys live here?"

"We're staying here until we find an apartment," Conrad clarified as he stood. "Most of her stuff is boxed up in storage with her furniture."

"Oh," he frowned. "I was hoping to see some of her things." His cheeks grew warm. "That sounded really creepy. I didn't mean it like that. I just want to get a better idea of who she is."

"You don't have to explain yourself, Zach, I get it." He replied and stood up when a soft knock rapped against the door. When Zach perked up hopefully, he laughed. "Kee wouldn't knock on her own door. It's probably Lucy."

"Duh." He murmured to himself in embarrassment.

The other wolf shook his head and opened the door. His heart sped up when Lucy stood there looking at him with her pale green eyes. "Hey," he greeted softly and stepped aside. "Do you want to come in?"

She shook her head, her white blonde hair slipping a little from its clip. "I'd rather talk out here. *Alone.*"

His stomach did a small slip. "Alright," he looked over his shoulder at Zach. "I'll be in the room across the hall, okay? Shout if you need something."

"Roger that." The teen replied with a mock salute.

He rolled his eyes and stepped out into the hall, closing the door behind him. He stepped past Lucy and opened the door. This room was decorated in hues of white and purple, but the furniture was the same. He closed the door behind her and walked over to the bed. He sat down on the edge of it and looked at her.

She crossed her arms over her chest and tried to ignore how hard her heart was beating. "Something you need to tell me?" She asked quietly. She swallowed as he ran his hands into his honey blonde strands and pushed them back from his face before looking at her with those intense amber eyes.

"I have a daughter." He confessed softly.

Her heart stuttered. "So I saw."

He sighed and hunched forward so he could put his elbows on his knees. "I wanted to tell you, but I was in a bad situation. I couldn't tell you about her without truthfully telling you why she wasn't with me. It's why I've been resisting my pull to you so much."

Her heart raced again at the thought that he was just as drawn to her as she was to him, but she shoved it down. She needed answers.

"Baby mama drama?" She bit out harshly.

He didn't comment on her attitude. "No, Mia's mother isn't in the picture."

Some of her ire subsided at that. "So, she's not your mate? Or, isn't anymore?"

"No to both. It was just a fling gone wrong," he rubbed his face. "It's a long story."

"Good thing it's slow downstairs." She shot back defiantly. "I have time."

He gave another sigh and nodded. "At least sit down," he patted the spot on the bed next to him. When she hesitated, he added, "Please?"

"Fine." She huffed and sat on the bed next to him but put space between them. She rolled her hand at him. "Go on."

"Mia's mother, Michelle, had been a mistake, but one I can't regret since it resulted in my daughter," he began honestly. "When I met her, I was eighteen and didn't know she was mated. I was in Newport Beach for the weekend with my friend Ethan. He's really good friends with someone who worked the front door at one of the bars. We had fake IDs so getting into bars wasn't usually a problem, but it never hurt to know someone who worked there.

"I met Michelle and we hung out together all night. We were drinking, flirting, and making out, and one thing led to another. We ended up hooking up my car in the parking lot. She was a wolf too so we didn't use protection. Wereanimals can't catch diseases, as you know, and conceiving and carrying a pup is difficult so I didn't think much of it." He scratched his head with an embarrassed blush. "Really, I wasn't thinking about anything except for getting laid."

"It was a one night stand, but she didn't tell you she was mated?" Lucy asked with a scowl. "Did she just not care about her mate?"

Conrad shrugged once. "I guess they were having some issues. Anyways, seven weeks later, Michelle just shows up at my alpha's house claiming she was pregnant with my pup. When I asked her how she knew it was mine, she broke down into sobs." He sighed and looked down at his hands as he clasped them together. "That's when she told me she was mated to someone in the Beach Cities pack. She said they had been together for decades and they hadn't been able to conceive. Even though her mate knew she had cheated on him, he thought the pup was his."

"But it wasn't." She said softly, her anger diminishing the more he spoke.

"Michelle knew it wasn't so she hunted me down. She said she called every pack until she found one that had a wolf with my name. When she found me, she drove all the way to Claremont to tell me." His eyes fluttered shut. "I was horrible, Lucy. I was almost nineteen, I didn't want a kid. I told her that to her face. I told her to go home and not to worry," his voice trembled slightly. "Because she would probably lose it anyways."

She sucked in a gasp, "Conrad!"

"*I know,*" he said in a strained voice. "But she didn't miscarry. She managed not to shift every month. At first, she would call Liam, my alpha, after every full moon, telling him to tell me that our pup was still there. After the fifth moon the idea began to grow on me so I gave her my cell phone number. I was anxious each time the full moon neared. By the seventh moon, Liam had to stop me from going to her. It would make everything worse, he told me. Her body was already stressed and she didn't need the emotional strain my presence would bring, especially with her mate there."

She reached out and put her hand on his. "What happened?"

"I got a call on the ninth full moon and it was from the Beach Cities' alpha." He bit off his story, his eyes turning angry as he recalled that phone call with vivid clarity. "She gave the alpha my number a couple weeks beforehand and told him the situation."

"What did he say?"

Conrad looked at her with a tormented expression. "He said Michelle was dead and to come get my daughter." He closed his eyes again. "I was told the strain of resisting the shift put her in labor even though it was a few weeks before her due date. She gave birth and her mate completely lost control of his inner wolf. His beast knew the pup wasn't his by the scent. The alpha had grabbed the baby while someone else tried to stop her mate from attacking her. They couldn't intervene in time and her body had been too weak to fight back."

Lucy scooted closer to Conrad and pressed her cheek to his shoulder, trying to comfort him. "I'm sorry, Con."

He leaned his head against hers. "I hurried over there and probably broke six traffic laws in the process. I got to the alpha's house and he handed me this tiny bundle swaddled in a pink, fleece blanket," he held his hands out as if he was holding Mia's small form for the first time once again. "She was so small and fragile." He whispered with a warm smile.

The werefox could hear the love in his voice, and all her irritation and resentment left her completely.

"As soon as I looked at her face, I was swept off my feet. I remember my wolf and I both saying, *'mine'*. I asked what her name was, but the alpha told me that Michelle never had a chance to name her. So, I named her Emilia Michelle Novak." He gave a forced, humorless laugh. "I was nineteen with this newborn and I didn't know what the fuck to do. I just knew that she was mine and I loved her."

"Oh, Conrad, I'm so sorry." She cooed.

"Why are you apologizing? You didn't get your daughter's mother killed," he pointed out.

"Because it's a sad situation. I know you blame yourself, but you shouldn't. You couldn't have possibly known what was going to happen." She said softly.

"But I should have. I know how wolves are, Lucy. I know how possessive they can be. I should have taken it more seriously from the start." He murmured.

She pulled away from him and cupped his face in both of her hands, angling his head so he looked at her. "You were eighteen when you found out she was pregnant, Con. Were your words harsh? Yes, but you came around. You manned up and took care of your daughter."

Conrad stared down into her understanding eyes and felt as if his heart had melted. He wanted to act on his feelings, but he still had to tell her why he hadn't told her, or Kee, about Mia.

"There's a reason I didn't tell you about Mia," he said softly. "My old alpha is the Alpha of Los Angeles County and he sent me here to gather information about Warren."

She frowned at this new information. "What about Kee?"

"Kee is my alpha," he stated vehemently. "She treated me with kindness and protected me even though she didn't know anything about me. She took me in and treated me as a person when I had spent almost two weeks as nothing more than a submissive punching bag."

"But, you're not a weak wolf, Con. Why act like that?"

"Because I had to, Lucy. I was *given* to the LA pack because Liam needed me to get them to lower their guards so that they would feel comfortable talking around me." He sighed and closed his eyes when her thumbs stroked his cheeks. "I didn't want to do it, but he held Mia captive from me."

Her eyes widened, her cheeks reddening in anger. "What? He kept her from you?"

He nodded. "Liam started acting weird when Mia turned seven. He began staring at her with a blank expression and became increasingly more hostile towards me. It got worse after every full moon. I think it's because she hasn't shifted into a wolf yet." As soon as the words left his mouth, he was reminded of Kee's story. "Oh gods, I finally understand why."

"What? Why?" She asked, thoroughly confused.

"I found out today that Liam is Kee's dad, Lucy. Kee never shifted into a wolf when she was seven. Instead, they found out she was shapeshifter. What if Liam is doing this to Mia and me because he's reminded of his own daughter?" He balled his hands into fists. "Was he keeping me from her because he thinks I'll turn out like him? Beating my daughter because she might not be a wolf?"

Lucy saw his eyes gleam gold with his wolf's presence. She didn't know the full story of Kee and her dad, but she didn't like what Conrad had just said about him. "Shh, Con, you'll never be like him. You'll never hurt Mia. Look at what you've gone through to get her back. *You* are a good dad."

His anger instantly left him as those words warmed him to his core. That's all he ever wanted to be: a good father to Mia. He gently set his hand on her cheek, his thumb brushing across her bottom lip. "Thank you for saying that," he breathed.

Butterflies exploded in her stomach at the light caress. "Y-you're welcome. I'm sorry I doubted you." She whispered back.

He lowered his head so his nose brushed against hers. He felt her body sway towards him and his heart skipped a beat. She wanted this just as much as he did. He tilted his head and ever so lightly pressed his lips against hers. He heard her breathe in sharply through her nose, her hands falling to his neck.

He pulled back just enough to give her a shy, but happy smile. "You're not mated, are you?" He teased.

Lucy gave a soft giggle and ran her fingers into his long hair. "No, so kiss me again."

Conrad happily obliged.

Eighteen

Kee carefully kept a few paces between her and Lucas as they ventured down the stairs. Once they reached the bottom, he held out his arm to her and she obediently tucked her hand in his elbow again. She hadn't heard Samson reply to her and it made her nervous.

What if it wasn't the mermaid that died? That it wasn't the griffin who was purchased?

"Ah! You have returned! How are you enjoying the blade?" The fae merchant with long hair asked as they passed his stall.

She gave him a smile and looked up at Lucas. "You would have to ask him. He's the one I gifted it to."

Lucas inclined his head ever so slightly. "Your blade is beautiful. I am glad to have it in my possession even now as we speak."

The merchant beamed and gave a bow. "Such praise from a lord vampire."

"I give credit where it is do," he replied then ushered Kee forward after Mr Smiley.

Samson? Are you here? Answer me. Kee tried to call in her mind, but she wasn't even sure if she was projecting. She wasn't telepathic; he had been the one to contact her last time.

Lucas glanced down and took in her concentrated expression. He felt a twinge of worry from her side of the bond and pulled her hand closer between his arm and side. He felt her squeeze his elbow in return and turned his attention back to Mr Smiley when they came to a stop outside the large black and grey striped tent. Reclining against one of the poles that held up the tent was a tall, lanky woman who smelled of poultry.

"Ringmaster," Kee greeted and gestured at Lucas with her free hand. "I've brought my lord, as I said."

Ringmaster grinned at her, sharp pointed teeth flashing for a second before they rounded out. "Lord of Los Angeles County, do you wish to look upon my treasures?"

"If they are indeed worth the title of treasure, then yes," he said and then slid his cool gaze down to Keira. "My wolf has already misled me, so I am not sure I can take her word as to what is deemed a treasure."

Oh, he's skating on thin ice. He's so going to pay for this. She seethed in her mind but put on an innocent expression.

"I did not mean to disappoint you, my lord," she dipped her head slightly. "And I am sure that I will not this time. The Ringmaster's inventory is breathtaking."

"You humble me, Miss Wolf of Vranas." The Ringmaster laughed with glee. "Come, allow me to prove that your wolf is indeed correct."

Lucas merely gave a soft scoff before following her inside, Keira still on his arm. As they ventured into the tent, he felt her stiffen beside him. The scent of rotting flesh and blood, both stale and fresh, hit their noses. There was a distinct fish odor that was mixed with salt and he was certain it was from the mermaid Keira had spoken about.

"Ringmaster, where is your mermaid?" Kee managed to keep her voice nice and even, her anger and disgust nowhere in her tone.

"Ah, she perished very early this morning. Apparently, you were right about the water and food." Ringmaster laughed as if it was a small, trivial thing. "I will keep your advice in mind next time." She said as she tapped her temple for emphasis.

"You brought me here for a mermaid? I have no use for such things." The vampire said coolly.

Kee glanced up at him from the corner of her eye. "Of course not, my lord. I know better than anyone that you have no trouble getting someone in your bed."

Little minx. Lucas thought to himself as the borrowed blood in his body warmed at her words. "Watch yourself, wolf. Make sure you do not see yourself removed from such an honor."

She had to fight to keep the grin off her face when she was filled with smugness. Then she heard his retort and clenched her jaw tightly. *That's it, I'm kicking his ass when we get out of here.*

Why did you come back?

She tripped on her own heel when Samson's voice invaded her head suddenly. If she hadn't been holding on to Lucas' arm, she would have hit the floor. Samson's words had been filled with venom, but his tone was strained. He sounded awful.

I told you I was coming back for you. I brought help.

Trap, he rasped.

She instantly stopped walking, her hand tightening on Lucas' elbow. *What are you talking about? She can't cage me. I'm here with a vampire lord.*

Not for you, he whispered into her mind with obvious difficulty.

"Wolf?" Lucas' question came out as impatient to those who were listening, but his concern reached her through their bond the same way her sudden panic did him.

She took one small step back, pulling on his arm. "My lord, I forgot something in the car." She said blankly, but her grey eyes stared straight into his with an empty coldness.

At that look, he confirmed that she knew something he didn't. Something dangerous to them. He released a forced, exasperated sigh. "My apologies, Ringmaster, but could you give us ten minutes to return?"

The faerie gave a sharp laugh before sweeping a hand out to the side. "What do you think, Ms Vampire of Jada?"

Lucas straightened his spine as apprehension crept across his skin. He pinned Keira's hand to his side with his elbow as a short woman stepped out from the shadows. Her skin was a little darker than the color of caramel, her hair a deep, rich brown. Her eyes were the color of milk chocolate with long, thick lashes lined around them. She wore a silk, amber colored dress that hugged her body in all the best ways to accentuate her curvaceous figure.

"You are a member of Jada's coven," Lucas stated calmly, trying not to show that he had been taken off guard. He didn't like how she had been able to hide her presence. She had to be one of Jada's vampire witches. "I did not expect to see one of you here."

"That was the point." She replied with a light tone. "I'm sad your pet ruined Lady Jada's initial surprise, but it couldn't be helped."

Kee dug her fingers into his elbow. Her instincts usually told her when something was off or wrong, so why hadn't she felt it when they first stepped into The Top? Why hadn't she sensed this new vampire?

"And what did you hope to gain from this surprise?" Lucas asked in a monotonous tone.

"A warning, of course. You are in my lady's territory and I have every right to destroy you." She reminded him in a sing-song voice.

"I was expected here by the Ringmaster," he corrected, not glancing at the faerie. "I entered your territory a guest."

"Faeries cannot lie." the Ringmaster said with a grin. "I didn't exactly invite you, but I did agree that you could come. However, I only allowed it because of your wolf. Word traveled that she had come on your behalf and Lady Jada came to make me a bargain. She would take care of you while I got your wolf."

"Why not just take me last night?" Kee asked, eyes narrowed in a glare. "Why wait until tonight?"

"Because of your warlock assistant, of course. We are not allowed to harm any magic user. That is what we agreed upon with the lady when we moved here." The Ringmaster answered with a grin full of sharp teeth.

"Why do you want me to begin with? I'm nothing exotic like the other creatures you had. I'm just a wolf." She pointed out, glancing over her shoulder at Samson's cage.

"You are the Lord of Los Angeles's bonded wolf. That will already fetch a higher price than a normal werewolf. You're more durable, faster to heal." The Ringmaster spread her hands out in front of her when Kee scowled. "What can I say? I'm a business woman."

"Come now, did you think Lady Jada would simply let you get away with killing Joseph? He was her favorite." The vampire mused. "Lady Jada has waited a long time to get back at you."

"That was over sixty years ago." He told her and released Keira's hand so he could step away from her. There was going to be a fight and they would both need the room to move.

"Sixty years is nothing for someone who is immortal, you should know that." She reminded him.

"Grudges are an unflattering thing," he mused as he undid the buttons on his suit jacket. "Tell me, did you come alone?"

The smile fell off her face, a glare replacing it. "I am made from Lady Jada's blood. I am strong enough to defeat you alone."

Lucas shrugged off his jacket and rolled up the sleeves of his white button up. "How very foolish of you." He glanced at Keira from the corner of his eye. "Will you be alright on your own?"

"I'll let you know," she replied honestly as she toed off her heels.

Lucas didn't reply, instead he and the other vampire clashed together with a blur of fists. She lifted her hands in front of her as she stared at the Ringmaster who was grinning in delight. "You're acting like you already won."

"I have, Miss Wolf of Vranas," she commented. "Your lord cannot kill the Riverside Lord's coven member in her territory. He would be punished by the Lord of California and probably killed. She gave me her word that you would be mine. Whether he kills her, or she him, I win. We take vows very seriously."

"I didn't agree to any of this," Kee snapped. "I will not belong to you."

Ringmaster laughed again. "Oh, you will."

"I *won't*," she growled then glanced at Lucas when she heard a loud thud. She saw the female vampire hit the ground several feet away from him, her hand wiping at her lip. She opened her mouth to tell him not to kill her but snapped her mouth shut, jumping back when she was attacked.

Ringmaster had the silver pole she had prodded Samson with in her hands, twirling it around like it weighed nothing. When she swung it again, Kee moved back. She thought she had moved far enough away, but the metal hit her and sent her tumbling to the side with a burn on her arm. The faerie jabbed the pole once again, Kee rolled out of the way but yelped when she felt a sharp pain in her calf.

She braced herself on the ground with her hand and swung her uninjured leg up at the Ringmaster. She caught the fae in the jaw, her top hat falling to the floor and white hair feathers falling around her shoulders as she staggered back. Kee tried to get to her feet but staggered at the pain in her calf. She looked down at the singed puncture wound and glanced at the silver pole.

It's round and blunt at the end, how did it stab me?

Glamour, Samson mumbled to her.

She jerked when comprehension hit her. "Fucking fae." She mumbled under her breath and forced herself to her feet.

Jada's vampire scooted back as the LA Lord approached her. She quickly began muttering something under her breath, and Lucas could make out some words that sounded like Latin. When his feet were suddenly rooted in place, his hands pinned to his sides, he mentally cursed the witch.

"You're trapped, Lucas." She laughed and gracefully climbed to her feet. She stuck her hand between the slit in her amber dress and pulled a small blade from the garter on her thigh. She approached the stoic lord with a triumphant smirk and didn't hesitate as she sunk the blade into his chest. "This is for my lady."

He grimaced slightly at the pain but otherwise held her gaze. "If this is what Jada's undead witches can do, I am disappointed." He said, emerald green eyes flickering to blood red for a second.

He flared his aura, his power coming out like a gust of wind and pushing her back a few paces. Regaining control of his hand, he slipped it into his pocket and withdrew the knife Keira had bought him. With a flick of his wrist, he sprang open the blade and stabbed it into his thigh. The emerald cleansed him of the spell, freeing the rest of his limbs.

Her eyes widened when he reached up to remove the blade she left in his chest. "Well then, I'll just make it stronger!"

When she tried to let out another spell, Lucas flashed in front of her. He hoisted her up by her throat and slammed her against a nearby empty cage. He stopped his habit of breathing when the stench of her burnt flesh invaded his nose. "Try to enchant me again, and I will kill you."

"You can't kill me in Lady Jada's territory!" She shouted, hands clawing at his wrist.

He leaned in close to her ear. "There are things worse than death."

He pulled back and gave her a pitying look. "You are nothing to Jada. You made a mistake by confronting me this night."

She hissed at him, fangs bared in both anger and pain. "I am doing as Lady Jada asked!"

"Do you not care that you are nothing more than a pawn to her?" He replied casually as he pulled her away from the silver bars. Skin hung between her body and the bars like melted cheese.

"I'm not a pawn, I'm a messenger!"

"And what message does your lady bring?" He asked, tightening his hold on her neck until he heard the bones in her neck creak.

She squirmed against his hold but managed to choke out, "A son for a son."

His eyes flashed to crimson again and he slid his hand up to her jaw, the other hand fisting her hair. "What did you just say?" He asked in a quiet, calm voice.

She gave him a smug smirk. "A son for a—" A loud crack filled the tent and she let out a blood curdling scream as her jaw was snapped down and out of place.

Lucas stuck his thumb in her mouth so that he had a strong hold on her broken jaw. With his emerald blade, he made a slice at each corner of her mouth and gave a quick, hard pull. The mandible separated from the rest of her face with a sickening, hollow pop, skin tearing apart unevenly at the cuts. He tossed it to the ground and released her neck. She dropped to her knees in front of him, screaming in pain as blood flowed from the bottom portion of her face. Her tongue flopped around uselessly as she tried to cover her exposed mouth.

"When your jaw heals back together, you can tell Jada that she can expect worse." He sneered before he swiftly punched her in the temple. She fell to the ground unconscious, blood pooling around her head.

Kee could feel the blood running down her leg, but she kept her eyes on the fae. Some of the Ringmaster's hair feathers were red and pink with blood, a couple sticking to the gash on her cheek. Hearing Lucas' opponent screaming almost made her turn to witness what Lucas had done, but the Ringmaster swung. Kee stumbled back from the long, silver pole's supposed reach and toppled against Samson's cage. She hissed as the silver bars burned her through the lace on her back. She tried to move away, but the faerie was on her. The Ringmaster pressed the silver pole against her throat, the lace giving little protection from the burn, and forced her back harder against the silver bars.

Kee put her hands on the pole and tried to push it away from her throat. She gasped at the pain from her hands and back but tried to kick at the fae. Clawed hands slipped through the bars behind her and buried themselves into the fae's hands as they held the silver pole. The Ringmaster screeched at the pain and tried to tug free, but the claws only dug deeper.

"I've got her." Samson rumbled from behind Kee.

When the Ringmaster tried to pull the pole back, Kee ducked under it and threw her fist straight into her opponent's throat. The fae hacked from the force of it and abruptly released her hold. Kee saw Samson's claws tear through the fae's flesh as he curled his fingers in when she jerked away. The pole fell to the paved floor with a loud *clank,* and Kee grabbed the hem of her dress so she could pick it up without searing her skin. She swung it at the Ringmaster, the hidden, sharp edge slicing across the fae's chest.

"I yield!" The Ringmaster cried out as she fell to the floor, dark tinted blood spilling from the slash on her chest.

Kee pressed the invisible tip against the faerie's throat, the grey skin dimpling in from the pressure. She felt a hand on her shoulder and glanced up at Lucas. "I should kill her for what she's done."

"She deserves worse," he agreed. "But we will spare her and gain a favor for doing so."

Kee glared down at the faerie. "Is this true?"

"Yes," the Ringmaster gasped out as her skin was pricked by her own weapon. "I will owe you a favor."

"Give me the dragon." She felt Lucas' bloodied hand flex slightly on her bare skin. "And let us leave unharmed." She demanded, pressing harder so that a thin trail of dark blood streamed down the Ringmaster's neck. "Or I can kill you and simply take him."

The fae bared her pointed teeth at her. "Fine! Take him! He'll be dead soon anyway," she sneered. "The key is on my belt loop."

Kee removed the spear from her neck so she could violently stab her in the shoulder with it. Ignoring the fae's screech, she made sure the sharp end went through the Ringmaster's body and into the floor so she was pinned there. She bent down and ripped the keyring away from the thin piece of fabric. She hissed when the silver bit her fingers and quickly grabbed the bottom of her dress once again to put a barrier between skin and metal.

Lucas followed her to the cage, catching her arm when she stumbled. His eyes narrowed at the deep cut in her calf. "You are hurt." He accused as she quickly unlocked the cage and flung the door open.

"You are, too. I only have a couple burns and a stab wound. I'll be okay." She reassured him as she hobbled to Samson's huddled form. She dropped to her knees next to him and cautiously reached out to touch his shoulder.

Lucas grabbed her dress and yanked her back as Samson turned on her with a swipe of his claws. His black eyes had taken on his dragon, the irises and pupils like slits. They were wide and glassy, his teeth exposed in a wordless snarl. A spasm shook his body from his abrupt movement, pain contorting his face into a wince.

"His beast is taking over, Keira." Lucas told her, keeping a firm hold on her dress when she tried to go near the dragon again.

"He's in pain," she argued as she tried to twist of out his grip. "I have to help him."

"He is *dying*. He is reverting to a primal mode to protect himself. He will kill you if he deems you a threat." He tightened his hold when she continued to struggle. "I am not willing to risk your life for his."

Kee glared at him. "That's not your choice to make," she snapped at him. When he narrowed his eyes at her, she swatted his hands away. "You don't control me, Lucas. You agreed to come here and help me. Now that we're here, I'm not abandoning him."

He stared down into her defiant, stubborn grey eyes and considered his choices. He could easily sweep her up in his arms and carry her out, kicking and screaming, but she would only resent him for it. He did not wish to fight with his shapeshifter again. Or, he could let her attend to the dragon and risk her life in the process. If she died, he would kill the dragon, as well as everyone on the Street in fit of rage. The easy choice was obvious, but nothing was ever easy with his shapeshifter.

He cursed in Greek. "Fine, but we need to hurry before the other fae decide to assist their comrade."

She nodded once and kneeled down next to Samson again. She heard the warning rumble in his chest but gently put her hand on his dirty, bruised shoulder anyways. "Samson," she cooed softly when he tensed under her touch and hissed. "It's okay, it's me. I told you I was coming to save you and I'm here."

Lies, he spat in her mind. *I'll die here.*

You helped me defeat the Ringmaster. Don't you remember that? She asked, lightly petting his skin as he talked to her telepathically.

Dreams? He suddenly groaned, the sound echoing in her mind and ears. *Everything blends.*

This is real. I spared her life and my favor is you, she told him seriously. *You're mine and I'm going to get you out of here, but I need you to calm down.*

Why? Samson croaked as he flexed his hands, his claws returning to fingers.

Because you asked for help. I know you told me to go away and not come back, but you'll learn I'm stubborn. She gave him a small smile when he turned his head to look at her, his black eyes back to their human shape.

"Keira?" Lucas called as he glanced at the Ringmaster when she tried to remove herself from the pole.

Samson tensed at the male's voice and he bared his teeth again. *Who's that?* He snapped. He closed his eyes tightly when he swayed, vision going hazy. Wait, when had he gotten to his knees?

Lucas. He's, um, she blushed. *My boyfriend, I guess. Anyways, he won't hurt you. He's a lord and he's come to help me get you out of here. You can trust him, okay?*

Vampires only want my blood. He snarled in her head but let her help him to his feet. What did it matter? It was just another one of his dreams of freedom. He would wake in a few hours to discover he was still on the soiled floor of his cage.

Trust me, he has very good control of his thirst. He wants my blood more than anything, but he's only tasted it once and that was a month and a half ago. He's given his word he won't drink from me again and I believe him. She blabbered to Samson as she finally got him to his feet, trying to keep him distracted.

Whatever.

Lucas handed his suit jacket to the slightly shorter male. He himself was almost six foot, but the dragon fell somewhere around between five foot nine and five foot ten. The dragon just looked at him with empty black eyes, and the vampire sighed. He tied the suit jacket around Samson's narrow waist so that the fabric covered his groin and backside.

Kee draped one of Samson's arms across her shoulders but grunted when he leaned on her for support. Her leg buckled, but she kept upright. "I can't support him and walk," she told Lucas, but her eyes were on Samson.

Samson, I'm hurt. I can't support your weight. Lucas is going to have to help you. She saw his lip turn up and patted his arm. *We don't have time to argue. It's only until we're out of here. Just remember what I said.*

When the dragon grunted, Kee looked at Lucas and nodded. "You can take him."

"I do not like that I cannot hear your conversations." He admitted as he hoisted the dragon onto his back.

She winced when she heard Samson groan in pain. "I'm sorry," she told Lucas. "I think it's easier for him to communicate that way when he's this weak."

"I understand; I just do not like it," he replied and started walking towards the tent entrance, his hands supporting Samson's legs around his waist. He frowned when Kee stumbled behind him, limping as she tried to keep up with him. "Keira, if you fall behind, I will drop the dragon and grab you instead. *You* are my priority."

She blanched at his serious expression but gave him a single nod. "I won't fall back." They stared at each other for a second longer before Lucas turned and led the way out of the tent, Kee following close behind him.

Nineteen

Samson was suddenly in the backseat of a car, the smell of leather invading his nose. He blinked when he heard someone pleading to let them go. His black eyes stared up to see the werewolf's face from his dream, but there was something wrong with it. It was scrunched up in pain, and there was a cut with a smear of blood on her cheek.

"Samson, Sam, *please*, let go." She called to him. "Lucas will kill you."

Let go? He asked himself. He was then aware that one of his hands was wrapped around her forearm. His fingers had shifted into black talons and were imbedded in her skin. With a start, he quickly unlatched his fingers, freeing her from his grasp.

He tried to sit up, but she pushed on his shoulder, keeping him down. "Don't move, Sam. You're really hurt and getting you in the car opened some of your older wounds."

"Keira, get in the front seat," a voice growled at her. "There is hardly enough room for him, let alone both of you."

"No, Lucas! What if he has another seizure?" She snapped.

"Then he has another seizure," the driver replied dryly. "I do not care as long as you are safe. He has already torn my leather, what if you are next?"

She sighed. "My touch is calming him down, I think. He starts flailing when I let go of him. As long as I keep petting him, I should be okay."

"Twice he has turned on you. If he mars you once more, there will not be a fourth time."

"He's not doing it on purpose," she pointed out softly.

She was looking forward so that Samson had a clear view of her neck and the underside of her jaw. He wanted to bury his face there and take in the comfort her voice and promises had brought him, even if it was all a dream. His head lifted from her lap, but he froze when a wave of pain crashed over him.

When he opened his eyes with a groan, she was suddenly looking down at him, worry etched on her face. "Hang on, Sam. Everything is going to be okay." She whispered softly to him, her hand stroking his matted hair.

His vision blurred, but he could make out the trails of blood slipping down her arm. "M'sry." *I'm sorry.*

"Shh, it's okay."

When he was jerked to consciousness the second time, there was an argument going on. "I am not leaving you here alone." The male voice from earlier was angry.

"I'm not alone. Nana is here." The werewolf replied calmly as she rummaged through a plastic, white box on the bed.

Bed? His mind swam. He wasn't in his cage anymore? Wait, wasn't he in a car? *Yes, with the werewolf and the other guy. The vampire. Her boyfriend. But when did the car stop? Where are we now?*

"He is a *dragon*, Keira! He has been losing control of his beast more and more since we left The Top. If he shifts, he will take you both down." The vampire protested indignantly.

"I can't take him to Byte, can I?" She finally snapped back. "I won't endanger everyone there with him. Plus, there's no way to get to my room without dragging him through the crowd. He's naked, beaten, and bloodied. He's practically a walking meal to your coven. Not to mention I'm also hurt and covered in blood."

"Keira—"

"No, you don't want me to flaunt my blood in your club and I won't show his off either." Her voice softened as she continued, "Lucas, please, I'm doing this for you as well. We will recuperate here."

Samson heard the vampire sigh and rolled his eyes towards that direction. He watched as this Lucas person grabbed Keira's hands in his, stopping her from digging through what he now comprehended was a first-aid kit.

The vampire pressed his pale lips to her knuckles and said, "I know it is the right course of action, but it still makes me uneasy." Samson's eyes closed briefly when Lucas lowered his voice. "Your shapeshifter blood is powerful, Keira. I remember it healed and empowered me, but it also made me crave it more. I have self-restraint, but you do not know this dragon."

"Samson is good," she defended him without hesitation.

She doesn't know me. How can she say that? And why would I crave her blood? He thought groggily. *Wait, shapeshifter?*

"You do not know that. You do not know *him*." Lucas stated.

His eyes blurred when they slid to look at her, but he could make out the flustered expression. "I know I don't know him, but it's just a feeling I have. Besides, we don't know if it'll come to that. Nana and I just said it was an option. Hopefully he will heal on his own."

"We can only hope that he does not fall prey to his wounds." His tone was *almost* bitter.

He felt the mattress under him shift when she stood from the bed and approached the blur that was her boyfriend. "You're also hurt." She had said it so softly, Samson almost didn't hear it. "I'm sorry."

Lucas pulled her towards him. "It is nothing; do not apologize."

"Thank you," she murmured. "For helping me."

Instead of replying, Samson could see his head dip down towards her and assumed they kissed. He didn't generally like vampires, but he had never seen one act the way this one did.

Dreamland is full of surprises.

"Make up your mind to leave or not, Vampire, but either way you're in my way." A new voice came with a huff. He tried to look at the shorter woman who had appeared in the room with something white in her hands but was sucked into the black void of nothingness once again.

A small, flicker of light appeared in the darkness around him when something warm dripped into his mouth and spread across his tongue. The liquid tasted like copper but had a sweet undertone to it. It rolled towards the back of his mouth and down his throat, leaving a tantalizing sensation in its wake. He tried to swallow it, but his body wasn't cooperating.

"I don't know if it's going to work, Kee." The other woman from earlier said from the left of him.

"It has to! I'm not going to let him go after all this!"

Why was the werewolf—no, that wasn't right. The vampire had called her a shapeshifter. Why was the shapeshifter shouting? He felt something hit him hard on his chest.

"Damn it, Sam! Breathe!" She yelled again.

Breathe? He was breathing. Wait, no, he wasn't. Why wasn't he breathing? *This is it. This is how I die. Finally free from the pain.* But, if that was true, why was he still dreaming of the shapeshifter?

"I'm giving him more." She declared, and he briefly heard the other woman protest before more of the delicious fluid filled his mouth.

Samson could feel it spread heat through his chest like a liquid flame. It seared through his body and across his skin. His inner dragon reared its head at the sudden feeling but didn't fight it. Instead, he basked in it. A roar rumbled from his beast as the liquid found the dying embers of his flame.

Embers? He suddenly panicked. A dragon's fire didn't go out. It just didn't. If it did, they would die. Suddenly, her shouts replayed in his mind. *I really am dying.*

However, whatever she had given him had worked as an accelerant and flared his fire back to life. His beast instantly took charge and his eyes few open. He sucked in a greedy, pained breath and choked when he inhaled some of the liquid lingering in his mouth. When his airway was clear he released a loud, triumphant roar. He felt hands on his face and jerked his head towards the owner of them.

Shapeshifter. His beast recalled and stilled his hand before he could swing his talons at her. *She did this. She saved us.*

She stared into his black slit eyes without fear. "You're here and you're safe," she told him softly. "But you're still hurt. Relax and let it heal you."

He stared back at her, chest heaving as his exhausted body thrummed almost happily from whatever she had given him. He searched her eyes for deceit and found none. Was this reality? Was he *really* freed from his torment?

Her eyes softened, the dove grey hue a stark contrast to the smudged eyeliner surrounding them. "You're safe," she repeated firmly as she gently stroked his cheek. "I won't let anything happen."

For the first time, he let himself believe her. Her presence soothed him, and he realized it wasn't the first time he had thought that. In the car, his beast had settled under her touch. He knew of two people who could have that effect on him. A mate, but they were most definitely not mated. The second option was much more probable.

You're an alpha. He said to her.

Her eyes widened for a second before a tired smile tilted her lips.

Not really.

You are.

She simply shook her head and slid her hand up to pet his hair. *Go to sleep. The worst is over. All you have to do now is heal. I'll be right here when you wake up.*

Samson was going to protest, but he could feel his body already arguing. She was right, he needed to rest so he could heal. Whatever she had given him had renewed his energy, but his body needed to focus that energy on healing, not being awake. Now that he had come to terms that he was actually free from the daily torture, he knew he would finally fall into a deep, peaceful sleep.

—

The smell of seared meat brought Samson out of his sleep. He stared up at a cream ceiling as his mind quickly processed his situation. He was no longer in the The Top, the ceiling and comfortable bed under him told him as such. He vaguely remembered his dragon telling him that they were free.

With a jolt he recalled that his fire had almost extinguished, that he had basically died. He went to lift his hand to his chest, but his left one was weighed down. Panicking at the thought of being restrained, he whipped his head to look at his restraint but stilled to see the werewo—*shapeshifter*, he corrected. She was asleep in a chair next to his bed and bent over the edge of the mattress. Her head rested on her arm, her hand holding his.

She wasn't wearing the black dress anymore. Instead, she wore a blue tank top. With her hair tied up into a messy bun, the bandages across her shoulders and around neck were exposed. The forearm of the hand holding his was wrapped and he winced, knowing he had inflicted that wound on her. Her wrist, hands, and fingers were wrapped as well, and a small Band-Aid had been stuck to her right cheekbone.

"She doesn't heal as fast as you do," a vaguely familiar voice told him. He looked away from the shapeshifter to see an elderly woman with curly dark red hair approach him. In her hands was a tray of food. A mostly rare steak and a half-dozen fried eggs filled a plate next to two steaming cups of coffee. Another plate on the tray had scrambled eggs, raspberries, and a piece of perfectly toasted bread.

Samson's stomach growled ferociously as the heavenly scents attacked his nose. His cheeks warmed in embarrassment. He slid his hand out from Keira's and sat up so he could lean back against the headboard, the blanket falling to his waist.

"How hurt is she?" He asked quietly as the older woman flipped the legs down from under the tray and set it over his lap.

"Not too badly. A few silver burns, some puncture wounds, and a few cuts. Honestly, the worst is the stab wound on her calf, but it's nothing she won't survive." She replied blandly and walked over to the other side of the bed. "I am Nanette, by the way; Kee's great-grand-mother. You may call me Nana, or Nan."

"Kee?" He echoed and watched as she approached the slumbering girl next to his bedside. "Short for Keira, I guess?"

"Yes, she prefers to be called Kee," she explained then looked at him again with a disapproving scowl. "Your manners are atrocious, young man. I offer you my home, my care, and cooking, and yet you can't introduce yourself?"

He flushed in embarrassment again and quickly dipped his head, his matted black hair curtaining around one half of his face. "I'm sorry. My name is Samson Richland. Thank you for your hospitality." He rushed out.

Nana grunted at him in acknowledgment. "Good," she said simply before she shook Kee awake. "You better wake up before your coffee gets cold."

Kee's head popped up at the mention of coffee. She blinked the sleep out of her eyes and leaned back in her chair, stretching her sore back as she did. She smiled tiredly at Nana and accepted the coffee. "Thank you," she said as she cupped the porcelain mug in her bandaged hands. She took a tentative sip and let out a content sigh. "This is heaven."

"Don't just drink coffee, Kee. Eat your breakfast." Nana demanded as she placed the plate with raspberries on the mattress in front of her great-granddaughter.

"Yes, ma'am," she laughed, her smile widening when she looked at Samson. "It's good to see you awake. How are you feeling, Sam?"

Sam? I haven't been called Sam in ages. "I feel better than I have in weeks. Months, maybe. It's hard to tell." He replied solemnly as he picked up the silverware Nana had provided him.

Her smile fell. "You were there for that long?" She asked softly as she set her coffee down on the nightstand. She grabbed her fork and scooped up some of the eggs Nana had made her.

He nodded once as he took a bite of his steak. "I can't tell you the exact amount of time, but it was a while."

"I'm sorry you had to go through that," Kee told him earnestly. "It makes me so angry that this happened to you. Seeing your body," she flinched. "It pained me."

"Try being the one who went through it," he snorted at her and took an angry bite of his steak. "She had people cut scales off my body. Not just a surface cut either, they wanted to make sure they had meat on the scales to go with it."

Her eyes fell on the random white, smooth patches of skin that was scattered across his shoulders and chest. The scars were faint, but he was a weredragon and shouldn't have scarred at all. That was how malnourished they had kept him. "They took some of your horns, too."

Samson glared at her. "I'm aware."

Her eyes softened. "Will they grow back?"

He shrugged once and turned his attention back to his breakfast. "I don't know. I've never had my horns cut off before."

"I'm sorry."

He dropped his fork to his plate with a loud *clang.* "Stop fucking apologizing!" He snapped and clenched his hands into fists. When she just stared at him with calm, empathetic eyes, he swallowed his anger. "You saved me. You of all people have nothing to apologize for."

She gave him another small smile. "You asked me for help, Sam."

"You didn't have to agree," he pointed out as he picked up his utensils again.

"I'm not going to abandon someone who asked me for help." She scrunched her nose up at him with a teasing look. "Even if they told me to go away and didn't believe me."

Samson's cheeks reddened in embarrassment again, and he looked away as he chewed on some eggs. When he swallowed, he glanced down at the food on his plate. His eyes fell on the bandages wrapped and taped to random places on his body and he pursed his lips hard together. These people didn't know him and yet they had taken care of him.

His black eyes fell on Kee's bandaged hands and arm. *She fought for me. Even when I told her it was a trap for her and her boyfriend.*

He felt someone looking at him and lifted his gaze to see Nana staring at him with her arms crossed over her chest. She mouthed '*manners*' to him and his brow furrowed. He looked at Kee again and slowly reached out. He hesitantly put his hand on hers, his fingertips brushing against the course fabric of her bandages. When she looked up at him, he swallowed nervously. "T-thank you."

Kee's heart warmed at his quiet, but sincere gratitude. "You don't ever have to thank me, Samson," she told him. "You owe me nothing and I would gladly do it again."

He gave her a tentative smile, the action almost foreign after not doing it for so long. "*Thank you.*" He repeated more seriously.

She patted the top of his hand with her other one. "Finish your breakfast. You need the protein to help regain your strength. Afterwards, we need to talk about what you're going to do after this."

He blanched slightly at the thought but nodded once and withdrew his hand. What would he do? Would she make him go with her? Would he be forced to return to his previous life? He shuddered but didn't say another word. He just turned back to his breakfast and resumed eating.

Twenty

Lucas stormed into Byte close to three am in a foul mood. The entire situation in Riverside had aggravated him, but driving home with Keira's blood smeared in his car had flustered him. If it had just been the dragon's blood in his car, he would have been fine, but he craved his shapeshifter's blood more than he cared to admit.

Thankfully the club had already been cleared out, leaving the main floor mostly empty. The last of his employees were leaving, having just finished up cleaning. He gave them a single nod of acknowledgement and ignored the curious looks at the blood stains on him.

"Mr Vranas," Lucy called as she stepped out from behind the bar after clocking out, purse in hand. "Are you okay?"

"Yes, Miss Rhodes." He replied coolly and headed to the stairs.

"Where's Kee?" She asked with a small frown and followed him. "That blood isn't all yours, is it?"

He stopped on a stair and turned to face her, his irritation rising. "She is at her Nana's house with her new pet. And no, it is not just mine."

"Do you require a bleeder?" Dante asked, suddenly appearing at Lucy's side. He smirked when she jumped in surprise. "We have a few humans who lingered behind for a bite."

"Yes," Lucas answered Dante then looked back at the concerned werefox. "Keira is fine. So long as her pet controls himself, she should survive."

She tightened the grip on the strap of her purse. "What does that mean?"

"Exactly as it sounds," he retorted shortly.

She narrowed her eyes at him. "If she was in danger, why didn't you stay to help?"

He titled his head ever so slightly at her. He was already frustrated and angry at the situation, he didn't need his employee making it worse. "Are you saying Keira cannot defend herself? Do you think my bonded wolf, *your* friend, is so weak?"

Lucy stepped back as if he had struck her. "No, of course not," she swallowed her trepidation and straightened her spine defiantly. "I just thought you would want to help the woman you love."

Every muscle in his body tensed at that last word. His eyes narrowed at her in a menacing glare, the green taking on a hue of crimson. "You had best watch what you say, little fox."

"Don't threaten her." Conrad growled as he came across the second story and down the stairs. He stopped on the stair in front of the vampire, amber eyes hard.

Lucas ground his teeth, lips pressing hard together as his fury grew. "Do not presume to tell me what to do, wolf. Your alpha is not here to protect you from me." Feeling bitter, he threw some salt in Conrad's wound. "But then again, I suppose she is not your alpha anymore, is she?"

Conrad blanched, the color leaving his face for a second before it blotched red with anger. "Where is Kee?"

"At her Nana's with her *new* pet. Perhaps she is finding a replacement for you." Lucas shrugged before storming past the hurt werewolf. He stopped when he got to the top of the stairs and looked down at the stunned werefox. "To answer your question, Miss Rhodes, I had to come back to handle a personal issue that involves my vampires. Also, as you know since you went there, Keira's guardian does not have a safe place for vampires to sleep while the sun is up. Love makes you foolish, and I am anything but that. Remember that before throwing around useless accusations and assumptions."

Conrad balled his hands tightly into fists, knuckles turning white. "Is she coming home tonight? Can you at least tell me that?"

"No." He replied as he walked towards his office.

"No to what?!" He shouted after him.

"Figure it out." He snipped before slamming the door shut to his office. He sank down in his office chair and buried his head in his hands. He let out a frustrated groan and rubbed his face.

He *could* not love Keira. He would not dare do so. Yes, he found her company soothing and being around her usually lightened his mood, but it wasn't love. It couldn't be. If people thought he loved her, then he had been foolish. He would have to pull away and immediately put emotional distance between them.

Dante knocked softly on the door before opening it. "I brought you a first timer, Lord Lucas." He announced with a grin.

A nervous, tan skinned woman was on his arm, teeth biting her full bottom lip. "H-hello." She greeted shyly.

Lucas tried to shove down his anger as he stood from his chair and walked towards her. "Good evening," he greeted with forced charm. He saw her eyes fall to the blood that stained most of his shirt and could almost taste her fear. "Is this correct? This is your first time being bitten by a vampire?"

She nodded once and swallowed audibly. "Yeah, I always wanted to try it though." She took a small step back when he moved closer to her. "Your shirt..."

He gave her a pleasant smile. "I have had a long night." He lightly touched her chin and tried not to smirk when she flinched. "Are you frightened?"

"Yes." She squeaked. She panicked when Dante untangled her from his arm, her hands grabbing for his sleeve.

"Don't worry, Lucas only hurts people who deserve it. Isn't that right, my lord?" He mused as he pried her fingers from his sleeve and put her hand in Lucas. "He'll take real good care of you."

She looked at Lucas, taking in his handsome face and welcoming smile. "If you're sure."

"I am quite sure. I will bring you nothing but pleasure with my fangs, I give you my word." Lucas said as he drew her closer, his hand sliding into her short, curly black hair. "Are you ready?"

She hummed in her throat when his fingers massaged her scalp. She followed his hand, eventually craning her head to the side so the right side of her neck was exposed to him. She could feel his cool breath brush across her suddenly sensitive skin. He repeated the question and she had trouble finding her words. "Y-Yes, please."

He ran his tongue over the spot on her neck he would bite, spreading the endorphins from his fangs on her flesh. When she writhed at the touch, he sunk his fangs in. He tried to drown out her groan as he drew out her blood. Her eyes closed, a moan escaping her lips with each hard pull of his mouth.

He closed his eyes as well, images of Keira suddenly filling his head. When his prey gave another moan, he imagined his shapeshifter naked on his bed under him. Her head was tossed back in ecstasy, pink lips parted as she panted and breathed his name. He could feel her legs over his hips as he bent down to her exposed neck. He kissed the spot there and opened his mouth wide, fangs brushing against her soft creamy skin. He could feel her nails biting into his shoulders as he bit her and quickly opened his eyes.

Disappointment hit him hard when he realized it was the petite Hispanic woman in his arms. She was clawing at his back, trying to draw him in closer to her body. Disgusted with his fantasy, he withdrew his fangs from her and didn't bother to lick up the mess. When she cried in protest and tried to pull him back, he retreated a few quick steps.

"Done already?" Dante asked lightly, but there was a stern edge to it.

Lucas wiped his mouth in frustration. "Yes, my mind is elsewhere."

"Do you want me to bring you someone else?" He offered as the woman sauntered up to him instead, asking him to bite her. He let her hang on to him, but his milk chocolate eyes focused on his lord. "Or, perhaps you thirst for something more...*wolfish*?"

Lucas shot him a glare. "Do not start with me, Dante."

He shook his head and wrapped his arm around the human's waist when she pressed her lips to his neck. "Giovanni is not here to be your reason so I'm standing in. There is nothing wrong with opening your heart. Even the undead need love. How long has it been?"

"Stop," he seethed furiously. "Do not say that. You have no idea what will happen, Dante. *I do.* I know what will happen and I cannot risk it."

He raised his free hand in mock surrender. "You're right, I don't know, but you better watch yourself. I have grown to like Kee. She doesn't deserve to have her heart broken."

"There is no love between us." Lucas could feel his patience slipping, but Dante's words hit him in the stomach. "It is purely physical."

Dante actually laughed, his fangs gleaming in the dim office light. "I hope you think of something better than that to tell her." Knowing his lord had reached his limit, he led the human out the door. "See you tomorrow." He called over his shoulder before shutting the door behind him.

Lucas stood there fuming, his jaw and hands clenched. He needed to hit something and just barely resisted smashing his new desk to pieces. He took a few deep calming breaths. Now was not the time to succumb to his fury. He had to focus on finding Jada and Alexander.

He let out a curse when he realized he didn't tell Dante what he learned at The Top. He was certain Jada was working with Alexander and that she had Giovanni.

He quickly threw open the door and poked his head out, "Dante!"

—

"What do you mean, she's not coming back tonight?" Zachary asked angrily, his hands balled into fists.

"She's at her Nana's house for the night," Conrad replied calmly. "I'd say we can stay and wait for her, but your father already demanded we come back an hour ago. He's going to be pissed when we come back so late."

He threw his hands up. "This might be the only time I can meet my sister!"

"Don't be dramatic, you'll see her." He assured him and carefully lifted Mia into his arms, her head lolling against his shoulder.

"Why isn't she coming home?" He asked, lips pressed together in a pout.

"My guess is that she saved someone and is taking care of them." Conrad answered as he headed to the door, Zachary following close behind. "At least, that's what I gathered from what Lucas said."

That fucking bastard, his wolf growled in agreement. *What the hell had him so angry?*

"What if you're wrong?" Zach pressed with a frown. "What if dad decides it's time to go home already?"

"I have a feeling Liam isn't going to leave until this mess with the LA pack is fixed." He answered as they traveled down the flights of stairs until they reached the main floor. He trekked through the kitchen and out the back door, heading to the parking lot where Lucy was waiting for them.

"Con!" Lucy called as she hurried over to him. When she got to the trio, she took in the mini-Conrad in his arms and smiled.

"Hey, let me buckle her in real quick." He said as he opened the back door and set Mia down in her booster seat. He fastened her seatbelt and pressed a kiss to her cheek before closing the door.

Lucy watched as the little girl curled on her side, her head resting against the window. She beamed up at Conrad when he looked at her. "She's really cute." She complimented.

His chest warmed in pride. "Thank you. You need to meet her when she's awake. She's too smart for her own good." He took Lucy's hand in his and pulled her closer, their bodies nearly touching. "I have to go." He said with a regretful sigh.

"I know," she murmured, cheeks red at their closeness. If her body reacted this intensely from just being close to him after kissing him, she couldn't imagine what would happen in the bedroom. Her face burned with embarrassment at the thought.

Conrad's breath hitched when the very faint scent of her arousal hit his nose. He resisted the urge to pull her flush against his body and instead settled for placing a firm kiss on her lips. "I'll be back." He told her after they parted.

"Promise?" She asked, hands resting on his chest.

"Yeah, I need to talk to Kee about everything. I have to tell her what I told you." His eyes hooded with shame. "I just hope she will hear me out. That she'll forgive me."

She cupped his cheek. "Don't let Lucas' words get to you. He was being an asshole tonight and you know it. Kee loves you. You two have a bond I can't even put into words. Just explain it to her, okay?"

He nodded once but was still uncertain. "What if she did replace me?"

"You can't be replaced, Con. She knows that. She's doing what she does best: helping people. Maybe she'll bring home a new pack mate for us." She said with a sly smile.

His head perked up. "*Us?*"

Lucy smiled at him. "Us."

Zachary dramatically cleared his throat and shot them a cool stare. When they looked at him with sheepish smiles, he introduced himself. "Hi, I'm Zach."

Lucy stepped away from Conrad and waved. "Lucy."

"So, you're also a part of my sister's pack? But, you're not a wolf." He accused.

She tucked a strand of hair behind her ear. "No, I'm a fox." Her eyes widened. "Wait, *sister?*"

"Yeah, Kee is my half-sister. And you're a werefox? That's cool. I've only met one before. Claremont doesn't have a skulk." He explained.

She was still staring at him with a shocked expression. She turned back to Conrad. "Does Kee know about him?"

"No. I planned on telling her everything tonight, but she's not here." He sighed and ran his hand through his hair. "It's going to be a lot for her to take in."

Zach's phone started to ring, and he paled when he saw the name on the screen. "It's dad."

"Fuck," Conrad cursed then pressed another kiss to Lucy's lips. "I'll try to keep you updated, okay? Just...have faith in me."

"I will. Do you want me to warm Kee up to everything if I see her before you?" She offered.

"That might be helpful. Can you also give her these keys? I forgot I had them yesterday." He handed her the pair of Jeep keys. After she took them, he opened the door to the Mercedes and slipped in. He then waved goodbye and pulled out of the parking lot, heading back to the Marriot.

Twelve minutes later, the trio opened the door to Liam's suite. Conrad's eyes instantly went to Liam, taking in his tense, fuming frame as he sat on the couch. His amber eyes then drifted to the bed where Natalie lay, her tired gaze on him as they entered.

"I told you to be here an hour ago." Liam said coldly.

"It's my fault, dad," Zach protested as he stepped forward. "I wanted to stay out."

The alpha detected no lie in his son's response and it made him marginally relax. "And why was that?"

Zachary swallowed once but met his father's stare. "I wanted to meet my sister."

Liam stood abruptly from the couch, hands balling into fists at his side. "You have no sister."

"You're lying! Why is it so wrong to admit that you have a daughter? That I have a sibling? It's all I wanted!" He shouted angrily.

Mia had roused from the yelling, her arms looping around her father's neck before she pressed her face there. "I don't like fighting," she murmured. "Please, stop."

Liam bit back his shout at Emilia's soft cry. He took a deep breath and flared his nostrils as he tried to find Kee's scent. "Did you see her?"

"No," Zach frowned with disappointment. "She's out for the night."

"Have you talked to Kee at all, Conrad?" Nat asked softly as she moved into a sitting position.

Conrad thought she had looked tired because they woke her up, but he could see now that she looked drained more than anything. Dark circles were under her red-rimmed eyes, her eyelids hooded with fatigue.

"No, I haven't," he answered. "Are you okay?"

Liam's lip twitched into a snarl when Conrad shot him an accusing glance. "I've done nothing to her. Warren's mental health is deteriorating and it's affecting her through their bond."

Natalie gripped a handful of blankets tightly in her fists. "Cain is getting stronger."

Conrad pet Mia's hair as she sighed tiredly. "I've noticed it, too."

"Being upset and anxious is common for an alpha when a wolf begins to rise in the pack, but not like this, Natalie. His wolf simmering on the surface and lashing out at you is not normal." Liam pointed out.

"But, with the three deaths in the pack..." She protested.

"Three deaths in the pack and a challenge for alpha may put them on edge, but not to this extent." He argued.

"Wait, a challenge?" Conrad asked in surprise.

Nat nodded gravely. "Cain declared it tonight."

Zach's brows rose. "When is it supposed to be? The next full moon isn't for two weeks."

"Cain doesn't want to wait that long," Natalie whispered worriedly. "Liam agrees that the sooner the better."

Conrad shifted Mia's weight. "How do you feel about that, Nat?"

She looked down at her hands. "I'm torn, Conrad. I don't know what to do anymore. He's been falling apart since Wyatt's death, and that was over a month ago. I know each death made it worse, but there's something more to it. Maybe Warren not being alpha is for the better."

"For him or for the pack?"

"Both," she murmured and put her hands on her stomach. "And for our pup."

Conrad gaped at her. "What? You're pregnant?"

She nodded once. "I held back my shift last full moon, and so far, everything is okay. I didn't want anyone in the pack to question me so I told them I wasn't feeling well."

"How far along are you?"

She shrugged. "I'm not sure. The last full moon was two weeks ago, and before that was four, so that leaves me just barely at six weeks." She swallowed. "Unless I was pregnant during the shift before that and it was too small for my body to harm it."

"It's possible," Liam commented. "You could have gotten pregnant somewhere between the full moons of September and October."

She pressed her face in her hands. "I have a doctor's appointment tomorrow."

"I'm going with her," Liam added then lowered his tone. "If Cain wins the alpha challenge, he has every right to kill Warren."

Conrad bristled. Warren had been the cause of all the negativity in Cain's life as of late. Death of his pack mates, death of his best friend, and his break-up with Kee. All of it led to the command that he couldn't mate her even if they rekindled. It was Warren's fault. "He has every reason to." He mumbled.

"I know." Nat cried, tears filling her eyes. "And I have no right whatsoever to ask him otherwise." She sniffled and noticed Conrad shifting Mia in his arms again. "Mia can sleep with me, if you're okay with that." She offered softly as she scooted over and patted the bed next to her.

"Thank you." He said as he walked closer to the bed.

Mia held tight to her dad when he moved to set her down. "Don't leave me." She whispered.

He hugged her tightly at the plea in her tone. "Baby girl, I'll never leave you again," he told her firmly. "You slept in my bed without me there and everything was fine, remember? You need to sleep and I'll be right here."

She shook her head. "That's because it smelled like you," she admitted in a small voice. "Nothing here has your scent."

He gave a small, sad smile before he kissed her head. "Alright,

Mia. I'll find a place for us to both sleep." When she nodded into his neck, he shot a pointed look at Liam before looking at Natalie. "Pups need their fathers, Nat."

"And women need their mate to help resist future shifts," Zachary added when Liam glared at Conrad. "Maybe Cain will understand that."

"Maybe." She said softly then sunk back down so she was flat on the bed. She didn't want to think about it anymore. "I'm going to try to sleep."

Zach clamped Conrad on the shoulder. "You can sleep on the bed with Mia in my room. I'll take the couch. Dad will stay here with Natalie." He looked at his dad for conformation. When Liam waved a hand at them, he led the father and daughter to the door.

"Zachary, you will not leave this premises without my approval. No more hunting for your sister." Liam told him before they walked out the door.

His face fell in disappointment. "Yes, sir." He growled bitterly and all but slammed the door behind him.

Twenty-One

"You look horrible. When was the last time you actually slept?" Nana asked her great-granddaughter in a strict mom tone. The two of them were sitting at the dining room table, waiting for Samson to finish getting dressed upstairs.

Kee blinked at the question as she sipped her third cup of coffee. She pursed her lips and looked up at the ceiling in thought. "Tuesday night, I guess, but even then, it was restless with three people in the bed." She responded. "And when I do sleep, I have nightmares."

Nana frowned at her. "What are these nightmares about?"

Kee frowned down at her bandaged hands and forearm. She looked like a mummy. "Mom and Liam," she answered and tightened her hold on the mug. "I saw him yesterday."

Nana touched Kee's uninjured wrist in concern. "Are you alright?"

She sucked in a breath. "I don't know," she admitted. "I couldn't do anything. I froze in fear, Nan."

"I see." Nana replied without judgement. "Is there a chance you will run into him again?"

"Yeah, I feel it in my bones," she responded and lifted the top of her lip in a sneer. "I won't freeze next time."

Nans stared at her. "Kee, it's okay that you were frightened."

Kee narrowed her eyes. "No, it's not. I'm not the same little girl. I'm stronger now, I can defend myself."

"Why is Liam in Los Angeles?" Nana asked.

"He's the LA County alpha." She shrugged. "I don't really know why he's here now, but my guess is because of what's going on with the pack. It's a mess." She then gave a soft snort. "Or, he came to take Conrad back."

"Your beta?"

"Mhm, turns out he was part of Liam's pack all along. Silly me." Sarcasm dripped from her tone.

Nan pursed her lips together. "That doesn't seem right. He's loyal to you. It was obvious."

"It is what it is." She replied coldly.

"You know how your father is. There has to be more than what you think is happening." Nana commented then looked up when Samson quietly walked into the room.

He wore her deceased mate's clothes, the dark blue jeans and white button up shirt the only things she could find that weren't terribly outdated. His black hair was clean and hung like a curtain below his right ear. The hair from his left temple down to his neck was short, but Nana thought that it had probably been shaved that way at one point. The dirt and blood had been washed away, revealing lightly tanned skin. With the exception of the bandages, dark circles under his eyes, and the fact that he was still too thin, he looked a lot better.

"The clothes fit." Nana commented.

He nodded. "They do. Thank you." He said as he ran his hand through the long side of his hair. It was still a little damp, but would dry straight. He looked over at Kee and couldn't help but stare at the white scars that were visible above the neckline of her tank top.

"This is the fourth time you've looked at them," Kee mused as she caught his gaze. "I know my scars are more impressive than my B-cups, but I'm going to start charging you." She laughed when his cheeks turned red.

"I'm sorry," he muttered but didn't look away. "How far down do they go?"

She would give him credit for his blunt forwardness. "To the opposite hip."

Samson's brow furrowed. "Are they claw marks?"

"Yep," she leaned back with her cup, balancing the chair on the back two legs. "Werewolf claws to be exact."

His black eyes shot to Nana before flicking back to Kee. "Shapeshifters don't heal like wereanimals do."

"Correct." Feeling Nan's disapproving look, she set the chair down. "Although I noticed I heal a little faster since blood bonding with Lucas." She admitted.

"Your boyfriend?" His eyes widened slightly. "You're really the bonded wolf of the Lord of Los Angeles?"

"Yep."

"But you're not a wolf."

She smiled ruefully at him. "Funny, isn't it?"

He rubbed his temples. "I don't understand."

"Sam, shapeshifters are supposed to be extinct. They were wiped out 200 years ago and are still a taboo subject. With the exception of the past month or two, only four people knew what I was. And two of them I'm related to." The smile was replaced with a serious frown. "You bring my count to seven. Only people I trust know my secret."

Samson met her gaze without flinching. "How do you know you can trust me?"

"I don't and I'm honestly a little miffed that you know about it when I wasn't the one who told you," she shot back. "So, I'm asking *if* I can trust you."

"You said I don't owe you anything for saving me."

"You don't."

His brow furrowed slightly as he stared at her, trying to figure her out. He released a sigh when she gave nothing away. "I won't tell your secret on two conditions."

Kee set her cup down and steepled her fingers. "Let's hear them."

"First, I don't want you to shift into me without my approval." He began.

That surprised her. "Let's get some clarification. What are you restricting me from? Copying your human image or your dragon one?" She decided not to go into detail about actually becoming him. She didn't have any of his DNA in her anyways.

He thought about it. "Not my dragon image, for sure. I guess if you have to, you can use my human image, but I would prefer you didn't."

Again, she was surprised by his answer. "I accept that," she said. "How about the second?"

Samson's jaw ticked. "Let me stay with you. I want to be part of your pack."

Her lips parted in shock. "I wasn't expecting that."

"Is that a no?" He asked it quietly, but there was a bite in his tone.

"I didn't say that," she defended calmly. "I'm just curious as to why you would want to."

"You're a shapeshifter. You can technically be anyone's alpha, and I would like you to be mine. You rescued and took care of me even after I yelled at you," he glanced down at the floor. "After I hurt you."

"As I said last night, I'm not really an alpha. I don't have a pack as of right now. I had a beta, but things aren't going well between us. I have an open invitation to a werefox, but she hasn't responded."

He crossed his arms over his chest and leaned against the wall. "So, what are you trying to say?"

"That even if we were all together, I have a small pack. However, we are really close," Kee explained. "I don't know you and I can't vouch that you won't cause a disturbance."

"But as of right now I would be your only pack member." He pointed out.

She pursed her lips. "You got me there."

"I'm fairly simple, Kee. I do what I think is right and observe when I think something is wrong. If it's really bad, I may step in. I've been called stoic, but I prefer calculative." He cracked his knuckles nervously. "But I'm loyal until you give me a reason not to be. If you take me into your pack, I'll be loyal to you and the other pack mates. I take oaths seriously. All dragons do."

Kee couldn't help but smile at him. "You *are* very straight forward, aren't you?"

Samson shrugged. "No point beating around the bush."

"Before I answer, can I ask why you don't want to go back to where you were before The Top?" She asked. "Surely you had a life before you were in a cage."

Samson looked away from her. "I did. Are you familiar with Muir Woods?"

"That's about seven hours north of Los Angeles, by San Francisco," Nana commented. "It's one of the only homes for the forest folk in California."

"You mean the elves and trolls and whatnot?" Kee asked.

"Fae and dragons, too," Samson added. "Dragons are the only wereanimal that are allowed to live with the forest folk."

"Why is that?" Nana asked. The last time she saw a dragon shifter had been in Ireland right after the shapeshifter hunt.

"We're more in-tuned with nature and most of us have an affinity for an element." He explained. "We're the first defense if someone attacks the forest folk."

"And you don't want to go back to that?" Kee guessed.

"No. We fall under the ruling of the elves despite having an alpha dragon." He scratched the short side of his head as he thought about the people he used to care about. "So, what they decree is law. Let's just say I stuck my snout where it didn't belong and I ended up in The Top."

"So, you *can't* go back?" Kee asked softly.

"It's probably not a good idea. If I do, there's a good chance I'll end up back where you found me." He sighed and shrugged off the topic. "If you're worried I'll ruin what little bonds you have, I'll figure something else out."

"Quit putting words in my mouth," she snapped. "I didn't say no."

"Then what do you say?"

She stood from the table and picked up her empty coffee cup. "That we'll play it by ear for now. You can come back with me to LA and we'll see how it pans out."

He blinked and followed her as she went to the kitchen to put the cup in the sink. "Seriously?"

She couldn't tell if he had asked it in disbelief or irritation. "Yeah, unless you changed your mind?"

"No, I'm just surprised. Where am I supposed to stay?" Samson asked.

"You'll stay at Byte with me until I find an apartment. I was hunting for one with my beta, but maybe it's better if I rent a house," she said as she turned to look at him. "But first, I have to do a job for Lucas. I have to get information about a missing person. Do you want to come with me?"

"Will it be dangerous?"

She thought about going to Warren's yesterday. "Potentially."

"I'm in." He followed her to the entryway of the house where Nana was waiting for them. "I can prove my loyalty to you."

Kee was about to argue with him but chose not to. *Honestly, I'm happy he's coming with me to Warren's. I may need the support if Liam is there.* Her eyes hardened. *This time I'll fucking kill him.*

Samson watched her expression turn hostile, the grey of her eyes darkening with anger. "Is that rage directed at me?"

She straightened her spine. "No, it's not. Sorry. My mind wandered."

"I was raised to fight, to be a soldier. I can help you fight whatever that anger is for," he offered earnestly. He refrained from adding, *it's the least I can do.*

"Thanks for the offer, but it's something I have to handle alone." She said and then turned to Nana when the older shapeshifter huffed at her.

"A pack exists to help one another. They give their alpha strength, and the alpha does the same in return. Don't be foolish and face Liam alone if you can't handle it. It would be a mistake that you may not live to regret." Nana scolded as she pulled Kee into a hug.

Kee sighed as she hugged Nana back. "We'll see." She pulled away and gave her a grateful smile. "Thank you for taking care of us. I'm sorry we bombarded you without any notice."

Nana waved a hand, dismissing her apology. "When John was alive, nightly visits with wounded werewolves were expected. It was nice to feel the adrenaline of it again."

Samson awkwardly hesitated before he stepped closer to Nana and gave a small bow. "Thank you again for taking care of me."

Nana patted his head. "If it all works out, I expect to see you at Christmas with the rest of the pack." She narrowed her eyes at him when he straightened and pointed a finger at him. "Don't disappoint me."

He flushed and nodded. "Yes, ma'am."

"Good boy," she praised then waved her hand again. "Go on. I have things to do today."

"Didn't Lucas drive? How are we getting to LA?" Samson questioned as they exited the house and stepped off the porch.

"Lucy's picking us up," Kee replied with a smile as they headed towards the sidewalk. She was still surprised that Nana had the fox's number. She must have liked Lucy more than she thought. It made Kee's smile widen. "She's the werefox I was telling you about."

"Okay," he said simply, and they stood in comfortable silence until a red Kia Optima pulled along the curb. He waited until Kee moved towards the passenger door before getting into the back.

Lucy was about to turn around and introduce herself to the newcomer, but she stilled when she saw all of Kee's bandages. "Studying ancient Egypt?" She teased but couldn't keep the concern out of her expression.

Kee gave a reassuring smile. "Just got in a fight with some silver." She gestured at the backseat. "Lucy, this is Samson. Sam, this is Lucy."

"Hello." He said as he buckled himself in.

"Hey," Lucy replied as she turned to look at him. She frowned when she saw bandages through the white dress shirt. "Did you also get in a fight with some silver?"

"You could say that," he answered evasively.

She pursed her lips together at him in a scrutinizing look. "Did you two get in a fight? Lucas said that as long as you behaved yourself, she would survive. I may have to kick you out if you say yes."

His brow furrowed and he looked away. "I regained control."

Kee turned and looked at him. "Sam, it's okay. I don't blame you. You gave me a few scratches, but I'm the one who cut my wrist."

"I sunk my claws into your forearm like it was a pincushion." He murmured.

"As you saw, I'm no stranger to claws." A few weeks ago and that statement would have given her painful flashbacks. She looked at

Lucy again. "Remember what I told you guys about The Top? He was the dragon."

Lucy gasped as she looked him over a second time. "Holy shit. Kee told us about what was happening there. I'm glad you made it out alive."

He was startled to hear the genuine tone. "It's only because of Kee and Lucas."

"Speaking of that dickhead!" Lucy suddenly shouted and turned to Kee with an accusing finger. "What the fuck happened between you two?"

"What?" Kee held her hands up in defense when Lucy poked her in the chest.

"He came back to Byte in a *mood*, Kee. Like, he was furious. He lashed out at everyone, including Conrad. It was bad." She informed her as she put the car in drive and began to head back towards the 60 freeway.

Her brows knit together. "I knew he was irritated about having to leave when Sam wasn't in complete control yet, but to yell at everyone?" She frowned. "What did he say to Conrad?"

"That you weren't his alpha anymore and that you were replacing him." Lucy clenched the steering wheel. "It really hurt him."

Kee sighed and ran her gauzed hand down her face. She still felt the sting of betrayal from the wolf, but a part of her was upset that Lucas had attacked him. "Why was Con even there?"

"To talk to you, of course. He has a lot he has to tell you, Kee." She glanced over at her friend. "Do you know who Mia is?"

"Do you?" Kee countered.

"Yes, and she's beautiful. You should see the way he's with her. It's like she's his everything."

She stared at her in shock. "And that doesn't bother you?" *Was I completely off about how Lucy felt about Conrad?*

"No way! She's a mini-Conrad, you wouldn't even believe it." She commented with a wide smile.

This time her lips parted in disbelief. "Wait, *what?*"

Twenty-Two

"Just think about what I said, okay?" Lucy asked as she pulled the car to a stop.

Kee sighed as her mind whirled with what Lucy had told her. She hadn't gone into details about Conrad's situation but had given her enough to get a general idea. "I will. Thank you for the ride." She replied before getting out of the car.

Samson got out after Kee and thanked Lucy before closing the door. He watched as Kee rubbed the bridge of her nose and tilted his head. "You okay?"

"Yeah, it was just a lot to take in," she explained and looked at Warren's driveway. The Jeep was still there, but no other cars were visible. No Liam. She tried to ignore the flutter of relief she felt. She felt Samson behind her as she moved towards the front door. She knocked once and opened it when she didn't get a response.

Samson was on alert as he followed her into the house. His eyes narrowed at the chaotic state of the living room. The couches were torn and knocked aside, the coffee table broken in pieces next to the shattered TV. He heard a loud growl and resisted the urge to step in front of Kee at the threat.

"What the fuck are *you* doing here?" Warren snarled as he stalked out of the bedroom, his body tense with taught muscles. Hostility radiated off of the alpha in almost tangible waves.

"I have a few questions for you." Kee answered calmly as she met his glare.

He bared his teeth at her. "Fuck you. You're the cause of all this! I've lost everything because of you!"

She actually laughed. "*I'm* the reason? I'm not the one who ordered your pack to attack me."

He narrowed his ice blue eyes at her. "You think I ordered it because I wanted to?"

No denial, she mused.

"Maybe you did it because I refused to fuck you," she shrugged. "Or, maybe you did it to help your vampire friend."

He balled his hands into fists. "You know nothing." His voice was rough with a growl.

"I know you're bonded to Alexander." Kee shot back and smirked when the muscle in his jaw ticked. "So, it's true."

"Nothing would have happened to you if you weren't associated with Lucas!" He spat angrily and closed the space between them with four quick steps. "This is *your* fault! Cain growing in power, my dead brother, my dead pack mates, Nat leaving, Liam coming here, everything! My wolf is almost always in control," he tapped his temple. "Always here and fighting any rational thoughts. Did you know I hurt my mate because of you? Struck her? I didn't even know I did it until afterwards! I'm losing lapses of time! I'm losing control and it's *your* fault! This is why your kind was slaughtered! You cause nothing but trouble!"

She held her hand out to stop Samson from interfering. How did he know what she was? She scowled when she remembered Noah. Of course, he told his precious alpha. He probably bragged about killing her.

She stared up at Warren as he sneered, not cringing under his gaze as his aura pulsed around her. The dominant alpha power barely affected her. He wasn't any more dominant than she was and didn't even compare to Liam.

"Does blaming me make you feel better?" She mocked.

"I won't be better until you're dead." He sneered

Kee tilted her head at him in a mocking manner. "You sent three of your wolves to kill me and look how that panned out. Do you really want to try, too?"

His hackles rose, and he snarled so loud it shook his body. "*You?*" He growled. "You killed my pack? A fucking shapeshifter?!"

"Kee," Samson warned as the wolf's energy rippled and contorted. "Careful."

She didn't flinch as Warren shifted into his hybrid wolf form, black fur spurting across his body. "Yes, *me*. Maybe I should thank you, Warren. If you hadn't sent your wolves after me, I wouldn't be the ruthless bitch I am now. You think you can kill me? You missed your chance and you won't get another." She hissed as she continued to hold his stare.

Warren snarled at the challenge and Kee leapt back as he swung at her, narrowly missing his massive paw. She quickly slid into a defensive position when he let out a furious howl. Warren lunged at her, but Samson intercepted. He threw his lithe body at the werewolf, knocking him away from Kee. The two tumbled into one of the torn couches in a flurry of limbs.

Samson grabbed a handful of scruff on the side of Warren's face to keep the snapping jaws away from his throat while his other hand delivered a quick, hard punch to Warren's diaphragm. Warren hacked out a breath and kicked his opponent off of him. Samson landed on his feet, wincing as his wounds were jarred. He didn't have time to fret about them because as soon as he touched the ground, the alpha was on him. Warren knocked him back and pinned him by the shoulders to the glass ridden floor.

Kee wasted no time jumping onto Warren's broad, furry back. She jabbed her fist as hard as she could to where she hoped his kidney was. Sometimes she wasn't quite sure where internal organs ventured when wereanimals shifted. She must have gotten somewhere close because Warren howled and released one of Samson's shoulders to grab at her. She ducked out of reach of his claws and grabbed his massive forearm instead. She pulled it backwards across his back, making his body turn towards the movement.

Seeing the strain in Warren's arm, Samson grabbed the werewolf's shoulder and yanked it forward in the opposite direction Kee was pulling. With a sickening, hollow pop, Warren's arm dislocated from his socket. Samson threw his free elbow up at the furry neck and rolled out from under him. He sprang back up onto his feet, standing next to Kee when she let go of Warren. He reached out to steady her when her wounded leg buckled.

Warren hacked as he clumsily got to his canine shaped feet. His right arm hung uselessly at his side as he sneered at them. His beast told him to attack, urged him to tear them both to pieces, but the diminishing, rational side of him whispered to think again. She was a shapeshifter and she had yet to shift into anything. He had no way of knowing what she would become. And the man? He was a wereanimal, he was sure, but not a wolf. That alone made him a danger. His arm was hurt and both of his opponents were unknowns.

When Kee was sure the pain in her calf wouldn't make her knee give out again, she gently pulled her arm free of Samson's hold. "Don't be stupid, Warren. There's two of us, and we already proved we can overtake you." She said when she practically saw the wheels turning in his head.

"I see what this is," Warren snarled, his voice thick and gravely from the pain. "Cain sent you here. He knows I'll kill you. He wants the rage of your death as a power source for the challenge. No, I won't give him what he wants. When I kill him, I'll go after you next. Then I'll get revenge for my pack! For my brother! For my mate!"

Challenge? "Cain didn't send me here. I came here for answers," she replied dismissively. "And in case you weren't paying attention, we just kicked your ass."

"Get the fuck out of here before I give him what he wants." He growled as if he hadn't heard her.

"Answer my questions and we will." She crossed her arms across her chest. "Who told you about my connection to Lucas?"

"Wyatt," he snapped in a harsh tone. "He saw you at the gun range and wanted to kill you right then and there. I should have let him." He let out a sarcastic snort. "Tell me, what's better? A dead dick or a live one?

"They both have their perks," she admitted without missing a beat. She wasn't going to let him bait her. "Where is Alexander?"

He sneered at her. "Do you think I would tell you if I knew?"

"Oh, I know you know. You're bonded to him. I know how blood bonds work. He took two people who belong to Lucas and I need to find them. Where is he?" She pressed.

"Good, I hope he experiences the same loss I feel!" Warren sneered and flexed his claws. "And you'll feel it too when I kill Cain!"

Kee pretended not to hear anything he said about Cain. "How good are you at getting information out of people?" She asked casually as she looked at Samson. "I mean, we already dislocated his shoulder. Shouldn't be too hard, right?"

"I'm very good at it. I was raised to be a soldier, remember?" He cracked his knuckles and smirked. "The question is, are you up for a round two?"

She mirrored his smirk. "Always."

Warren bared his teeth and snapped his jaws at them. "You think I'm scared of you? I'm the Alpha of the LA Pack!"

"And I'm a Dragon Guard for Muir Woods," Samson replied and let his fingers shift into black talons.

Uncertainty flickered across Warren's eyes. "Weredragons are extinct."

Kee laughed. "Like shapeshifters are?"

Samson's smirk grew. "You want to take a chance?"

Warren scoffed at them. "This is another test from Cain, I know it. He'll do anything to ruin me! To win! He won't get to me! It's my pack!" He howled, that edge of crazy taking over again. "Mine! Cain can't have it!"

"Have you ever considered that *Alexander* is the reason for all this?" His eyes flickered and Kee could tell she hit a nerve. "Aren't you supposed to be a team? I thought a bond was like a partnership."

"You know nothing." He snapped.

She was correct though; Alexander was also on Warren's shit list. There was no point going along with the vampire's plan if he lost everything because of it. He wanted to kill Alexander for the havoc his plan had created but knew he couldn't do it with their bond. It would try to protect itself. It wouldn't be strong or have an effect like an alpha's order, but he would be tempted to obey. With his beast in his current state, he wasn't sure what would happen.

She sighed and shrugged again. "Tell me where Alexander is and we'll leave." She reminded him.

He forced himself back into his human form, his naked body drenched in sweat from the effort. If Lucas killed Alexander instead it would fix the predicament he had. "He's holed up in the Arcadia coven," he bit out, rubbing his dislocated arm. "He's keeping Lucas' people there as well."

"Where in Arcadia are they?"

His expression hardened again. "Figure it out," he retorted. "And tell your dad that if he hurts my mate in any way, there'll be hell to pay."

Kee snorted and turned around to leave. "Tell him yourself. I don't keep in touch with Liam."

"I mean it, Kee, Natalie is everything to me." He said with a fierce glare.

"Maybe you shouldn't have put your paws on her then." She tossed unsympathetically over her shoulder.

He made a move towards her with a loud growl but stopped when the so-called dragon stepped in his path. He balled his hands into fists. "After I kill Cain, I'm coming for you. I will finish what my pack started."

What is this shit with Cain? She tilted her chin up defiantly. "I look forward to killing another wolf. I know exactly how I'll do it, too."

He sneered at her again. "I'll send you to the grave like the rest of the abominations that were your ancestors."

She laughed and started walking towards the door again. "Good luck, you'll need it."

"Don't die to Alexander, shapeshifter." He called to her as she walked out the door.

Samson kept his eyes on Warren as he followed Kee out the door, not trusting the crazed wolf. Once they were outside, he walked alongside her until they got to the Jeep. He slid into the seat when she did and looked at the watered-down Starbucks cups in the drink holders.

Kee scooted the seat forward so she could reach the pedals before grabbing her phone. She hit the home button and was surprised that it still had some battery life to it. She had a missed call from Lucas and a handful of unread messages from Lucy, Conrad, and Cain from the day before. She ignored Conrad's and read the others. Lucy's had asked if she was okay and where she was, but Kee didn't respond since she had already talked to her. She opened Cain's message and frowned at it.

I issued the challenge for alpha tonight.

Kee immediately tapped on his name to call him.

"*Hello?*" Came the tense greeting.

"Hey, I just got your text." She responded quickly.

"*Oh, I thought maybe you were ignoring me after yesterday.*" He commented with a sigh of relief.

"No, I wouldn't ignore something that important, Cain," she replied softly. She glanced at Samson as she felt him staring at her.

"*That's good to know,*" he mumbled before he raised his voice and yelled at someone on his side of the call. "*Sorry, I'm at a job site.*"

"Do you want me to call you back?" She offered.

"*No, they're just a bunch of idiots that don't know what the fuck they're doing.*" Cain growled in irritation.

She gave a soft laugh. "Ouch."

"*It's true. It's been harder around here without—*"

He broke off, but she knew what he was going to say. "Without Noah," she finished for him in a gentle tone. "You can say his name, Cain. I'm not that much of a bitch."

He was quiet for a moment. "*I never said you were a bitch.*"

A real laugh escaped her lips. "You didn't have to. I know I've changed."

"*You have,*" he agreed, but there was no heat or judgement in the words. "*But I think I have, too. Maybe we both needed to.*"

"Maybe," she drawled. She cleared her throat and changed the subject. "So, when did you start working on Saturdays?"

"*It's a rush job. They're paying us extra to hurry the framework for this building.*" He grumbled. "*And I'm the foreman so I have to be here.*"

"Foreman? Wow, congratulations, Cain. That's great." She said, genuinely happy for him. He was such a hard worker and he deserved it.

"*Thanks.*" She could almost hear the smile in that one word.

She smiled as well and a comfortable silence stretched between them. "So, you challenged Warren for alpha?" She asked quietly.

"*Yeah.*" His tone had turned anxious.

"Are you nervous?"

"*...yeah.*"

She closed her eyes and titled her head back against the seat. "What made you decide to challenge him?"

"*Everything,*" he sighed. "*It was time, Kee. After seeing him try to avoid all my questions with Liam yesterday, it was just the last straw. He's guilty and he knows it. He's the reason I've lost you, Noah, and other pack mates. He hurt Nat and that was it. I don't trust him to not further endanger my pack.*" He let out a soft sigh and lowered his voice. "*I just hope I can beat him.*"

"You can do it, Cain. You're strong and you're *good.*" She told him vehemently. "You will be an amazing alpha. I know it."

"*I would be a better alpha if I had you as my mate by my side,*" he muttered softly. Before she could reply, he continued. "*I know, I know,*" he sighed even though she hadn't responded. "*Can I ask that you be there for the fight?*"

She opened her eyes and glanced at Samson as he continued to watch her. "You think it's a good idea if I go? What about your pack?"

"*This fight is for them, for the future of the pack,*" he told her. "*But if I fail-*" She didn't like the pause he made. "*-well, I want to see you before I die.*"

Her brows drew together in anger. "You're not going to die, Cain. Don't say that!"

"*Kee, I'm not stupid. I need to consider it as a possibility. Plus, you've always given me strength and I could use all I can get for the fight.*" He took in a soft inhale. "*Please don't make me beg.*"

She pursed her lips together. "When is the challenge?"

"*Tomorrow night. It'll be at Warren's,*" he said. "*I have to warn you, Liam will be there.*"

"Gods damn it," she cursed and rubbed her temples. "Cain..."

"*I know,*" he huffed. "*But he's the reining alpha of Los Angeles County so he has to oversee all challenges.*" When she didn't respond, he pleaded, "*Please, Kee.*"

She let out a heavy sigh and, despite all the voices in her head telling her no, gave in. "Alright, I'll be there." She conceded unhappily. "What time?"

"*Sunset. You can meet Katie and me outside. We'll walk in together.*" He said and then added, "*Thank you, Kee. Really. You don't know what this means to me.*"

"I do," she argued. "And you're welcome. I'll see you tomorrow night."

"*See you.*"

She hung up and let her forehead fall to the steering wheel. "I'm such a sucker." She murmured miserably.

"Who's Cain?" Samson asked curiously. "He's clearly someone strong in a pack. The LA pack?"

"Yeah," she said as she started the Jeep and backed out of the driveway. "Cain is my ex-boyfriend and the beta of the LA wolf pack."

He continued to look at her in a calculative manner. "Ex? What happened? Who's Liam?"

She sucked in a breath. *Fuck, I forgot how straightforward he was. I really don't want to tell this story again. How many times would this make in the past three days?*

He tilted his head at her when she glared at the road and didn't say anything. "If you tell me a story, I'll tell you one in return."

She blinked and peeked at him before turning her attention back to the road. "Tempting."

"Tempting enough to get you to agree?"

She gave a small smile. "Yeah, but only if you go first."

"Fair enough," he relented and crossed his legs on the seat. "I wasn't originally from Muir Woods. I was born human in San Jose and lived with my dad until I was ten. When I was thirteen, I went on a trip with my school at Muir. My friend and I went off the marked trail, trying to make our own adventure instead of listening to the boring tour guide. My friend was sure that he knew where we were going, but I found out too late that we had passed into the northern Forest Folk territory."

Even though she wasn't looking at him, he could tell she was listening intently to him. "Before we knew it night had come. It was a full moon, so there was some light, but we were lost. I was terrified, but he kept insisting we were heading in the right direction. A member of the Dragon Guard thought otherwise."

Kee could see where this was going but let him continue.

"The dragon who attacked us killed my friend. He bit me, tried to tear me to pieces with his claws and fangs, but I kicked him right in the eye. I remember being dropped and landing on the ground, but when I woke up, I was lying in a bed of silk sheets." He tilted his head back against the headrest. "Apparently I was deemed worthy of life. Ever since then I've been living in Muir Woods."

She glanced at him from the corner of her eye. "What about your dad?"

He looked at her. "That's the first time someone asked me that question," he told her. "Usually, people ask how I felt."

"I'm curious about how you felt waking up as a dragon shifter, but that wasn't my first question."

He nodded. "My dad died when I was ten. I was in foster care so there was no one to miss me. I was a kid and had just been bitten by a dragon on the full moon; they weren't going to let me leave. Besides, dragons are a tight clan and they're not like other wereanimals."

"You mentioned that before. More in-tuned with nature and the elements," she recited. "So, how *did* you feel being a dragon?"

"I didn't believe it at first. I convinced myself I had dreamed about the dragon killing my friend. I ignored the way the wounds on my body healed too quickly and refused to listen to these people who had kidnapped me. For a month I tried to escape, attempted multiple times to run away through the forest, but they caught me each time. Sometimes it took them a day or two, but they always found me.

"Finally, on the next full moon, I was forced to come to terms with it when my body turned into a red and black dragon. It was hard to swallow at first, but it's not like I could have cured myself. So, I told myself that I would make the best of it." He opened his eyes. "I shifted as frequently as my body allowed so I could control the change better. I talked to my beast, came to terms with him so that we were more in sync than others. Because of that I learned to fly and wield my flame within the first couple of changes. Nathan, the alpha of the dragons, noticed my dedication. Next thing I knew I was training to be a soldier for the guard."

Kee shot him a look as she pulled into Byte's back lot. "How long ago were you infected?"

He shrugged. "I'm twenty-three now so about ten years."

"Do you resent them?"

Again, her question caught him off guard. "I did at first, then didn't, and now I do again," he admitted. "I didn't have a family, Kee. My dad died when I was ten and my mom died years before that. After a year, I thought I finally found a family. Not just with the other dragons, but the other people living there. I made friends and allies wherever I could. Elves, fae, centaurs, etcetera."

"I see," she commented softly.

He ran his hand through the long part of his hair. "I rose through the ranks of the Dragon Guard faster than most. I was entrusted with the job of protecting one of the elder's daughters after she was kidnapped." He let out a sigh as he remembered Bay with her black hair and wide, innocent cerulean colored eyes. He briefly wondered who was protecting her in his stead. They would have their hands full, of that he had no doubt.

"Then I caught wind of something bad going on in parliament. As I said earlier, I stuck my snout in it and was accused of treachery. Elder Creal told me he was banishing me, but instead of being escorted out, I was shoved into the Ringmaster's hands. Not only did my so-called new family not believe me, but they disowned me and set me up for death without a second thought."

Her brow was drawn together in both anger and disbelief. "I'm so sorry, Sam." She reached over the console and put her hand on his shoulder. "You're free from them now."

"I didn't want to be free, Kee. I considered them *family*," he reiterated. "I guess they just didn't feel the same way."

She tightened her grip. "I know the sting of family betrayal." When he looked at her curiously, she told her story once again.

Twenty-Three

Liam glanced at his silent driving companion. Natalie was sitting in the passenger seat, staring down at her hands with a vacant look. The doctor had confirmed that she was 11 weeks pregnant and that the pup was healthy with a strong heartbeat.

Even though she wasn't in his pack, she was still under his rule and he could feel her anxiety. He reached out and put his hand on hers. He felt her jump, but she didn't pull away. "What are you thinking, Natalie?" He asked softly.

"I'm scared," she admitted to her alpha, eyes watering. "I keep thinking of all these 'what ifs'."

"Like?" He pressed.

"What if I had told Warren of the pregnancy? I wanted to wait until after the last shift to tell him, but he's so erratic right now and I was scared to. What if I told him earlier? Would he have still gone crazy?" She murmured. "And what if I do tell him, he calms down, and I lose it? And he gets worse? What if," she choked on a sob. "What if Cain kills the father of my pup?"

Liam quietly listened to her troubles and squeezed her hand when she let out another sob. "You can't focus on what might have happened. As for what may happen, you have people who will protect you should he get worse." He began as he pulled the Mercedes into the valet line at the Marriot. He turned to look at her. "And if you are left without a mate after the challenge, I will take responsibility for keeping your pup alive."

"Responsibility?" She echoed, eyes wide.

He nodded once. "I'll make sure you don't shift for the remaining months. I will keep you safe and be there until you give birth," he explained. "If you need it, I'll help you raise the pup."

Her mind went to Zachary, and then to Kee. "But, Kee..." She said and covered her mouth when he growled.

"What happened with Kee will *never* happen again," he said in a deep tone as the valet opened their doors.

She got out of the car and quietly walked behind him, chewing on her bottom lip. "I'm sorry to bring her up," she whispered. "I just don't understand."

"It's not for anyone to understand but her and me," he answered as he led them through the lobby to the elevators.

Nat's brow furrowed as they stepped into the elevator and silence stretched on between them. She was startled when he suddenly spoke again in a quiet voice. "Because of her, I had to obey an order and I lost everything."

She stared at his broad back, mouth slightly open in surprise. "Then do you truly hate your own daughter?" She breathed. "Or the person who gave you the order?"

His hands flexed into fists before relaxing back at his side. "Your pup will be safe, Natalie." He stated as he stepped off the elevator when it arrived at their floor.

She decided not to question his change in subject. She was surprised by his offer to take care of her and the pup but was glad for it. Liam was strong. His alpha power would almost certainly ensure she didn't shift. However, her heart still yearned for her mate.

Before Liam led her further down the hall, he stopped at his son's door. He frowned when he didn't sense or smell anyone on the other side. With a growl in his throat, he pulled out his cell phone from his pocket and called Zachary.

"*Hey, dad!*" Came the too enthusiastic reply.

"I thought I told you not to leave without my permission," he growled, unable to believe his son had broken his order. "Where are you?"

"*What's that? I can't hear you.*"

"Don't play games with me, Zachary. Come back to the hotel. Now." He ordered.

There was a beat of silence before a terse, "*No.*"

Liam glared down at his phone after the line went dead. Clearly, he should have used his power as alpha on his son instead of assuming that he would simply obey. He knew without a doubt that his son was searching for his sister again. Clearly, Conrad and Emilia were with him as well. Kee had barely resurfaced in his life and was already managing to cause mayhem.

Natalie watched as he let out another growl before storming down the hall to his room. She trailed after him, keeping a safe distance from him in case he decided to lash out like Warren had. She wanted to believe that he wouldn't hurt her, but knowing what he did to Kee and Conrad made her keep her guard up.

—

"You're going to be the death of me, do you know that?" Conrad asked from the passenger seat of Lucy's car. "Your dad is going to kill me for taking you away again."

Zach scoffed. "I'll take all the blame, Conrad. I'm determined to meet my sister," he said then looked at Mia when she scowled at him. "What?"

"Don't get Daddy in trouble!" She pouted and crossed her arms across her chest.

He ducked his head as if ashamed. "I said I'll take the blame, Mia. Your dad will be okay."

"He better be!" She huffed at him angrily.

Lucy grinned as the little girl berated the teen. "She's feisty," she commented to Conrad. "I like her."

Conrad smiled at her. "You have no idea," he replied then reached across the console to grasp her hand. "But I'm hoping you will soon."

She smiled shyly and laced their fingers together. "Me too."

Mia stared at them, a small frown turning down her lips. Her eyes focused on their interlocked hands and narrowed slightly before looking out the window.

"You're sure she's at Byte?" Zachary asked, leaning forward slightly as he addressed Lucy.

She nodded. "When I drove by, I saw the Jeep. She's a little banged up and I can't imagine anywhere else she would go."

Conrad frowned at that. "Is she okay?"

"She's covered in bandages, but she said she's alright. Samson looked beat too so they're probably recuperating." The werefox explained.

Zach almost bounced in his seat with excitement. "I can't wait!"

Conrad twisted in his seat to look at him. "I need to talk to her first, Zach. I have a lot to say to her."

"Yeah, yeah, I get it. Just as long as I get to meet her." He said and grinned when Lucy pulled into Byte's parking lot. He quickly unbuckled his seatbelt when she put the car in park and all but leaped from the car.

Mia got out of the car and followed behind her dad. When she saw him approach Lucy, she quickly moved between them and grabbed his hand. "Is Kee nice?" She asked as she looked up at him.

He smiled down at her. "Yes."

Lucy gave a smile of her own. "She's feisty like you," she teased and gave the little wolf a wink when she looked up at her. Her smile slipped a little when Mia gave her a blank expression before looking back up at her father. Lucy nervously picked at her nails. "Um, it's a good feisty, of course."

Conrad glanced at Lucy when he suddenly felt her nerves. He leaned towards her and pressed a kiss to her temple. "I like the bad kind, too." He murmured in her ear.

She blushed and gave him a flirty smile. "Good."

Mia clenched her jaw and tugged on her dad's hand, pulling him after Zach. "Come on, Daddy! Zach is already there!"

He gave Lucy a heated, hungry look before letting his daughter drag him away. When he joined Zachary at the door, he gave Miguel a smile. "Hey, Miguel."

"Mr Novak, welcome back! Your alpha arrived a couple hours ago with a new young man. He's quiet but seems nice enough."

His smile faltered at the mention of the newcomer. Lucy had told him that Kee had brought someone back, but Lucas' words echoed in his mind. "Thanks, Miguel." He said as he walked past the werebear and into the back area of Byte. His nose instantly inhaled the scent of garlic and tomatoes, and his mouth watered a little.

"Something smells good," Zachary commented as they walked further into the area. He stilled when they reached the kitchen, his eyes falling on the woman at the restaurant sized stove. Her back was to him, but she had the same hair color as him, tied up into a messy bun. She was just a tad shorter than him, probably putting her at five foot seven or so.

"Kee," he said in awe before he could think better of it.

She turned her head and looked at him. Her brow furrowed in question before looking at the others. Conrad dropped his gaze as she looked at him so she turned her attention to the little girl holding his hand.

Lucy wasn't kidding, she looks just like him.

She turned back to the stove and stirred the marinara sauce before putting on the lid so it could simmer. "Are you guys hungry?" She asked nonchalantly as she grabbed one of the large pots from a rack next to the dishwasher.

"Starved!" Lucy chimed in, trying to ease the tension in the room. She moved towards where Samson sat on the counter and waved at him. When he waved back, she smiled at him. She was determined to help him feel welcome in their small pack.

"I love pasta!" Mia said happily. "We just had it yesterday, but it's my favorite and I could eat it all the time!"

Kee set the pot in the sink and began to fill it with water. "Me too," she replied and smiled at the mini-Conrad. "What kind of noodles do you like?"

"The really skinny ones!" She answered, moving away from her dad so she could approach the woman cooking. "Is that what you're making?"

At her big, hopeful eyes, Kee laughed. "I think I can manage that." She lifted the pot from the sink, but the fabric around her hands made her lose her grip. Almost instantly, larger hands were there to catch the pot before it could crash to the floor.

"You okay?" Conrad questioned, taking in the bandages around her hands and neck.

Kee wanted to hate how his presence brought the same comfort it had since her attack but couldn't.

"I'm fine, just got in a fight with some silver. Will you put that on the other burner?" She gestured towards the stove. When he turned to do so, she bent down so she was more eye level with the girl. "And who do we have here?"

"Emilia, but everyone calls me Mia!" She stated confidently and stuck her hand out.

Kee laughed again and took the small hand in hers. "I'm Keira, but everyone calls me Kee."

Mia beamed at her then pointed to the slack-jawed wolf still standing at the edge of the kitchen. "That's Zachary, but you can call him Zach. He really wants to meet you!"

"Oh?" She asked as she straightened and looked at the blonde teen again. She blinked when she realized he had been at Warren's house with Liam. "You're one of Liam's wolves."

He flinched at her cool tone. "Yeah, but it's more than that!" He quickly said and took a couple steps towards her, jerking to a halt when she scowled at him in warning. "He's my—you're—we—argh!" He shoved his hands into his hair in frustration. He then took a deep breath and shyly looked at her again when he released it. "You're my sister." He stated in a quiet, unsure voice.

Kee could feel everyone's eyes on her as she stared dumbfounded at Zach. "What?" She murmured. The longer she looked at him, the more she saw the resemblance between him and Liam. His pure blue eyes were just like Liam's, but they looked so nervous, almost scared. His hair was the same shade as hers, his nose was the exact replica of Liam's. She swallowed twice as she tried to digest the information. "How old are you?"

He blinked, not expecting the question. "Sixteen."

Nine years younger than her. Liam moved on two years after he killed her mom. "Oh," she looked away from him, down at the floor as she tried to not show him her anger.

It's not his fault our father is such a piece of shit. Her heart skipped a beat. *Our father. Fuck, I've had a little brother for sixteen years and had no idea.*

"Kee?" Zach questioned softly, wringing his hands anxiously.

She looked up at him and saw the lingering hope in his eyes. What had Mia said? He really wanted to meet her? How long has he known about her?

She patted Mia's head and stepped around her so she could approach her brother. His eyes widened as she neared, and he took an unsure step backwards. Seeing him retreat, she scoffed, "I'm not Liam." She then wrapped her arms around him, hugging him to her. He took in a sharp breath before his arms encircled her shoulders.

"I've wanted to meet you for so long," Zach whispered, face buried in her neck. "I was told you were dead."

"Not yet." She answered with a wry smile. Her heart did a little flip when he tightened his hold on her, and she felt his tears soak through the bandage around her neck. "Shh, it's okay, Zach. I'm alive and we're here together for now. Let's enjoy it."

He nodded and reluctantly pulled away. He wiped at his face, drying the tears, and gave her a sheepish grin. "I don't normally cry."

She smiled at that familiar statement. "I don't either."

"I have so much I want to say to you, but I know your beta is dying to talk to you, too," he admitted and looked over at Conrad, who was sneering at the man who held a napkin out to the crying Lucy.

Conrad tore his glare away from the male on the counter and looked at the siblings. He cleared his throat when Kee's gaze turned neutral. "Can we talk, Kee? Please?"

She let out a heavy sigh and turned her attention to Lucy. "Will you please watch the sauce and put the noodles in soon?" She winked at Mia. "I think we have some angel hair in the walk-in pantry."

"Yay!" Mia beamed at her then skirted around Lucy when the werefox approached the stove. She hugged Zach around the waist and slipped over to Samson to introduce herself. "Hi, I'm Mia!"

Samson shifted awkwardly on the counter. "Samson," he introduced and shook her tiny hand when she thrust it at him.

"Can I call you Sammy?" She asked with wide, pleading eyes.

"I'd rather you didn't," he countered, but she ignored him and started prattling on about her hobbies.

Kee grabbed Conrad by the elbow as he stiffly watched the dragon interact with his daughter. "Samson won't hurt her," she stated then pulled him out of the kitchen. She led him to the empty bar and sat down on one of the barstools. She propped her feet on the railing and looked at him expectantly.

"Is he my replacement?" Conrad murmured, crossing his arms across his chest defensively.

She lifted her eyebrow at him. "I'm guessing you mean Samson. Why would you think he's your replacement?" Her tone turned sour. "Could it be because you lied to me from the beginning? That you stabbed me in the back? That you feel guilty?"

He looked down and shuffled his feet. "I guess I deserve that."

"You *guess*?" She mocked.

"I don't want to fight with you, Kee," he said with a furrowed brow. "I just want you to hear me out. Give me a chance to explain myself. Please."

She leaned back so her elbows rested on the bar's counter. "Fine, let's hear what you have to say, *beta*." She put a heavy emphasis on that last word.

His face scrunched in anger. "Am I even your beta anymore? Lucas suggested you were finding someone to replace me since you're not my alpha anymore."

She was surprised that Lucas said that. Still, she kept her tone passive aggressive. "He was irritated because he had to leave Nana's. I felt his anger through the bond, but I didn't know he would take out his frustration on you. He was only mad because he couldn't stay and protect me from Samson."

His brow furrowed. "Samson hurt you?" He tossed his hands up in disbelief. "And you brought him here? To be part of our pack? That's not okay, Kee!"

She held up a finger at him. "First of all, that's not your decision to make." She lifted another finger. "Secondly, he didn't mean to hurt me. He was dying and his beast was lashing out. He just sort of clung to me, but with his talons." She gestured at the bandages wrapped around her forearm before adding a third finger. "Lastly, *our* pack?"

Her words hit him in the gut. "So," he mumbled. "He *is* replacing me."

They stared at each other for a long moment, the tension mounting until she let out a heavy, defeated sigh. She rubbed her forehead and mumbled, "Of course not, Conrad."

Conrad frowned and looked down at his shoes. "You sure? You said you didn't want to see me again."

She let out a frustrated noise and sat up straight with a glare. "I was fucking hurt, Conrad! What did you expect?" When he lifted his gaze to hers, she softened her expression. "You and Lucas were all I had, and to hear that you had never really been mine *hurt*," she held up a hand when he opened his mouth. "At least, I thought I was hurt then, but it was worse when I realized that you didn't trust me with the truth of your situation. Lucy had to tell me. Do you think that was fair? For me to find out from her? You trusted her enough with your story, but not me? What the actual hell?"

His shoulders hunched in shame. She was right, of course she was. He thought Lucy telling Kee would ease the tension, but he didn't consider how it would have come off. "I'm sorry. I was desperate to talk to you, and I thought if Lucy eased you into it then you would hear me out."

"Well, you were wrong." She pursed her lips and took another deep breath. "Kind of, I guess. Yes, it stung that you told her and not me, but if you hadn't told her, I may not be sitting here listening to you. I heard it from her and now I need to hear it from you. Why did you lie to me?"

He closed his eyes. "I was scared to tell you. I had finally found an alpha worthy of the title, and I didn't want you to reject me. It grew harder and harder to tell you the truth as time went on."

"How much of it was a lie?" Kee demanded.

"I'm not a submissive wolf," he began. "That was an act I had to put on for Warren's pack. Liam sent me to the Los Angeles pack when he heard that Warren was doing something wrong."

"Wrong?"

"Liam thought that Warren was just trying to take his role of Alpha of LA County so he sent me here. When wolves started dying, he knew it was something more. It wasn't until I figured out that Warren was in league with Alexander that he decided to come here." He explained.

She scowled at him. "Did you tell him I was the one who killed the wolves?"

"No, I made sure to keep your name out of it. I told him about Cain's intended mate. I mentioned later that you worked for Lucas because that was the proof I had that Alexander was involved." He said. "But I never said your name in conjunction with the murders."

The scowl softened into a furrowed brow. "If you were acting this whole time to do a job, why did you even come to me for help in the first place?"

Conrad clenched his jaw. "I didn't act with you, Kee," he stated firmly. "I asked to stay with you because I wanted you to be my alpha."

"But your alpha is Liam." She pointed out in a cold tone.

"I was looking for a *new* alpha," he clarified. "I wanted to find a new home for Mia. When Liam used her against me, I knew we weren't safe. I wanted an alpha we could rely on. One who wouldn't hurt us or abuse their status." He raised his eyes to meet hers. "And then I found you."

Kee tried to ignore the way his statement cooled her anger. "Weren't you concerned that Liam would find out?"

"No, I knew the likelihood of him finding out was slim. He *gave* me to Warren and told him he didn't want a submissive wolf. He wouldn't call to check on me because he didn't want to give Warren any indication that something was off. Why would he ask about a wolf he threw away?" He shrugged. "Besides, I kept doing as Liam asked so he had no reason to question me. I continued to spy on Warren and his pack while living with you."

She raised her brows in surprise. "When?"

"When you were at Shifters or working for Lucas. Then when you were recovering and the other times you already know of." He replied as he uncrossed his arms and flexed his hands at his sides. "Look, I was trying to do what was best for my daughter, Kee. She's everything to me and I needed to find a new home for her—for us."

She rubbed her face again and let out a heavy breath, the anger nearly diminished. "I get it, Conrad. If anyone knows how dangerous Liam can be, it's me," she said as she rose to her feet. "But I'm still hurt you didn't trust me enough to tell me."

"It's not that I didn't trust you," he protested. "I was just nervous you would think it was too much baggage."

"Baggage?" She echoed in surprise.

He gestured at the kitchen. "Mia," he responded. "And the fact that I'm coming from a different pack."

She gave him a disapproving look. "Conrad, I don't care that you have a daughter. Will it be a change? Yes. I'm not particularly used to being around kids, but she's a part of you and I accept that."

"Then, you'll let us stay in your pack?" He asked as she stopped to stand in front of him.

Kee leaned forward and looped her arms around his waist. She let out a final, caving sigh and pressed her cheek to his chest. "Of course, Conrad. You're not just my best friend; you're my beta."

The tense muscles in his body relaxed, his shoulders slumping in relief as he hugged her back. "Thank you," he breathed and tightened his hold. "I'm so sorry for lying to you. You don't know how sorry I am."

She pulled back from him with a small smile. "No more lies, okay? Is there anything else you need to tell me?"

He shook his head. "No, nothing. I promise."

She smiled at him. "Good," she said then raised both hands to pinch his cheeks. "You need to be nice to Sam. Don't think I didn't see you glowering at him."

He winced and rubbed his tender cheeks when she released them. "He was too close to Lucy."

"What, so no one can touch her now that you've finally admitted your feelings to her?" Kee put her hands on her hips.

Conrad pursed his lips together. "Not a man I don't know," he grumbled.

"So possessive." She rolled her eyes but couldn't stifle the smile that curved up her lips. "So, how *are* things going with you and Luce?"

"Good," he replied honestly. "I mean, it's only been a day since we first kissed, but I'm hoping we can spend more time together soon. With Liam here it's been hectic. Then there's Emilia. I don't want to leave her alone ever again, but I also want some alone time with Lucy. Is that horrible of me?"

She shook her head. "No, it's okay. Of course, you wouldn't want to be separated from your daughter after spending months apart. However, I also know how it feels to want to spend time with someone you've fallen for." She began walking back towards the kitchen, Conrad following behind her. "Maybe the three of you could do something together and then when Mia goes to sleep you and

Lucy can be alone."

"Yeah, maybe," he agreed as they walked back into the kitchen. He saw Samson now sitting on the floor, Mia tying tiny braids into the long section of his hair. The dragon had his eyes closed, nodding every once in a while as Mia went on about all the things she learned from watching crime shows on television.

Kee nudged Conrad in the side with her elbow. "See? Mia *and* Samson are going to fit in just fine."

Twenty-Four

"Did you hear about the alpha challenge?" Conrad questioned as he handed Mia a napkin. The small group had claimed one of the large, round, high-top tables in the bar area so they could sit together. He had taken the seat to Kee's right and Mia had claimed the one on his other side.

Kee nodded and took a sip of her water before speaking. "I talked to Cain earlier today. He wants me to be there."

"Are you going to go?" Zach asked with a mouth full of pasta. "Dad's going to be there."

She let out a heavy sigh. "I know, but I'm still going. Cain needs my support and I want to give it to him. He deserves to be alpha."

Samson, who was sitting between Mia and Lucy, looked up from his plate. "How do alpha challenges work?"

"It's basically a fight for dominance. The winner becomes alpha of the pack. However, most challenges only happen when it's obvious the challenger is rising in power, or if the alpha is unsuited to rule," Conrad explained to the newcomer without looking at him.

"In this case, both are happening, right?" Lucy asked, looking across the table at the beta then at Zach sitting to her left. "Why will your dad be there?"

He swallowed his mouthful of pasta and cleared his throat. "Because he's the alpha of the county. The wolf that wins the fight will be part of the alphas under dad's rule. He wants to make sure it's a clean fight. He doesn't want someone who plays tricks to be part of his governors. Plus, he always gives the winner a prize for their effort."

"Oh," she frowned. "I guess the alpha who wins is a direct reflection on the county alpha."

Zach pointed his fork at her. "Exactly."

"What kind of prize does he give?" Samson asked curiously. He looked down at the little girl, who had demanded he sit next to, when she patted his arm.

"It can be anything!" She told him in a matter-of-fact way. "Zach once told me Uncle Liam gave the Glendora alpha his old Porsche."

Kee shuddered when Mia addressed her father as uncle. *Just like how I used to address Christian.* "That's interesting." She hummed. "I can't imagine what he would give Cain though."

"You seem so sure your ex-boyfriend will win," Samson pointed out.

"Hopeful, I suppose," she admitted with a shrug. "I want Warren out."

The dragon narrowed his black eyes at her. "You do realize that if Cain fails, Warren is coming after you."

"So he said," she replied dismissively.

"Wait, what? When did this happen?" Conrad asked with a furrowed brow.

Kee told him what happened earlier at Warren's house. "He's pretty intent on killing me," she shrugged. "He can try."

"Liam is making me go so I'll be there. I won't let him hurt you, Kee." Conrad said seriously.

"I'll be fine." She protested.

Samson scoffed. "I'm going with you tomorrow night. I don't trust this Warren guy. Plus, you're still recovering from last night."

She shot him a knowing look. "And you're not?"

"I heal faster than you," he stated with a deadpanned expression.

"I'm going, too!" Lucy interjected. "Unlike you two, I'm not hurt at all."

Kee shook her head. "It won't be good to have everyone go. I'll be fine with Cain and Conrad."

"I'm going with my pack, Kee." Lucy stated defiantly.

Kee went to protest until Lucy's words sunk in. "Your pack?" She echoed softly.

Lucy grinned at her. "Yes. Although I guess I should say *our* pack." her smile softened and turned a little shy. "If the offer still stands?"

Kee pushed her chair back and stood. She walked over to where Lucy was and hugged her tightly from behind, rubbing her cheek on the top of Lucy's head. "Welcome to the pack, Luce."

Lucy squeezed Kee's forearms. "Thank you for giving me a family."

"Thanks for trusting me to give you one." She responded and then looked at Mia as the little girl stared at her with wide amber eyes. Kee released Lucy and walked over to stand between Mia and Conrad.

She gave Conrad a wink before turning her attention to Mia. "Miss Emilia Novak, would you do us the greatest honor and join our pack as well?" She knew she didn't have to ask Mia since her father was her beta, but she remembered not having a lot of choices when she was younger and she didn't want that for Mia.

Her eyes widened before she looked at her father for approval. When he gave her a proud nod, she looked at Lucy then at Samson. "Is Sammy part of your pack, too?"

She stifled a laugh at the way Samson snorted at the nickname. Still, she shot him a meaningful look. "If things work out, then yes," she said before looking at Mia again. "What do you say?"

Mia looked down at her hands. "Does that mean you'll be my alpha? Like Uncle Liam?"

"Not like Liam, but yes, I would be your alpha." She responded honestly.

"You won't take me away from Daddy."

It had come out as a statement rather than a question, but Kee nodded. "I won't."

She glanced at her dad again then shyly up at Kee. "Yes, I want to be part of your pack, too."

Kee smiled kindly at her and smoothed out her hair before placing a kiss to the top of her head. "Welcome to the pack, Mia."

Conrad beamed at Kee when she straightened then leaned towards his daughter, pressing a kiss to her temple. "I love you, baby girl."

She gave him a wide smile. "I love you, too, Daddy."

On her way back to her chair, Kee ruffled Samson's hair affectionately. "You're on the right course." She whispered to him. He gave her a tentative smile and turned back to his food without responding.

After dinner, Samson and Lucy took it upon themselves to do the dishes while Conrad and Mia raided the kitchen's pantry for sweets. Zach had pulled Kee to the side in the bar so they could speak alone before he left.

"I think it's cool you ask them to join instead of just forcing them." He complimented her as he swiveled on his barstool.

She frowned at him. "Does Liam force wolves into his pack?"

He hummed. "I guess force is a strong word," he said. "He claims rogue werewolves who stay in his territory for too long. If he doesn't think they'll be a good fit for our pack, he'll send them to different packs. He makes sure the rogue submits to the authority of that pack's alpha before leaving."

"Wait, rogue?"

He nodded. "Mostly people who were turned. You know, people

who were once human and know nothing about werewolves except for what Wikipedia tells them."

She sneered. "He doesn't even give them a choice, does he?"

Zach glanced at her. "He can't afford to, Kee. He's not just responsible for the actions of his pack in Claremont, he's responsible for *all* the werewolves in LA County. If the rogue doesn't submit to the alpha of the pack he gives them to, he'll give them another shot at working with our pack. If they continue to cause issues, he kills them."

Kee gave him a sour look. "You're saying there's no other way to deal with them?"

He sighed. "Most werewolves *want* to be part of a pack. It's a part of our instincts. The ones that don't are dangerous. Like I said, most rogues Dad bring in are rehabilitated to other packs without trouble." He rubbed his face. "But some aren't. There have been at least four in the past two years that wanted nothing to do with packs or alphas. When the full moon comes, or they lose control of their beast and turn, they kill anything in sight.

"One time, a rogue killed one of our female's mates when he tried to calm him down. Dad let her rip his throat out." He shuddered. "Dad dealt with the other three. They are given multiple chances, Kee. What else is he supposed to do with a wolf that's a danger to himself and others?"

Kee went silent, not wanting to agree that she would have done the same thing. If a random person showed up and attacked her pack mates, she wouldn't hesitate to kill them. Her body tensed when she thought of Samson. Conrad and Lucas were right, she *didn't* know him. She could be putting her small pack at risk. Would she be able to kill him if he turned on them?

If I could kill Noah after knowing him for a year, I can kill Samson, she sternly reminded herself.

"Can I show you something?" Zachary suddenly asked as he pulled his phone out of his back pocket.

Kee blinked out of her thoughts and looked at her little brother as he scrolled through his phone. "Sure," she said as she pulled out her own phone and checked the time with a yawn. "We're running out of time though. The club opens in an hour and a half, but I need to talk to Lucas beforehand." Also, some cuddling would be ideal.

He nodded as he scrolled until he found the picture he was looking for. He clicked on it so it filled the screen and showed it to her. "Do you know what this is?"

She looked at the screen and froze. Her breath caught in her throat and her heart felt as if it stilled. She gingerly took the phone from him and brought it closer. There was no mistaking the dark grey and white stuffed animal in the picture. His white paws were discolored with age, the fur not as smooth as it had once been. There were several black streaks on the grey from where a little girl had once tried coloring on markings to match the father she had idolized so much. The plastic blue eyes had lost some of their gleam and gained a few scratches, but none of that was new.

"Wolfie," she whispered in disbelief as she ran a fingertip over the screen. "I lost him when I was a kid. Where did you find him?"

Zach ducked his head. "I found it in the bottom drawer of Dad's desk," he murmured. "It's normally locked, but when I went to use his computer, it wasn't closed all way and I was curious."

She recoiled like he hit her. "Liam has this in his desk?"

"Yeah, all locked up," he repeated. "I didn't understand what it was so I took a picture of it. I didn't put it together until I realized you actually existed."

Kee sighed heavily and handed the phone back to him. "What do you mean?"

He pocketed the phone and looked away from her. "Originally, I was told I didn't have any siblings. One of the older pack members told me that once upon a time, I had a sister, but that you and your mom disappeared. I asked Dad, but he said you were dead. I asked what happened, and he said that an order was given and he complied."

She snorted. "Zach, Liam killed my mother, *his mate*, right in front of me. He tried to kill me too, but my grandpa got to me first and took me to the San Bernardino County line. He couldn't come after me." She gestured at his pocket. "That was the night I lost Wolfie. Running for my life as my dad killed my mom."

Zach closed his eyes tightly and clenched his hands into fists. "The same pack mate told me a story after I was sworn to secrecy, but I didn't believe it until now." He took a shaky breath and looked at her. "He told me that before my dad was alpha, when he was still a beta, he had a family. He said he had a beautiful mate and a little girl."

When Kee just stared at him, he continued. "He said that everyone expected great things from his daughter. She came from a powerful line of wolves, and they all expected her to shift as soon as she was six years old." He winced. "But she didn't. Her seventh year came and still no shift. He said that Dad started to keep her from the pack, keeping her isolated while he tried to coax out her wolf."

She scoffed and crossed her arms across her chest. "Coaxed?" She mocked. "He beat me, Zach. When I continued to fail to be what he wanted, he hit me. My mom tried to protect me, but even she couldn't stop him after a while. He would constantly accuse me of being the reason he lost everything."

Zach's eyes stung as her words sunk in. "He's never struck me," he murmured as he squeezed his eyes shut. "He was, um, *intense* when I was little, though. He would constantly have me around him when he was in wolf form. He would insist I be with him and the pack when they changed for the full moon, but he never hit me."

She met his gaze and tried to keep the contempt and jealousy from her eyes. "Let me guess, he eased up after you changed for the first time?"

He nodded. "It was three months after I turned six. He was so... relieved," he whispered. "Like a visible weight had been lifted from his shoulders."

She swallowed the sudden lump in her throat. "That's because he realized he wouldn't have to repeat the past," she mumbled. "You weren't someone who could destroy everything he had. Was he mean to his new mate, too?"

Zach tilted his head at her in question. "If you mean my mom, she's not his mate. He doesn't have one."

"Does that bother you?"

He shook his head. "No, Dad made it clear to my mom that all he wanted was a pup. He treats her well though. She never has to want for anything, he gives it freely." He shrugged. "She gained some status from having me, so I think she's okay with it, too."

"Ah," she commented, trying not to focus on the small amount of relief she felt.

Zach frowned when she released another yawn. "Maybe you should go to bed, Kee."

"I plan on it. Maybe I'll get some spooning time in with Lucas." She laughed when Zach rolled his eyes. "I've been running on fumes the past couple days and I sleep better when I'm with him."

"I'll let you go to sleep then." He slid off his barstool with a shy smile. "I'm really glad I got to meet you. I know you don't care for Dad, but you're still my sister."

She gave him a tired smile and hugged him. "I'm glad, too. Hopefully the bastard will let you come visit me. If not, I'll find a way to come kidnap you for a day."

He grinned as he hugged her back. "I'd like that."

She pulled away from him then led him back towards the kitchen. "I know Conrad said he has to go tomorrow, but is Liam making you go, too?"

He nodded as he walked alongside her. "He wants me to see all the alpha fights," he pursed his lips. "Unless he makes me stay at the hotel with Mia."

"No way is he getting his hands on her again. She's staying here with Lucy and Samson. She'll be safe here, especially when Lucas is awake." She stated confidently.

Zach grinned at her. "I might just join your pack next."

She gave a soft chuckle. "I think Liam would rather die than see me take you away from him."

He shrugged. "Yeah, you're right. He'd challenge you, of course." A soft frown turned down his lips as he glanced at Conrad and Mia as they shared a bowl of ice cream. "What will you do if he doesn't let Conrad join your pack?"

She lifted a brow at him. "Con wants to stay with me, isn't that enough?"

He gently grabbed her arm and brought her to a stop. "Not always, Kee," he said seriously. "If he's vindictive enough he'll order Conrad to stay with him. Your power as alpha and your bond to Conrad has to be stronger than Dad's."

Her brow furrowed. "And if it's not?" She asked quietly.

He sucked in a breath. "You'll have to fight him."

She cursed and felt everyone's eyes fall on her. She knew she would have to fight Liam eventually. She *wanted* to fight him, wanted to redeem herself for becoming a fear-ridden statue upon seeing him again. She needed to see his blood spilled for what he did to her mom, for what he did to her. And yet a part of her still feared him.

This isn't about me, or even Mom anymore. Now it's about Conrad and Mia, too. They're my pack and I will protect them. They're mine.

She squared her shoulders and stared her brother in the eye. "Then I'll fight him."

"Kee—" Conrad began, but she cut him off.

"No, you and Mia are mine now," she stated without breaking eye contact with Zach. "He won't get you back."

Zach held her stare for a moment before giving her a proud grin. "I'll be rooting for you then, sis."

She relaxed and smiled at the nickname. "Thanks." She hugged him a final time. "I'll see you tomorrow night then."

"See you." He replied.

She turned to Conrad. "Are you staying here?"

He shook his head. "I have to take Zach back and go with Liam tomorrow."

She nodded. "Bring Mia here before you go to Warren's." She turned to Lucy and Samson. "I want you two to stay here and watch Mia while we are gone."

Samson bristled. "Kee, I'm going with you."

"No, you're not," she countered firmly. "This is a wolf ordeal."

He gave her a deadpanned expression. "Then why are *you* going?"

She glared at him. "Because Cain asked me, and I have wolf blood in me," she saw him start to argue and cut him off. "Sam, I'm trusting you and Lucy to keep Mia safe. Can you do that or not?"

He pinched his lips together and turned his head away from her. "I can." He grumbled unhappily.

"Good." She looked at Lucy, who nodded in return. "Thank you. Can you show Samson the fourth floor so he can pick a room for now? I would, but I need to see Lucas."

"Of course, Kee," the werefox said before approaching Conrad and Mia. She bent down to Mia's level and gave her a wide smile. "Tomorrow we'll have a girl's night! What do you say we paint each other's nails and watch Disney movies?"

Mia stepped back from her, her hand finding her dad's. "I watch true crime shows." She muttered.

Lucy raised her eyebrows and looked at Conrad. "True crime, huh?"

He gave a shake of his head and lifted his free hand in defeat. "I don't know. Believe me, I've tried to dissuade her from watching them, but she's adamant about it. It honestly freaks me out a little bit. Especially when the victims are little girls who have been kidnapped, killed, and...violated." He shuddered and his inner wolf growled. "She's stubborn and won't let me change the channel. She claims she learns stuff from it."

"Did you know that most kidnappings are done by people who know the victim?" Mia stated.

Lucy laughed at Conrad's exasperated expression. "I didn't," she commented as she turned her attention back to Mia. "Have you ever seen Cold Case Files?"

Mia perked up in interest. "No," she admitted. "But I know what a Cold Case is. It's when a case hasn't been solved after a really long time and has no leads."

She nodded. "Yep! It's a really good show about them. Do you want to watch it with me tomorrow? Maybe chow down some pizza?"

Mia shuffled her feet but gave a small nod. "I guess," she mumbled. She liked crime and loved pizza, but she didn't want to leave her dad or stay with the woman who was trying to take him away from her.

Lucy's smile widened. "It's a date then!"

"I'll be expecting one next." Conrad said and smirked when Lucy straightened with red tinged cheeks. He dipped his head down and pressed a kiss to her lips.

She eagerly kissed him back and pulled away when Kee whistled at them. She looked down in embarrassment. "A date would be nice," she agreed before shooting a half-hearted glare at her new alpha. "That way nosey people don't interrupt!"

Kee stuck her tongue out and glanced at the stiff little girl at

Conrad's side. She wasn't sure if anyone else had seen it, but Kee clearly saw the angry gleam that had crossed Mia's eyes. She didn't seem to be a fan of Lucy and that worried Kee. Maybe she would have to run some interference.

"Alright, we'll see you all tomorrow. Sleep well everyone." Conrad said as he headed to the back door with Mia and Zach.

"Night, guys," Kee responded then covered her mouth as she yawned again. She turned towards Lucy and Samson and gave them a tired wave. "I'm going to the basement. You two going to be okay?"

"I work the bar tonight," Lucy answered and brightened as she looked at Samson. "Why don't you come down to the bar and keep me company? You can meet the other bartenders and the staff here!"

He tilted his head. "I guess that's okay. I don't have my ID, though. All my possessions were taken from me when the Ringmaster grabbed me."

"We'll work on getting you a new one, as well as some new belongings." Kee frowned when he looked away with a tight jaw. "It's not weakness to accept help, Sam."

"Isn't it, though?" He bit out.

"No." She reiterated. "If you feel bad about letting me help you, then I'll ask Lucas and Dante what they think about extra security. I know they just hired Conrad, but maybe they need someone else as well."

"I'd prefer that," he mumbled. "I don't like taking handouts. I've always held my own, even in Muir."

"Think of it as a loan then," she replied. "Take in the bar tonight, but if anyone tries to ID you, tell them you're with me. Otherwise, try to avoid being carded. I don't want Lucas to get in trouble."

"Alright." He agreed.

She gave him a weak, tired smile and made her way to the door leading to the coven. "Have a good night, guys. Stay safe." She said before shutting the door behind her.

She tripped going down the stairs, her legs reminding her just how tired she was, but managed to stay upright. She staggered down the hall until she reached Lucas' room. After she shut the door behind her, she walked towards the bed, feeling for it in the pitch dark. When she got to it, she made her way around to her side and quickly stripped off her clothes.

She shivered with the sudden exposure to the cold and practically burrowed under the thick covers of Lucas' bed. She wiggled her way over to his side and sighed in content when she made contact with the smooth, cool expanse of his torso. She snuggled into his side, resting her cheek on his chest and draping her arm across his stomach. He didn't have a heartbeat, didn't have any body warmth, but his mere presence soothed her. Her bunched muscles relaxed and another content sigh left her lips. She closed her eyes and let sleep finally claim her.

Twenty-Five

Lucas snapped awake as soon as the sun sunk into darkness, the moon rising high in the sky to take its place. He stared up at his ceiling for a moment as his body started to hum with life. He glanced at the clock next to him and saw that Byte was supposed to open in thirty minutes, but he couldn't care less at the moment.

He heard a soft, rumbling noise and jerked his attention down towards his chest. His undead heart clenched to see his shapeshifter curled up against his side, her head propped up on his chest as she snored softly. He looked at the dark circles under her eyes then the bandages wrapped around her hands and forearm.

He lifted his hand and lightly trailed his fingertips up and down the soft skin of her arm. He smiled when she hummed and pressed her body closer to his. His fingers slid into her hair and detangled a few of the snarls that had developed during her sleep.

"I just thought you would want to help the woman you love." Lucy's voice suddenly echoed in his mind, followed instantly by Dante's words, *"There is nothing wrong with opening your heart."*

Lucas abruptly pulled his hand away as if he had been burned. He scowled and let out a curse. She shifted at the sound and parted her puffy eyelids. She lifted her head to look at him, and his hand automatically moved to gently push her hair back from her face. This time he cursed *mentally*.

"You look terrible." He commented softly.

"Feel terrible." She croaked.

His glaze slid over the bandages again. "I take it your new pet behaved himself."

Her eyes fluttered closed. "He ended up dying, but he's okay now."

His muscles went tense as jealousy and irritation welled up in him like a spring. "So naturally you gave him your blood despite me advising you not to."

Kee propped herself up on her elbows to look at him. "There it is," she mumbled. "That same feeling from last night. I've never really felt anything from your side of the bond before, but your emotions are screaming at me right now."

He immediately shielded his feelings, face going blank. "Oh?"

She frowned at him and struggled to sit up. Once upright, she straddled his lap and flattened her hands on his abs. "What exactly are you mad about?"

His hands went to her smooth thighs, his thumbs tracing circles on her skin. Noticing what he was doing, he drew his hands away as if her flesh scalded him. "I am not mad."

"Bullshit," she said. "Are you pissed off about me helping Samson? About giving him my blood? I couldn't let him die, Lucas. And he's a good guy. He helped me at Warren's house."

His eyes narrowed at her as he sat up, his hands going to her hips. "What happened at Warren's house?"

She rubbed her face. "I told him I was the one who killed his wolves. He tried to attack me, but Samson interfered." She looked at him with a grim expression. "He knows I'm a shapeshifter, Lucas. Noah must have told him after my attack. I don't know why I didn't consider it before."

He tightened his hold on her hips out of reflex from his anger. "Which means Alexander may know as well."

She lowered her gaze to his collar bones. "It's a possibility, but there's also the chance he still thinks I'm dead. Warren only found out I was alive when I went to his house yesterday with Conrad. I think Warren hates Alexander so there's a chance he hasn't relayed the information."

"But we do not know for sure." He sighed. "What else did you find out?"

"Alexander is at the Arcadia coven with Gio and Aubrey." Her hands flew to his shoulders when he suddenly pressed a hard kiss to her lips.

"Well done," he purred and kissed her again with elation. He lifted her from his lap and gently tossed her on the bed. He stood and eagerly ran his hands into his hair. "We are going in a few hours to get them."

She frowned up at him as she rose into a sitting position. "Lucas, I can't. I'm too exhausted. I've been running on fumes these past couple of nights and my body is protesting. Plus, I'm still recovering from saving Samson."

Lucas clenched his jaw tightly. He could take on Alexander and Jada separately, probably even together, but he did not trust either of them to play fair. He wanted her there with him. She was a weapon and they both knew it. He would bring Dante as well, just in case Alexander had another ally besides Jada.

He took a deep breath and slowly released it. "I do not know if I can wait until tomorrow night." He saw her body go rigid as she looked away and scowled at her. "What, Keira?"

She was too exhausted to flinch at his tone. "Cain is challenging Warren tomorrow at sunset. I told him I would be there."

"You would choose your ex-boyfriend over your obligation to me?" He seethed. Why did Cain always arise in subject when things were uncertain between them?

She glared back at him. "I'm not choosing anyone over anything. I want to kill Alexander for what he did to me. Yes, I want to make him pay for taking Gio from us, but that doesn't mean I'm obligated to do anything *for* you. My need to kill him is not for you, it's for me."

The green of his eyes darkened with his anger. "So, you assume I will wait for you to be ready to attack Alexander? To get my people back?" He bent over the bed so he could put his face inches from hers, a sneer marring his handsome face. She tried to draw back from him, but he cupped the back of her neck to keep her in place. "I will not make Giovanni suffer another night in my enemy's hands, Keira. Not even for you." *I do not love her.* "Giovanni is my priority."

They stared at each other in a tense silence, neither one breaking eye contact with the other. She wanted to shout back that she wasn't asking him to wait, but technically she was. He was right about Giovanni. She knew he came first to Lucas.

Finally, she closed her eyes in defeat. "I know Gio is more important to you," she mumbled. "I'm sorry I asked you to wait. But, if you can hold off a few more hours, even two at least, I'll go with you. I just need some energy."

His fingers flexed on the back of her neck. "I do not *need* you to go, Keira. I asked you to locate Alexander for me, and you did. Dante and I are more than capable of handling the rest."

Kee opened her eyes again to meet at his cold glare. "I know you don't need me, but I would like to help. Both for Gio, and for myself. If Alexander really doesn't know I'm alive or that I'm a shapeshifter then we'll have an advantage on him."

"And if he does?" His ire flared at the thought of her falling into his enemy's hands like Giovanni had. "Did we not just discuss this the other night? About him getting his hands on you?"

She almost flinched as his emotions burned through their bond. "How will he know who I am if I'm someone else?" She leaned in and brushed her lips against his, trying to cool his anger. "Let me help, Lucas. You know how much I want to kill him."

Every last bit of him urged him to kiss her back, but he refrained, Lucy and Dante's words coming back to haunt him once again. He pulled back from her, releasing her neck as he did. "Two hours, that is all I will give you."

She frowned. "Okay." She grabbed his hand before he could move too far away from the bed. "You never answered me. Why are you really mad? What did I do?"

Lucas clenched his jaw again when he saw the vulnerable expression on her face. *You made me feel something I am not supposed to.* "Nothing." He replied curtly and pulled his hand away from hers. "Go to sleep, Miss Quinn."

Her lips parted both in shock and hurt, but before she could comment on it, he disappeared into his closet. He emerged a few minutes later dressed in a pair of a black slacks and black collared shirt. "Lucas!" She called in disbelief as he walked out the door and shut it behind him.

Lucas stood there outside his room and stared down at the floor with a bitter scowl. He had to do this. He had to put distance between them. It was for her own safety. Look at what his feelings had done to her already. His affection had scarred her both mentally and physically due to Alexander. What would love do to her?

He shut his eyes as the image of her lying motionless and dead in her own pool of blood flashed in his mind. He had seen the sight of it in her apartment already. She hadn't been dead then, nor had the two of them been as close. If she truly died now, with him feeling how he did, it may very well break him.

Swallowing, he pushed his emotions down and stepped away from his door. *This is for the best,* he repeated to himself even as his heart argued otherwise.

———

"Are you sure you want to include Kee in your plans for tonight?" Dante asked casually as he leaned back in the chair across from Lucas' desk.

Lucas narrowed his eyes. "And why would I not?"

"Because Alexander already tried to kill her once. Then possibly killed Giovanni and your bleeder," he replied as he met the glare. "Wasn't sure you would like to tempt fate with her."

"She wants to go." He stated bluntly.

Dante continued as if he didn't hear him. "Oh wait, I don't suppose it matters, does it?" He lifted a mocking brow at his lord. "Since it's just physical, right?"

Lucas slammed his hands down on his desk as he lurched to his feet. His power crackled in the air around him causing Dante's eyes to widen. "Do not make me repeat myself from last night, Dante. I have no qualms forcing you to your knees to remind you of your place."

Dante swallowed but didn't back down. "And I feel I need to remind you that I have never seen you as happy as you are when you are with Kee."

"That is none of your concern!" He shouted, pushing down and locking up the feelings that persisted. "She—"

"Am I interrupting?" Kee asked in a raised voice as she stepped into the room.

Lucas sucked in a breath as he looked at her. She wore a pair of dark blue skinny jeans and a long sleeve black shirt that hugged her torso. Her hair hung over her shoulder in a loose braid, the ends of it falling to her waist. The two hours of sleep had done nothing for the dark smudges under her eyes, and he could see the obvious tension in her shoulders.

Dante turned his head to look at her and gave a somewhat forced smile. "I'm not sure," he hummed and gave Lucas a knowing look. "Is she interrupting something you were saying, *my lord?*"

Lucas could have decapitated him then and there. If Keira had not been there, perhaps he would have then regretted his decision later. "No," he bit out and ran his hand into his hair. "We were just discussing the plan for tonight."

"Yes, *that's* what we were discussing," Dante gestured at the man standing quietly behind Kee. "And who's this?"

Kee stared at Lucas for a few seconds longer, trying to figure out what was wrong with him, before turning and putting her hand on Samson's shoulder. "This is Samson. I wanted to introduce him to you two."

Samson cautiously watched as Dante approached him. When the vampire held his hand out to him, he shook it.

Dante appreciated the firm grip. "Welcome, Samson. I'm Dante, head of security here at Byte as well as second-ranked in the Los Angeles Coven." He held on to the man's hand when he tried to release him. "Interesting. You're not a wolf."

Samson gave him a neutral expression as he pulled his hand back. "I didn't say I was."

His fangs were visible when he grinned. "True, but when I heard Kee had a new pet, I assumed it was another wolf."

Kee bristled when Sam shot her a glare over his shoulder. "He's not a pet!" She snapped and pointed an accusing finger at Lucas. "Quit saying that Conrad and Samson are my pets! They're people, damn it!"

Lucas waved his hand at her dismissively. "You take in strays, give them a place to go, and care for them. That sounds like a pet to me."

"This must be the boyfriend that wanted to kill me," Samson

mused as his black gaze fell on the other vampire.

Dante laughed when Lucas tensed and Kee blushed in embarrassment. "Oh, this is a story I would love to hear. Anything with her *boyfriend*."

"Is that what you told him I was?" Lucas asked in a tone that was soft but icy. He violently shoved down the swell of joy that tried to rise when she referred to him as her boyfriend. It was such a mundane term and yet he wasn't blind to the implications of it.

Kee's brow furrowed, but her cheeks remained pink. "Well, yeah."

"Is that so?" He pressed.

Dante clenched his jaw as all humor left him. "Lucas, don't."

Kee's eyebrows drew together in confusion, her eyes darting to Dante then back to Lucas. "What else should I call you?"

"Bonded?" Lucas suggested frigidly.

She recoiled like he hit her. "Excuse me? Are you telling me that is all we are? Bonded?"

"There is a modern, crude phrase for what else we are, I suppose. What do they call it?" He pretended to ponder it.

Samson scoffed, surprising everyone in the room. "Fuck buddies doesn't include feelings. I may have been in and out of consciousness when you guys rescued me, but I heard enough to know you're more than that."

Dante clapped with another laugh. "See? Even the new guy knows that's bullshit."

Kee ignored the two of them as she stared at Lucas, dumbfounded. He met her stare, and she tried searching the green depths for any indication of what he was feeling. Now that she knew how it felt to feel something from him through their connection, she knew what to look for. She reached for the bond that bound them, trying to decipher what was going on.

At first, she didn't feel anything then realized it was something similar to a cold numbness. She focused harder on it and could slowly make out a few of the emotions he was trying to hide. Irritation and reluctance hovered over anger, but she could feel the tendrils of longing and satisfaction.

What the hell was going on with him?

"Lucas? What is going on?" She asked, her voice stern. "What did I do to mess things up between us? Is it because you had to leave? Because I gave Sam my blood? Or is it because I didn't listen to you?" When he simply held her gaze, she glared. "Or did you decide to belittle our relationship because I told you I was going to help Cain tomorrow night? Are you that insecure?"

Lucas was aware of everyone's eyes on him, curious to his response. "You left me once before to go back to him."

"You and I got into a fight and I had just learned that your enemy was the reason behind my attack. I officially broke up with him that next day, Lucas." She threw her hands up. "I chose you. I want to be with you. I don't know how else I'm supposed to prove that. Clearly introducing you as my boyfriend is not enough and was the wrong thing to do." She cleared her throat and straightened her spine. "Sam, let me introduce you to my bonded vampire, Lucas Vranas, Lord of Los Angeles County."

Samson crossed his arms across his chest looking unimpressed. "I think I like Cain better and I haven't even met him."

Kee stepped protectively in front of Samson when Lucas' eyes bled red. "Don't." She warned with a menacing glare.

"I don't need to be protected from someone who hides from himself." The dragon commented as he stepped out to stand beside her.

"I like this guy." Dante grinned and sat down on the leather couch. "Why don't we save this fight for after the one tonight? That way Giovanni can get in on it."

Kee sobered at the mention of the vampire doctor. She sighed as she looked at the fuming Lucas once again. "Dante is right. Gio is more important right now. We can deal with this later. Tell me what you have planned."

Lucas closed his eyes, and when he parted them a few moments later, they were back to their normal color. He walked around his desk and leaned against the edge of it. "The Arcadia coven is a strip club. It has a second story for private rooms and a basement for the vampires."

"Do we assume Gio and Aubrey are in the basement?" Dante asked.

"I think that would be too obvious, wouldn't it? I bet they're upstairs in one of the rooms." Kee suggested.

"Hmm, that may be true. He could be keeping Giovanni in a room just barely dark enough to save him from burning. It would keep him weak. Maybe Aubrey is with him." He added with his chin in his hand. "If they're both still alive, that is."

Kee winced and peered at Lucas' rigid posture. "I have faith they're still alive, Lucas," when he gave her a somewhat grateful look, she added. "What's my role?"

Dante grinned. "How's your dancing?"

She gave him a deadpanned stare. "You're kidding."

"I'm not." He answered with another fangy grin. "The Arcadia lord has a rotation of girls on Saturday nights that tend to cater to the needs of vampires. If you know what I mean."

"Let me guess, you want me to be one of those girls." She said with a blank stare.

"Yep. You could audition and say that you're open to feeding as well. Lucas and I will go there as customers and use you as an excuse to get upstairs." He explained.

"That's too many coincidences. If they have any brains, they'll figure out what you're up to." Samson commented. "A new girl starts and suddenly two of the vamps from the LA coven show up the same night to take her upstairs? I'm guessing it's no secret to other vampires that your people were taken and that you are looking for them."

Kee caught Dante's suspicious look. "Samson was raised as a soldier. You should listen to him, Dante."

"And what would you suggest, Mister...?" Lucas asked.

"Richland, but call me Samson," he said. "It would be better if one of you went instead of both. Maybe one of you could keep tabs on the outside? Or perhaps subdue the security detail, but both of you going inside as customers is too suspicious." He glanced at Kee. "If you're really going to putting yourself in a vulnerable position, I could go in and pose as a customer as well. No one knows who I am."

Kee wanted to protest, but she knew he was right. "Do you feel well enough to do that? If Alexander is there with Jada, there's going to be a fight."

"Do you?" He countered. "You look like shit. My wounds are mostly better, but if I can wear someone's long sleeve shirt, it will cover my bandages." He tilted his head at her. "You can't cover yours if you're prancing around basically naked."

"I forgot about your scars, too," Dante murmured. "Maybe we should ask Lucy."

"No," Kee snapped. "I'm already not comfortable including Sam, but he has a point. We would have the element of surprise with him."

"The best thing," Samson began. "Would be if one of you already knew one of the girls there. That way you can say you came back to meet her for seconds." He shrugged. "Do you know any of them?"

"Not personally, but we know who will be working. They post the rotation on their website," Lucas said then glanced knowingly at Keira. "There is one way to solve that issue. It also solves the issues of how you can hide your scars and wounds."

Samson also looked at Kee. "Is that something that you can do?" He didn't know what kind of limits shapeshifters had, but now he was curious to find out.

"You suggesting she go in furry form?" Dante asked skeptically.

For the plan to work, Kee would have to shift into one the dancers. She would also have to tell Dante exactly what she was. She rubbed her face and let out a sigh. "Dante, I've been keeping something from you," she looked uncertainly at Lucas but continued on when he nodded at her. "I'm not exactly a werewolf."

Twenty-Six

"Lord Lucas, welcome!"

Lucas glanced up at the Lord of Arcadia as he hurried over to his table. The man was a short, scrawny thing. His shoulder length, brown hair was greased back into a low ponytail and clashed with his gaudy, black sequined suit. Lucas still had a hard time understanding how Jeremy hadn't been challenged for his position yet. Since Arcadia was part of LA County, Lucas had appointed Jeremy as lord but didn't expect him to last as long as he had.

"Jeremy," Lucas stood and shook the man's hand before sitting back down. "I see your club is as prosperous as always."

And it was. Tips was packed with patrons. The strip club was decorated in black furniture and different hues of red for the walls, carpet, and lighting. The club had a wide stage with a pole in the middle, and each chair that lined the tip rail was taken. The tables that were scattered in front of the stage and DJ booth were full of eager men of all species. The bar, situated off to the far right of the club, was busy with people trying to order. Lucas could barely make out Samson sitting at the bar, a half-empty glass of beer sitting in front of him.

"Tips is doing well!" Jeremy agreed with a grin full of fangs. "I mean, it managed to capture your attention! Not that I am displeased, but may I ask what brought you in?"

Lucas leaned back in his seat with a small smirk. "I am sure you know of my missing bleeder." He saw the vampire swallow but continued on as if he hadn't. "I met a young woman last evening who piqued my interest. She told me she works here and so I have come to pay her a visit." His smirked turned predatory. "I am looking to have another sample before writing up a contract."

Jeremy visibly relaxed. "Oh? And who is it? I'll be happy to bring her over to you."

"I believe she said her stage name is Scarlett." He answered calmly.

His smile faltered. "Scarlett, you say? She's one of my best."

"I can see why. She is quite the charmer." He gave the other vampire a knowing look. "And delicious in more ways than one."

"Y-yes, she is. It would just be a shame to lose her." He mumbled.

He tilted his head. "Is it not the greatest compliment to have your lord take her as his bleeder?" He lowered his tone. "Or have I insulted you, Jeremy?"

"N-no, of course not, my lord!" He quickly stammered in reply. "I would be honored."

Lucas cut off his reply when a seductive laugh reached his ears. He watched as a tall woman with long, black hair approached their table. Her eyes were a light brown and lined with thick eyeliner and smoky eyeshadow. Her lips were painted a deep crimson and matched the push-up bra she wore. The bottoms she wore were black and a couple inches wider than a thong. Her long legs had black, sheer stockings that went up to her thighs and clipped in place by a red garter belt. He appreciated the way the elastic dipped into the meat of her thigh, making a small dip between the edge of the stocking and her skin.

"You came," she cooed as Lucas stood to greet her. "I'm surprised, Mr Vranas."

He took her hand in his and pressed a gentle kiss to the inside of her wrist. "I do not go back on my word, Miss Scarlett."

She batted her thick, fake eyelashes at him then turned to her boss. "Are you going to hog my new friend?" She asked with a pout as Lucas sat back down.

Jeremy gave her a grim smile. "Of course not, Scarlett. I just didn't realize you wanted to be tied down with a contract."

"It only takes one man to change your mind." She teased and slowly slinked down until she was sitting in Lucas' lap. She swung her legs over the chair's arm so her ass pressed directly against his crotch.

Lucas' hand came to rest on her thigh, his fingertips trailing along the edge of the elastic. "I can be very persuasive." He almost purred as he looked at Scarlett with a hungry expression.

"Well, I suppose I will leave you two alone. Don't forget about our regular when he comes, Scarlett. You know he fancies you more than anyone else. He throws a fit if he doesn't get his time with you." Jeremy reminded her.

Lucas' fingers twitched on her thigh before he tightened his grip. He shot the lord a cool stare. "Am I being limited on the time I can spend with my potential bleeder?"

Jeremy flinched. "Of course not, my lord." He gave a forced, nervous laugh. "She's just a very hot commodity around here and business is business."

"I'm sure he will pay me for my time." Scarlett leaned into Lucas, her hand sliding up his neck. She ran her fingers into his hair, her painted red nails scraping along his scalp. "Right, Mr Vranas?" She hummed into his ear.

He didn't break eye contact with Jeremy. "Of course."

She glanced at her boss again. "See?"

Lucas brushed his lips along the side of her neck. "May we continue our night now, Jeremy? I grow...eager."

A muscle ticked in Jeremy's jaw, but he nodded. "Of course. I hope you have a pleasant night, my lord. Should you need anything, please don't hesitate to ask."

"I will remember that," Lucas murmured against the column of Scarlett's neck. When the club owner walked away, he waited until he was out of ear shot to lightly scrape his fangs along her soft skin. "This is quite the outfit."

Kee smirked. "What, you don't like it?"

The four of them had taken an SUV with tinted windows to the club. Dante had waited for the real Scarlett at the back entrance of Tips while Kee, Lucas, and Samson waited in the car. It didn't take long for Dante to compel her, guiding her to the car and encouraging her inside. While Dante put her to sleep with his compulsion, Kee copied her image and snagged the bag of outfits the girl brought for the night.

When the bouncer at the door had asked her what happened, she gave a flirty laugh and winked at them, telling them a lady doesn't kiss and tell. They merely rolled their eyes and let her into the club. Scarlett didn't seem to have the best reputation.

"I did not say that," he rebutted. "It looks good on this body, but what about yours?"

Kee pulled back from him and looked at the stocking on her thighs. "I guess you'll never know since we're only *bonded*." She shifted and purposefully added more weight to his crotch. "Pity."

Lucas almost couldn't stop the groan from escaping his lips. "We can discuss that later. How are the shoes?"

She looked at the black, 8-inch stilettos strapped to her feet. "They're actually not too bad, but ask me again when I get off stage." She gave a heavy sigh. "If I fall on stage, just continue without me because I'll be dead from embarrassment."

"I rather look forward to it." He replied with a smirk.

She narrowed her eyes at him. "Don't flirt with me. You can't say we're nothing and then act like we're something two hours later. Make up your mind or stay away." She whispered so no one else would hear over the loud music.

Her harsh words startled him, as if he hadn't considered that she would give him an ultimatum. Because, quite frankly, he hadn't. Emotional distance was one thing, but could he physically stay away from her?

He was about to answer but was cut off when the DJ's voice boomed out over the music. "Scarlett, stand by!" He announced.

"Damn it," Kee cursed as her stomach fluttered with nerves. She stood from Lucas' lap and eyed the people seated at the chairs lining the stage. She cursed when Jeremy moved towards their table again. She cleared her throat and turned on her charm again. "You can wait another three minutes before taking me upstairs, can't you, Mr Vranas? I'm sure Jeremy can keep you company while I am dancing." She winked at him then turned towards the stage with a sway in her hips.

Lucas leaned back in his chair with a grim expression, Kee's words ringing in his ears. He glanced at Jeremy when he cleared his throat. "Yes, Jeremy?" He asked, trying to keep the irritation from his voice.

"Can I get you a drink while you wait, my lord? We have plenty of willing bleeders here. All different blood types, too!" He said with wide smile, the dim lights reflecting on his fangs.

"I appreciate the offer," he answered. "But I will wait for Scarlett for my drink."

"Of course," he murmured with a hint of disappointment. "Well, enjoy the show."

Lucas turned his attention to the stage when the song began, zeroing in on Keira as she sauntered onto the stage. She may have been wearing someone else's image, but all he could see was her. She approached the center of the stage with a sway in her hips, her hands gingerly wrapping around the pole once she reached it. She did a small spin that left her facing the club. He sucked in a breath when she slowly traced her hands down her body, fingers skimming over her breasts and down her waist. Her back slid down the pole, her hands running down and across her thighs as she dipped down into a squat.

He clenched his jaw tighter and tighter as he watched Keira continue her show. He gripped his hands tightly as he watched her interact with the customers at the tip rail, her flirty smile and batted eyelashes causing them to carelessly throw their money at her. He almost shot up from his chair when one foolish man slid a dollar bill into the side of her bottoms, his hand brushing over the curve of her ass.

Rage burned through him at the image of someone else's hands on Keira's body. True, it wasn't technically her body at the moment, but it was still *her*. He had every intent to deny his feelings for her and push her away in order to keep her safe. To keep her alive. But the question still stood: *could* he stay away from her? Could he handle knowing that someone else would eventually have her? And that it could very well be Cain of all people? The answer was almost blindingly apparent.

No, he thought miserably.

The thought that she would give her body, and her heart, to someone else was enough to bring him to his knees. He was foolish to think crass words and actions would change the truth. He knew it was dangerous and reckless to admit what he felt. But she was not Janrie nor Bridgette. What he felt for Keira was deeper. Stronger. She was stronger. Maybe he didn't have to fear for her.

Feeling eyes on him, he glanced up to see Samson staring at him with a smug, knowing smirk. Samson then turned his attention to the stage and Lucas felt his blood boil. Was the dragon after Keira? Did he want her, too? He was scowling at Samson when the shifter suddenly swiveled in his seat, his back to the stage. He blinked away his glare and looked at the stage again.

He wish he hadn't.

Keira had taken off her top, the enlarged breasts of Scarlett's body freely exposed to the crowd. He couldn't see the scars that decorated her torso, but he imagined them there, bared for the club to see. He hated it. He knew she was growing more accustomed to the four pale lines, sometimes exposing the top of them with certain shirts she wore, but only *he* saw them entirely. He was the one to adore her scars with his hands and mouth. She trusted him to not judge her, to not look at her differently.

Lucas ripped his eyes away from her and forced himself to look down at the table. He unclenched his jaw when he felt a molar crack from the pressure and stuck the tip of his tongue to one of his fangs. The prick of pain and the ooze of blood helped him clear his mind of the sudden urge to slaughter every male in the near vicinity.

After a few tense minutes, he stood when he saw Keira walking towards him. He held out his arm to her and felt the rest of his ire settle when her warm hand settled into the crook of his elbow. "Shall we?"

She quirked an eyebrow at him as they made their way to the VIP area. "What, no comment on my stunning performance?"

He decided not to confess how angry and jealous it had made him. "You did not fall."

Kee laughed despite the disappointment she felt. "Bonus points, right?" She had tried to make eye contact with him while she was dancing, but every time she had looked at him, he was looking somewhere else. Maybe he really didn't feel the same way she did.

They walked through the dance area, past the rows of single dance booths, and reached a flight of stairs. They climbed it in silence and came to a stop when they reached the second story. In front of them was a long, narrow hallway, the left side containing five doors while the other remained a solid wall. Two of the doors were open, leaving three to be investigated.

Lucas held his arm out as she clutched his elbow for balance and quickly removed each of her high heels. "Are you going to stay like that?" He questioned when she was done, heels dangling from her fingers by their straps.

She shook her head and let the skin drop. She closed her eyes tightly as her body readjusted down to her height. A wave of nausea hit her, leaving her light headed. She didn't realize she had swayed until Lucas grabbed her shoulder and steadied her.

"I'm okay. Let's get to work," she whispered as she pulled away from him.

He frowned at her but nodded, heading to the first closed door. He pressed his ear against the wood and heard a couple laughing. He went to the next closed door, but only silence greeted him. When he tried the handle, it was locked.

Kee had gone to the third door and shook her head when she heard moaning and grunting. She went to stand beside Lucas and nodded at the door she just walked away from. "Unless Gio and Aubrey are having sex, it's not them."

"This door is locked, but I do not hear anything on the other side," he said as he grabbed the handle again. "Prepare yourself, just in case."

"I'm ready." As soon as she finished speaking, he twisted the knob hard enough to break it off. She sucked in a breath when he shouldered the door open but frowned when she didn't see anyone. The room was decorated in dark purple tones, but the plush love seat was made of crushed black velvet to match the rug. Lights were hung on the wall, but they were set to low and cast most of the room in shadows.

Lucas walked into the dimly lit room first, Keira soon standing beside him. He saw the small window and narrowed his eyes when he saw that curtain rings still hung on the rod above it, the actual curtains nowhere to be found. He slowly scanned the room and saw a huddled shape hiding in the couch's shadow. He instantly noted that it was on the side of the couch opposite of the window.

Kee saw it at the same time and took a small step forward. "Gio?" She called softly.

Lucas saw the form twitch and slowly uncurl to reveal his blood son. Even in the darkness, he could see how thin and pale Giovanni was. His chest was bare, showcasing how frail he had become. His ribs, sternum, and collar bones jutted out of white, paper thin skin. His veins scattered across his body in stark, contrasting blue lines. His cheeks were sunk in, his shoulder length brown hair matted and tangled. Bright red irises took the place of a usual warm, hazel color, and the white of his eyes were tinged pink.

"Giovanni," Lucas warned when the younger vampire stared hungrily at Keira. When Gio didn't blink or give any indication that he heard him, he cursed. "Keira, get—Giovanni!" He shouted when his son launched himself at the shapeshifter. He caught Gio's arm before he made contact with Keira and tossed him back onto the couch.

Gio hissed at Lucas, fangs elongated and nearly black. Lucas kneeled over him, holding him down by throat to pin him to the couch cushion. Gio writhed under him, red eyes still fixated on the only living body in the room. Being this close to him, Lucas could see the raw patches of skin from where the sunlight had scalded him. Oh yes, Alexander would pay dearly.

"He needs blood," Lucas explained before he stabbed his fang into his wrist. As expected, Giovanni's nostrils flared and his head whipped towards the source. "Drink, Giovanni." He cooed as he held his wrist to his lips. He didn't flinch as Gio eagerly sunk his fangs into the offered wrist and drank deeply.

"Do you want me to have Samson bring one of the blood girls up here? You can't feed him too much, Lucas, we still have to deal with Alexander and Jada." She said softly, not wanting to startle or draw Gio's attention to her again.

"Yes," he said and stared down at Gio as he gently stroked his hair, trying to comfort both of them.

Sam, can you hear me? She called out.

Everything alright? He answered almost immediately.

We found Gio, but he's in bad shape. He needs blood. Can you bring up one of the girls who lets vamps feed on them? Act like you're taking them to the VIP. We're in the middle room.

Give me five minutes.

"Sam says he'll be here in five. We need to tell Dante. He can get Gio out of here, right?" Kee asked.

He glanced at the window. "The window would be the only way to do it without raising too many questions."

She walked over to the window and didn't find a single latch or way to open it. "It's sealed."

Lucas flexed his hand as it started to tingle from the amount of blood he was losing. He cupped Giovanni's bottom jaw and applied pressure to the joint. He pulled his wrist away and used the hold to pin Gio's head back down. His son looked only marginally better, but he knew it would take a lot more blood to get him even remotely close to what he was.

Kee watched as Gio began thrashing under Lucas again, his fangs trying to bite into the arm holding him down. With a solemn expression, she looked away and covered her mouth with her hand.

Is it safe to come in? Samson's voice came.

She quickly moved to the door and opened it. She looked at the startled dancer and gave her a reassuring smile. "We have a vampire who needs a donation." She stated as she closed the door behind them.

"T-that's not what I agreed to." She stammered, looking at the crazed vampire on the couch.

"You don't allow vampires to feed on you?" Kee asked.

She blushed. "Well, I do, but I thought I was doing a normal VIP. It's extra for blood."

"I will pay you whatever you want," Lucas assured her, his gaze serious.

"Five hundred dollars?"

"Done. I just need your blood *now*."

The girl swallowed nervously, but she kicked off her heels and cautiously walked over to the loveseat. She winced when the starved vampire instantly stared at her with wide, ravenous eyes. "Will he hurt me?"

"I will compel you so you feel nothing." Her fear spiked and Giovanni let out a low, rumbling groan of need. "I swear he will not kill you."

"You promise?" She whispered.

"Yes," Lucas replied and held his free hand out to her, reaching for her. When she put her hand in his, his eyes shifted to red. He captured her stare and deepened his voice as he worked his spell. "My friend is going to feed upon you. He will not be gentle, but you will not feel it. In fact, it will be delightful. You will yearn for it. It will bring you pleasure, won't it?"

Her eyes glazed over and became glassy as she listened to the melody that was his voice. "Yes, yes it will."

"Good girl." He didn't break eye contact with her as he guided her wrist to Giovanni's mouth. "Remember, the initial bite will be the best."

"The best." She echoed with a drunken slur.

Lucas released Gio's jaw, and the younger vampire instantly attacked the wrist in front of him. The stripper gave a loud moan and tossed back her head when the fangs pierced her flesh. Lucas stood from the couch and approached Samson and Keira as they stayed near the door.

"Thank you." He said stiffly to the dragon.

"You're welcome," he answered and looked down at Kee. "You guys going downstairs?"

"Is it safe to leave her alone with Giovanni like this?" She asked Lucas.

"No, he'll drain her dry in the state he's in. He should only be allowed to feed from her for another ten minutes before her life is at risk." He admitted and ran his hands into his hair. "We need to get him out of here."

"Jeremy has to know that Alexander and Jada are here. This is his coven," Kee began. "So, if he sees Giovanni leaving, he'll know we caught them."

"Yes, but Jeremy is a weak coward," Lucas said as he inspected the damage done to his wrist. "He would rather run than face me."

"Yes, but will he tell your enemies that they have been found out?" She pointed out.

Lucas dropped his hand and looked at her. "It is possible. If so, then our time will be limited once we take Giovanni out of this room." He glanced over at the couch as Gio swallowed greedily. "After her, he should be subdued enough to not lash out at any moving, living person on the way out of here, but he will need more blood on the way back to LA or he will attack one of us in the car."

"I can take him out to Dante," Samson offered. "And you two can head to the basement."

Lucas nodded. "Dante will probably feed him as well to keep him content." He looked at the weredragon. "If Keira and I take too long, you two need to take Giovanni back to Byte and get him more blood."

He narrowed his eyes. "I'm not leaving my alpha behind."

Kee couldn't help but smile at the title. She put a hand on his arm and felt the surge of anger through her and Lucas' bond. She looked at him and saw him glaring at the hand touching Samson. She rolled her eyes and pulled her hand away. "I think it's better if Samson stays. He could help us if we need it. Dante can take care of Giovanni."

Lucas turned his scowl on her. "As it pleases you." He replied before turning and walking back towards Gio. He pulled out his phone and called Dante so he could relay the plan.

She sighed and looked at Samson. "Sorry for all this."

"Don't apologize," he said and tapped his nose while looking at hers. "You have some blood in your nostril."

She cursed and wiped at her nose. She pulled her hand away and saw a small smear of blood. Had it just started? Or did it happen when she felt nauseous? If so, why hadn't Lucas said anything? "I'm okay."

"Don't push yourself." He warned.

She gave a soft, forced laugh. "Too late for that." When his brow furrowed, she patted his arm again. "I'll be okay, Sam. We just need to find Aubrey and kill two other vampires."

"Just." He mocked.

Another tired laugh. "*Just.*" She agreed.

Twenty-Seven

Kee helped the unconscious dancer recline against the chaise, her body limp and heavy. She would wake up feeling like she had been in a deep, relaxed sleep, not as if she had been nearly drained dry by a starved vampire.

Samson draped one of Giovanni's arms around his shoulders, supporting his weight as he stood on unsteady legs. "Dante is going to meet me at the back?"

"Yes," Lucas replied, opening the door for him. "If we are fortunate, Giovanni won't be recognized until then. If that is the case, we will have more time to find Aubrey."

"And if we aren't?" Kee asked.

His eyes met hers. "Then Alexander and Jada will have time to set a trap. We have to also accept the very real likelihood that Jeremy already told them that I am here."

"Well, let's hope for the best," she said as she followed behind him.

"L-Luc—," Gio suddenly rasped, his voice rough and quiet. It was the first time he had spoken since they found him.

Lucas was there, standing in front of them. "I'm here, Giovanni."

Gio's brows knitted together before his eyes closed tightly. "Sorry."

His chest tightened. "You have nothing to apologize for, Giovanni. This is my fault. It is me they are after."

Gio shook his head, but then a pang hit him hard in the stomach. He felt as if his insides were bared to the sun, burning him from the inside. "*Blood*," he cried.

"Get him to Dante," Lucas ordered and was thankful when Samson didn't give him any lip. Instead, he simply pushed past him with Gio, swiftly carrying him down the stairs. Maybe the dragon wasn't quite so bad.

"What do you want me to do?"

He turned towards Kee as she walked towards him. "I want you to do what you have to in order to survive."

She pursed her lips together as he took her hands in his. "Didn't I just get done warning you about this?" She asked, but her tone lacked any heat. "Or are you just making sure your bonded wolf stays alive for your benefit?"

A muscle ticked in his cheek, but he bit back his irritation. "After this, we are going to have a long, overdue conversation, Keira. I will explain everything to you and we will go from there."

"Will it explain your sudden change of heart?"

"Yes," he answered and leaned forward to place a gentle kiss to her lips, pleased when she didn't pull away. "Survive this night, Keira."

Her expression grew serious. "You too."

He gave her hands a light squeeze. "I intend to."

She released his hands and shifted back into Scarlett's image. She then gave him a slight nod before following him down the stairs. Once they reached the bottom, Lucas brought them to a door on the other side of the stairs. It was marked with a sign that said "Authorized Personnel Only", but he twisted the handle and walked through.

Kee sent Samson a mental note of where the door was located as she followed Lucas down the narrow staircase. Unlike Byte's basement stairs, these weren't illuminated with any sort of light. It was pitch black, and she had to put her hand on Lucas' shoulder to keep from tripping.

Once they reached the bottom, the floor opened up to a room half the size of the club. There were two doors to the back of the room, but otherwise it reminded her of a wide, luxurious living room. One massive, grey fur rug covered the concrete floor and Kee wondered just how many animals had died to make it. Plush black couches, like the ones from the VIP room, were situated in the direct center of the room. They faced a black marble coffee table that had a familiar unconscious woman on top of it.

Lucas quickly went to the coffee table, turning the pale, naked body onto her back so he could look at her. He clenched his teeth at the various puncture wounds marring Aubrey's skin from neck to calves. He pressed his pointer and middle finger to her pulse point, avoiding a bite mark as he did. It was faint and weak, but her heart beat.

He tried to lightly shake her awake, but her body was unresponsive. She did not have long. He would need to give her his blood as soon as possible to start the transition. He began to lift his wrist to his mouth but froze when he heard one of the doors open.

He looked up and saw Alexander strolling towards him, a smug smirk on his lips. His face had healed from the previous damage Lucas inflicted, the skin smooth and perfect once again. He heard footsteps behind him but didn't take his eyes off Alexander.

"Lucas, so happy you could make it." Jada purred from behind him. "And you brought us a snack! How polite."

Kee stepped back so that both vampires were in her sight, but she kept her gaze on Jada. The female vampire was beautiful. Her skin tone a perfect caramel hue, the white silk dress she wore contrasting against it. Her curled hair was the color of honey and fell to the middle of her back. Her eyes, however, were cold, dark, and hungry.

"Jeremy wouldn't like you drinking from his top human girls." She commented, trying to keep Scarlett's persona.

"Oh, my dear, he will deny us nothing, not even you." She hummed as she sauntered towards her. "I do love a brunette."

"Please don't." She pretended to tremble, moving closer to Lucas and Aubrey.

"Why even bother bringing a weak human down here, Lucas?" Alexander asked with a harsh laugh. "Did you think to tempt us with her?"

His eyes narrowed slightly. "I hoped to trade her for my bleeder." He gestured at Aubrey's limp form.

"Maybe we'll just take both." The blonde shot back as he shoved his hands into the pockets of his pants. "Along with your blood son."

"The son is mine!" Jada suddenly snarled, making Kee ball her hands into fists. "A son for a son! You agreed!"

Alexander gave her a placating smile. "So I did."

"Grudges are an unflattering thing," Lucas commented as he stood and looked at Jada. "Your blood son violated my bleeder at the time and I avenged him."

"A bleeder and a blood son are not worth the same amount!" Jada growled, her eyes hard.

Lucas simply stared at her for a second before looking at Alexander again. "And what about a bonded wolf? They are nearly as equal as a blood child. Between the two of you, you have killed my wolf and nearly drained my bleeder. And what of Giovanni? You have taken all three of my closest connections, and for what? Because I beat you in a fight? Because I sought vengeance for my bleeder? You have both crossed the line."

Jada clucked her tongue at him. "We are going to dethrone and kill you, Lucas. Alexander will take your place and our two territories will be unstoppable."

Lucas cocked a brow at Alexander when he grinned. "Still going on about taking over the other preternatural creatures? You are more a fool than I thought."

His grin vanished, pale gold eyes narrowing once again in a glare. "You're hardly in a place to throw insults. You came here with a little human and you'll die for it."

Kee remained silent through the exchange, trying to emanate fear as she considered their options. If Lucas took on Alexander again, she would fight Jada. She wasn't sure she could win against the Lord of Riverside County, especially since she dabbled in magic, but she would at least keep her busy while Lucas was preoccupied.

"Come at me then, Alexander." Lucas replied calmly as he stepped away from Aubrey's form.

"But can you beat me without your curse?" He taunted as he flexed his fingers at his side, eyes locked on his opponent's.

"How about you? Do you believe you can win without your talons?" He shot back in a mocking manner.

"If it comes down to simple combat, I know I can beat you."

"Doubtful."

Kee barely finished blinking before the two clashed together in a flurry of blurred movements. She could hear the sound of flesh hitting flesh, but she could only see some of their fight. She had faith Lucas would win but didn't trust Alexander to play fair.

Keeping an eye on the sneering Jada, she cautiously made her way towards Aubrey. Reaching her still form, she kneeled down next to the table and checked for a pulse as Lucas had.

"Aubrey?" She called, lightly tapping Aubrey's cheek.

"There's no point in trying to wake her, human. She will be dead soon," Jada hummed as she stalked towards Scarlett, a smooth leg peeking out from the slit in her cream, silk dress. "Tell me, why did he bring you down here? Did he compel you?"

Kee hesitated slightly before answering. "I-I don't know," she said, pretending to think about her answer. "He asked me to be his bleeder and then asked where the coven hideout was."

Jada laughed. "Oh, little blood bank, he used you. Which I don't particularly blame him."

Her retort died on her tongue when Alexander crashed into the coffee table, knocking Aubrey's body into Kee's. She sat back against the floor under Aubrey's deadweight as Lucas straddled his opponent. She watched as he grabbed Alexander by the throat, jerked him forward, and slammed his head back against the floor. Kee winced at the sound as he repeated the action over and over again.

There was blur of white then Lucas hit the wall at the back of the room, his body crashing through the installed drywall. He lifted his lip in a soundless snarl as he held up his arms to stop the onslaught of attacks from Jada's steel-like nails. He clenched his jaw and tried to ignore the sizzling sensation that came from her scratches. He caught one of the glowing green hands that came at him and yanked her close as he placed a foot against her torso. With a hard kick of his leg, he sent her sprawling back towards the recovered Alexander.

She landed lightly on her feet, eyes gleaming with smug satisfaction. "How do you like my poison magic? I had to drain a few warlocks to obtain it, but it was quite worth it."

Lucas glanced down at his arms and noted the open wounds that bubbled with green tinted blood. However, despite the fizzling blood, his skin began to knit together, albeit slowly. "It will heal."

"Will it once we gut you, though?" Alexander asked, the blood trickling down his neck not phasing him in the least bit.

"You are welcome to try." Lucas replied coolly as he rose to his feet. He calmly lifted his hand to his chin and turned it to the right, cracking his neck. He supposed he could use his golden flame now that it was two against one, but he didn't want to risk it hitting Keira or Aubrey.

Kee shoved Aubrey's body off of her and stayed on the ground as she mentally rummaged through her collection of skins. Her body throbbed with exhaustion, but she would push on. No way would she leave Lucas to fight them both alone. But, what skin did she choose? What would give her the right edge?

Me. She felt a rumble deep within her chest and an echo of a growl within her mind as that familiar rough voice called to her.

Her nostrils flared with apprehension, but the beast knew how to fight and Cain's strength would only benefit her. Giving in, she closed her eyes and let the beast step forward. Just like last time, the cold slammed into her, making her shudder. However, instead of the warmth that came afterwards, a different sensation racked her. This pain she knew. She was all too familiar with the feeling that came from shifting into an animal. Last time she shifted into Cain, it was his human form, not his wolf one.

"I believe it's time to level the playing field." Lucas commented as soon as the other two vampires grew tense with the shift of energy in the room.

As soon as Alexander turned towards her, Kee was on him, jaws clamping down hard around his neck and pushing him back against the ground. He gagged and tried to push the massive wolf off of him, but she refused to budge. Taking a page from Liam's book, she shook her head hard, trying to tear out the vampire's throat.

Kee was aware of Lucas and Jada clashing again from the corner of her eye, but she kept her attention on Alexander. He grabbed the scruff of her neck in a painful grip and yanked. Cain's beast snarled in response, and she dug her claws into the vampire's chest, anchoring herself in place. She would not lose.

We won't, came the growl, reminding her she wasn't alone. Alexander took something precious from each of them.

For Cain, his mate. For Kee, her security.

They would kill this vampire who turned their worlds upside down.

They would win this fight.

"Where the *fuck* did you come from? Are you his wolf then?" Alexander choked on his words, blood spluttering from his lips. "You can't be. You're supposed to be dead!"

Kee and the beast growled in response, flexing their paws so that their claws sunk deeper into the flesh beneath it. They tried shaking their head again, but the grip on their fur stopped them. So, they flexed their jaw instead, trying to get to the spine.

Alexander pulled harder at the scruff and smirked when there was a slight whisper of pain in response. "I won't be done in by Lucas' pet!" He twisted his grip and gave a hard pull so that the wolf staggered to the side. Once he had his opening, he kicked her off him and rolled back onto his feet.

He gingerly touched his throat and scowled when he felt a chunk of it missing, leaving behind a wet, gaping hole. Fucking bitch. He would finish her off and get back to killing Lucas.

She hesitated when he crouched, not sure how to anticipate his next move. The beast, however, had better instincts. As soon as he charged at her with a slash of his long nails, her body was moving out of the way before she could comprehend it. She forgot how fast vampires could be.

"Stay still, mutt!" Alexander rasped, his voice barely more than a gurgle with the hole in his neck.

With the help of Cain's beast, Kee continued to dodge the attacks, ducking and leaping this way and that to avoid damage. She had almost evaded the last one, but a sudden wave of fatigue made her stumble. The edge of the attack grazed their leg, splitting open their skin enough so that blood matted the brown fur.

Alexander's nostrils flared at the smell of blood. The heady scent filled his nose and made him salivate. What was this blood? It wasn't like Warren's, nor like any other wereanimal he had fed from before. It was rich and smelled warm, if temperature had a scent. A strong need tore through him. His fangs lengthened and pulsed as a raw, primal hunger took over him. He felt starved, as if he hadn't fed in days.

Kee snarled at him even as her body began to tremble. She could feel blood dripping from her nose and gathering in her triangular ears. A fuzzy feeling filled her head, making it feel both heavy and light at the same time. Fuck, this was not happening. Not now!

Alexander lunged for her, pupils dilated and iris red with blood lust. She tried to leap back, but her tingling back legs tripped on a piece of the broken table. The remaining legs slipped out from under her and the beast disappeared with a growl. She cried out at the spasm that racked her body when she shifted back into herself. Red blurred and burned her vision so she tried to blink it away. It was only a split second, but when she opened her eyes, Alexander was looming over her, fangs bared as he went for her neck.

She instantly threw her arms out, hands going to his shoulders to keep distance between them. Red filled her vision again, making her eyes burn. Her temples were pounding, her head tingling like her limbs. Her arms shook and right as they caved, Alexander was gone. She rolled onto her side, propping herself up on a weak elbow to see what happened.

The relief was immediate and she couldn't help but say his name like it was a prayer, "Samson."

Samson had one hand underneath Alexander's jaw, the other cradling the back of the blonde's head. When he gave Kee a questioning look over Alexander's head, she hesitated. Alexander's death is what she wanted. It was the endgame to all of her plans, the climax of her vengeance. His death at her hands was supposed to make everything. . .better. She wasn't naïve enough to think it would take away all her pain and anger, but it was supposed to be the starting point.

But she had to face the facts, she couldn't do it. He had bested her and she was too weak to try fighting him again. So, with a swallow of her pride, she gave him a single nod. She watched with satisfaction as Samson twisted with all his might. The vampire's head nearly did a full circle with a chorus of loud cracks. The hole that had been made with her teeth was now a wide fissure across his neck.

Vampires could heal from a broken neck. Only decapitation or a stake through the heart would kill them. So once his neck was broken, Samson wrapped his hand in Alexander's hair and placed the other hand on his shoulder for leverage. With a violent tug, he pulled the head free from the body. Blood spurted out from the arteries in his neck, but Samson dropped both body and head to the ground without a care.

The weredragon looked at Kee and went to her side, unbuttoning his shirt as he did. Ignoring her nude body, he inspected the blood on her face with a frown. "You're bleeding from every opening on your face."

"I pushed myself too far," she mumbled as he helped her into a sitting position. She slid the shirt on, but her shaking hands couldn't manage the buttons. Red stung her eyes once again and she cursed, pressing the hem of the sleeves to them. When she pulled them away, she saw the crisp white material was smeared with blood. "Fuck, my eyes too?"

"I told you," he replied then looked up as Lucas approached them.

"Are you hurt, Keira?" He asked, holding the shredded skin on one of his forearms.

Jada, like Alexander, had been distracted by the tempting scent of Keira's blood. He had tackled her to the floor before she could get to his shapeshifter. Using his fists, he bashed in her skull. She clawed at his arms, doing real damage before her face finally caved in under the pressure of his punches. He then broke her neck and ripped her head from her body, giving a petty kick to her head to send it flying into the nearest wall.

Kee shook her head and was aware that her body swayed with the action. Samson put a steading hand on her shoulder, and she was grateful for it. She looked up at Lucas and her mouth fell open at his tattered arms. The blood seeping from the wounds was nearly black, a bubbling green liquid mixed in with it. "Lucas! What the hell did she do to you?"

He glanced over at Jada's limp body and glared. "Poison." When she sucked in a startled breath, he added, "I will heal once I feed, Keira."

She shook her head. "You gave Gio your blood, fought two lord vamps, and now you have to feed Aubrey. When are you going to have time to feed? Will you even have enough to spare her?"

Lucas turned his attention to Aubrey and frowned at the grey tint her skin had taken on. When exactly had she passed? He would have to give her blood now if he were to turn her. But his shapeshifter was correct, did he have enough to spare without jeopardizing himself? He wasn't sure, but he couldn't break the contract with Aubrey.

Kee took a deep breath before reaching a hand out towards Lucas. He took it with a puzzled expression. "I can't stand," she huffed. "Come down here."

He did as she asked, but his jaw clenched when she pushed her hair over her shoulder. He knew what she was doing, what she was going to offer. "No."

She ignored him and shrugged one shoulder free of Samson's shirt. "Feed from me."

"I promised you I would not," he said, his voice low and angry. He moved to stand, but she grabbed his shirt and stopped him. "Do not make me break my word to you, Keira."

"You need my blood," she pointed out. "We both know what it did for you last time you were hurt. I'm giving you permission to drink my blood, Lucas. Do it."

Samson's brow furrowed. "Kee, you're in no shape to donate blood. You're already weak."

She cut her eyes to him before looking back at Lucas. "I just pushed my shifting limits. You've seen me do it before." His eyes fell to the bloody cut on her leg and she tugged on his shirt to get his attention. When those angry green eyes met hers, she softened her expression. "It's just a cut. You know you need to do this."

"And if I lose control like last time?" He questioned, his tone cold.

She looked at Samson again, giving him a reassuring smile. "You will stop him if that happens, right?"

Samson pinched his lips together, unhappy with the situation. "If this is what you want."

"It's what needs to be done." She turned her attention back to Lucas and gave him a small, loving smile. "You're not breaking your promise. If Aubrey dies, you'll be punished. I don't know what that means the Lord of California will do, but I need you. Please do this. For us."

Lucas' eyes softened, his body relaxing slightly. "Damn it, Keira," he sighed but shifted so he was kneeling in front of her. He opened his arms to her and she crawled into his lap, straddling him. His hand cupped the underside of her jaw while the other arm wrapped around her waist. He ignored the pain in his arm and stared into her face, searching for any hint of fear or regret.

"You can still say no." He whispered. *Please say no.*

"I trust you." Kee pressed her lips lightly against his, giving him a gentle kiss. "Bite me," she demanded when she pulled away.

With a tick of his jaw, he angled her face to the side and lowered his mouth to the sweet spot where her neck met her shoulder. He kissed it tenderly before flicking his tongue along the warm skin, making sure his endorphins were active this time. He gave her a gentle squeeze of warning before he bared his fangs and bit down. She tensed in his arms for a few seconds, but with a hard pull of his mouth, she let out a keening noise.

Just like the first time, her taste exploded on his tongue. Sweet, tangy, and rich. Her blood slid down his throat and seemed to fill his veins with power. With each swallow of blood, warmth consumed him as if he had stepped straight into the sunlight after centuries in the dark. He felt the wounds on his arms throb and knew they were knitting together like last time.

She moaned softly in his ear and he tightened his hold around her, sucking harder on her neck. He felt her hand rest on the back of his head, her fingers lacing into his hair and he continued to drink, the taste and feeling of her blood eliciting his own groan. Her moans of pleasure in his ear turned to breathy sighs and he felt her tug on his hair. He rumbled in his chest and flexed his jaw to embed his fangs deeper into her skin.

"Lucas," she mumbled into his ear as her hand fell away.

He wanted to keep drinking, but that edge of pleading in her voice made him hesitate. He blinked when he heard a growl, the warning in it clear and deadly. He lifted his eyes to see the dragon snarling at him. He blinked again, forcing himself out of the haze her blood had trapped him in. He instantly removed his fangs from her skin and gently ran his tongue over the angry puncture wounds.

Lucas pulled back from her neck and realized she had become deadweight in his arms. He gently cradled the back of her head when it started to fall back and frowned at her pale face. Worried, he gave her a little shake. "Keira," he called and felt a surge of relief when one eyelid parted for a brief moment before sliding shut again.

"I was this close to ripping you away from her." Samson growled, eyes narrowed into a seething glare.

"You should have sooner," he replied but kept his tone soft. He pressed a tender kiss to her lips and readjusted his hold on her so that he could lift her. "Take her. I have to tend to my bleeder."

Samson awkwardly took Kee's body from the vampire and supported her weight against his chest. He looked away as Lucas fixed her shirt, buttoning it shut before standing. "How long will this take?" He questioned.

"Not too long." Lucas answered as he rolled Aubrey onto her back. His arms were still healing so he chose the least damaged wrist and bit into it with his fangs. Once the blood welled up, he pressed it over the human's mouth, letting it drip inside. As he had done with Keira, he rubbed her throat and coaxed the liquid down, hoping it wasn't too late.

"Don't you think taking two unconscious, naked women upstairs will draw some attention?" Samson asked with a frown.

"At this point, I do not care. We will figure it out once I am done."

A minute or two went by before Samson spoke again. "What do you intend to do afterwards? Didn't the owner help them?"

He removed his wrist from Aubrey's mouth and lifted her into his arms before turning to the dragon. "I plan on burning this place to the ground, of course."

Samson stared at him for a second before a small smirk titled up the corner of his mouth. "Can I help?"

Twenty-Eight

Kee twitched awake when someone shook her. She tried to open her eyes and winced when she felt resistance. She rubbed at them, clearing away the crust she felt. When she pulled her hands away and looked at them, she saw flaked blood speckled on her skin. Aware of eyes on her, she looked up and couldn't help but smile at Conrad and Lucy.

"You look like shit." Lucy commented with a small smile as she approached the bed with a wet cloth.

"So I've been told." Kee gave her a wry smile and sat up, graciously accepting the towel. "Thanks, Luce." She wiped at her eyes and then at her nose when the scent of old blood hit her.

"Pushing your limits again, hm?" Conrad asked as he sat on the edge of the bed.

"Apparently," she answered as she moved to her ears, cleaning up the remaining traces of blood. She set the cloth down on the night-stand and rubbed her face again. Gods, her body hurt. It felt heavy and stiff. Her head was killing her, her chest tight and cold. "I'm exhausted. What time is it?"

"Close to five." Lucy responded as she went to the dresser and pulled out a pair of dark jeans and a long sleeve white shirt. "You need to get ready for the alpha challenge."

Kee groaned, burying her face in her hands. "Fuck, I forgot. Last night drained me."

"Literally." Lucy shot her a pointed look as she rummaged through Kee's underwear drawer, pulling out panties and a bra. Once the outfit was complete, she handed her the pile of clothes. "Samson told me about last night. Lucas drank from you, hm?"

Kee grazed her fingertips over the two puncture holes on the side of her neck. "He didn't have a choice and I offered." She explained as she unbuttoned the shirt.

Conrad turned his head away as Kee stood from the bed and began dressing. "I thought Lucas refused to drink from you." He then turned his attention to Lucy with a raised brow. "When did you talk to Samson?"

"Early this morning." She walked to him, stepping between his legs and framing his face with her hands. "I was sitting outside Byte, worried about Kee and the others. After a while, they showed up and I helped them get everyone inside. He told me what happened."

His hands went to her hips, pulling her in closer with a smile. She angled his head up, and he met her halfway for a kiss. He swiped his tongue over her bottom lip and resisted the urge to grin when her lips parted.

"You know that I'm still in the room, yeah?" Kee commented dryly as she watched them swap spit in front of her. Still, she couldn't help but smile.

Lucy pulled back at their alpha's comment and giggled when Conrad's hands went to her ass, pulling her in again. "Con! Don't be bad!" She scolded, but her cheeks were flushed.

Kee rolled her eyes then looked up when the door opened. She couldn't help but laugh. Samson walked in with a bemused expression, Mia hanging on his back with a huge grin on her face.

That was until the little wolf spotted her dad holding Lucy. She frowned and slid off Samson's back, landing lightly on her feet. "You're going to be late, Daddy."

Conrad sighed at the reminder. "I know, I know," he pressed another kiss to Lucy's lips before standing from the bed. He kneeled down in front of his daughter and smoothed her hair back. "You be good for Lucy and Samson, okay?"

"I will," she mumbled in reply. A reluctant smile curved up her lips when he kissed her forehead. "I love you."

"Love you more, baby girl. Have fun tonight." He straightened and turned to Kee. "I'll see you at Warren's?"

She nodded. "Yeah, I'll be there." She blinked when Samson whipped his head towards her, eyes narrowed.

Samson stepped aside so Conrad could walk past him but kept his angry gaze on Kee. "Are you kidding me?"

Kee lifted a brow. "What?"

"You're still going tonight? After the shit you went through?" He asked, hands balling into fists.

"Hey! Watch your mouth around Mia, Samson." Lucy said, crossing the room to stand next to Mia. "Come on, Mia, let's go watch that crime show I told you about."

Emilia scowled at the hand that was held out to her before turning her gaze on Kee. "Do I have to?"

Kee gave her an encouraging smile. "Sam and I need to talk, okay?"

"Fine." She gave a heavy sigh and turned to leave, Lucy following behind her.

Waiting until they were gone, Kee looked at Samson. "Why are you so angry?"

"Because you're in no condition to do anything." He answered. "You haven't had any rest since you rescued me and you're still hurt."

"I appreciate your concern, Sam, but I'm only going for moral support. You don't have to worry."

"Warren wants to kill you. What is Cain fails?" He pressed.

She gave a hallow laugh. "Warren isn't the only one who wants me dead." When he cringed, she moved closer to him, putting her hands on his shoulders. "I'm sorry, that was a bad joke. I'll be okay."

"You don't know that. You haven't been sleeping, have multiple wounds, pushed your shifting limits, and fed a vampire. You should be here recuperating." He pursed his lips together. "If you insist on going then I should go with you."

"Samson, it's not your job to protect me, but mine to protect you and the rest of the pack. It's why I need you to stay here and watch over Mia and Lucy. I need you to do it in my stead." She explained softly.

"But I'm not pack." He argued.

She tsk'ed and squeezed his shoulders. "Of course, you are. You proved yourself to me last night. I know you don't know me or the other members yet, but I knew you were mine as soon as you spoke to me at The Street." At his torn expression, she wrapped her arms around him in a hug. "I trust you."

He stiffened, his spine going ramrod straight. With the exception of his time with Kee and Mia, he hadn't been touched in a nonviolent way in months. When no pain came, he felt an unfamiliar comfort begin to seep into his body. It wasn't just comfort though; it was security as well. A feeling of home and belonging.

Kee smiled when his arms tentatively looped around her shoulders, returning the hug albeit awkwardly. When his arms loosened again, she released him and patted the top of his head. "Welcome to the pack, Samson."

"Thanks." He murmured with a small smile.

She then lightly tapped his cheeks. "So, your first order is to stay here and protect your pack mates." When his face fell, she gave him a grin then made her way to the door. "I'll see you later."

He let out a heavy sigh. "Fine. Just be careful."

"I will. Try to have fun tonight."

—

"Thanks for coming." Cain said earnestly as Kee walked up the driveway towards him.

"You're welcome." She replied, but her focus was on the black Mercedes.

"Kee—" Katie blurted then suddenly stopped herself, gaze on the floor as she anxiously wrung her hands together.

Kee blinked then lifted a brow. "Yes, Katie?"

Her jaw clenched before she let out a quiet, "Sorry."

The shapeshifter blinked in surprise before letting out a soft sigh. "I'm not exactly sure what you're apologizing for, but don't. We were both wronged, okay? Let's just not forget the common factor of why we suffered."

"Warren," Katie hissed out, hands clenched. "It's all his fault."

She nodded once. "Cain will make him pay today so everything will be worth it. We killed his bonded vampire last night. He has to be hurting from that."

Cain stared at her in surprise. "You did? For me?"

She deadpanned at him. "No, not for you. For Lucas and for myself. It just happens to benefit you as well."

He looked smarted by her answer but didn't comment on it. "Let's get this over with."

Kee swept her arm out. "After you."

Cain led them to the house. They entered the front door and made their way through the cluttered mess on the floor. It looked like a bomb went off. The furniture was broken, curtains and rugs ripped and torn. Even the doors and drywall had holes in them.

The trio stepped into the backyard and the hair on Kee's neck stood up in warning. She glanced around the wide clearing and saw that the LA pack was situated off to the left, their eyes darting between Cain and Warren who was standing in the middle of the backyard. Liam, Conrad, and Zach were standing next to a trembling Natalie off to the right. Two other unfamiliar wolves stood with them. She made eye contact with Conrad and Zach, who each gave her a small nod.

"Cain Donovan," Liam called, his voice loud and rippling with power as he spoke. "Are you here to challenge the current Los Angeles City alpha, Warren Erickson?"

"I am." Cain declared confidently.

The pack murmured to themselves, eyes darting between their current alpha and the possible new one. Kee realized that no one else knew what was going on. They didn't know what their alpha had done.

"The winner will become new pack alpha, the loser's life forfeit should the winner deem fit," Liam announced and ignored the way Natalie stiffened at his side. "Fighting form is to be chosen by the current alpha."

Warren glanced over at Natalie then back to Cain, hands fisting at his sides. "Wolf."

"A battle of beasts, then," Liam stated and made a waving gesture. "Start when both sides are ready."

Cain pulled off his t-shirt and sweats and handed them to Katie. The setting sun warmed his skin, despite the chilly fall breeze blowing past him. When he turned back to Warren, he saw his old alpha making his way towards Natalie. He moved to stop him, but Liam had already stepped in front of her, a warning growl vibrating loud enough for everyone to hear.

Warren held up his palms in defense. "I mean her no harm." He said in a low voice, tortured eyes falling on his mate's form over Liam's shoulder. "I just want a chance to apologize should anything happen to me."

Natalie's bottom lip trembled as she stared at her mate. He was back, she was sure. She could see it in his eyes. The crazy edge to him was gone, but now he seemed somewhat hollow. She pushed past Liam and flung herself into her love's arms holding him tightly. "Warren," she cried, burying her face in his chest.

His beaten beast whined. He closed his eyes and held her to him, nuzzling her hair. "I can never apologize enough, Nat. Everything got away from me, but it's not an excuse. Nothing can excuse what I did to you. Ever. I don't deserve to even hold you right now."

"You're back now," she said, pulling back to look up at him. "You're my mate again."

He gave her a weak smile when she cupped his face in her hands. "I love you, Nat."

"I love you, too." She then took one of his hands and pressed it to her lower stomach. "We love you."

His ice blue eyes widened as he stared down at his hand. His eyes darted back to hers with a pained expression. "That's why you didn't join the last pack run," he murmured and pressed his forehead against hers. "I lost myself and was blind to something so important."

"I'm sorry I didn't tell you," she whispered, eyes stinging with unshed tears. "With how you were acting, I was scared."

He gently stroked her stomach, imagining the tiny life within her. "Don't apologize. I understand, Natalie. It's my fault, not yours. I should have never bonded myself to that vampire. It cost me everything."

"Warren," Liam interrupted. "It's time."

He pulled back and brushed away his mate's tears with his thumbs. He felt a surge of relief when she pressed her lips to his. He returned the kiss then forced himself to back away from her. He pulled off his clothes, and she took them from him before he could toss them on the ground.

Cain shifted into his wolf form, his body contorting and twisting until he stood on all fours, covered in fur ranging from dark brown to beige. He took calming breaths through his snout when Warren's black furred form approached him. His beast anxiously paced back and forth within him. His wolf wanted blood. Demanded retribution.

Warren stared at the wolf who had always been like a second brother to him. He knew this day would come eventually, but he never thought it would come in a violent, spiteful way. He always assumed their fight for alpha would be one of pride, not revenge. Just another thing he messed up.

The backyard was silent, everyone feeling tense and holding their breath for the first strike. They didn't have to wait long; Warren lunged first, his body nearly a blur as he moved. Cain crouched down then sprang forward when Warren was close enough, their heads knocking together.

Kee winced at the sound of them colliding. The two rolled together on the ground in a flurry of snarls and growls. Each fought for the upper hand while fangs and claws dug into their opponent. Feeling eyes on her, she lifted her gaze to see Liam staring at her. She sneered at him, pushing down the fear that swelled in her as he walked towards her.

She wouldn't back down. Not this time.

"Did you need something, Liam?" She bit out when he was close enough. Conrad had followed Liam and stood close behind him, his body tense.

"Why are you here?" He asked, eyes narrowed.

He then glanced over at the two when a loud yelp echoed out. Warren had bitten down on Cain's shoulder, rolling the other wolf under him. Before he could successfully pin him down, Cain pushed all four of his paws against Warren's chest and kicked him off.

Kee gestured at the fight. "To watch Cain win, of course. Say goodbye to your shitty subordinate."

Liam lifted a brow at her sudden attitude. It was a far cry from the trembling mess she had been. He assumed he had made her that way from childhood, but there was some small spark of pride at her backbone.

"I suppose it makes sense that you would want to support your intended," he mused, turning back to her. "Just know that once you mate him, you'll be under my ruling."

She let out a bitter laugh. "You would love that, wouldn't you? To have some sort of power over me?" She crossed her arms over her chest and turned her attention back to the fight. "Too bad Cain and I are over. I'm dating someone else."

Liam narrowed his eyes at the holes in her neck and remembered what Conrad said two days ago. "The vampire?"

"Lucas Vranas, maybe you've heard of him," she responded in a flat tone. She sucked in a breath when Warren knocked his head against Cain's making the younger wolf sway and shake his head. "Fuck, come on, Cain." She muttered as her brow furrowed.

"The Lord of Los Angeles County. He's my equal, then."

She whirled on him with a familiar growl that didn't belong to her. "He's nothing like you, you son of a bitch. Unlike you, he'd never hurt me, never hurt the ones he supposedly loves. You're nothing but an abusive, murdering—" She abruptly cut herself off when a loud snap followed by a high-pitched whine sliced through the air.

She quickly turned back to the fight in time to watch Cain roll Warren under him, his teeth clamped down on the other wolf's throat. Kee could see Warren's back leg twisted at an odd angle, flipping awkwardly when he tried to kick Cain off of him. Cain snarled and bit down harder on his neck, claws digging into Warren's shoulders.

It was a tense minute of struggling before Warren finally went limp under his opponent, his head tilting further back and to the side in submission. Cain flexed his jaw before releasing Warren and stepping back. Some of the werewolves broke out into cheers. Kee wanted to join them, but it wasn't done yet. There was one more thing that had to be done.

Cain shifted into his human form first, breathing raggedly. His handsome face was slightly swollen in some places, blood gushing out from both nostrils. Bloody bites and scratches were scattered over his body, but he didn't feel the pain yet. His wolf howled within him with victory. Pride swelled in his chest, the blissful adrenaline of the win still coursing through his veins.

"Cain has won the battle for alpha," Liam announced. "But the battle isn't over until Cain decides."

The new alpha of LA sneered down at Warren as the other man shifted into his human form. Cain's wolf still hovered on the surface, ready to do what was needed. Warren was battered like Cain, but it was clear he received the brunt of the damage. When Warren rolled onto his side, trying to support his bad leg, Cain kicked him onto his stomach and pressed his knee into his back as he cupped the back of Warren's head in one hand and grabbed his jaw in the other.

Natalie felt a new wave of terror grip her at the sight. Cain looked like he was going to twist Warren's head off. Only very strong, healthy werewolves could survive a severed spinal cord and even then, it was rare. Warren wouldn't survive it in his condition. There was no way.

"Cain!" She cried, her voice almost a scream as she ran to them. Zach and Conrad intercepted her at Liam's command, but that didn't stop her from pleading. "Please, Cain, *please*! You can't kill him! You can't!"

Cain's nostrils flared at his pack mate's cry. His wolf didn't like that she was hurting, but his rational side couldn't be swayed. "Why?" He growled out without looking at her. "He hurt you. He hurt the pack!"

Nat didn't bother to wipe the tears that rolled down her cheeks. She ignored the pack's questioning murmurs to one another and continued to beg. "I'm pregnant," she cried, both hands clutching at her stomach. "I need him to not shift. I need him to help me raise our pup. I know I have no right to ask you this after what he did, but I'm begging you."

Gods dammit! His lips pressed together in a hard line, his fingers tightening on Warren's head as he did. Could he kill Warren and let Natalie suffer? He knew she always wanted a child. The couple had been trying for decades. After everything, could he possibly take that away from her? Be the reason she lost her mate and her child?

"Cain." Kee warned, her tone like ice.

His chest heaved with indecision. Warren was the cause of his problems. He deserved to die for trying to kill Kee, for indirectly killing his three pack mates. He looked at his pack, and they stared back at him with confusion and horror. They didn't know what Warren had done. If he killed him, they would fear him, maybe even hate him. He didn't want that.

Cain shook Warren's head with a growl. "You want to live to help your mate and pup?" He asked in his wolf's rough, angry voice.

Hope surged through Warren. He didn't expect to be spared. "Yes." He croaked, blood bubbling from his lips.

"Tell the pack what you did," he felt Warren tense and snarled again. "All of it!"

Warren looked at the pack through a swollen eye. They stared back at him with uncertainty. If it meant being with Natalie and their pup, he would take their hate and add it to his regret. "I'm the reason everyone is dead." He said in a low soft tone.

More murmurs before Alyssa stepped forward, her blue green eyes narrowed into a hard glare. "What do you mean, Warren?"

Kee glanced at the auburn haired girl who had verbally attacked her at the pack barbecue. Had that really only been two months ago? It felt like a year.

"Start at the beginning." Cain demanded, beginning to twist Warren's head.

"Okay!" He shouted desperately. Once Cain's hold relaxed, he continued. "I blood bonded with the Lord of Pasadena. He wanted me to help him take over humans. We put a plan in place, but the Lord of Los Angeles County found out.

"When Alexander lost the fight, I thought that was it, but it wasn't. He was even more determined to succeed. He wanted to ruin Lucas and started picking off his people." He looked over at Kee and saw her cold glare. He swallowed and looked down at the grass. "Wyatt found out Kee works for Lucas. When I told Alexander, he ordered me to have her killed. So, I did."

A few wolves sucked in a startled breath. Some looked at Kee while others split their attention between Cain and Warren.

"Tell them who you sent to kill her!" Katie yelled.

Kee jumped at the sudden shout and looked at the girl next to her. Her body was trembling, whether from anger or sorrow, Kee couldn't tell. She gently set her hand on Katie's shoulder, trying to offer her some form of comfort.

Katie's chin dimpled as she tried not to cry. She fisted her hands tightly together as she accepted the other girl's comfort. "Tell them, Warren!"

The former alpha looked at his stunned pack. "Wyatt, Noah, and Brandon." He muttered miserably. He closed his eyes when a chorus of snarls and shouts rang out.

"Brandon?" Mason asked, eyes wide with shock. Another were-wolf went to his side and put an arm around his shoulders, consoling him. "You sent my mate?"

"How did they die?" Alyssa asked when Warren nodded.

"I killed them," Kee answered, not flinching when the pack snapped their attention to her. "They almost killed me. I would have died if it wasn't for Lucas."

Liam's aura cracked through the air, the wolves flinching under it. "You killed my wolves?" He asked in a low, deep growl.

Kee met his gaze unwaveringly. "I did."

"They didn't die at the same time." He countered, jaw clenching. He may have noticed that she grew a backbone, but to have grown strong enough to kill three werewolves? There was no way.

"No, they didn't. I killed Wyatt before he finished me off. Then, once I was healed, I hunted down the other two." She gave him a rueful smile. "I must have learned it from you, *Daddy*." She spat the last word with as much hate and venom as she could muster.

Some wolves were stunned into silence by the entire revelation. Cain strained his hearing to listen to the ones who talked amongst themselves.

How could Warren order our beta's intended mate to be killed?

How could Cain still want her after she killed our brethren?

She was entitled to it!

Was she? She killed Wyatt in self-defense, wasn't that enough?

She's the daughter of an alpha! If I was an alpha female, I would have gone after the people who tried to kill me, too!

"Enough!" Liam shouted, making the pack fall silent. "Make your choice, Cain."

Cain glanced at Natalie's tear streaked face then at his pack. Some stared at him with hostility, but he wasn't sure if it was directed at him or at what Warren had done. Other wolves had wide, pleading eyes. A couple seemed conflicted while a few seemed indifferent. Their reactions were torn and so was his decision.

Ultimately, he had to do what was best for everyone. That's what alphas did, and that's what he would do.

He tightened his hold on Warren's head once again and jerked it to the side before stopping. He bent low so that his mouth was close to Warren's ear. "You better make sure your pup survives because that's the only reason you are." With that, he released Warren with a shove and stood.

Warren rolled onto his back and sat up, looking up at Cain with wide, disbelieving eyes. Natalie rushed over and fell to her knees next to him, but he kept his eyes on Cain. "You're letting me live?"

"No, I'm giving your unborn child the best chance at survival. Don't make me regret it." He growled and turned away from him.

Katie ran over to him, handing him his clothes while congratulating him. "You won, Alpha! I knew you would!"

He pulled on his sweats and gave her a weak smile. "Thanks, Katie." He turned to Kee and damn near flinched at her scowl. "Kee—"

"Don't," she hissed, her chest tight with betrayal. "Just don't, Cain."

He frowned but didn't regret his decision. Pups were rare and precious. He wouldn't put Natalie's innocent child at risk because of Warren's crimes. He turned to his pack and looked at their expectant gazes. It was time to claim his wolves.

He straightened his spine as his eyes took on the presence of his wolf. "Los Angeles wolf pack!" He called as he expanded out his aura, filling the backyard with his energy.

They stood at attention as their beasts responded to their alpha's power. Their auras flared, eyes mirroring their inner wolves and growls rumbling in their chests as they prepared for their claiming.

"Your troubles are mine! Your safety is mine! Your lives are mine! I claim you as *mine*! From here on out, I am your alpha!" His beast paced as he blanketed their auras with his, his power settling over all of them and coaxing out their beasts. In unison, they shifted into their wolf forms and tossed their heads back to release howls of acceptance.

Cain felt a surge of power slam into him from his claiming, making him stagger. This was what it meant to be alpha. He received power from his pack and they gained a leader that would protect them.

"Well done, Cain," Liam praised as he approached his newest alpha subordinate. Cain looked at him with his beast's predatory eyes, making Liam smirk. He set his hand on Cain's bare shoulder and called upon his own beast.

Cain started at the sudden power Liam pressed onto him. He was on an adrenaline power high, his inner wolf too close to the surface to be pushed back down. If Liam antagonized him and his wolf, they would strike. "What are you doing?" He ground out through clenched teeth.

"Giving you your prize for winning alpha." He said as he pinned his stare on Kee.

She instantly tensed at the cruel look Liam was giving her. Apprehension crept down her spine and her instincts told her to turn tail and run, but she refused. She wouldn't run from him again.

Pride can be a foolish thing.

"Your prize is your mate," he replied lightly and tightened his hold on Cain's shoulder. "Claim Keira as your mate, Cain."

Cain's wolf immediately howled in excitement, but Cain tried to rein it back. "I can't," he bit out through his wolf's whine. "She's not mine."

"But she can be," Liam pressed. "All you have to do is mark her."

Conrad couldn't believe his ears. Liam was trying to make Cain mark Kee. "Don't do it, Cain! Don't listen to him!"

"Dad, stop!" Zach protested as Liam pressed more of his power on Cain, making his beast squirm and shudder in response. "It's not right!"

"Hold them," Liam ordered his two other wolves. Conrad and

Zach instantly struggled when the other two men grabbed them, but Liam ignored their pleas. "Cain, as your direct *alpha*, I am ordering you to mark Keira as your mate."

Cain felt the command lock into his muscles as it settled over his wolf. If his beast wasn't on a power trip, wasn't so close to the surface, he may have been able to deny the order. Might have been able to fight against it. But his wolf wanted Kee too badly for Cain to hold him back like this.

Kee paled as Cain whirled towards her. "Cain, you can't." She said and took a step back as he began to advance on her. His blue eyes were dark with his wolf's presence, and she felt a stab of fear at the hungry look in them. "Cain!"

"Run. . .Kee." Each word was bit out with strained difficulty as Cain tried to dig his heels in the grass, trying to stop his march towards her.

"No!" She shouted and continued to back up, panic setting into her system. She glared at Liam over Cain's shoulder. "You made your point, Liam! Cancel your order!"

"No, I don't think I will, Kiki. You killed three of my wolves and clearly need to be leashed and tamed. Tying you to Cain will tie you to me as well," he said with a pleased smile on his face. "It's the perfect solution."

"I'm in love with someone else," she declared and flinched when Cain's beast snarled angrily, his pupils now like black pinpricks in a sea of blue. Her heart beat hard with anxiety, her chest heaving. "You already ruined my life once, Liam. Do you really need to do it again?"

"Liam..." Natalie whispered in horror, clutching Warren to her as they watched.

Liam ignored her and deepened his voice with authority. "Cain, I'm ordering you to mark your mate!"

Another shudder shook Cain's body as the command won. He

looked at Kee with misery as he began moving towards her again. "I'm sorry."

Kee turned and ran. She needed to shift and immediately Cain's wolf within her responded. She didn't care what or who it was, she just needed to get away. As soon as her mind accepted the image, her body collapsed. Her vision went black, knees buckling under her. She managed to catch herself, but the damage was already done.

Cain was on her, tackling her to the grass. She threw an elbow behind her, but he caught her arm and pinned it above her head. She started bucking and writhing, trying to throw his body off of her, but he was too strong and her body was too exhausted. He put a stop to her thrashing by shifting his weight on her back, pinning her other arm to her side with his legs.

"Cain, please," she begged, desperation sinking in as she realized she couldn't fight her way out of this. "Don't do this. Fight the command! You just won as alpha. You're better than this! Please!"

"I'm trying," he bit out, his voice gravely and deep with his wolf. He mentally begged his wolf to stop, trying to tell him that she would hate him, but the beast refused. He believed it was time to mark his territory. He didn't want another man to have her. "I'm sorry. I'm so sorry, Kee."

Lucas! She screamed in her mind, but she could see the setting sunrays shining on the grass by her head. Even if he could hear her or feel her fear, he couldn't come to her. It was just as he said, the sun would always prevent him from going to her.

She heard Conrad and Zach yelling at Cain as he wound her hair around his free hand. She felt his head move closer so she flung hers back as hard as she could. She felt the impact with his face, and his snarl nearly deafened her in response. She cried out when he used his grip on her hair to force her head forward, lengthening the back of her neck.

"Don't!" She cried, her lips brushing against the grass from the force of his hold. She felt something drip onto her neck as he bent closer to her once again, the scent of blood heavy in the air. She broke his nose and still he wouldn't stop? She felt his breath fan against her neck and her breath hitched. "Cai—!" His name ended on a scream as he sunk canine teeth into her skin.

The beast sank his teeth in but withdrew once he spilled her blood. Biting his tongue and drawing his own blood, he lapped at the punctures, mixing their blood together. His tongue soon stopped bleeding, but he continued to lick at the wounds he inflicted on her, making soft growls in his throat to soothe his hurting mate. Once satisfied that he cleaned her wounds, the wolf looked down at his mating mark with satisfaction before slinking back behind Cain's consciousness.

Cain snapped back in control once his beast disappeared. He stared down at the mark in horror before looking at the hand fisted in her hair. He quickly untangled it and abruptly stood. Once on his feet, he covered his mouth with his hand in repulsion, ignoring the pain in his busted nose. He couldn't believe what his wolf had done, what Liam ordered him to do.

He turned to Liam and growled low in his throat. "Why?"

"Because I need her tamed," he replied simply and nodded his head at the two wolves pinning Conrad and Zach down on the ground.

As soon as Conrad was free, he ran to Kee's side, Zach a step behind him. "Kee, are you okay?" He asked, helping her stand and supporting her weight when she staggered.

Zach sucked in a breath at the blank look on his sister's face "Kee?"

She felt numb. Of all the times she felt someone betrayed her, it was nothing to what Cain had just done to her. It felt like a fissure had ripped open her chest. She was livid while simultaneously feeling so fucking helpless. She was tied to Cain the same way she was connected to Lucas and she didn't know how that would affect her relationship with the vampire. They were already in a delicate spot; they didn't need this extra stress.

"Kee," Cain began, taking a hesitant towards her. "Please believe me, I didn't want this."

"Didn't you?" She shot back, fury taking over the cold emptiness as her neck began to pulse with pain. "Isn't this exactly what you wanted?"

Disgust twisted his face. "No. Not like this. *Never* like this, Kee. To force you into something against your will? I would never—" Her fist suddenly slammed into his broken nose and he stumbled back, not expecting it. She came at him again, but he caught her wrist and pulled her forward so their bodies were flush against each other. His body warmed at her touch, the bond doing exactly what it was supposed to.

Her body started to press harder against his, but she quickly stopped herself and threw her knee up to his groin. He had to release her to protect his balls. She hated how her body now craved to be close to his. "Don't you fucking dare! Don't *ever* touch me again, Cain, or so help me I will kill you. I am not yours. I do not, and will not, ever belong to you. Do you understand me?"

His brows pinched together in anger. "You made it quite clear that you're done, but we're mates." He glanced down at Katie in her wolf form when she bumped her head against his leg. He pat her head but turned his attention back to Kee. "As much as you want to, you can't ignore the bond. We're pack."

"Watch me," she sneered and turned a spiteful look at Liam. "This isn't over between us."

"No, it isn't," he agreed. "Conrad, Zachary, come. It's time to go."

Kee latched on to Conrad's hand, holding him tight. "Conrad is my wolf. He's staying here with his daughter and girlfriend. In *my* pack."

Liam looked between Conrad and Kee and lifted his brow. "You think your alpha bond is stronger than mine?"

"Yes." She immediately replied without hesitation.

"Would you like to test that theory?"

"Liam," Cain began with a growl. "You gave me a prize for winning the alpha fight, but it's not what I asked for."

Liam shot him a curious look. "And what is it you want?"

"Give Conrad to Kee without a challenge." When he saw Liam hesitate, he pushed on. "You claimed my gift was Kee, but it wasn't what I wanted. What I want is for Conrad to be Kee's."

Feeling eyes on him, Liam looked at the LA pack sneering at him with disgust. Natalie had helped Warren into his clothes and the two of them stared at him expectantly. He finally sighed and waved a hand. "Fine, keep him."

Conrad squeezed Kee's hand. "Thank you."

"You're mine, Con. I'll fight for you anytime, but I'm glad it's not today." She admitted and fixed Cain a flat look. "This fixes nothing."

He shrugged, defeat in his shoulders. "I didn't say it did." He then shifted back into his wolf form and released a deep howl. With a nod to his pack, they took off into the foothills, hunting in honor of their new alpha.

"Zach, come here," Liam ordered and jerked his head to Warren and Natalie. "You two will be coming to the Claremont pack with us."

"I-I want to stay," Zach protested. "With Kee and her pack."

"Zach," Kee said softly, touched by his declaration.

"Absolutely not. Get over here, *now*," Liam snarled, eyes narrowed into a glare.

Kee felt her heart clench when her little brother looked at her for help. "Zach, I can't fight today." When his face fell, she drew him in for a hug. "If you're serious, we will figure something out, okay? But if I fight now, I'll lose."

He nodded reluctantly and hugged her back tightly. He gave her a small, weak smile when they broke apart before heading over to his dad. He didn't look at Liam as he glared, just kept his attention on the floor as they made their way back to the house.

Conrad saw Kee sway next to him and put his hands on her shoulders to steady her. "Hey, you okay?"

"No," she mumbled. "Let's just go back to Byte. I need everything to be over."

Twenty-Nine

Conrad kept his hand on Kee's back as they approached the back door of Byte. She insisted on walking into the club on her own, but that didn't mean he wasn't going to support her. She wanted to be strong, and he got that, but she was pushing herself too much.

"What happened?" Samson asked as soon as the duo walked through the backdoor.

"Were you waiting here for us to come back?" Kee questioned with a lifted brow.

"Yes," he answered simply as he moved closer, eyes roaming over her pale face. "What happened?" He repeated.

"It was a shit show, Sam. You're right, I shouldn't have gone."

He frowned, glancing at an equally solemn Conrad. "I didn't want to be right."

"Well, you were." Her face softened as she looked at his concerned expression. "I should have let you come. If I had, maybe it wouldn't have turned out like this."

Samson's hands flexed anxiously at his sides. "Kee, what the hell happened?"

"I'm Cain's mate," she laughed without humor. "Totally against my will, might I add?"

His jaw dropped a little before he looked at Conrad accusingly. "Why didn't you help her?"

Conrad growled low in his throat and took a threatening step towards the dragon. "Don't you think I wanted to? I couldn't! I was pinned down!"

"Stop it," Kee ordered over their growling and weakly glared at them. "Tuck away the attitudes. I'm too exhausted for this shit right now, okay?" When they grumbled in agreement, she nodded and turned towards the door that led to the coven. One of her knees gave out and she cursed as she braced herself against the doorframe. She took a deep breath and forced herself not to punch the metal in frustration.

"Are you going to see Lucas?" Samson asked, moving to her side when she pushed away from the doorframe.

"Yeah, I need to talk to him, I—" She jerked back when the door to the basement flew open, Lucas standing there at the entryway. "L-Lucas."

He looked down at her, opened his mouth to say something, but then spotted the other two men standing nearby. He stepped aside and gestured at the stairs. "Come, we do not have long to talk."

Samson looked at his alpha. "Do you need help getting down the stairs?"

"I have it covered, Mr Richland," Lucas answered, lifting Keira into his arms without hesitation. He didn't give her pack a second glance before kicking the door to his coven shut.

Conrad sighed and ran his hand through his hair. "It's been a long night. I'm going to go see my girls."

"They're upstairs watching some homicide show." Samson told him.

He sighed in exasperation. "Of course they are." The wolf started to leave through the kitchen but stopped when he noticed Samson was staying behind. He turned and lifted a brow. "Coming?"

The other male looked startled at the offer, especially since they almost got into an argument moments earlier. "Uh, do you want me to?"

He shrugged. "You're pack. After the shit I've seen today, I just want to be around a pack that's actually worth being in."

Samson blinked before that foreign, odd contentment warmed him again. His lips quirked up in a small smile. "Alright."

—

Kee looped her arms around Lucas' neck as he carried her down the stairs. He tightened his hold on her and she melted against him. She still couldn't believe how just his touch could calm her, make her feel as if everything was alright. Even when it wasn't.

"We have to stay over here," Lucas began softly as he set her down on her feet when they reached the bottom of the stairs. "If Aubrey smells you, she will go into a fit. She is not strong enough to overcome the urge to feed mindlessly."

"How is she doing?" She asked, looking up at him. He was wearing a plain black tank top and pajama pants that sat low on his hips. His hair was disheveled, black strands falling down to brush his brow. She reached out and combed them back from his forehead before sliding her hand to his cheek. "How are you doing?" She added softly.

He leaned into her touch, turning his head to press a kiss to her palm. "I am always better when you are here, Keira," he murmured. "As for Aubrey, she is adjusting. The first night is done and that is always the worst. It will only get easier for her from here."

"Good," she stepped forward and wrapped her arms around his waist, hugging him as tightly as her weak body would allow. She needed the comfort he provided after the day she had.

His arms went around her shoulders, even as his apprehension flared. He was not used to the anxiousness that settled uncomfortably within him. "I heard you calling for me, Keira," he began, knowing they didn't have time to beat around the bush. "You were screaming my name, Keira. I almost rushed out the doors before I realized the sun was still out."

"I'm sorry," she replied, meeting his concerned green eyes. "I didn't mean to put you in that situation. Yes, I was desperate for your help, but I would never want to endanger you."

He framed her face in his hands, brow furrowed in concern. "*Why* were you desperate? What happened? You were terrified, but that's all I received from you. Did Cain lose the fight?"

Kee put her hands on his, making herself hold his gaze. "No, Cain won the alpha challenge," she started. "He made Warren tell the pack what he did, but he didn't kill him."

"I am sure that did not make you happy."

She scoffed. "Not at all, but his mate declared she's pregnant so I'm sure that was Cain's deciding factor. Kids are important to every pack."

His thumbs traced over her cheekbones. "I see. Then what happened?"

She took in a shaky breath. "Liam gives presents to those who win alpha challenges." Her fingers slid to his wrists as she dropped her gaze to his chest. "I was Cain's gift."

He went utterly still. "What does that mean, Keira?"

She almost flinched at his distant tone. She was nervous. Scared to tell him the truth. "Cain marked me as his mate against my will."

He blinked once, replaying her words in his mind. "You are Cain's mate?" The question came out strangely calm despite the ice rapidly filling his veins.

"Yes, but—" She cut herself off when he suddenly put distance between them. In a blink of any eye, he was several feet away from her. The distance he put between them hurt more than she thought. "Lucas?"

"You are Cain's mate," he repeated stoically, trying to hide the ache in his heart. This was his fault, of course. He didn't have the time to tell her the truth. To explain the mistake he had made.

Kee balled her hands into fists and tears stung her eyes. "It was forced on me! I don't want to be his mate, Lucas!"

"Do you not? I pushed you away and Cain was there to catch you." The flare of jealousy was expected, but it still startled him when it reared its head within him.

"Yeah, you did push me away," she agreed, taking a wobbly step towards him. "But you said we were going to have a long talk about why you were acting the way you were. I've been waiting to hear it, so tell me."

He retreated back another step. "It does not matter anymore. You belong to another man."

Her anger sparked to life even as a tear slid down her cheek. "Excuse me? I don't belong to anyone, least of all Cain!" A wave of exhaustion hit her, fizzling out the ember of rage. "I told you I ended things with him and I meant it. I want to be with you, Lucas. Nothing has changed that."

"And yet you end up back with your ex once again." He countered with bite in his tone.

His spiteful response almost knocked the wind out of her. "That's not fair." She whispered. "We talked about that."

"Go back to your mate, Keira." He said, turning from her. The ice in his veins was slowly turning into a fury so hot that he feared his golden fire would start seeping out of his pores.

Her heart cracked at his words. "We have already been through so much shit and you're going to just give up on us? Because of something I had no control over? Or, are you just using this as an excuse to end things between us? So you don't have to explain anything?"

Once again, her words hit him hard. Was he using this as an excuse? No. He decided back at Tips that he would amend things between them. But his worst fears came true, Cain won her before he could apologize and make things right with her. Right as his resolve faltered, a loud crash echoed in the hallway.

Aubrey was awake.

"You need to leave." He said and began walking back to his room.

"Lucas!" She shouted, but he didn't turn back. She watched his form until it disappeared around the corner and felt her heart crack a little more. With eyes burning, she whirled towards the stairs and used the steel banister to help her climb. When she reached the door, Dante was leaning against it with his arms crossed.

"You hear all that?" She mumbled.

"He'll come around, Kee." He simply said in response.

She wiped at her stinging eyes. "Maybe I don't want to wait for him to. I'm tired of this."

He frowned. "That's your choice, but I don't think it's what either of you want."

She held up her hand. "Please, I don't want to talk about this right now. I'm exhausted and I hurt. I just want to go to bed."

His chocolate colored eyes scanned her over. He held out his arm to her. "Come on, I'll help you to the fourth story."

She shot him a grateful look and took his arm. "It's been a long couple of days." She murmured as he led her through the kitchen and across the empty club.

"It has indeed," he agreed, supporting her weight as they climbed the stairs to the second story. "Much more eventful for you than for me."

She nodded, her vision swimming with the action. "Fuck yeah it has. I feel like it's been weeks since I slept properly."

"Looks like it, too."

Kee swatted at his arm. "Asshole." They reached the stairwell that led to the rest of the stories, and she groaned at the two flights that had to go up. "Have you seen Gio? How is he doing?"

"Much better," Dante replied. "He's still hungry, but his body has mostly filled back out and the blood lust has passed. Another night of feeding and he should be fine by tomorrow."

"Good. I was worried for him," she commented then tugged on his arm to stop at the fourth story landing. "Are you mad I didn't tell you sooner about me?"

"Mad? No, Kee. I understand. If anything, it makes me question how trustworthy I am."

She frowned. "I trust you, Dante. It's just that I've spent almost twenty years hiding my secret and suddenly it feels like I'm telling everyone. It's scary, to be honest. It only takes one spiteful person or one slip of the tongue to put me on the receiving end of a manhunt. You know?"

He nodded and resumed their walk to the door where he knew her pack was at. "Again, I understand. I know you were forced to tell me your secret, but I'll take it to my death, Kee. I'll prove my trust-worthiness that way."

She let go of his arm to give him a hug. "Thank you." She said softly, touched by his declaration.

He returned the hug before stepping back and gesturing at the door. "Enjoy the rest of your night, Kee. I'll see you later."

She smiled as he walked away then opened the door. The sight that greeted her soothed the ache in her chest. Her pack was on the California-King sized bed watching TV. Conrad and Lucy were propped up against the headboard as they cuddled while Samson lay on his stomach, facing the television. Mia was sprawled out next to him, the two sharing a bowl of popcorn. They all turned to look at her when she walked in, each one smiling.

"Kee! Come watch Cold Case Files with us!" Mia exclaimed, patting the mattress.

"Careful, this one hogs all the popcorn," Samson warned, dipping his hand into the bowl.

The little wolf stuck her tongue out at him. "It's not my fault you eat slow, Sammy!"

Kee laughed as she stepped into the room and closed the door behind her. She crawled onto the bed before flopping down on the other side of Lucy. She dropped her head to the werefox's shoulder and let out a soft sigh when Lucy lightly pet her hair, silently giving her comfort without pressing for information.

"I needed this," Kee murmured, feeling the past days of fatigue finally overwhelm her body. "Being with you guys."

Conrad leaned forward to look at her around Lucy, a knowing smile on his face. "We're always here when you need us, Kee. That's why we're pack."

She must have fallen asleep because she was jerked awake from a nightmare. She blindly stared at the ceiling, trying to get her breathing under control before looking around at her room. Her pack was gone, making her feel unexpectedly lonely. But, what did she expect? Conrad was probably with Lucy or Mia, and Samson didn't know her well enough to share a bed.

She reached for her phone and found it plugged in next to the bed. She winced when the light stung her eyes. Blinking the bright light's effect from her eyes, she glanced back down at her phone and groaned at the time. 5:41 am. She almost threw her phone in irritation. She knew she needed to sleep. Her body craved it, but her mind was fighting tooth and nail.

Seeing she had two text message notifications, she decided to read them instead of breaking her phone. The first one was from Cain, sent a few hours ago. What the fuck could he possibly have to say to her?

I'm not trying to make this right because I know I won't be able to. With that said, I have to move into the alpha house now that Warren is gone. That leaves my house free. I want you and your pack to have it so you guys have a home base. No strings attached. I don't expect anything in return. I'll sign the deed over to you if that makes it easier. You know where the spare key is hidden.

Kee sighed and closed her eyes, weighing the options. As much as she hated it, Cain was right. With her pack growing they needed a place bigger than an apartment. Lucy had her own, but Conrad and Samson both stayed with her. And now they had Mia, too. Yeah, they would need a house. She didn't want Cain's house per say, but they could revamp the whole thing, couldn't they? Make it their own?

I'll talk to my pack.

She sent the short message and went to the second text waiting for her. It was from Lucas and sent seconds before she woke up.

I saw your nightmare of Cain's marking. My harsh words were unwarranted. I was angry and jealous. I still am, to be frank, but I understand more now. I have three more nights with Aubrey before I am free. Shall we both collect our thoughts and emotions and then try speaking again? I do not know if the damage is already done, but I still wish talk to you about the topic at the club.

She wanted to stay furious at him. Oh, and she was, but she was curious as to what he had to tell her. What could he possibly say to excuse him pushing her away so harshly? The other night and last night as well? What could possibly explain it? She didn't think anything might. Still, she wasn't going to make this easy for him.

Cain gave me his house. You can meet me there four nights from now.

She sent the text before she could second guess the pettiness of it then silenced her phone. She didn't want to talk to anyone else until she slept for at least twenty hours. Or, whatever time was needed for her body to finally recover.

Thirty

"You ready to talk to Lucas?" Conrad asked conversationally as they unpacked the boxes from her storage.

Samson snorted as he finished setting up the television on the entertainment center. "You shouldn't give him a chance."

"It's been four days," she responded, pulling a lamp out of the box and removing the bubble wrap. "I'm still angry, but we need to at least talk about everything."

"He threw a fit like a child," the dragon pointed out. "He can't fight his feelings for you and then cry when he thinks you moved on."

She silently pulled out some frames from a different box, mulling over his words. "It's not like that."

"The fuck it's not." Samson countered.

"Samson," Conrad warned. "I've been here, you haven't. Lucas is good for her. They are good *together*."

"Sam, like I said, I'm still pissed with how he acted, but he saw what happened to me in my nightmare and wants to talk. He said there's something he has to tell me that will explain his mood. I want to hear it. After that I'll make a decision, okay?"

Samson walked over to her to help go through another box. "You just don't need to be hurt."

Kee gave him a small smile. "Thank you for looking out for me," she said and stood, but she promptly stumbled as the persistent ache in her chest grew. She put her hand to her sternum, rubbing the skin to try and alleviate the pain.

"Kee, you okay?" Conrad asked, watching as she righted herself.

"I'm fine," she answered and bent to pick up another box. As soon as she did, her chest felt as if it hollowed out, leaving her nauseous. She dropped the box and went to her knees, clenching her jaw as she tried to take deep breaths. She suddenly felt drained and empty. Where was this coming from?

Samson squatted down next to her, hand on her shoulder. "What is it?"

"I don't know," she gasped out then winced when the back of her neck flared with heat. "Fuck!"

"Where does it hurt?" Samson pressed.

"The back of my neck. I have a sinking feeling in my chest, like there's a gaping hole there."

"I think I've seen this before," Conrad murmured, kneeling down next to her. "It's because of the mating bond. How long has it been bothering you?"

"It's been a dull ache since it happened, but it's been getting worse." Kee responded with a groan. "I thought it was just my anxiety."

"It'll get worse the longer we're apart." The three looked at Cain as he stood in the entryway to the living room.

"The fuck do you want?" Kee snarled, her anger at him flaring.

He held up his hand to show a key, knowing better than to push her when she was like this. "I was just bringing by the second house key."

Conrad walked over to Cain to collect the key. "Thanks." He said, tone neutral.

The alpha wolf nodded once before his eyes fell back on his reluctant mate. "Are you okay?"

"No, I'm not fucking okay!" She snapped. She didn't look at him in fear of caving to the bond. As soon as she heard his voice, something in her hummed, making her fingers twitch with the need to touch him. She hated it. She needed him to leave.

Cain walked towards her, ignoring Samson's warning growl. "I can make it better. All I have to do is touch you, Kee." Seeing her about to deny him, he sighed. "My weakness is why you're suffering. At least let me ease your pain."

"He's right, Kee," Conrad added. "He's here, might as well let him help you."

Again, she went to protest, but Samson squeezed her shoulder. "Think of it as using him."

Cain deadpanned at the newest member of Kee's pack. "Gee, thanks."

With Cain so close to her, the fire that was burning her neck started to spread down her spine and shoulders. "*Fine*," she said through clenched teeth, gripping her knees in a white knuckled hold. "Just get it over with."

Cain bent a knee behind her and gently pushed her long hair over one shoulder, holding it there to keep the back of her neck exposed. The puncture holes had healed but still held an angry red tint to them. His beast growled in approval even as guilt washed over him. Ever so lightly, he pressed his other palm over the mating mark.

Kee sucked in a breath at the instant cooling his touch brought on. She squeezed her eyes shut when the bond purred happily, making it feel as if something was fluttering in her chest.

She detested it. Vivid flashbacks hit her from his forced marking and her stomach hollowed out.

Cain's body jerked at the overwhelming feeling of touching his mate. His beast preened at her reaction and rumbled happily. He pressed his palm harder and lightly stroked the side of her throat with his thumb.

Kee was helpless to stop the soft moan that escaped her lips in response. She could briefly make out the sound of the doorbell, but she was too distracted with the relief she was feeling to care.

"Better?" Cain asked in a hushed, husky tone.

"*Yes*," she bit out, hating herself for it. Hating him for it.

He leaned closer to her ear. "Good," he all but purred.

She snapped her eyes open, lip curling up at his audacity. She started to turn towards him, but he was gone with a snarl so loud it nearly deafened her. She leapt to her feet and whirled around in time to see Cain crash against the wall.

Cain quickly righted himself and launched at the vampire standing in front of her. Lucas bared his fangs in a silent sneer and caught the fist that was thrown at him. With his other hand, he punched the alpha hard in the stomach. Cain got back to his feet, poised himself to attack, but froze when Kee stepped between them, her back to Lucas.

Lucas stared at his very pissed off shapeshifter as she stood in front of him, blocking him from Cain. "Allow me to deal with him." He rumbled.

"No," she said simply, eyes still on Cain. "You need to leave, Cain."

Cain's eyes turned pleading. "Kee—"

"No," she repeated and gestured towards the door. "Go back to your pack."

"I just wanted to make us both feel better." He explained.

She crossed her arms over her chest. "I know, and you did, but this isn't easy. I'm still so livid with you. Lucas shouldn't have attacked you, but this isn't easy for him either. You need to respect that."

He would be lying if he said he wasn't somewhat hopeful that they would breakup. Not that he would tell her that. "I didn't ask for any of this to happen."

She sighed. "I know, but I need time to process this. Time to calm down."

Cain nodded and made his way towards the door. "Alright. I know I said it, but I *am* sorry."

"Good night, Cain." Kee said firmly, not bothering to watch him leave.

Silence filled the room after the alpha wolf's departure. Tension mounted in the room as the seconds ticked by. Conrad and Samson looked between their alpha and Lucas before sharing a knowing look.

Samson cleared his throat. "Well, at least no one died." He pointed out.

Conrad shoved him towards the door. "So, uh, we're going to stay at the club tonight." He said, holding up the Jeep keys. "Tomorrow we'll get back to unpacking the rest of the boxes. The girls will want to come help now that paint is dry and assembling the furniture is done. That cool?"

Kee rubbed her arms. "Yeah, sounds good, I'll see you guys tomorrow."

Conrad patted her shoulder as he and Samson passed her. "Good luck."

She gave him a nod before turning around to face Lucas.

Lucas watched his shapeshifter standing stiffly in the living room. The living room of *Cain's* house. With everything that happened, the knowledge that she was living in her unwanted mate's old house bothered him. However, he knew better than to comment on it. At least until he solved the mess between them.

He could see the muscles in her neck grow taught with nerves as she looked at him. Or, perhaps it was with anger? He wasn't sure at this point. It had been four nights since they had seen each other and so much had gone wrong between them at that time.

No, before that, he admitted. *I truly made a grave mistake the night we went to Arcadia. I was foolish to push her away.*

"So, what do you want?"

Her hissed question ripped him out of his thoughts. She stood in the living room but stayed near the wall, far from the couch he sat on. "I want many things, Keira."

She crossed her arms across her chest. "Allow me to rephrase. What do you want from *me*?"

He gave a wry smile. "The answer remains the same."

"Fuck off, Lucas. I'm done with these games. I can't play this mind chess with you anymore. Checkmate, you win. Now get out."

He frowned and narrowed his eyes. "I presumed we were going to talk," he snipped out as he rose to his feet.

"Yeah, well, now I'm not feeling so chatty." But that wasn't the truth, was it? She had missed him. She wanted to hate the part of her that warmed at just seeing him but couldn't. Still, she was done with this back and forth. She never thought being in a relationship with him would be so difficult.

"We have a lot to discus," he began. "We can still fix this."

"We?" She mocked. "No, there is no we, Lucas. You're the one who got cold feet and pulled back from me. You decided we weren't anything more than fuck buddies. Or, do you not remember that?"

He sighed as her anger began to swell within the bond. "I remember, but—"

"I was physically and mentally exhausted after the fae fight, but I chose to go with you to Tips even though you said you didn't need me. You didn't need me because I'm nothing to you, right?"

He ground his teeth together, trying to stop her rage from consuming him as well. "I handled that poorly, but there was a reason for it. I—"

"I know that was my choice, but damn it, Lucas, I could barely move the next day! I hadn't *really* slept in days. My body hurt from holding Scarlett's skin and from donating blood to you. Still, Warren needed to be put down and I wanted to see it happen. I wanted to see the last cause for my attack get dethroned. But could you accept that? No! You had to give me a gods damn guilt trip!"

Lucas ran his hands into his hair in frustration. "Keira—"

"I'm not done!" She screamed and kicked a nearby box across the room. When he pressed his lips in a hard line, she continued, "I couldn't defend myself, Lucas!"

Lucas felt her anger twist into loathing as she brought up the event of the alpha challenge and his brows knitted together. He knew what happened from her nightmare, but he should have let her talk about it the night it happened. *I should have listened.*

"Liam gave a command to Cain as his alpha and he couldn't fight it. And I couldn't fight *him*. We both tried. Even Conrad and Zach couldn't help; they were literally pinned down by other wolves. Cain forced his mating mark on me and I could do *nothing*!" The word came out in a harsh, vicious whisper. "I was scared. I felt like I was back in my apartment during my attack but so much weaker."

"You are not weak, Keira."

She scoffed and met his sincere stare. "I am, Lucas, because I only thought of one thing when it was happening, and that was you."

Lucas balled his hands into fists. "I heard you calling for me. Felt your distress and panic. I could taste it as if it was my own," he told her in a soft tone. "I wanted to go to you, but I was confined to my room."

She shook her head. "I know you had to spend five days locked up with a girl who's obsessed with you." His lips parted to say something, but a deep growl from Cain's beast ripped from her lips and kept him from speaking. "I know you had to turn her! I *know* that! But that didn't make it any easier for me even with the cold shoulder you were giving me. I still wanted you there to help me."

"I *wanted* to be there, Keira. I would have stopped him." Of that he was certain. The sun will forever be his worst enemy, an enemy he could do absolutely nothing about and never win against. "I would have rather died again than let Cain claim you as his!"

Kee startled when he shouted at her, but she held her ground. Her voice, however, had lost some of its heat. "I was so vulnerable and confused after I was marked, Lucas. My body physically craved Cain, but my heart and mind wanted you. I just wanted you to tell me it was going to be okay, that we would make it work."

Her voice trembled, but he resisted the need to hold her until he knew for sure she wouldn't push him away. "Despite me knowing how you felt at the time, I was angry. I felt that you were taken away from me, and by your ex of all people. The fact that he marked a part of your soul infuriated me. But most of all, I was furious at myself. I pushed you away and my fear that someone else would sweep you up became true. I felt nothing but rage over the whole thing and I took it out on you." He admitted softly.

She gave a jerky nod. "I was forced to become someone's mate and yet you basically accused me of wanting it while you stayed locked up in your room with Aubrey."

He took a few hesitant steps towards her until he was standing an arm's length away. "I was foolish."

"No, foolish was going after Cain," she responded, her eyes fixated on his chest. "You were *cruel*."

He closed his eyes and let out a sigh. "I was."

"You don't understand what you mean to me," she whispered.

His chest tightened and he forced his eyes back open. "Tell me."

She swallowed at his soft response. "You are my safe place," she began. "I let down my walls when I'm with you. I allow myself to give in to my weakness, to let my emotions go. I try to keep myself so controlled, but when I'm with you, I let it all go."

Lucas gave in to the need to touch her and gently framed her face in his hands, tilting her face up so he could look into her eyes. "Keira, I feel the same way. You are my comfort." He rested his forehead against hers, happy that she didn't pull away or throttle him. "That was why I tried to push you away. You make me feel things I have not felt for many years and it's dangerous."

Her heart squeezed in her chest, but she wouldn't let it win. For days she all but agonized over what she did to screw things up between them but had finally allowed herself to accept the fact that he had done it, not her. She wouldn't beg for him or take blame for what he did. "Dangerous, how, exactly?"

He ground his teeth together and pulled back so he could meet her gaze again. "Love is an emotion I told myself I would never feel again." The hurt in her eyes had him pressing a soft kiss to her lips. "But then you stumbled into my life and all of my plans were destroyed.

"You intrigued me from the beginning, Keira. We slowly got to know each other, even as boss and employee. I will admit that after a few months I wanted you. Yes, I wanted a weapon, but then I wanted *you*. Mind, body, and soul. I was saved from giving in to the desire when you began dating Cain. I told myself it was a sign that it was not meant to be." He swiped his thumb over her cheek. "But then you broke up and the year of holding myself back became too much. I had been hopeful that you felt the same pull when we kissed at the gun range."

"I was always attracted to you, but I thought you only saw me as an employee." She murmured as she held his smoldering gaze.

"I tried to," he agreed.

"But, why? These are all pretty words, Lucas, but it doesn't explain why. I shouldn't even be listening to you after how you treated me."

She tried to force anger in her voice, but it only came out exasperated.

"You are correct. You should not be giving me this chance, but I am thankful for it." He paused as he contemplated his next words, his thumb gliding back and forth over her cheek again. "There have been two women I have loved before you," he finally said in a hushed tone. Her grey eyes widened slightly and he continued. "I am over four hundred years old, Keira. Can you see that I do not take the word for granted? There have been flings, yes, but only twice did I feel the strong emotion."

"What happened?" She pressed.

"My maker happened," he explained. "Remember when I told you about Florence? How she saved me from my human master's wrath after I burned his son to death? Well, that day she marked me as hers. Indefinitely. Shortly after I was turned, she found out about my affair with our maid and killed her." His thumb continued its caress. "In the 1800s, I found love once again with a fellow vampire. We were awful together, but in all the right ways."

Kee saw the pain in his eyes and tried to stop her hands from flattening against his chest, but they had minds of their own. "Florence found out?" She guessed.

He dipped his head into a single nod. "Yes. We had parted ways before that nearly a hundred years earlier, but she still came and ruined my happiness. I did not even see her, Keira. She simply came back to England, killed my Bridgette, and then left."

"Lucas," she whispered, her heart hurting for him. "I'm so sorry."

"No, *I* am sorry," he replied seriously. "You deserved an explanation from the beginning. I thought that perhaps if I could deny myself what I felt for you, if I could push you away enough, I could keep you safe." He let out a bitter laugh. "But I am utterly miserable without you."

Her breath hitched. "Miserable?"

"Yes, and selfish. Loving you puts your life at great risk, but I need you. You are the sun that I have been denied for centuries."

Her pulse quickened as her hands fisted his shirt. "Say it," she demanded. "Say what you feel for me."

He held her gaze as she trembled before him and did not hesitate. "I love you, Keira. It may very well get you killed, but I love you."

"You're such an asshole," she whispered before she yanked him towards her and pressed her lips hard against his. "I love you, too," she breathed when she broke away.

He gave her a tender smile before kissing her back. He ran his hands down to the small of her back and pulled her against him. Her lips parted against his and his tongue slipped past them to stroke hers. Gods, he had gone too long without her touch and it had nearly driven him mad.

She made a whimpering sound in the back of her throat that made him want more. His hands slid down to her ass, and he used it as leverage to lift her from the ground. She instantly locked her legs around his waist, pressing their groins together.

She let out a breathy moan when he pressed her against the wall, applying more pressure where she wanted it most. She slid her hands up his neck and into his silky black hair when he moved away from her lips to lay a trail of kisses down the column of her neck. She shuddered when he ran his fangs lightly over the skin he bit at Tips.

"I will not do it again." His breath fanned across her skin as he spoke.

"I told you to do it," she whispered back. "I'm not mad."

He pulled away from her neck so he could meet her eyes. They were glassy with need, but he could feel the twinge of something else from the bond. "You may not be mad, but you are feeling something. What is it?"

Her fingers threaded through his hair again, eyes not leaving his.

"Wariness." She admitted.

"Why?"

"Because I'm afraid we will fall into a cycle," she murmured. "Fight, separate, and then make up." She tugged on his hair, but he didn't flinch. "I won't do it again. I caused our fight the first time, you did this time. I won't do the back and forth anymore. I don't want this to end."

He saw that the words hurt her just as much as they did him. The possibility of them. He rubbed their noses together before pressing his forehead against hers. "It is all we need," he cooed. "We may spat and bicker, but we are not separating again. For better, or for worse, you are mine."

A soft laugh escaped her. "That sounds like marriage vows."

"Is that what you want?" Lucas asked, looking down at her intently. "If it is, I will give it to you. We love each other and are blood bonded. Why not make it official in human standards?"

She blinked up at him. "You're serious."

"Of course I am," he answered. "I'm also selfish. I will tie you to me in every way possible if it means keeping you."

Her lips tilted into a small, happy smile. "Kiss me."

He obeyed, kissing her gently at first, but she pressed her chest into his and his kiss turned possessive and hungry. He devoured her moan as he rocked his hips against hers, earning him another. With his hands on her thighs, he pulled her away from the wall and carried her down the hall to the master bedroom.

The room may have been Cain's at one point, but Keira had made it her own. The room was done in hues of charcoal grey with accents of white and dark purple. He remembered her bed used to be a light green, but now it was grey with purple sheets and pillows.

Lucas laid her down on it and went to his knees between hers. He pulled her T-shirt over her head, her bra soon following it to the floor. He cupped one of her breasts and flicked his tongue over the hardened peak of the other. Once she let out a pleased sigh, he switched his mouth to the other nipple, his tongue tracing the scar that ran next to it. As he adored her chest with his mouth, he slid the fingertips of his free hand down her body until he got to her jeans. He undid the button and tugged them, along with her panties, down her toned legs and tossed them aside with her other garments.

Kee went to her elbows but almost instantly fell back flat against the bed when she felt a finger trace her core. He opened her legs wider and dipped his head down to trace his tongue over her clit. She jerked under him, a soft moan encouraging him to continue. He licked down to her opening and back up before pressing his pointer finger into her. Her walls clamped down on his finger and he bit back a groan.

His tongue flicked and swirled over the bundle of nerves for a few more minutes before moving to her inner thigh, lightly scraping his fangs along the soft, tender skin. While his forefinger thrust and curled into her, his thumb rubbed firm circles against her clit. She moaned his name and bucked, making him pull back so he didn't accidentally break skin.

Right when she was on the verge of release, he sat back on his knees and unbuttoned his shirt. She sat up and pressed hot, open mouthed kisses along his chest that made him groan. He helped her with his slacks and soon his clothes joined hers on the floor. She flopped back against the mattress, and he moved between her legs once again. He rested a hand on either side of her head and simply looked down at her nude body. Her long hair spilled over the pillow like a waterfall of dark gold. Her eyes shined with desire as she met his gaze and he knew he would never tire of seeing her like this.

He was foolish to ever think he could stay away from her.

"Lucas?" Kee whispered his name and her chest warmed when he gave her a tender smile.

"I love you," he said earnestly and then gave her an almost embarrassed smirk. "Now that I have said it, I seem to not be able to stop."

She gave a soft laugh. "I don't want you to." She put her hand on the back of his neck and pulled him down to press her lips against his. "I love you, too." She gave him a sultry smile. "Now *make* love to me."

"As my lady wishes," he purred as he readjusted his position. He went down to one elbow by her head while his other hand guided his cock to her slick heat.

She gasped as he entered her with a languid thrust. She tossed her head back and let out a breathy moan as he slid out and slowly back in. Her eyes closed as pleasure consumed her at the full feeling.

"More," Kee demanded.

Lucas was all too happy to comply. He watched her intently as he increased the speed of his thrusting. Her chest flushed, making her pale scars stand out beautifully. He grabbed one of her knees and hiked it high on his hip so he could sink in deeper. She let out a curse that was far from spiteful and his pride swelled.

He took her wrists in one hand and pinned them above her head. She liked someone else being in charge and taking away her control in the bedroom. Dominating her. After her attack, and after becoming alpha, he suspected that she subconsciously tried to have control over everything. It must have bruised her to have that taken away with Cain's mating. He knew she needed this, and he would admit that he loved having her at his mercy.

He released her knee, but she kept it propped up as he continued to piston his hips in quick, hard movements. He bent towards her, kissing her breasts when her chest arched towards him. Freeing her wrists, he kissed the column of her neck and groaned when she raked her nails down his back.

Kee whimpered when he pulled out, but her stomach tightened

in anticipation when he flipped her over. She immediately lifted her hips and let out a loud moan when he smacked one of her ass cheeks before thrusting back into her. She felt him lean over her, his hand winding into her hair.

Lucas sucked in a breath as he saw the four teardrop shaped scars on the back of her neck. He could see the fading marks from where Cain's other canine teeth had broken her skin, but he knew the four biggest ones would remain forever.

He pressed his lips to each of the large white scars, resisting the urge to sink his fangs in to make them his own. He felt her tense under him and released her hair so that it covered her mating mark once again.

"I chose *you*." She reminded him as she rocked back against him.

He didn't realize he had stilled his hips until she moved. He moved his lips to her shoulder as his hand slid around to cup her throat. "Good," he cooed in her ear as he applied just the right amount pressure to her neck and began thrusting again. "Because you are mine, Keira."

"And you're mine," she declared with a wanton moan.

"Good answer." He praised and rewarded her with an increased vigor.

"*Fuck!*" Kee gasped as she squeezed her eyes shut in ecstasy. She felt heat blaze across her skin as her body climbed towards that peak. As if sensing her nearing climax, he released her neck and grabbed her hips, quickening the pace of his thrusting.

He grunted when her walls fluttered and clenched around his cock with her orgasm, bringing him to his as well. He shuddered as he finished emptying his lifeless seed inside her and slowly slid out with a groan. He collapsed next to her on the bed and looped an arm around her waist to pull her back against his chest.

Her lips curled up in a tired, lazy smile as his lips grazed her temple. "Mmm, I love you," she murmured.

His heart warmed and, if it were alive, would have skipped a beat. "I love you, Keira." He rested his head against hers and watched as her eyes fluttered shut, a content smile on her face as she finally fell into a deep, restful sleep.

To Be Continued in. . .

Sever

Book three in the Skin series!

Coming 2022

CPSIA information can be obtained
at www.ICGtesting.com
Printed in the USA
LVHW031536091221
705747LV00005B/831